THE STEAMPUNK TRILOGY

VICTORIA

HOTTENTOTS

WALT AND EMILY

THE STEAMPUNK TRILOGY

VICTORIA

HOTTENTOTS

WALT AND EMILY

BY PAUL DI FILIPPO

FOUR WALLS EIGHT WINDOWS
NEW YORK/LONDON

TO MY VERY OWN NEWT(ON)

Published by:
Four Walls Eight Windows, Inc.
39 West 14th Street, #503
New York, N.Y., 10011

First printing April 1995.

"Victoria" first appeared in *Amazing Stories*, June 1991. "Walt and Emily" first appeared in *Interzone*, November and December 1993.

Library of Congress Cataloging-in-Publication Data:
Di Filippo, Paul, 1954-
The steampunk trilogy/ by Paul Di Filippo.
p. cm.
Contents: Victoria — Hottentots — Walt and Emily.
ISBN: 1-56858-028-2
1. Nineteenth century—Fiction. 2. Science fiction, American.
I. Title.
PS3554.I3915S74   1994
813'.54—dc20   94-42282
                                    CIP

10 9 8 7 6 5 4 3 2 1

Designed by Cindy LaBreacht
Printed in the United States

VICTORIA

"I was tired, so I slipped away."

—*Queen Victoria, in her private journal.*

1

POLITICS AT MIDNIGHT

A rod of burnished copper, affixed by a laboratory vise-grip, rose from the corner of the claw-footed desk, which was topped with the finest Moroccan leather. At the height of fifteen inches the rod terminated in a gimbaled joint which allowed a second extension full freedom of movement in nearly a complete sphere of space. A third length of rod, mated to the first two with a second joint, ended in a fitting shaped to accommodate a writer's grip: four finger grooves and a thumb recess. Projecting from this fitting was a fountain-pen nib.

The flickering, hissing gas lights of the comfortable secluded picture-hung study gleamed along the length of this contraption, giving the mechanism a lambent, buttery glow. Beyond rich draperies adorning the large study windows, a hint of cholera-laden London fog could be detected, thick swirls coiling and looping like Byzantine plots. The sad, lonely clopping of a brace of horses pulling the final late omnibus of the Wimbledon, Merton and Tooting line dimly penetrated the study, reinforcing its sense of pleasant seclusion from the world.

Beneath the nib at the end of its long arm of rods was a canted pallet. The pallet rode on an intricate system of toothed tracks mounted atop the desk, and was advanced by a hand-crank on the left. A roll of paper protruded from cast-iron brackets at the head of the pallet. The paper, coming down over the writing surface, was taken up by a roller at the bottom of the pallet. This roller was also activated by the hand-crank, in synchrony with the movement of the pallet across the desk.

In the knee-well of the large desk was a multi-gallon glass jug full of ink, resting on the floor. From the top of the stoppered jug rose an India-rubber hose, which traveled upward into the brass tubing and thence to the nib. A foot-activated pump forced the ink out of the bottle and into the system at an appropriate rate.

Fitted into the center of this elaborate writing mechanism was the ingenious and eccentric engine that drove it.

Cosmo Cowperthwait.

Cowperthwait was a thin young gentleman with a ruddy complexion and sandy hair, a mere twenty-five years old. He was dressed in finery that bespoke a comfortable income. Paisley plastron cravat, embroidered waistcoat, trig trousers.

Pulling a large turnip-watch from his waistcoat pocket, Cowperthwait adjusted its setting to agree with the 11:45 passage of the Tooting omnibus. Restoring the watch to its pocket, he tugged down the naturopathic corset he wore next to his skin. The bulky garment, with its many sewn-in herbal lozenges, had a tendency to ride up from his midriff to just under his armpits.

Now Cowperthwait's somewhat moony face fell into an expression of complete absorption, as he composed his thoughts prior to transcribing them. Right hand holding the pen at the end of its long arm, left hand gripping the crank, right foot ready to activate the pump, Cowperthwait sought to master the complex emotions attendant upon the latest visit to his Victoria.

Finally he seemed to have sufficiently arrayed his cogitations. Lowering his head, he plunged into his composition. The crank spun, the pump sucked, the pallet inched crabwise across the desk along an algebraic path resembling the Pearl of Sluze, the arm swung to and fro, the paper travelled below the nib, and the ink flowed out into words.

Only by means of this fantastic machinery—which he had been forced to contrive himself—was Cowperthwait able to keep up with the wonted speedy pace of his feverish naturalist's brain.

May 29, 1838

V. seems happy in her new home, insofar as I am able to ascertain from her limited—albeit hauntingly attractive—physiognomy and guttural vocables. I am assured by Madame de Mallet that she is not being abused, in terms of the frequency of her male visitors, nor in the nature of their individual attentions. (There are other dolly-mops there, more practiced and hardened than my poor V., to whom old de Mallet is careful to conduct the more, shall we say, demanding patrons.) In fact, the pitiable thing seems to thrive on the physical attention. She certainly appeared robust and hearty when I checked in on her today, with a fine slick epidermis that seems to draw one's fascinated touch. (Madame de Mallet appears to be following my instructions to the letter, regarding the necessity for keeping V.'s skin continually moist. There was a large atomizer of French manufacture within easy reach, which V. understood how to use.)

Taking her pulse, I was again astonished at the fragility of her bones. As I bent over her, she laid one hand with those long thin flexible, slightly webbed digits across my brow, and I nearly swooned.

It is for the best, I again acknowledged to myself, to have her out of the house. Best for her, and above all, best for me and the equilibrium of my nerves, not to mention my bodily constitution.

As for her diet, there is now established a steady relationship with a throng of local urchins who, for tuppence apiece daily, are willing to trap the requisite insects. I have also taught them how to skim larval masses from the many pestilential pools of standing water scattered throughout the poorer sections of the city. The boys' pay is taken from V.'s earnings, although I let it be known that, should her patronage ever slacken, there would be no question of my meeting the expenses connected with her maintenance.

It seems a shame that my experiments had to end in this manner. I had, of course, no way of knowing that the carnal appetites of the Hellbender would prove so insusceptible to restraint, nor her mind so unamenable to education. I feel a transcendent guilt in having ever brought into this world such a monster of nature. My only hope now is that her life will not be overly prolonged. Although as to the proper lifespan of her smaller kin, I am in doubt, as the authorities differ considerably.

God above! First my parents' demise, and now this, both horrible incidents traceable directly to my lamentable scientific dabblings. Can it be that my honest desire to improve the lot of mankind is in reality only a kind of doomed hubris...?

Cowperthwait laid his head down on the pallet and began quietly to sob. He did not often indulge in such self-pity, but the late hour and the events of the day had combined to unman his usual stern scientific stoicism.

His temporary descent into grief was interrupted by a peremptory knock on his study door. Cowperthwait's attitude altered. He sat up and answered the interruption with manifest irritation.

"Yes, yes, Nails, just come in."

The door opened and Cowperthwait's manservant entered.

Nails McGroaty—expatriate American who boasted a personal history out of which a whole mythology could have been composed—was the general factotum of the Cowperthwait household. Stabler, trapdriver, butler, groundskeeper, chef, bodyguard—McGroaty fulfilled all these functions and more, carrying them out with admirable expedience and utility, albeit in a roughshod manner.

Cowperthwait now saw upon McGroaty's face as he stood in the doorway an expression of unusual reverence. The man rubbed his stubbled jaw nervously with one hand before speaking.

"It's a visitor for you, ol' toff."

"At this unholy hour? Has he a card?"

McGroaty advanced and handed over a pasteboard.

Cowperthwait could hardly believe his eyes. The token announced William Lamb, Second Viscount Melbourne.

The Prime Minister. And, if the scandalous gossip currently burning up London could be credited, the lover of England's pretty nineteen-year-old Queen, on the throne just this past year. At this particular point in time, he was perhaps the most powerful man in the Empire.

"Did he say what he wanted?"

"Nope."

"Well, for Linnaeus's sake, don't just stand there, show him in."

McGroaty made to do so. At the door, he paused.

"I done et supper a dog's age ago already, figgerin' as how you wouldn't take kindly to bein' disturbed. But I left some for you. It's an eel-pie. Not as tasty as what I could've cobbled up if'n I had some fresh rattler, but not half bad."

Then he was gone. Cowperthwait shook his head with amusement. The man was hardly civilized. But loyal as a dog.

In a moment, Viscount Melbourne, Prime Minister of an Empire that stretched nearly around the globe, from Vancouver to Hyderabad, stood shaking hands with a baffled Cowperthwait.

At age fifty-nine, Melbourne was still possessed of dazzling good looks. Among those numerous women whose company he enjoyed, his eyes and the set of his head were particularly admired. His social talents were exceptional, his wit odd and mordant.

Despite all these virtues and his worldly successes, Melbourne was not a happy man. In fact, Cowperthwait was immediately struck by the famous Melbourne Melancholia. He knew the source well enough, as did all of London.

Against the wishes of his family, Melbourne had married the lovely, eccentric and willful Lady Caroline Ponsonby, only daughter of Lady Bessborough. Having made herself a public scandal by her unrequited passion for the rake and poet, George Gordon, Lord Byron (to whom she had ironically been introduced by none other than her own mother-in-law, Elizabeth Lamb), she had ultimately provoked Melbourne to the inevitable separation, despite his legendary patience, forbearance and forgiveness. Thereafter, Lady Caroline became so excitable as to be insane, dying ten years ago in 1828. Their son Augustus, an only child, proved feeble-minded and died a year later.

As if this recent scandal were not enough, Melbourne still had to contend against persistent decades-old rumors that his father had in reality been someone other than the First Viscount Melbourne, and hence the son held his title unjustifiably.

Enough tragedy for a lifetime. And yet, Cowperthwait sensed, Melbourne stood on the edge of yet further setbacks, perhaps personal, perhaps political, perhaps a mix of both.

"Please, Prime Minister, won't you take a seat?"

Melbourne pulled up a baize-bottomed chair and wearily sat. "Between us two, Mister Cowperthwait, with the information I am about to share, there must be as little formality as possible. Therefore, I entreat you to call me William, and I shall call you Cosmo. After all, I knew your father casually, and honored his accomplishments for our country. It's not as if we were total strangers, you and I, separated by a huge social gap."

Cowperthwait's head was spinning. He had no notion of why the P.M. was here, or what he could possibly be about to impart. "By all means—William. Would you care for something to drink?"

"Yes, I think I would."

Cowperthwait gratefully took the occasion to rise and compose his demeanor. He advanced to a speaking tube protruding from a brass panel set into the wall. He pulled several ivory-handled knobs labeled with various rooms of the house until a bell rang at his end, signaling that McGroaty had been contacted. The last knob pulled had been labeled PRIVY.

The squeaky distant voice of the manservant emerged from the tube. "What's up, Coz?"

Cowperthwait bit his tongue at this familiarity, repressing a justly merited rebuke. "Would you be so good as to bring us two shandygaffs, Nails."

"Comin' up, Guv."

McGroaty shortly appeared, bearing a tray with the drinks. A bone toothpick protruded from his lips and his shirttails were hanging out. He insouciantly deposited his burden and left.

After they had enjoyed a sip of their beer and ginger-beer mixed drinks, the Prime Minister began to speak.

"I believe, Cosmo, that you are, shall we say, the guardian of a creature known as Victoria, who now resides in a brothel run by Madame de Mallet."

Cowperthwait began to choke on his drink. Melbourne rose and patted his back until he recovered.

"How—how did you—?"

"Oh, come now, Cosmo, surely you realize that de Mallet's is patronized by the *bon-ton*, and that your relationship to the creature could not fail to become public knowledge within a few days of her establishment there."

"I wasn't aware—"

"I must say," Melbourne continued, running a wet finger around the rim of his glass, thereby producing an annoying high-pitched whine, "that the creature provides a novel sensual experience. I thought I had experienced everything the act of copulation had to offer, but I was not prepared for your Victoria. Evidently, I am not alone in appreciating what I take to be her quite mindless skills. In just the past week, I've run into many figures of note at de Mallet's who were there expressly for her services. Those scribblers, Dickens and Tennyson. Louis Napoleon and the American Ambassador. Several of my own Cabinet, including some old buggers I thought totally celibate. Did you know that even that cerebral and artistic gent, John Ruskin, was there? Some friends of his had brought him. It was his first time, and they managed to convince him that all women were as hairless as your Victoria. I predict some trouble should he ever marry."

"I am not responsible—"

Melbourne ceased to toy with his glass. "Tell me—exactly what is she?"

Having no idea where Melbourne's talk was leading, Cowperthwait felt relieved to be asked for scientific information. "Credit it or not, William, Victoria is a newt."

"A newt? As in salamander?"

"Quite. To be precise, a Hellbender, *Cryptobranchus alleganiensis*, a species which flourishes in the New World."

"I take it she has been, ah, considerably modified...."

"Of course. In my work with native newts, I have succeeded, you see, in purifying what I refer to as a 'growth factor.' Distilled from the pituitary, thyroid and endocrine glands, it has the results you see. I decided to apply it to a Hellbender, since they normally attain a size of eighteen inches anyway, and managed to obtain several efts from an agent abroad."

"And yet she does not look merely like a gigantic newt. The breasts alone...."

"No, her looks are a result of an admixture of newt and human growth factors. Fresh cadavers—"

"Please, say no more. Although here in a semi-private

capacity, I am still a representative of the law."

"It was my intention to test the depths of her intellect, and see if I could educate her. In the end, she proved lamentably intractable. Not wishing to destroy her, I had no choice other than de Mallet's."

"Why, if I may ask, did you name her Victoria? Was it a bad joke? Are you aware that in so doing you might have been guilty of *lèse majesté*?"

Cowperthwait was taken aback. "No, no, it was nothing of the sort. A chance resemblance to the new Queen, a desire to dedicate my scientific researches to her—"

Melbourne held up a hand. "I believe you. You need go no further."

There was silence in the study for a time. Then Melbourne spoke, apparently on an unrelated topic.

"When the Queen came to the throne a year ago, she was incredibly naive and unsophisticated. Not lacking a basic intelligence, she had been reared in a stifling and cloistered atmosphere by her mother, the Duchess of Kent. My God, all she could talk about was horses and tatting! She was totally tied to the apron strings of her conniving mother and the Duchess's Irish lover, John Conroy.

"I soon realized that, in her current condition, she would never do as the matriarch of our nation. It was up to me to form her personality along more regal lines, for the good of the Empire.

"I knew that the quickest way to do so involved becoming her lover.

"I will not bore you with the rest of my tactics. Suffice it to say that I believe I have succeeded in sharpening the Queen's wits and instincts, to the point where she will now make an admirable ruler, perhaps the greatest this sceptered isle has ever known."

"I fail to see—"

"Wait. There is more. I have steadily increased the Queen's work schedule, to the point where her day is taken up with reading dispatches and listening to her ministers. I thought she was bearing up admirably. However, I now fear I might have taken things too fast. The Duchess and Conroy have been bedeviling her lately with picayune demands. In addition, she has been nervous about her Coronation, scheduled for next month. Lately in bed together she has been complaining about feeling poorly and faint, miserable and nauseous. I'm afraid I brushed off these sentiments as idle vaporing."

"Surely you could let up a little on the poor girl...."

Melbourne passed a hand across his brow. "I fear it's too late for that.

"The Queen, you see, has just this day fled the throne."

Cowperthwait could scarcely give credence to his ears. "Impossible. Are you sure she has not been kidnapped, or injured while riding? A search party must be mounted—"

"No, it's useless. She's not lying senseless on some bridle trail somewhere, she's gone to ground like the cunning vixen she is. Certain personal items are missing, including her diary. To rouse a general search would only insure that her abdication became public knowledge in a few hours. And with political matters as they stand, Britain cannot afford even temporarily to be without a sovereign. Schleswig-Holstein, the Landgravine of Mecklenburg-Strelitz, the Spanish Succession—No, it's impossible that we advertise the disappearance. There are members of the nobility who

would like nothing better than such a scandal. I am thinking particularly of Lord Chuting-Payne. And besides, I
don't want Victoria to lose the throne. I have a conviction
about that girl. I think she's going to make a splendid
monarch. This adolescent impetuousness should not be held
against her."

"Oh, I agree," said Cowperthwait heartily. "But why
come to me? How can I help."

"I am asking you to contribute the services of your
Victoria. I want her as a stand-in for the Queen, until the
real Victoria can be found."

"That's ludicrous," expostulated Cowperthwait. "A newt
sitting on the throne of England? Oh, I concede that with a
wig, she might deceive from a distance. But up close—never!
Why not just bring in another human woman, perhaps of
low degree, who would impersonate the Queen and keep
silent for a fee?"

"And run the risk of future blackmail, or perhaps of
capricious misuse by the actress of her assumed position? No
thank you, Cosmo. And despite what people say of me in
connection with the Tolpuddle Martyrs, I am unwilling to
have such a woman later assassinated to preserve the secret.
No, I need a mannequin, someone utterly pliable. Only your
Victoria fits the bill. Loan her to me, and I'll handle the
rest."

"It's all so strange.... What can I say?"

"Simply say, 'yes,' and the nation and I will be forever in
your debt."

"Well, if you put it that way—"

Melbourne shot to his feet. "Wonderful. You have no
idea how relieved I am. Why, perhaps my Victoria, weary of

playing commoner, might even now be on her way back to
Buckingham Palace. But in the meantime, let us go secure
your Victoria from her bed at de Mallet's. You understand
that you'll have to fetch her, for I cannot be seen bringing
her away."

"Oh, of course...."

Only when they were in the shuttered landau driven by
McGroaty, rattling across the nighted town, with the womanly newt Victoria seated damply between them, a veil
demurely drawn across her elongated features, did
Cowperthwait think to tell Melbourne about the peculiar
diet of his charge.

"Flies?" said the Prime Minister dubiously.

"Fresh," said Cowperthwait.

"I assume the stables—"

"I can see, sir," complimented Cowperthwait, "how you
became Prime Minister."

2

A TRAIN STRAIGHT TO CHINA

The grandstand was draped with gay bunting in gold
and blue. Local personages of note, politicians and
members of the railroad corporation, sat in orderly rows on
the wooden platform, the women in their full bombazine
skirts protecting themselves from the summer sun with frilly
parasols. A brass band played sprightly tunes. Birds trilled
counterpoint from nearby branches. A crowd of farmers and

merchants, their wives and children, filled the broad meadow around the grandstand. Peddlers hawked lemonade and candy, flowers and souvenir trinkets.

The place was the small village of Letchworth, north of London; the year, 1834, shortly after the passage of the Poor Law, which would transform the rural landscape, sequestering its beggars into institutions. The occasion was the inauguration of a new rail line, a spur off the London-Cambridge main.

A few yards from the grandstand lay the gleaming new rails, stretching off to the horizon. The stone foundation of the station, its brick superstructure only half-completed and surrounded by scaffolding, stood south of the scene.

On the rails—massive, proud, powerful—rested an engine of revolutionary design. Not far off nervously hovered its revolutionary designer, Cosmo Cowperthwait, age twenty-one.

Next to Cowperthwait stood a fellow only slightly older, but possessed of a much greater flair and obvious sense of self-confidence. This was the twenty-eight-year-old Isambard Kingdom Brunel, son of the famous architect and inventor, Marc Isambard Brunel, genius behind the Thames Tunnel, the first underwater construction to employ shield technology.

The association between the Cowperthwaits and the Brunels went back a generation.

Clive Cowperthwait, Cosmo's father, had been engaged to the lovely Constance Winks. Not long before their scheduled nuptials, at a ball thrown by the Royal Association of Engineers and Architects, Clive had chanced upon his fiancée in a compromising position with the elder Brunel, in a niche partially occupied by a bust of Archimedes. The offended man—doubly incensed by the joint desecration of both his bride-to-be and the ancient philosopher—had immediately issued a challenge to duel. Brunel had accepted.

However, in the interval between the challenge and the event, the two men had chanced to discover the mutuality of their interests. At first frostily, then more warmly, the men began to discourse on their shared vision of a world united by railroads and steamships, a world shrunken and neatly packaged by the magnificent inventions of their age. Soon, the duel was called off. Clive and Constance were married as planned. Marc Brunel became both Cowperthwait's business partner and frequent house guest, bringing his own wife and young son along. Upon Cosmo's birth, he and little Isambard Kingdom ("I.K.," or "Ikky") had been raised practically as brothers.

Now the young Cowperthwait turned to his companion and said, "Well, Ikky, what do you think? She's keeping up a full head of steam, with only a few ounces of fuel. Is it a miracle, or is it not? Stephenson's Rocket was nothing compared to this."

Ever practical, Ikky answered, "If this works, you're going to put an end to the entire coal-mining industry. I'd watch my back, lest it receive some disgruntled miner's dirty pickax. Or what's even more likely, the silver table-knife of a mine-owner."

Cosmo grew reflective. "I hadn't thought of that aspect of my discovery. Still, one can't retard progress. If I hadn't chanced upon the refinement of Klaproth's new metal, someone else surely would have."

In 1789, Martin Heinrich Klaproth had discovered a

new element he named "uranium," after the recently discovered celestial body, Uranus. Other scientists, among them
Eugene-Melchior Peligot, had set out to refine the pure
substance. Cosmo Cowperthwait, inheritor of his father's
skills, raised in an atmosphere of practical invention, had
succeeded first, by reduction of uranium tetrachloride with
potassium.

Casting about for new uses for this exciting element,
Cosmo had hit upon harnessing its heat-generating properties to replace the conventional means of steam-production
on one of his father's engines. Clive Cowperthwait had
reluctantly acceded, and today saw the trial run of that modified engine.

"Come," said Cosmo, "let me instruct the engineer one
last time."

The two youths clambered aboard the train. In the cab
the crew welcomed them rather coldly. The chief engineer,
an old fellow with walrus mustaches, nodded ceaselessly as
Cosmo talked, but the young inventor felt he really was not
paying attention.

"Now, remember, there is no stoking of this engine, or
addition of fuel. Depressing this lever brings the two portions of uranium closer together, producing more heat, while
pulling it out increases the distance and diminishes the heat.
You'll note that this pin and cowling arrangement prevents
the depression of the lever beyond the danger zone—"

Cosmo halted in alarm. "The cowling—it's split and
ready to fall off. It seems a deliberate breach of all my safety precautions. Who's responsible for this malfeasance?"

The crew looked idly at the ceiling of the cab. One insolent superfluous stoker whistled an air Cosmo recognized as

an indecent folk tune by the title "Champagne Charlie."

Cosmo realized it would be futile to attempt to assign guilt now. "Come with me, Ikky. We must fix this before the trial." The two descended the engine. Some distance away on the grandstand, Clive Cowperthwait had just kissed his wife and moved to the front of the podium to give his speech.

"I am sorry that my partner could not be here today, but I'm sure I can speak long enough for both of us...." There was mild laughter from the crowd.

Cosmo was in no mood to join in the gaiety of the spectators. "Where can I find some tools?" he demanded frantically of Ikky.

"How about the blacksmith's, back in town?"

"Good thinking. Let me tell Father to delay the start of the engine."

"Oh, let's just dash. You know how long your father speaks. We'll have plenty of time."

Cosmo and Ikky hurried toward the village.

While inside the blacksmith's they faintly heard the resumption of the music, which had ceased for Clive's speech. Cosmo and Ikky rushed outside in alarm.

At that instant an enormous explosion knocked them off their feet, shattering every window in the village. A hot wind rolled them along the ground. When they managed to regain their feet, they saw the remnants of a mushroom-shaped cloud towering high up into the sky.

With immense consternation, mixed with not a little trepidation, the pair of friends hastened back toward the site of the dedication.

Still many furlongs away, they encountered the rim of an

immense smoking crater that sloped away into a glassy plain, the start of an excavation aimed at Asia.

Cosmo yelled into the desolate smoky waste. "Father! Mother!" Ikky laid a hand on his arm. "It's plainly no use, Coz. There can't be anyone left alive there. They've all been blown to Jehovah by your invention. I read this as a mark of Providence, which even your father's usual loquacity could not forestall, signaling that the world is not ready for such knowledge, if it ever will be.... You may console yourself with the thought that it must have been a painless death, thank God. In any case, I venture to say we won't find enough mortal flinders to fill an umbrella-stand."

Cosmo was in a state of shock, and could not reply. (Later, his old friendship with Ikky would be forever somewhat strained, as he recalled Ikky's callousness in the light of such a disaster, for which, by any fair measure, he was partly culpable.)

Feeling for some reason that it would be unwise to linger at the scene of the disaster, Ikky dragged his friend away.

Back in London, after a period of a few days' insensibility, Cosmo, now sole heir to the Cowperthwait name, had gradually recovered his mental faculties. One of the first things he had noticed had been the appearance of strange sores on his body. Ikky turned out to be suffering from the same manifestation of their experience, as were the few surviving Letchworthians. With the help of a pharmacist, Cowperthwait had derived a Naturopathic remedy, which, kept continuously against the skin, seemed to stem the plague. (Four years later, the sores would be all but vanished, yet Cowperthwait continued to wear his Naturopathic garment, more out of extreme caution than any scientific reason.)

After attending to his own ills, Cowperthwait realized he must set about arranging a ceremonial funeral for his parents. He was ready to step forth from his home one day to visit a local undertaker. Opening his front door, he was shocked to encounter someone already standing there.

The fellow was on the shortish side of average height, wiry and eager-eyed, dressed in loose American style. He hailed Cowperthwait vigorously.

"Friend, I been observin' of you in your bereavement, as you wander stupefied and pole-axed about this here town, and I come to the conclusion that you are in need of some moral companionship and support. In short, a personal valet."

Cowperthwait knew not what to make of this character. "Are you from the undertaker's?"

"Better'n that, young fellow. I'm from the Yew-nited States of Goddamn America, and I can get anything done that you order."

In his confused and guilty condition, Cowperthwait latched on to this offer eagerly. "What—what's your name?"

"Nails McGroaty, if it please you, Chief. Hell, even if it don't. So-called since I am tougher than my namesake, and twice as sharp. Now you just put your affairs in my hands, and let your mind be at peace. We'll show this town a wake, funeral and reception the likes of which they ain't witnessed since ol' Henry the Eighth threw snake-eyes."

Cowperthwait made up his mind. McGroaty was hired on the spot.

True to his word, the brash American arranged a first-class cortege to honor Clive and Constance Cowperthwait. There was enough black crepe to cover Westminster Cathedral.

After this performance, Cowperthwait grew assured that McGroaty was indeed no confidence trickster but apparently just a man in need of a permanent position with a lenient employer. Cowperthwait, apparently, had fit the bill.

McGroaty carried out his new household duties with dispatch. So invaluably, in fact, had he acquitted himself on a hundred occasions since, that Cowperthwait felt him more an older, more worldly brother sometimes, than servant.

The man's selling points were not his personal appearance, nor his insouciant demeanor. McGroaty was flippant, wry and occasionally abusive—hardly the marks of a good servant. He affected a casual dress reminiscent of a frontiersman, a kind of roughneck dandyism. McGroaty neglected shaving, and had never been known to bathe—a failing somewhat mitigated by his liberal use of strong toilet-waters.

McGroaty was, as he liked to remind Cowperthwait at frequent intervals, "one hunnerd and ten per cent American." His colorful history made his master wonder how one nation, even large as it was, could hold millions of such individuals, granted the representative nature of McGroaty's past.

McGroaty claimed to have been with the Stephen Austin expedition into the territory of Texas. ("G.T.T.," or "Gone To Texas" was currently American slang for fleeing the law, and Cowperthwait wondered if such had been

McGroaty's motives.) The man also maintained that he had been initiated into the Chickasaw tribe as a warrior, after saving the life of Chief Ikkemotubbe, and had willingly fought against his fellow whites who had sought to remove the tribe from their desirable lands in Mississippi. (A permanent weal on his buttocks, eagerly displayed to any chance female acquaintance, however reluctant she might be to view McGroaty's bare arse cheeks, was alleged to represent tribal scarification.) He bragged that he had been a mooncusser in New England, and would slyly exhibit, upon much cajoling, a small flat ingot of gold known as a "smuggler's bar," which fit neatly into his vest pocket.

Cowperthwait never learned what had made him seek permanent refuge in England, but suspected it was an illicit affair of titanic proportions.

All in all, a man of remarkable dimensions—the shortest of which was culture—and a companion Cowperthwait felt helped to offset his tendency toward dreaming abstraction.

Under McGroaty's stewardship, the years passed rather amiably. Ikky and his father ran the joint Cowperthwait-Brunel enterprises alone, insuring Cowperthwait, as absentee proprietor, of a guaranteed income and allowing him to indulge in his scientific investigations. Needless to say, he had lost all interest in further uranium-based transportation.

He had thought himself safe in turning his attentions to biological matters. What harm could come, after all, of experiments with tiny amphibians?

But woman-sized ones—Cowperthwait was beginning to suspect they were another matter altogether.

3

THE MAN WITH THE SILVER NOSE

In the days following the establishment of the false Victoria on the throne, as May shaded into June, Cowperthwait found himself disbelieving at times that he had ever experienced such a queer witching-hour visit from the Prime Minister, or that the product of his laboratory now sat in the regal seat reserved for the Hanoverian line. It seemed too much like a dream or nightmare born of a visit to one of the opium dens of Tiger Bay or Blue Gate Fields in the Old Port section of the city.

Yet such periods of doubt were dispelled by certain stern and irrefutable facts. The salamandrian Victoria was no longer at de Mallet's. The white velvet cushions in the landau were permanently stained. Dispatches detailing the unfolding of events arrived daily from Melbourne, hand-delivered in laminated and inlaid cases which normally contained official state documents. The functionaries who passed on these missives were members of the Queen's Messengers, those agents entrusted with the most privy of communications.

June 1

Still no trace of the veridical V.. I have employed certain confidential agents with the story that they are searching for my ille-

gitimate daughter. Naturally, their first step will be to comb all the most obvious hideyholes, including brothels like de Mallet's. Should they ultimately fail, I might have to bring in the Yard.

In the evenings, with pseudo-V. locked in her room, I search the teeming city myself, so far all to no avail.

Hopefully,
W. L.

June 3

Have kept contacts between V. and her ministers to a minimum. Let it be known that the Queen's "neuralgia" prevents her taking much interest in matters of state. All ceremonial duties are indefinitely postponed. Don't believe anyone suspects the imposture yet, tho' V. did eat an insect in public. I talked coolly right over the general consternation. The Ladies of the Chamber are hardest to put off. Many are the spies of Conroy and others. Have told them the Queen is experiencing an unusually difficult and prolonged menstrual period, and has armed herself with a pistol and threatened to shoot anyone who sees her naked, water-bloated form. The Ladies seemed one and all to comprehend. Yet how long can I believably prolong this...?

Frantically,
W. L.

June 5

Still no ray of light. Much of the time I might spend searching is taken up with satisfying V.'s predatory sexuality in order to keep her tractable. Her capacity is awesome. Find myself drained. Losing hope.

Despairingly,
W. L.

Cowperthwait read these missives with growing concern. All his experiments were pushed aside and forgotten. Even the eight-legged calves from Letchworth failed to sustain his attention. His mind was preoccupied with Melbourne's dilemma. The nation's dilemma, though the general populace was all unwitting. What would happen if the real Victoria were not found by the day of her Coronation? Would a newt be solemnly consecrated by the Archbishop of Canterbury as the Queen of England? It would be worse for England than the papacy of Pope Joan had been for the Romish Church.

And what of the awful travails the real Victoria must be undergoing? Here was a girl who had never in her short life even been allowed to ascend a staircase by herself, for fear she might stumble and fall. Now she was adrift in the urban squalor that was London. Cowperthwait could not rid his mind of a series of images of degradation and humiliation that were both disturbing and strangely exciting.

In the end the hallucinations threatened to rob him of his sleep, and he realized that he had to do something to rid himself of this excess of nervous humours. Science had temporarily lost its allure. There was nothing for it but to join the search for Victoria himself. Any other option would leave him feeling he hadn't done enough.

It would not do to tell Melbourne, however. The Prime Minister seemed somewise reluctant to further involve Cowperthwait, and the young inventor, as a loyal subject, was not willing to risk being told definitely not to contribute his help.

Thus it was that the nine-fold chiming of the tall timepiece in the hall one foggy evening found Cowperthwait, cape athwart his shoulders, standing indecisively at the door to his Mayfair residence.

Where should he begin to look? Where would a young girl on the run likely end up, here in this metropolis of sin and greed? Other than a brothel—and Melbourne had already had them all searched—Cowperthwait realized he hadn't the slightest idea.

Cowperthwait felt a hand on his shoulder and turned to confront Nails McGroaty. His manservant was dressed for the night chill with a stained bandanna knotted around his otherwise bare throat, and obviously intended to accompany Cowperthwait.

In confirmation McGroaty said, "Don't worry, Coz, it's all jake. I ain't lettin' you go out alone. I knows the whole dismal story, knowed it since that first night when I was a-listenin' at the study door. And though it don't matter nuthin' to me—your precious royalty bein' jest a bunch of whangdoodles to a born demmycratic American—I cain't stand by and let you expose yerself to all kinds of danger. You need a ripsnortin' bobcat sech as myself by your side, when push comes to shove. As I says to Mike Fink when we was workin' on the same barge up and down the Big Muddy, 'Mike, there ain't nuthin' more important in life than friendship.' That was jest before I walloped the tar out of the mean bastard and tossed him overboard."

Cowperthwait felt vastly relieved, and showed it by warmly clasping McGroaty's hand. "Your noble offer is accepted, Nails. Let's go."

As they were leaving, Cowperthwait's eye fell on a malacca cane protruding from the elephant's-foot umbrella-stand by the door, and he snatched it up.

"Just in case," he told McGroaty with a wink.

"Air you sure, Guv? You remember the last time—"

"I've fixed it since then."

"Suit yerself."

As they left behind the exclusive district where Cowperthwait maintained his household, the streets became more and more thronged with citizens of every stripe. Blind beggars, elegant ladies, coarse streetwalkers known as "motts," hurdy-gurdy operators, men with dancing bears, a fellow running a movable shooting-gallery where participants banged away with spring-loaded pellet guns at targets moved like Cowperthwait's writing pallet by a crank.... A fight broke out between two match-girls, and one knocked the other into a horse-trough. This was the least remarkable incident Cowperthwait and McGroaty witnessed.

When they reached Oxford Circus, McGroaty indicated that they were to cross the thoroughfare. Cowperthwait hesitated.

The actual streets of London were in many cases running sewers and rubbish bins. Offal and manure presented an obstacle ankle-deep. Springing up to capitalize on this phenomenon were the "crossing-sweeps," homeless boys and girls who, for a token payment, would brush a path across the street for a citizen. Seeing his master's hesitation to imbrue his footwear in the muck, McGroaty now moved to engage such a one.

"You there, ol' carrot-top! C'mon and clear us a path!"

The shoeless youth thus addressed hurried over. His clothes were in rags and he was missing several teeth, yet he flashed a broad smile and radiated a kind of innocent happiness. His one possession appeared to be a broom worn almost to its nubbin.

Doffing his cap, he said, "Tiptoft's the name, gents. Reasonable rates and swift service is me motto. Anytime you're in the neighborhood, ask for me."

Without further ado, the boy stepped squarely into the horrid slop with his bare feet and began to sweep industriously. Cowperthwait and McGroaty followed in his wake.

On the far side of the street Cowperthwait asked, "How much?"

"One pence apiece, if it's agreeable, gents."

Cowperthwait handed the lad a shilling.

The sweep was ecstatic with the over-payment. "Thank'ee, guv'nor, thank'ee! Won't I eat elegant tonight!"

Cowperthwait and McGroaty moved on. The inventor seemed touched by the incident, and at last chose to comment.

"Here you see an example of the trickle-down theory of material improvement, Nails. Thanks to the fruits of the Cowperthwait-Brunel enterprises, I am enabled to endow those less fortunate. A rising tide lifts all ships."

"I done heard that trickle-down stuff compared to a sparrow what gets whatever oats a horse shits out undigested."

"A crude and imprecise analogy, Nails. In any case, someday, thanks to science, the streets of London will be clean of organic wastes, and such poor urchins, if they exist at all, will be maintained by a wealthy and benevolent state."

"Ayup," was McGroaty's laconic comment.

Continuing their walk in silence for half an hour through the clammy streets—Victoria the Imposter would have no need of her atomizer in this weather—Cowperthwait finally thought to ask where they might be heading.

"Well," said McGroaty, "I figger ol' Horseapple is always needing people for the treadmills. Perhaps your little lady was press-ganged there."

Cowperthwait nodded sagely, although he was truly no further enlightened.

Through the cobbled dismal streets, past shabby forms slumped against splintered doors in shadowed entryways, ignoring the outstretched hands and more lascivious solicitations of the ragged throng, Cowperthwait followed McGroaty. They seemed to be trending toward the Thames. Soon, Cowperthwait could contain himself no longer.

"Exactly where are we heading, Nails?"

"Horseapple's pumping station."

Soon the air was overlaid with the murky odors of the river that flowed through the city like a liquid dump. Water sloshed over nearby unseen weed-wrapped steps. Cowperthwait heard the muffled dip of oars, presumably from one of the aquatic scavengers who made their meager living by fishing from the river whatever obscure refuse they might encounter—not excluding human corpses.

A building loomed up out of the fetid air. Light leaked out of its shutters. A vague rumbling as of vast machinery at work emanated from the structure. McGroaty knocked in a mysterious fashion. While they waited for a response, the servant explained to Cowperthwait the nature of the enterprise run by his friend.

"Horseapple heard they was lookin' for someone to supply water to them new houses out in Belgravia. He greased a few palms with the old spondoolicks, and got the contract. He's been addin' customers right steady ever since. 'Course, every new client means more manpower's needed."

Cowperthwait was astonished. "They're drinking Thames water in Belgravia? Why, this stuff is positively pestilential."

"Oh, it ain't so bad as all that. Since they put the grates up on the intake pipes, nuthin' bigger'n a rat can get through."

The door opened and a belligerent poxed and bearded face thrust out. Squinting, the man recognized McGroaty.

"Come in, come in, Nails. Another volunteer for the treadmills, I take it. Does he need further persuasion?" Horseapple flourished a truncheon.

"Not this one, old man. It's my mate, Cosmo. He's lookin' for a lady friend of his, and thought she might be gracin' your establishment."

"Let him look then. But don't disturb their rhythm. It makes for bad water pressure and the toffs complain."

Horseapple conducted the visitors through some cob-webbed antechambers and into a dimly-lit cavernous interior. The building must have been at one time a brewery or warehouse. Now, however, ranked across the quarter-acre or so of floorspace were five dozen wooden treadmills, all hooked by an elaborate system of gears, cams and shafts to a brace of huge pumps. The treadmills were manned by rag-clad wraiths chained to their stations. Whip-bearing over-seers marched up and down, applying persuasion whenever a unit flagged.

Cowperthwait turned angrily to Horseapple. "My Christ, man, this is absolutely barbaric! A steam engine or two would easily outperform all these poor wretches."

Horseapple stroked his hirsute chin. "You're talking heavy capital investment now, Carmine. The bleedin' pumps cost me enough as it was. And besides, what would these poor buggers do with their free time? Just drink themselves silly and lie in the gutter. As it stands, they've got a roof over their head and three meals a day, albeit it's usually only whatever's fouling up the grates."

McGroaty laid a hand on Cowperthwait's shoulder. "No time for social reform now, Coz. We got an important lady to find."

So saying, the pair trooped up and down the ranks, looking for the missing Queen. For purposes of comparison, Cowperthwait carried a silhouette that had been published in the daily papers.

No luck. Horseapple invited them to check the sleeping off-shift laborers, which they quickly did, making all haste to escape the urinous and bedbug-ridden common dormitory.

Horseapple saw them to the door. "Remember, Nails— ten shillings a head. The way this city is growing, I'll be forced to double my operations in a year."

The door slammed behind them, and Cowperthwait stood motionless a moment, stunned and disheartened by the experience. With such pits and cesspools of inhumanity, how could he ever hope to imagine the Queen was still alive and unhurt, and able to be found? The task seemed hopeless....

McGroaty was whispering in Cowperthwait's ear. "Don't let on, but there's someone watchin' us. To your left, behind that pile of crates."

Cowperthwait slowly turned his head. A glint of light flashed off something silver.

"I'll handle this," Cowperthwait whispered back. He raised his cane. Then, in a loud voice: "Step forward and declare yourself, man!"

From the shadows emerged the form of a giant. A swarthy native of India, he appeared at least seven feet tall, although some of that height might have been attributable to his voluminous headwrap. Dressed in colorful silks, he bore a long scimitar by his side.

"Holy Andy Jackson!"

"Have no fear," declaimed Cowperthwait, his voice quavering. The inventor raised his cane and pressed a spring catch in its handle. The lower portion of the cane shot off, taking the concealed sword-blade with it and leaving Cowperthwait holding a stubby handle.

The two waited for the Indian to advance and decapitate them both with one mighty blow.

Instead, the thuggee was joined by another figure.

The Man with The Silver Nose.

Lord Chuting-Payne.

In his late fifties, Chuting-Payne possessed the athletic build of a Olympian. Impeccably attired, the master of vast ancestral estates at Carking Fardels, he had once been deemed the most handsome man of his generation. That had been before the duel he had fought with Baron Leopold von Schindler of Austria.

One evening in the year 1798, the eighteen-year-old Chuting-Payne, only scion of his line, had been hosting a dinner for various ambassadors, in an attempt to further his political ambitions. Present had been his sovereign, the demented King George the Third. The Austrian Baron von

Schindler, somewhat tipsy and of a fractious nature, had criticized with Teutonic wit Chuting-Payne's wine list in front of the royal guest of honor. Humiliated beyond tolerance, Chuting-Payne had immediately challenged von Schindler to pistols at twenty paces.

Von Schindler, revealing himself as coward and caitiff, had fired while Chuting-Payne was still turning, blowing off the man's nose.

Immense quantities of blood streaming down his face, Chuting-Payne had then calmly drilled von Schindler through the heart.

The jewelry firm of Rundell, Bridge & Rundell—the very makers of the new lightweight crown that was to be used in frail Victoria's upcoming coronation—had been employed to melt down some family sterling and fashion a prosthetic silver nose to replace Chuting-Payne's missing flesh one. They had exerted all their skill, and the resulting simulacrum was a marvel to behold. Affixed by gutta-percha adhesive, the nose was said to be capable of exciting the most jaded of women.

But the attainment of a new nose was hardly the end of the affair. Pressed by the Austrians, King George had sworn out a warrant for Chuting-Payne's arrest. The man had been forced to flee the country. As the tale went, he had ended up in India, in the Province of Mysore, still an independent nation at the time. Turning his back on his own country, Chuting-Payne had allied himself with the Maharaja of Mysore, Tippoo Sahib, and his French backers against the British. He had lived in Mysore for a year, until it fell to a joint attack by British and Mahratta troops.

Escaping from the siege of Seringapatam, Chuting-Payne had then traveled among the other independent Indian nations—Sind, Rajputana, Punjab—until the death of George the Third in 1820. Somehow he had amassed a large enough fortune to bribe King George the Fourth to rescind the long-standing warrant against him. He had returned to his native land over a decade ago, a figure of enigmatic Oriental qualities, sunbrowned and distant, more wog than limey.

Having been mistreated by Victoria's ancestor, Chuting-Payne had conceived a stupendous hatred of their whole line. As Melbourne had intimated to Cowperthwait, the man would like nothing better than to involve the throne in any sort of scandal.

"Mister Cowperthwait, I believe," said the silver-nasaled nobleman, his voice imbued with queer resonances. "I don't think we've ever had the pleasure of meeting. My name I assume you know. Allow me to introduce my servant, Gunputty."

Gunputty bowed. Cowperthwait croaked out something. The bizarre pair completely unnerved him.

"What brings you so far from your retorts and alembics, Mister Cowperthwait? Looking for more amphibious subjects among the slime? By the way, where is your creation lately? I've noticed her absence from de Mallet's."

"She's—I've—that is—"

"No matter. She's not the only unique lady missing. Or so my spies report."

"I—I don't know what you mean...."

"Oh, really? I think differently. In fact, I believe we are

both abroad in search of the same thing, Mister Cowperthwait. Lest the *hoi polloi* overhear, we'll just call her 'Vee' among ourselves, shall we?"

"You're—you're hallucinating."

"Far from it, Mister Cowperthwait. Although I must admit that your addlepated clodpoll of a servant, who appears the byblow of a New World savage on a warthog, does resemble some of my less pleasant nightmares."

"Put up your dukes, Tinface, them's fightin' words."

Chuting-Payne snugged his white gloves for a more precise fit. "Tell your man, Cowperthwait, that the last fellow who engaged in fisticuffs with me is now so much wormsmeat, and that he would be well-advised to steer clear of his betters. Gunputty—fetch the carriage. Mister Cowperthwait, farewell for the nonce. I sense our paths will cross again."

In a moment Lord Chuting-Payne's phaeton was rumbling away. Cowperthwait felt his wits gradually returning, and was mortified that he had let Chuting-Payne treat himself and McGroaty in such a cavalier fashion.

Seeming similarly embarrassed, McGroaty said, "I thought you said you done fixed that cane."

"It acted precisely as I wished," extemporized Cowperthwait. "Had it struck that lascar, it would have knocked him senseless."

"I suggest more diereck tactics in the future, Coz. That air Gunputty don't seem the type to be stymied by no flyin' baton."

"Suggestion acknowledged, Nails."

4

Cowperthwait spread mint jelly across his scone. The transparent greenish substance reminded him of the egg mass of the Hellbender. He still recalled the shivery thrill he had felt upon receiving the crate from his American compatriot, S. J. Gould of Harvard, containing the glass vials packed with fresh Hellbender eggs, nestled snugly in wooden cradles set in sawdust and straw for their transatlantic journey. The many nights of feverish experimentation, the innumerable abortions and teratological nightmares which had to be destroyed, the refinements in technique and purification, all resulting in the unique miracle that was Victoria.... A wave of sadness and nostalgia crossed over him. Would he ever see his progeny again, or would she remain forever immured inside Buckingham Palace, a slave to the needs of the state?

The only solution lay in finding the real Victoria, a creature no less fabulous than her salamandrine counterpart. Where, oh where could she be? In the three days since their visit to Horseapple's, Cowperthwait had racked his brain for any likely burrow she might have found, all to no avail. Even at this moment, Cowperthwait had McGroaty out scouring the city for any possible clue, however wild and far-fetched.

A knock resounded on his study door. Cowperthwait tugged down his Naturopathic corset beneath his dressing gown, adjusted the silk scarf around his neck, and called out, "Yes, who is it?"

The door swung open and McGroaty entered, propelling a scurvy character before him. The fellow clutched a battered cap with both hands in front of him, high up on his chest. This position for his headgear was necessitated by his having a withered right arm only a few inches in length. In compensation, his whole left arm was an overdeveloped bulk of muscle.

"Coz, this here's Shortarm. He runs a sewing shop down in the Seven Dials. Shorty, tell the guv'nor what you told me."

Shortarm attempted to compose his features into a semblance of innocence, but succeeded only in looking like a fox with chicken feathers stuck to its lips. "Wurl, it's like this, see. I got me a daughter, a lurvely gell—"

"He fathered the poor thing on his older daughter, so you might say she's his granddaughter too," interrupted McGroaty.

Cowperthwait winced. "Yes, go on."

"Wurl, she's all of six, so's I figgered she was old enough to start earning her keep. Otherwise, she was gonna find herself eatin' air pie, if you get my meanin'. So I puts her to work in the shop, stitchin' up breeches—"

This time it was Cowperthwait who interrupted. "You know, of course, that in so doing you were in direct violation of Lord Althorp's Factory Act, regarding the employment of minors."

Shortarm wrinkled his brow in genuine bafflement. "Can't say as how I ever heard of no Fackery Axe, sir. And she warn't doin' no minin' of any sort."

Cowperthwait sighed. "Pray, continue."

"Wurl. One evenin' aroun' seven, just as the gells was finishin' their day by receivin' their nightly strappado, in busts these two wimmen. One's an older lady with the pinchy face of a do-gooder, so's I know I'm in for trouble right away. The other 'peared to be much younger, but I couldn't be sure, for she had a veil 'crost her face. And not no lacey thing either, but a piece of muslin with eye-holes in it.

"Next thing I knows, the older bitch—parm me, sir, lady—had me good arm what was holdin' the whip doubled up behind me back, fit to snap. Gord, she was a strong un!

"'Sisters,' she says, 'I'm a-here to offer any of you what wants it sanctuary at my school. Which of you will come with me?' Next thing I knows, all my gells is hollerin' and shoutin', 'Me, me, I'll go, take me!' Even me own two daughters joined in the tragic chorus."

Shortarm paused to sniffle and wipe a tear away. "I can tell you, guv'nor, it hurt me deep inside. To think of all the attention and money and high-quality wittles I done lavished on those gells, and then to have 'em turn on me like that. It cut me to the quick."

"Nails, I fail to see what any of this has to do with our search...."

"Hold on, Coz, it's comin'." McGroaty prodded Shortarm, who resumed his tale.

"The elder gell turns to the one in the veil then and says, 'Vicky, escort the wimmen to the carriages.' When my shop is empty, she boots me headfirst against the wall. I didn't wake up for half an hour, and there was no way of tracin' 'em by then."

A thrill had shot along Cowperthwait's nerves at the name of the assistant rescuer. Trying not to betray his eagerness, he fumbled in his purse to reward the sweatshop owner, coming up with a five-pound note.

"Gord, a fiver! Thank'ee kindly, sir. This'll be more'n enough to replenish my workforce, so to speak." Shortarm turned to leave, then halted. "Oh, if you find my gells, you're a-welcome to the older one. She's kinder used up. But as for the younger—" Shortarm smacked his lips obscenely.

Cowperthwait shot to his feet. "Nails, eject this brute before I give him a good thrashing!"

McGroaty picked up Shortarm by his trousers and shirt. "Them's the words I been waitin' to hear, Coz!"

When McGroaty returned from tossing Shortarm out, Cowperthwait was pacing his study, rubbing his hands together. He stopped and grabbed McGroaty by the arm.

"Nails, it all makes sense! The Queen, frustrated by the glacial pace of her government and her remoteness from her subjects, has joined forces with a private benefactress, and now seeks to remedy the ills of her empire firsthand! It's a noble attempt and speaks well of her character, but we must find her and persuade her that she can do more good from her throne."

McGroaty rubbed his whiskery chin thoughtfully. "Ackshully, Coz, it shouldn't be too hard. I can't imagine any sech school as can house dozens of gals can remain much of a secret from its neighbors."

"Precisely, Nails. Let us begin our enquiries."

By that very afternoon McGroaty's inspired ferreting had met with success. Cowperthwait clutched in his clammy hand a pasteboard bearing a name and address in nearby Kensington:

LADY OTTOLINE CORNWALL'S
LYCEUM AND GYNOCRATIC MISSION
NUMBER TWELVE NOTTING HILL GATE
EDUCATION, LIBERATION, VINDICATION
"SORORAE SE FACIUNT ID"—SAPPHO

Cowperthwait hurriedly snatched up a large maple cane from the stand by the door. "Come, Nails, let us be off while it is still light out."

McGroaty eyed the cane dubiously. "Is that a plain walkin' stick, or some new infernal device, Coz?"

Cowperthwait chuckled. "The latter, I fear, Nails. Observe." Cowperthwait opened a breach in the cane, revealing a large-caliber shell. "The trigger is here in the grip. I wager even a superhuman specimen like Gunputty will not be able to easily fend off a charge of this size."

"With any luck, we won't run into that towel-headed furriner at all today. Meanwhile, don't go a-pointin' that cane at no helpless merchant who wants a few pence extra fer his termaters, like you usually do."

The pair exited the Cowperthwait manse. There, on the sidewalk, they encountered a familiar face: the gap-smiled countenance of little Tiptoft, the crossing-sweeper.

"Hullo, kind sir. I seen your man scurryin' about the town and took the liberty of followin' him back here. This seems like a ritzy neighborhood with a lack of sweeperly competition. I shall reside here henceforth."

"God's wounds! You—you can't encamp outside my house like this. This is Mayfair, after all, not Covent Garden. What will the neighbors say?"

"Doubtless they will be forever in your debt, sir, for securing such an asset to clean-footed traffic."

To illustrate his utility, Tiptoft dashed out into the street and begin switching away at a huge pile of accumulated manure, sending showers of offal left and right, bespattering passersby who paused to flourish their fists and utter imprecations.

"Stop, stop, that's enough! Look now, will you take this money and go away?"

"I'm sorry, sir, but I've got me mind fixed on a steady income."

"All right, all right. Let's see—do you have any objections to living in my mews, with the horses?"

"Horses is me bread and butter, so to speak, sir. I do not."

"Very well. You may live in the mews and receive meals and a weekly stipend, provided you ply your trade elsewhere."

"Agreed! And furthermore, it is to be understood that your honor will have unqualified first-call on me services."

The two shook hands on the deal. Then Cowperthwait said, "I cannot spend anymore time here dallying. We are in search of a woman."

"I could help there, too, sir."

"No, no, that's fine. Goodbye for now, Tiptoft."

"Allow me to conduct you partway, sir."

With Tiptoft sweeping ahead like a dervish,

Cowperthwait and McGroaty proceeded toward Kensington, eventually parting ways with their escort near Hyde Park, where the confluence of traffic provided a fertile field for his broom.

Number Twelve Notting Hill Gate was a large edifice in the early Georgian mode, with freshly washed steps and starched curtains in the windows serving to conceal the interior. Using the knocker, which was shaped to resemble the ancient symbol of the Labrys, or double-headed ax, Cowperthwait sought admittance. The door was soon opened part way by an elderly maid, stopping at the short extent of a stout chain.

"No visiting privileges for menfolk," she said, and slammed the door.

Cowperthwait was both baffled and slightly enraged. "I say—" He resumed knocking. The door opened once more, this time to reveal the snout of a large old-fashioned pistol aimed at his head.

A stern and cultivated female voice spoke. "Perhaps you failed to comprehend my maid's injunction. We do not permit husbands, fathers, brothers, uncles, employers or lovers entrance. When we admitted your wife, daughter, sister, niece, employee or paramour, it was under tragic circumstances which your presence would only aggravate and reinforce. Now, will you depart, or shall I blow your head off?"

Cowperthwait's ire won out over any fear. "Madam, I do not know any of the young ladies in your care, unless possibly it be the one whom I seek. My name is Cosmo Cowperthwait, and I merely wish to speak to you about, um, the missing wife of a friend."

The pistol dropped away. "Did you say Cowperthwait?"

"Yes, that was the appellation."

"Author of the monograph 'Sexual Dimorphism Among The Echinoderms, Focusing Particularly Upon The *Asteroidea* and *Holothurioidea*'?"

"The same."

"One moment."

The door shut, the chain rattled off, and the door swung wide.

Revealed was an imposing figure of womanhood. Clad in a strange kind of one-piece white cotton garment that ended at the elbows and knees, the woman stood six feet tall with a deep bosom and large hands and feet. Striped lisle stockings and flat athletic shoes completed her outfit. Her hair was sequestered under a plain mob-cap. Her gray eyes radiated a fierce intelligence. Her full unpainted lips were quirked in a smile, as she dangled the pistol by her side.

"You and your servant may enter, Mister Cowperthwait. But just remember that you are here solely on my whim, and may be ejected—or worse—at any moment, if your misbehavior merits it."

Cowperthwait was somewhat embarrassed at this odd woman's revealing attire, but sought to meet her on her own unconventional terms. "Madam, I assure you that you are dealing with two gentlemen of the highest propriety and social standing."

"When one contemplates the deeds that are daily done in society's name, such a description is no high recommendation. But please enter."

Once inside, Cowperthwait said, "I assume I have the honor of addressing the proprietor of this establishment?"

"Indeed. I am Lady Ottoline Cornwall, and this is my

school. Perhaps you would care to see its functioning?"

"Certainly. I have already been intrigued by what I have heard of your recruitment methods."

"Desperate times demand desperate measures, Mister Cowperthwait. I am not one of those who believe that idle bemoaning or passivity will accomplish anything. When I see an evil, I move vigorously to remedy it. There is much wrong with this world, but I limit my scope to ameliorating the sorry condition of womankind. I have pledged my family fortune to this establishment, which is dedicated to helping unfortunate girls from every stratum of society. From the warrens of Lambeth to the drawing-rooms of my own posh precinct I extract the abused and maltreated and try to inculcate a sense of their own worth in them."

Lady Cornwall had brought them to a closed door, upon which she now gently knocked, then opened. Cowperthwait saw inside rows of desks at which sat a class of girls of various ages, all dressed identically with their headmistress. At the front of the room stood a teacher. Cowperthwait eagerly scanned her face for a resemblance to the missing Queen, but was disappointed.

"Here you see some of the girls at their lessons. Latin, Greek, French, geography, and many more subjects are here covered, particularly the natural sciences. We use several of your monographs in this latter area, Mister Cowperthwait."

Cowperthwait was flattered, and did not know where to look. "I—that surprises me, Lady Cornwall. My papers are not intended for the layman. Ah, laywoman."

"Our girls are up to it. Thank you, Miss Fairbairn, you may get back to your teaching."

Shutting the classroom door, Lady Cornwall continued

the tour, bringing them to a capacious ballroom. The large
space was fitted out with gymnastic equipment of all sort,
barbells, skipping-ropes, punching bags. Bales of hay with
targets on them even afforded the possibility for some of the
girls to practice archery.

"I do not neglect the physical side of my charges either.
Eight hours of sleep nightly in our well-ventilated dormitory, plenty of good food and exercise, along with the wearing
of sensible clothing—no stays or contorted footgear here—
can work wonders in their self-image."

When McGroaty saw the bows and arrows, his face lit
up. "Criminy! I ain't handled a bow nor arrow since leavin'
the Chickasaws! Here, now, Missie, you're a-holdin' it all
wrong. Let me larn you what Chief Ikkemotubbe showed
me."

Soon McGroaty was surrounded by enthusiastic young
Amazons. Tongue protruding from the corner of his mouth,
he placed an arrow in the bullseye. Then he presented his
hindquarters to the target and, bending over and firing
between his legs, split the first shaft with a second.

Applause and huzzahs filled the air. Lady Cornwall said,
"Your servant seems to have found something to occupy
him. Shall we adjourn to my private office and discuss what
brings you here?"

"By all means."

Seated in Lady Cornwall's sanctum, holding a glass of
port sangaree, Cowperthwait regarded the formidable
woman before speaking. She had impressed him mightily
with the acuity of her intellect and the strength of her met-
tle. He knew he must choose his words with care, so as not
to anger or insult her.

"Ah, Lady Cornwall—"

"Please, I disdain titles. Call me Otto. And I shall address you by your Christian name also."

"Yes, um, Otto, then. Otto, would it be safe to assume that you look with favor and hope upon the ascension of our new Queen to the throne, as an exemplar of competent womanhood?"

Lady Cornwall snorted. "After a year, she has yet to prove that she's more than a poppet to Viscount Melbourne. I yet have my hopes. But she'll have to do more than she's done so far to merit them."

Cowperthwait studied the depths of his sangaree. "Suppose I were to tell you that the Queen, in an assertion of her independence, has run away."

Lady Cornwall jumped to her feet. "I'd shout bravo!"

"Please, Otto, calm down. While the Queen's hypothetical desertion might appeal to your romantic side, if you stop to consider it practically it presents more cause for grief than rejoicing. If we don't want to see the Queen lose the throne, then she must be cajoled to return to it."

Dropping into her chair, Lady Cornwall favored Cowperthwait with a calculated look and said, "How does any of this relate to me and my school?"

Dropping all subtlety, Cowperthwait said, "I have reason to believe that you employ a veiled woman referred to as 'Vicky.' Might it be she of whom we speak?"

"What if I tell you no? Then I suppose you'll demand that I haul poor Vicky before you, so that you can satisfy yourself. Why should I subject poor Vicky to your male imperiousness?"

Cowperthwait had no ready answer to this. Lady

Cornwall eyed him piercingly, then spoke. "Cosmo, I respect you as a man of science, a male whose intellect and self-control raises him above the brutish level of his fellows."

Such talk made Cowperthwait nervous. What would she think of him if she knew of the newtish Victoria, and how he had satisfied his base lusts upon it?

"Therefore, I will allow you to speak to my Vicky, but only on one condition. That you accompany me this moment on a mission that will perhaps open your eyes to the real condition of women in this isle. What do you say?"

"Well, if it's the only way—"

"It is."

"I consent."

"Capital!" Lady Cornwall rose and took a dress off a peg and donned it unconcernedly. She changed her shoes, then pulled off her mob-cap, spilling out long auburn curls. Clapping a flat straw hat on her head and grabbing a reticule, she said, "Let's go."

"But my servant—"

"Are you afraid to venture unaccompanied someplace where I am not?"

"By no means!"

"Then we're off."

Leaving by a back door, Cowperthwait and Lady Cornwall made their way to an omnibus stand and were soon on their way cross town.

"Exactly where are we heading?"

"To Bartholomew Close, in the Smithfield Market. The central exchange for stolen goods."

Cowperthwait fingered his cane nervously.

They disembarked at a dilapidated three-story building

with gingerbread trim, whose lower floor held a meat-market. The sight of so much raw red meat and the smell of animal blood made Cowperthwait feel faint.

"We are looking for Liza, a flower girl. She normally stations herself here, although I do not see her now. I have been arguing for weeks with her parents, trying to enroll her in the school. I feel they are almost ready to consent."

"What are we to do now?"

Lady Cornwall cupped her chin. "We'll have to visit Liza's home."

Down several noisome alleys they treaded, arriving finally at a ramshackle tenement. Lady Cornwall went confidently in, Cowperthwait tentatively following.

Upstairs, in a darkened hall illuminated only by what light penetrated a small filthy cobwebbed window, the schoolmistress knocked on a door.

The door cracked open and a bearded, greasy face thrust itself out. "Which family?" said the man gruffly.

"The Boffyflows."

"That'll be one pence for crossing the Swindle establishment, one pence likewise for the Scropeses, and a third for the Snypes."

"Very well. We'll pay. Now let us in."

The man opened the door fully. They entered.

The tiny candle-lit unpartitioned room held four families and their miserable possessions. The high-status Swindles occupied the quarter closest to the exit, and hence had to pay no tolls. Next came the Scropeses, then the Snypes. Lowest in stature were the Boffyflows, who cowered—mother, father, infants and adolescents—in the farthest corner.

Dispensing the pences, they made their way to the Boffyflows.

Father Boffyflow was a lardy fellow sitting in a rickety chair and nursing a black eye. Lady Cornwall accosted him. "Where's Liza?"

"On her doss, snifflin' and sobbin'."

"Why wasn't she at work today?"

"Argh, she warn't makin' nuffin sellin' flowers, so I decided she had to go out as a cripple."

"Cripple—?" Lady Cornwall hastened to the girl on her pallet and lifted up the slack form.

Liza's fresh wrist-stub was wrapped in bloody rags.

Lady Cornwall wailed. "Oh, that I should have temporized with these savages! Now must I live with this on my conscience for the remainder of my life!"

She made to leave, carrying the unconscious girl. Boffyflow interposed himself, thrusting his stomach against the schoolmistress. "'Ere now, where are you takin' my girl—"

Before Cowperthwait could interpose there was a gunblast, and Boffyflow fell back in his chair, shot in the gut.

Lady Cornwall's hand was in her reticule, which exhibited a smoking hole from the derringer within.

"Anyone else object?" she asked.

Mister Snype advanced cautiously. "No argyment from us, Ma'am, long as we get our pence on the way out."

"Cosmo, see to it."

With shaking hands, Cowperthwait paid the exit tolls.

The trip back to Number Twelve Notting Hill Gate passed for Cowperthwait as in a dream. Only when he was once more sitting in Lady Cornwall's office and soothing his nerves with a rum and shrub did reality begin to resume its wonted dimensions.

When Lady Cornwall returned from letting out the female physician who had tended to Liza's wounds, she said, "And now, Cosmo, I'll keep my end of the bargain. Here is the woman you wished to see."

Cowperthwait could hardly contain his excitement at the appearance of the veiled woman. At last, the real Victoria would be restored to the throne and his Victoria would be returned to him....

The woman slowly lifted her muslin veil.

At first Cowperthwait could hardly believe that the face revealed to him belonged to a human, let alone a woman. A mass of keloid scars and twisted discolored flesh, it resembled that of some hobgoblin or creature out of Dante's Inferno.

"A combination of acid and flame, administered by her bawd. Even women may hurt women, you see."

Cowperthwait struggled for something to say commensurate with the horrible injustice of the situation. "I—my growth factor—perhaps it might repair some of the damage. I can't guarantee anything. But regular applications might help."

"Vicky would appreciate that. Wouldn't you, Vicky?"

The woman nodded mutely, shedding a tear from one ruined eye.

"Thanks you, Vicky. That will be all."

When the girl had left, Lady Cornwall came up by Cowperthwait's side.

"Cosmo, you stood up admirably during that little contretemps at Smithfield Market. And your pity toward Vicky touches me. I would like to reward you, if I may."

So saying, Lady Cornwall grabbed Cowperthwait in a grip of iron, tilted him backward and kissed him in the Continental manner, thrusting her tongue deep into his mouth.

Cowperthwait's cane discharged thunderously into the floor.

5

THE FATAL DANCE

For several days after the visit to Lady Cornwall's Lyceum, Cowperthwait moped about like a love-sick schoolboy. The surprising denouement to his visit, in which Lady Cornwall had revealed the passion which lurked beneath her competent exterior, remained vivid in his mind, obscuring all other matters. Even the notion of finding the missing Queen was cast into shadow.

Cowperthwait had for years dreamed of marriage to a perfect companion. The woman would have to be smart and amiable, literate and lusty, free-minded and foot-loose. Truth to tell, his creation of Victoria had been something of an experiment along crafting the perfect bride he could not find.

Now, in the person of Lady Cornwall, he was convinced he had found her. Smitten by her soul-kiss, he could think of nothing but joining their fortunes and estates together. A woman who could appreciate "Sexual Dimorphism Among the Echinoderms" was not to be found every day.

Seeking McGroaty's opinion of the woman, Cowperthwait was somewhat dismayed by the manservant's undisguised disdain of her.

"She puts me in mind of a sartin Widder Douglas I knew, back in Hannibal, Moe. Always a-trying to reform and change people, which in my book is about as pointless as tossin' a lasso at the horn o' the moon. Plus she's all-mighty bossy. You mark my words—if'n you two get hitched, she'll have you scrubbin' her knickers on washday faster'n spit dries on a griddle."

Cowperthwait would have liked to have McGroaty endorse Lady Cornwall, but it this was not to be the case, then McGroaty would have to simply lump it. After all, an opportunity like this came along only once in a lifetime....

The lone difficulty in Cowperthwait's view lay in how best to broach his proposal. It would have to be handled just right....

When scarred Vicky visited shortly thereafter, for her first treatment with growth factor, Cowperthwait entrusted her with a note for her mistress.

Dearest Otto,

Our adventure is etched in flames upon my cortex. If you could possibly see fit to entertain me again, I would like to consult with you upon making our alliance a permanent one, so that we may offer each other mutual aid and comfort.

Your earnest admirer,

Cosmo.

The reply he received with Vicky's next visit was rather brusque.

Dear Sir:

*I am not at present of a mind to agree to any such permanent
and exclusive arrangement as, if I read you aright, you are ten-
dering. Let us submerge our feelings for the nonce, and remain
simply friends.*

Otto.

This cold water dashed on his marital hopes threw
Cowperthwait into a blue funk. He spent the next few days
homebound, reading and rereading a passage in Blore's
Exceptional Creatures about the Giant Rat of Sumatra.
Eventually, however, he realized that such behavior ill-suit-
ed him. Thrusting aside all consideration of personal happiness, he plunged once more into his quest for his vanished
sovereign.

Every waking hour was devoted to the increasingly futile
search for the vanished Queen. Accompanied by McGroaty,
the young natural philosopher combed the festering warren
that was lower-class London, silhouette in hand, feverish,
sleep-deprived brain alert for any trace of Victoria.

By daylight and gaslight, aboveground and below,
amidst the noisy market crowds or alone in a rooming house
with a work-worn suspect female, Cowperthwait pursued
the mirage of Victoria.

From fish-redolent Billinsgate to the prison hulks at
Gravesend, where convicts lay sickly in bilge-water; from
Grey's Inn law offices where pitiful petitioners pled their
cases to tubercular sanitariums where angels like one named
Florence Nightingale escorted him from bed to bed; from
filthy dockside to plush gambling parlor—Through every
stratum of the underworld, in fact—guided by McGroaty,

whose knowledge of such places seemed encyclopaedic—
Cowperthwait journeyed, footsore and obsessed.

And everywhere he searched, it seemed, a nemesis
would greet him.

Lord Chuting-Payne, the arrogant, evil tempered
enemy of the throne.

Either Chuting-Payne was there waiting for him; or had
just departed; or arrived as Cowperthwait was leaving. No
matter what hour it was, the cruel and sardonic nobleman,
always accompanied by the silent and forbidding Gunputty,
appeared fresh and dapper, as unruffled as a calm lake. At
those times when he and Cowperthwait came face to face,
they usually exchanged no more than a brittle *bon mot* or
two. Sad to relate, Chuting-Payne could be counted on to
triumph in such exchanges, his rapier wit honed by a lifetime among the cynical rich.

Cowperthwait came to loathe the sight of the arrogant
Lord with his precious-metal nose that made him seem half
machine. He soon regarded the man as his own evil doppel-
ganger, and the only comfort he could find in Chuting-
Payne's continued appearances was that it meant the Lord
was having no more luck in his search for Victoria than
Cowperthwait was.

Victoria. The name itself began to sound unreal to
Cowperthwait. Who was this phantasm, this woman he had
never met in the flesh? She lay at the heart of
Cowperthwait's life, at the center of the Empire's power. On
the one hand, although only on the throne a year, it could be
generally sensed that, after a succession of old, doddering
Kings, she was already the very lifebreath of a fresh new era,
the embodiment of the sprawling political organism that

stretched its tentacles across the globe. On the other hand, she was only one woman among millions, no more important in the ultimate scheme of things than the fishwife or costermonger Cowperthwait had just interviewed, no more to be loved and admired than the stoic Vicky whom Cowperthwait continued to treat. (And with some measure of success....)

And what of his own Victoria? Melbourne's dispatches had trailed off, and Cowperthwait had heard nothing of the hypertrophied Hellbender in days. The last missive had not been reassuring.

June 10

I fear the "black dog" of Melancholia has me in its jaws. I and the kingdom are positively undone, unless V. makes her reappearance. Whilst hopelessly waiting, I contemplate the merits of your creature: if only all women could be so tractable...!

From Stygian depths,

W. L.

Something of the same despondency gripped Cowperthwait. He hoped that the Prime Minister in his funk was not neglecting Victoria's needs, but he had no way of finding out. It would hardly do to approach Buckingham Palace and ask whether the Queen's skin appeared suitably moist....

Three weeks passed. There were now less than seven days until the coronation, and no sign of Victoria.

This evening found Cowperthwait preparing to embark one more time on another fruitless round of searching. On the point of setting out, a wave of ennui swept over him. He felt as if all his bones had been instantly removed.

"Nails, I fear I cannot continue this Sisyphean task. At least not tonight."

"Cain't say I blame you, Coz. I'm plumb tuckered out myself. What say we swing 'round to de Mallet's, and take it easy for one night?"

"A capital idea, Nails. Although I fear I'm too weary to endure the embraces of any doxy, the atmosphere should prove congenial."

Leaving the house, they encountered Tiptoft asleep under the front portico. Stepping quietly over the lad, so as not to awake him and be forced to endure a whirlwind of sweeping, they set out for Regent's Street.

At the carven oak door of de Mallet's luxurious establishment they employed the gilt knocker in the shape of a copulating couple and were quickly admitted by the major-domo. Their hats were taken, glasses of champagne were proffered on a golden salver, and soon Cowperthwait and McGroaty were seated in the large ballroom, watching couples dance to the stately strains of Mozart flowing from a gilt pianoforte, and eyeing appreciatively the corseted trollops sprawled on velvet chaises around the four walls.

The only incident momentarily to jar Cowperthwait's composure occurred when he thought he detected a flash of reflected candlelight in an oddly fluted piece of silver borne aloft at nose-height across the crowded room. But if the glint indeed indicated the presence of Lord Chuting-Payne, that spectre did not materialize any more solidly, and Cowperthwait, by dint of his mental discipline, soon succeeded in banishing such fears.

Cowperthwait switched from champagne to Madeira, and the room soon took on an ethereal glow. The cande-

labra appeared to waver and flare, like will-o-the-wisps.
McGroaty disappeared at one point, presumably to display
his Chickasaw scars to some lucky roundheels, and
Cowperthwait found himself nodding off to sleep. He
dozed for awhile and awoke feeling more refreshed than
he had in ages. It was at this point that Madame de Mallet
approached him.

Tall and buxom, swamped with jewels, perhaps overly
made-up for some tastes, in the fashion of an older period,
de Mallet was a well-preserved seventy. Rumor had it that
she had been a chambermaid to Marie Antoinette (and
sometime bedpartner of Louis), and had barely escaped the
Revolution with her life.

"*M'sieu* Cowperthwait, may I interest you in a lady
tonight? We have a new addition to the house." Here de
Mallet bent lower, and spoke in a whisper. "She is someone
très special, un bijoux. I do not offer her to *tout le monde*, only
my favorites. I can guarantee that it will be the chance of a
lifetime."

Cowperthwait was momentarily intrigued, but, not
wishing to disturb his serenity with the rigors of carnal love,
he ultimately declined. With a shrug, Madame de Mallet
said, "*Très bien*, as you wish."

Feeling a pressure of a different sort emanating from his
bladder, however, Cowperthwait said, "I could make use of a
chamber pot, though."

Madame de Mallet waved her beringed hand airily.
"You are familiar with the house. But piddle," she advised,
"with discretion and a minimum of noise, please. *La cham-
bre à côté du pissoir*, it is occupied."

Cowperthwait got unsteadily to his feet. He made his

tipsy way up the grand staircase, colliding off various couples in an illustration of Brownian motion which appealed to him.

In the second-floor corridor he began counting doors, but soon lost track. Cowperthwait opened what he recalled to be the correct door.

It was not.

Two women were in the room. One, clothed in a plain chemise, sat at a veneered secretary, her back to Cowperthwait as she vigorously scribbled in a small book. Upon hearing the door open, she cradled her arms around the diary, as if to shield its contents, and dropped her face down upon it.

The second woman, a veritable Amazon, filled the rumpled bed with her Junoesque naked body. Lying spread-eagled on her back, hands clasped behind and pillowing her head, she wore on her features an expression most obviously betokening sexual satiation.

"Otto!" exclaimed Cowperthwait.

Lady Cornwall was not embarrassed. "Yes, Cosmo, it's I. How may I help you?"

Cowperthwait sank into a handy chair and held his head in his hands. "A daughter of Lesbos. No wonder you had no interest in my proposal. I should have guessed, from your mannish ways. How convenient for your perversion, you keeping all those young helpless chicks as your wards—"

Lady Cornwall leapt from bed and slapped Cowperthwait across the face. "How dare you impugn my motives! My girls are treated as chastely as nuns. Why do you think I'm buying my love in this place, if you imagine I sate my desires at the school?"

Lady Cornwall sat down on the bed and began to cry.

Cowperthwait could think of nothing to say or do except to mutter a useless apology and leave.

Finding the privy, he relieved his bladder. What a farce life was, he thought as he piddled. Missing queens, newts on the throne, Sapphic saviors....

Ruefully buttoning his fly, Cowperthwait returned to the main salon.

The current piece of music was just ending. Cowperthwait was startled to see McGroaty standing next to the piano. A borrowed fiddle was tucked under his chin.

"Ladies and gents, pick up yer feet. Yer about to be ennertained by some authentic Virginny foot-stompin' reels. Hit it, Wolfgang!"

McGroaty immediately began an enthusiastic sawing, the pianist managed to master the beat, and the floor was soon filled with energetically twirling couples. Cowperthwait found himself engaged by a red-haired whore and spun about. Reluctant at first, he found the lively music to be just the tonic his tired blood needed, after the dismaying revelation upstairs, and he was soon performing more spiritedly than anyone. Within minutes the dancers had stepped back to form a circle at the center of which Cowperthwait and his enthusiastic partner performed.

Cowperthwait's head was spinning. He couldn't remember when he had felt so wonderful. Damn all his troubles! By God, he'd give everyone a show! He hoped Otto was watching. Picking up his partner by the waist he began a particularly acrobatic maneuver. At that moment, two things happened simultaneously. From the spectators a disdainful voice said, "What an ignorant and savage display—" At the same instant, Cowperthwait lost his footing and launched his partner out of his sweat-slick hands and through the air.

After Cowperthwait had picked himself up off the floor and dusted himself off, he thought to look for the red-haired girl.

Her fall had been inadvertently cushioned by the body of Lord Chuting-Payne, who in so doing had lost his nose. The dead tissue and gaping holes in the center of face were revealed before the whole room. Strong men fainted and woman screamed.

Chuting-Payne calmly accepted his nose back from Gunputty and stuck it back on his face. Unfortunately, it was upside down.

"Dawn tomorrow at my estate, Cowperthwait. Your choice of weapons."

Watching the misassembled nobleman haughtily depart, Cowperthwait wondered briefly if he could convince Chuting-Payne to agree to flying sword-canes at fifty paces.

6

TREACHERY AT CARKING FARDELS

In the flickering light of a candle, Cowperthwait peered into the looking glass atop the chiffonier in the hallway and nervously adjusted his cravat. It wouldn't do to meet his predictable death looking less than a fashionable gentleman. He wouldn't give Chuting-Payne the satisfac-

tion of standing over his corpse and uttering some cutting
remark about the failings of his haberdasher.

A door creaked. In the mirror, Cowperthwait saw
McGroaty appear behind him, carrying a package wrapped
in oiled cloth. He turned.

"It done took me some time to find where I laid it up,
but here it is."

"Here what is?"

"The key to you blowin' that dirty skunk offen the face
of the earth." McGroaty began to tenderly unwrap the
object within the greasy rags. Soon lay revealed an enormous
weapon, a product of the Colt Arms Manufactory in
Connecticut. The gun had a barrel as long as loaf of French
bread, with a bore of commensurate diameter. The chamber
appeared designed to hold projectiles the size of
Cowperthwait's fingers.

The naturalist attempted to pick up the pistol. He found
himself unable to heft it one-handed, and perforce had to
grasp the giant's weapon with both. He made as if to draw a
bead on the stuffed orangutang at the hall's end. His arms
shook with the effort of supporting the pistol's weight, and
the gun barrel wavered through an arc of several inches.

McGroaty was smiling earnestly at Cowperthwait's
target practice. (Those teeth of his not missing were
chipped.)

"That's the trick, Coz! Yer onto it now! You may not
reckon it, but yer holdin' the world's finest Peacemaker. I
done toted this little honey all over the globe, and she never
let me down once. Hellfire, you don't even got to hit nothin'
vital to kill that polecat. Jest whang him in the fingertip and
he'll likely die of shock. I blowed the head offen a buffalo
with this darlin' from a hunnerd yards away."

Cowperthwait laid the monstrous gun back among the rags. His arms were quivering. "No, Nails, I'm afraid not. It simply wouldn't be sporting, since we haven't its mate to offer Chuting-Payne. And I fear I'd be stone-dead before I could lift your Colt up to fire. No, you'd best fetch my father's set. It's time we were off."

Reluctantly McGroaty wrapped up his gun, breathed a sigh of consternation, as if unable to fathom Cowperthwait's finicky morals, and went off to secure the aforementioned pistols.

Soon he returned with a mahogany box. Cowperthwait lifted the lid. Inside, nestled in velvet depressions, were a brace of small pearl-handled pistols.

The selfsame guns purchased by Clive Cowperthwait in anticipation of his duel with Marc Isambard Brunel.

Cowperthwait shed a tear at the thought of his father and mother, and the whole tragic family history. He thought also of Ikky Brunel, who had just promised him a guided tour of *The Great Western*, the marvelous transatlantic steamship about to have its maiden voyage. Now it looked as if he would never get a chance to witness that marvel of this wondrous age. Ah, life—how bittersweet....

"Very good," said Cowperthwait, closing the lid. "That leaves only a few points of unfinished business. Nails, keep this on your person. It's my last will and testament. You'll find that you're my sole heir."

McGroaty wiped his eyes. "Reckon I'd better make out my own then, cuz I'll be coolin' my heels in the calaboose afore I swing by the neck."

"Why?"

"Cuz when Chuting-Payne croaks you, I aim to croak him."

"Nails, I appreciate the sentiment, but please don't. It would stain the family honor."

"Ain't nothing you could do to stop me, Coz, but I promise anyhow."

"Very good. Now, here is a letter for Lady Cornwall, along with the last of my growth factor for her ward, Vicky. Please make sure she gets them."

McGroaty overcame his disdain of the Lyceum mistress enough to agree to this.

"Excellent. Finally be so good as to fetch Tiptoft."

When the sweep appeared, straws in his hair and rubbing crumbs of sleep from his eyes, Cowperthwait handed him an envelope.

"Tiptoft, here's a draft on my bank for a hundred pounds. You are hereby discharged from my services."

"Hurrah!" shouted the lad. "I'm off to Australia to make my fortune!"

Cowperthwait patted the sweep on the head and saw him out the door. Turning to McGroaty, he said, "Let's depart. We don't want to keep the noble bastard waiting."

In the trap, rattling through the empty pre-dawn London streets, Cowperthwait tried to gauge his feelings. He was remarkably calm and clear-headed, especially considering neither he nor McGroaty had gotten any sleep since the fracas at de Mallet's just a few hours ago. He was surprised to find that the prospect of his imminent death did not trouble him in the least. It seemed, rather, a relief to know that everything would soon be over. The failure of his experiments with the salamander known as Victoria, followed by the frustrating and enervating quest for the human Victoria and his disillusionment with Lady Cornwall, had left him weary and dispirited. There seemed little left in life to engage his interests, and, despite his physiological youth, he felt himself a veritable greybeard. Better to have it over with now, than drag through life with this premature ennui....

Soon they had left the sprawling metropolis behind. In under an hour, they were approaching Carking Fardels, the ancestral estates of the Chuting-Payne family, of whom Cowperthwait's nemesis was the last direct descendant. The sky was lightening in various sherbert tones, birds were trilling, and breezes were stirring the mists that writhed among the underbrush. It looked as if it would be a fine day on which to meet one's demise.

McGroaty turned the trap onto a lane that diverged from the tollroad. Beneath fresh mint-green foliage they rolled, until they came to a large pair of gates. Waiting there was the magnificent figure of Gunputty.

Leaning close to his employer, the American said, "Iffen you can ee-liminate ol' Tinface by some scientific slight-o'-hand, Coz, go for it without worryin' about facin' his second. I got a scheme to sap that fuzzy-wuzzy's will."

Cowperthwait sighed deeply. "Please, Nails, no shennanigans that will spoil my exit from this mortal coil."

"Just leave that human mountain to me, Chief," finished up McGroaty mysteriously. At this juncture, the fuzzy-wuzzy in question leaped silently up as postillion and, clutching the carriage's superstructure, waved them on toward their mortal rendezvous.

Across a dewey field, the trap leaving glistening tracks, and to the edge of a copse of speckled alders. Gunputty disembarked and led the way beneath the trees.

A small discreet clearing was to be found amidst the trees, just wide enough for the requisite paces.

Standing nonchalantly there was Lord Chuting-Payne, dressed in morning-coat and spats. His nose was correctly positioned, and had been buffed to perfection. Cowperthwait could see himself in it.

"I had my doubts as to your showing up," said Chuting-Payne. Cowperthwait let the insult pass. He felt serenely exalted above such pettifogging. "I trust you brought suitable weapons...."

Cowperthwait silently held up a hand, and McGroaty laid the pistol-box in it. Chuting-Payne advanced, opened the receptacle and selected a gun. "A splendid model, if a bit antique. I recall that the last time I used such a gun was to perform a trick for the Earl of Malmesbury. He tossed a deck of cards into the air, and I shot only those which would beat the hand of euchre which he simultaneously flashed before my eyes."

McGroaty spat into the grass. Chuting-Payne sneered. "There will soon be a brighter, more vital fluid staining the lawn here, my man, so don't waste your precious substance. Well, there's no point in delaying any further, is there?"

McGroaty and Gunputty stepped aside. Cowperthwait noticed his man whispering into the lowered ear of the turbaned Titan, and the next thing he knew, the two seconds had vanished behind a tree.

But there was no time to ponder their actions further.

Cowperthwait and Chuting-Payne advanced to the center of the clearing and stood back to back. Mist coiled around their ankles.

"On the count of three, we commence walking for twenty paces, turn—completely, mind you, for I have no second nose to lose—and fire at will. One, two, three—"

The walk seemed miles. Cowperthwait felt a small wild animal striving to claw its way to freedom within him, but suppressed it. Soon, soon....

Twenty paces. Turn.

Chuting-Payne stood negligently, with arms folded across his chest, allowing Cowperthwait first shot. The inventor raised his gun, shut his eyes, and fired.

Lifting his eyelids, he saw a robin fall dead from the tree behind the Lord.

Chuting-Payne smiled and brought his pistol up. "Before you die, Mister Cowperthwait, I just want you to know that I have found our common Grail. And the scandal I intend to cause with what I have learned will topple the throne, and more than adequately recompense me for the insults I have suffered. Now, address your prayers to your maker, Mister Cowperthwait."

Chuting-Payne aimed confidently at Cowperthwait, who closed his eyes again, for the last time.

The shot rang out.

Miraculously, Cowperthwait felt nothing. How grand.... He had been right not to fear.... Paradise, hello!

Cowperthwait opened his eyes.

Chuting-Payne lay dead on the turf, the back of head blown off in a gory mess.

It dawned slowly on Cowperthwait what must have happened. "McGroaty! Goddamn you, McGroaty, you promised! That was hardly sportsmanlike!"

Out from the trees stepped a figure.

It was Viscount Melbourne. The Prime Minister clutched a smoking pistol.

"William—I don't—How? Why?"

The dapper nobleman calmly removed the spent cartridge from his gun and substituted a fresh one. "I could hardly let Chuting-Payne continue to live now, Cosmo, could I? After what he just said about his plans to embroil Victoria in a hideous scandal. Not after all the work the two of us have put into keeping her name unsoiled. And besides, I rather like you, and owed you a favor. I consider that debt discharged."

"But I thought you said you didn't believe in assassination."

"That was of women, boy. Entirely different set of rules for the other sex. No, I fear Chuting-Payne's treasonous intentions earned him his death. And besides, without heirs his estate devolves to the throne. I've had my eye on it for years."

A thought occurred suddenly to Cowperthwait. "The Queen! He knew where she was! Now the knowledge is gone with him."

Melbourne seemed queerly unconcerned. "Yes, rum bit of luck, that. But I could hardly wait any longer to bag him."

A sudden malaise swept over the young scientist, leaving him disinclined to press the matter further. All he wished now was to be home in bed. Thoughts of those welcoming counterpanes brought up an associated matter, which he now put to the Viscount.

"My creation—it's been so long since I've had any news from you. Is she flourishing? Does she ever seem to—to pine for her old surroundings?"

Melbourne sought to brush the matter aside. "She does well. Her needs are simple, and easily fulfilled. Most of them, at any rate...if you know what I mean, eh?"

Cosmo opened his mouth to adjure the Minister not to overtax the chimeric creature, but Melbourne cut him off.

"Well, you'd best be heading home. Oh, don't worry—there'll be no legal repercussions. The Crown will handle matters."

From out of the woods there appeared McGroaty, accompanied by Gunputty. Melbourne raised his pistol, anticipating deadly action from the servant on behalf of his wronged master. Cowperthwait too fully expected that the loyal Indian servant would attempt to revenge his master's death.

But instead, the Indian merely beamed a bright smile their way! Picking McGroaty up like a child, he trotted eagerly toward them.

"Nails, what—?"

"Everything's jake, Coz. I just finished explainin' something mighty beneficial to ol' Ganpat here. That's his real name, by the way, after some heathen god or other. I managed to instill some demmy-cratic ideals in him, made him see that iffen his master was to die, he'd be a free man, able to make his fortune with his good looks and exotic ways. We're plannin' to get him a job with P. T. Barnum, who's blowin' in through town soon. He does a mean snake-charmin' act."

Cowperthwait sighed. A regrettable lack of remorse all around here.

But life must go on, he supposed.

Mustn't it?

WHAT EVERYONE ELSE KNEW

Cowperthwait slept for a day and a half. His dreams, if any, were painless, and vanished upon waking. Standing over him was McGroaty, bearing a tray heaped high with lavishly buttered scones, a decanter of tea, and a lidded crystal pot full of fresh strawberry jam.

"I thought you might need some vittles by now, Coz."

Cowperthwait sat up in bed, plumping the pillows behind himself. "Quite right, Nails. Time to fortify the body before attempting to tackle the problems of the mind that yet beset us."

"I couldn't'a phrased it no better myself."

Cowperthwait dug hungrily into the repast. He was amazed at his hunger, having expected to bear some lingering anxiety and consequent loss of appetite over the death of Chuting-Payne. However, even the resemblance of the strawberry jam to Chuting-Payne's spilled brains was not sufficient to dismay him.

As he ate, Cowperthwait pondered the problem of Victoria.

Chuting-Payne had claimed to know her hiding place. It was obvious the knowledge was fresh, for during a recent meeting last week—at the establishment of a Jewish moneylender reputed to occasionally harbor runaway children—Chuting-Payne had been as obviously ignorant as ever.

Therefore, he must have discovered it just prior to the contretemps at de Mallet's—

De Mallet's. Cowperthwait ceased to chew. An image of the old bawd materialized vividly before his slack-jawed face.

"Someone *très spéciale*....the chance of a lifetime...."

It couldn't be—could it? De Mallet's establishment was the first place Melbourne would have searched. The only reason Cowperthwait hadn't bothered himself was that certainty. And yet—

Tossing back the blankets, Cowperthwait sent his breakfast flying. "Nails! Nails!"

McGroaty ambled in unconcernedly while Cowperthwait was attempting to insert both lower limbs into a single trousers-leg.

"Nails, we must hurry with all dispatch to Madame de Mallet's."

McGroaty winked. "Takin' care of some other needs now, I reckon."

"Oh, Nails, you're hopeless. Just ready the transportation."

Soon Cowperthwait found himself admitted by a sleepy and disheveled majordomo into the empty parlors of Madame de Mallet's. (McGroaty was waiting outside; should Cowperthwait's hunch prove correct, it would hardly do to have the uncouth ruffian present to embarrass the delicate sensibilities of the woman he now fully expected to meet.) The gilt fixtures and flocked wall-coverings appeared tawdry in the light of day that diffused through the drawn heavy drapes. There was a nauseating odor of spilled champagne and stale bodily exudations. The place wore a face far different from its glamorous nighttime image. Cowperthwait wondered which manifestation, if either, was closest to reality.

Hand on the staircase rail, Cowperthwait was hailed by the servant. "'Ey now, Guv'nor, you can't disturb the girls at this hour—"

"Oh, shut up, man! I'm not here for a roger. For Agassiz's sake, why is everyone so blasted fixated on their privates?"

In the upstairs corridor something drew Cowperthwait unerringly toward the room that had once held the salamander Victoria. At the door, he knocked softly. A feminine voice responded.

"Is it night already? I feel like I've hardly slept. Come in, then, come in, I'm ready...."

Cowperthwait twisted the handle and entered.

The chamber was curtained from the daylight, and lit only by a single candle. The match that had just ignited the tallowed wick was being puffed to extinction by the pursed lips of the woman in bed.

Woman, yes. Now she was plainly girl no longer.

Victoria's long hair was a soft brown, halfway between the flaxen color of her youth and the foregone darker shade of her maturity. Her face was round and still somehow innocent, her nose and chin somewhat pronounced. She would, Cowperthwait suspected, never look more radiant. These looks, he knew, were slated to be soon captured by the court painter, Franz Winterhalter.

The Queen possessed a commanding gaze which Cowperthwait now found hard to disengage from his own. At last doing so, he took in the rest of Victoria's dishabille.

She lay with the covers thrown back, wearing the sheerest of peignoirs. Her bust and hips were full, giving some hint of a future stockiness, and she looked ripe for bearing many children. Cowperthwait was suddenly certain that it would not be long before a new little Prince or Princess graced the land.

Yet this maternal aspect of Victoria was still implicit, not dominant. At the moment, she looked anything but motherly. Her exquisite body yet unmarred by any pregnancies, she was as inviting a woman as any Cowperthwait had seen.

On a card-table in a corner was a partially completed dissected picture, one of the puzzles Victoria enjoyed assembling. Next to it rested her inevitable diary.

Cowperthwait dropped to one knee. "Your Majesty—"

Victoria's voice was throaty. Cowperthwait knew she had trouble with septic tonsils. "You can forget all titles now, silly boy. I'm not queen here. In this house, there are others who know so much more than I, and deserve that title. But I'm learning. Come here, and I'll show you."

Victoria lifted her arms out imploringly. Shocked, Cowperthwait stood and came to sit on the edge of the bed where he could press his case more convincingly.

"Your Majesty, I realize that the demands of your high office have caused you untold grief, and that it is only natural you would seek to forget all your troubles by adopting a wanton's role. But you must realize that the nation needs you. The coronation is imminent. And do not forget the personal anguish you have caused your Prime Minister. Viscount Melbourne is beside himself, wondering where you are."

"Whatever are you talking about, you foolish man? It was Melbourne who put me here."

Cowperthwait felt as if his brain were about to tear itself apart. "Melbourne—?"

"Yes, Lambie told me it would be part of my education. And he was so right. Why, I've met many of the most important figures in the country, on more intimate terms than I could ever achieve in the sterile corridors of state. Writers, artists, members of Parliament, educators. Men and women both. Why, there were even some common laborers who had saved up their money for ages. And the talk has been almost as stimulating as the loving. The secrets I've learned, the bonds I've forged, the self-confidence I've cultivated, not to mention the tricks I've learned that will certainly please my darling Albert when we've married—These will stand me in good stead for my whole reign. I shan't have any trouble getting my way from now on, I feel. Oh, I've enjoyed it so! It's a shame it's almost over."

Cowperthwait tried to find his tongue. "Then you have no intention of abdicating—?"

"Of course not! I'm returning to the Palace tomorrow, for the Coronation rehearsal. It's all arranged. Now, forget all this talk of matters politic, dear boy. Come here to your little Victoria, and let her make everything all better."

Victoria flung her arms about Cowperthwait, pulled him down and began unbuttoning his fly.

At first hesitant, Cowperthwait soon began enthusiastically to comply.

After all, one simply did not casually disobey one's sovereign, however demanding the request....

It was no trouble to break into Buckingham Palace under the cover of darkness. Security was quite primitive. As an example, in December of that year 1838, "the boy Cotton" would finally be apprehended, after inhabiting the Palace uncaught for several months. Twelve years of age, he was perpetually covered in soot, having often concealed himself in chimneys. He blackened the beds he chose to sleep in, broke open sealed letters to the Queen, stole certain small geegaws and food, and when caught was found to be wearing a pair of Melbourne's trousers.

Cowperthwait did not encounter "the boy Cotton" as he made his way down the echoing passages that night toward the Queen's private bedroom. He followed the directions Victoria had graciously given him earlier that day, after their bout. Cowperthwait had explained his involvement in the subterfuge surrounding Victoria's absence. It turned out the Queen knew nothing about the mock-Victoria occupying her bed with Melbourne, and he thought he could detect no small jealousy on her part. He did not envy Melbourne the explaining he would have to do tomorrow.

At the same time, Cowperthwait was quite angry with the way the Prime Minister had duped him. He was now determined to secure his Victoria, and have it out with the man.

Only once did Cowperthwait encounter anyone, a patrolling Beefeater whom he avoided by ducking into a niche holding a bust of Ethelred the Unready.

At last Cowperthwait stood outside the royal bedchambers. Without knocking, he let himself in.

Melbourne lay abed with the salamander. When the newt saw Cowperthwait she let out a croak of joyous recognition and slithered out of bed. Completely hairless, her sinuous form combined mammalian and amphibian characteristics in an unearthly beauty. The wig she used to impersonate the Queen graced a stand across the room.

Melbourne leapt naked out of bed, his burly hairy body a gross contrast to the ethereal, sylphlike splendor of the Hellbender.

"Sir," uttered Cowperthwait, "I know all! You have tricked me in a dastardly fashion. I suppose you had the interests of the country at heart, but I believe there was also a component of unholy lust in your actions. I now reclaim my ward, and leave you to your conscience."

Cowperthwait took Victoria's hand and turned to go.

Melbourne grabbed her other hand and held on. "No, don't take her. You're right, I am besotted with this creature of yours, have been from the moment I first had her at de Mallet's. I couldn't stand the notion of others enjoying her. The Queen's sojourn away, already long planned, seemed the perfect excuse to arrogate the newt to myself. I can't do without her now!"

"Sir, let go," Cowperthwait urged, tugging on Victoria. "Do not make me employ force with you!"

Melbourne did not listen, but instead continued to pull on the newt. Cowperthwait pulled back, and there ensued a tugging match which soon grew to ferocious proportions.

Without warning Melbourne suddenly shot backward onto the bed.

Looking down, he found himself holding Victoria's severed twitching arm, from which dripped a pale fluid.

"My God!" cried the Prime Minister. "Where have my brutish lusts led me!" He dropped the limb and, cradling his head in his hands began to weep.

Cowperthwait looked at the Prime Minister with disgust. "You have abused a helpless animal, and now feel the appropriate pangs. Let it be a lesson to you that even the highest worldly powers are not exempted from common morality. You may take comfort from the fact that Victoria will quickly regenerate her arm, as she still possesses that newt-like faculty."

Tossing a blanket around the uncomplaining creature, Cowperthwait said, "Come, dear, let us go." He left Melbourne weeping.

In the hansom cab heading home, cradling Victoria's elongated head against his chest, Cowperthwait mused aloud.

"I could wish it were Lady Cornwall by my side at this moment, dear Victoria, but what good would such impossible longing do? No, it is you and I, poor thing. You and I once more."

Cowperthwait stroked her head, and Victoria butted it against the underside of his chin.

"Ah, my dear, you have been through many rigors in your unnatural life. And much as any man loves his creations, I can only hope that your existence is not further prolonged by very many days. If only I knew your natural span...."

And with that sentiment echoing in the coach, the vehicle rolled on through the night—

—through the decades—

—through sixty-three years, until February 1, 1901, when the same city thoroughfare, draped with purple and white banners (Victoria had in her will asked that the black hangings she abhorred be banned) was thronged with weeping crowds watching the horse-drawn gun-carriage bearing the short coffin of their elderly Queen make its slow way from Victoria Station to Paddington Station, on its way to the mausoleum at Windsor.

Among the mourners was a hunched figure dressed in black, her face veiled from sight. She was accompanied by an elderly bald man with a moony face, leaning on a cane whose hairline joint revealed it to be of a deadly nature. The duo were soon joined by a gap-toothed old codger who was slyly tucking a wallet not his own into his breast pocket.

"So long ago," said Cowperthwait. "But the cards at Christmas never stopped coming."

"Wimmen air like elleyfants," said McGroaty. "They never forget."

And as if in silent agreement, Victoria pulled back her veil and snapped a passing fly from the air.

HOTTENTOTS

1

THE FACE OF AN APE

The big fish was plainly stitched together at its mid-section. Sloppy looping overhand whiplashes formed of black waxed twine ran around its entire circumference like the grin on an insane rag doll, holding its two disparate halves together. Mismatched slightly in size, the halves of the hybrid did not fuse neatly, but revealed the pinkish white inner meat of the larger front. With its long tapered head, protruding lower jaw and leading grasping teeth, the forepart plainly belonged to the family *Sphyrænidæ*: one of the Barracudas. The rear portion was less identifiable, although a highly educated (Lausanne, Zurich, Heidelberg, Munich, Vienna, and Paris) guess would place it within the family *Acipenseridæ*: the Sturgeons. One fact, however, was incontestable: the tail was mated upside down to the head, so that the ventral fin was now impossibly in a dorsal position.

The monstrous miscegenation lay on a piece of damp canvas with ripped edges and a single brass grommet, its eyes glassy, pale serum slowly leaking from its jointure. The canvas lay in the lap of a seated man.

This man was Louis Agassiz.

Swiss-born scientist, master of paleontology, ichthyology, and zoology, doctor of medicine, public lecturer, formulator and popularizer of the *Eiszeit* Theory, Naturalist

Laureate (in journalistic parlance) to his adopted America, Agassiz had only recently turned forty. Tall and strong, yet somewhat portly, he was dressed in wool pants, vest and double-breasted suitcoat, with a white foulard at his neck. His face was dominated by brown eyes as sharp and piercing as the spikes of a sea urchin (or common echinoid), and a broad square jaw. His lips and nose were rather fleshy. He was clean-shaven, save for longish sideburns, and possessed of a rather florid complexion. The tide of his still dark hair, now ebbing slightly, revealed a highly philosophical brow. (Samuel George Morton, distinguished Philadelphia colleague of Agassiz, had estimated his peer's cranial capacity at 115 cubic inches, plainly above average for a specimen of the white race ((and hence for all races, white representing the pinnacle of creation)), and Morton, although he had refrained from revealing his desire, had already made plans to secure Agassiz' skull for his immense collection, should he, Agassiz, chance to perish before Morton himself....)

Agassiz now regarded the abomination on display in his lap. He hardly knew what to say. Was he supposed to take this crude hoax seriously? Just how gullible did these Americans imagine the average European to be?

During the ten months of his American experience to date, Agassiz had formed certain conclusions regarding the national character. The typical citizen of the United States was brash, cunning, energetic and liberally supplied with glibness and low morals. At their most likable, they were spoiled children, full of a youthful enthusiasm. Good in a sprint, they had no endurance. The best of them, such as his compatriots at Harvard (those who had managed to establish clean breeding lines within their own class) were intellectually and ethically equal to the best of the Europeans. The bourgeois, such as John Lowell and Samuel Cabot— well, bourgeois were the same the world over. But the mass of Americans, unlike their Old World counterparts, were wild and unpredictable.

It stemmed, of course, from interbreeding. The country was a hodgepodge of races, all mixing their bloods without proper regard for the ancient geographic divisions that had prevailed since the Creation. Aryan, Anglo-Saxon, Gallic, Slavic, Iberian, Mediterranean, Hibernian, Celtic, Mongol, Han, Semitic, Scandinavian, Baltic, Red Indian—Was it any wonder that the progeny of such egregious mongrelization were capricious, unorganized and avaricious, or that they should assume that their betters would be as easy to hoodwink in a business transaction as their own simple-minded fellows?

And the worst component of the mix, the vilest, most polluted stream feeding into the muddy river that was America, the most offensive taint in any putative white man's blood, a contamination which recked to heaven and violated all moral order, was—

The Negro.

Agassiz shuddered, recalling his first encounter with American blacks—with any member of the African races, for that matter—which had taken place just last year. He had written about it last December, in a letter to his sainted mother, Rose, thankfully safe at home in Neufchâtel.

It was in Philadelphia that I first found myself in prolonged contact with Negroes; all the domestics in my hotel were men of color. I can scarcely express to you the painful impression that I received, especially since the feeling that they inspired in me is contrary to all our ideas about the confraternity of the human type and the unique origin of our species. But truth before all. Nevertheless, I experienced pity at the sight of this degraded and degenerate race, and their lot inspired compassion in me in thinking that they are really men. Nonetheless, it is impossible for me to repress the feeling that they are not of the same blood as us. In seeing their black faces with their thick lips and grimacing teeth, the wool on their head, their bent knees, their elongated hands, their large curved nails, and especially the livid color of the palm of their hands, I could not take my eyes off their face in order to tell them to stay far away. And when they advanced that hideous hand toward my plate in order to serve me, I wished I were able to depart in order to eat a piece of bread elsewhere, rather than to dine with such service. What unhappiness for the white race—to have tied their existence so closely with that of the Negroes in certain countries! God preserve us from such a contact!

Eyeing the piscine horror in his lap, Agassiz suddenly saw embodied in it all his fears of cross-breeding. With a shiver, he recalled the similarly stitched creature born in Mrs. Shelley's imagination. What if Nature should ever permit such monsters? Even the fancy was too much—

Agassiz tore his gaze away and confronted the man standing expectantly before him.

A rough-hewn fisherman of indeterminate age, with a seamed face like tanned leather in which were set squinty eyes, dressed in a turtle-necked cabled sweater greasy with lanolin, watch cap and baggy trews, a long-stemmed unlit clay pipe poking out of one corner of his mouth, the hopeful seller now deemed it appropriate to speak up in favor of his wares.

"So, young fella, what d'ye think? The boys down at the wharves all say you're lookin' for queer specimens, and you'll not see many queerer than that 'un."

Agassiz was astonished at the man's temerity. The Professor's Swiss accent—which so many of the ladies had found charming, and which consisted mainly of Frenchified vowels—became highly pronounced now, in an attempt to cow.

"Do you expect me to believe, sir, that this fish ever swam whole and entire through the seas of this world?"

The old salt scratched under his cap. "Ah, them eagle eyes of yourn has done detected the slight repair which I was forced to make in the rascal. One o' my crew was preparin' to fillet the critter for our shipboard supper when I comes upon him and, recognizin' its scientific value, put a halt to his butchery. Unfortunately, not before he had separated snout from flipper. Seein' as how it's slightly damaged, I will consider lowerin' my price. Which is four bits, cash on the barrelhead."

Agassiz removed the canvas and its contents from his lap and stood up. "Please, go now. You've wasted my time."

"Wait, old hoss, I can see ye be too many for me. Hold on, and I'll tell ye the truth. I was only holdin' back cuz I warn't sure ye could appreciate it."

"Very well, proceed. I am all ears, as you say."

Cupping his chin and squinching his eyes even further, so that he looked like a mole (*Talpa europæa*), the fisherman said, "Well, we pulled our nets aboard, and in them was a barracudy and a black sturgeon—"

"That much I had deduced."

"Mebbe so. But what ye cain't know was that there was also a swordfish with 'em. Now, that there swordfish had the most peculiar instrument. Namely, a spike with a hole in its tip like the eye of a needle! Before my unblinking gaze, that swordfish proceeded to slice them two other fishes in half. Then it flopped across the decks to where we was mending our sails. It got the end of some cord in its eyelet, and proceeded to stitch the fishes together, just as ye seen 'em. I merely brung them by as proof, since the swordfish was too big to lug along. And it's this swordfish what I propose ye should buy offen me!"

Concluding triumphantly with a huge grin, the fisherman awaited Agassiz's reaction.

For a moment, Agassiz was stunned. Then he began to roar in laughter. The foul mood he had been laboring under all day—which had many unavoidable causes—evaporated in a moment under the flow of the typically American tall tale.

When he had mastered himself, Agassiz said, "Very good. You bring me this surgeon swordfish, and I'll pay you handsomely."

The fisherman extended a horny hand, and Agassiz took it. "That I'll do, old hoss, or my name's not Captain Dan'l Stormfield out o' Marblehead."

And with that, Captain Stormfield departed, taking with him both the vivisected fish and also a pleasant personal briney odor Agassiz only noticed in his absence.

Spoiled children, indeed!

Agassiz's study was a comfortable den where he had spent many a lucubratory hour since his arrival on these foreign shores. Several glass-fronted bookcases held ranks of large scientific volumes from Linnaeus to Lyell; their open lower shelves were devoted to the well-read volumes of the elephant-folio edition of *Audubon's Birds*. A sideboard was scattered with the fruits of recent composition, neatly stacked into separate monographs. A round-topped table pushed into a corner was littered with correspondence to be answered. A comfortable couch, occasionally used for post-prandial naps, was now occupied by large cardboard portfolios secured with ribbon ties and containing various expeditionary sketches. Several leather-cushioned chairs and throw-rugs were scattered around the wooden floorboards. (Hardly Biedermeier, but what could one expect from such a rude nation...?) A watercolor of Agassiz's birthplace, the lake-surrounded village of Motier, composed by his long-time artistic assistant, Joseph Dinkel, who had regrettably chosen not to accompany his master to America, graced one wall. On another hung a map of North America, studded with green-flagged pins indicating points already visited—Niagara Falls, Halifax, New Haven, Albany, Philadelphia—and red-flagged ones betokening planned jaunts: Lake Superior, Charleston, Washington, the Rockies....

Having holed up here in his atelier all morning indulging the black melancholy which had been dissipated so effectively by Captain Stormfield's fable, Agassiz now enjoyed a return of his accustomed energies. He felt inclined once more to be out and about in the world, uncovering Nature's secrets, classifying and discovering, collecting and theorizing, and, not incidentally, making his name resound from the lips of the masses as synonymous with modern nineteenth-century science.

Stepping from his study, Agassiz headed toward the workrooms located in his East Boston quarters hard by the bayshore, which had been so graciously donated by one of his patrons, John Amory Lowell, textile magnate and financier. The establishment was sufficient for the moment, and daily inspired in Agassiz feelings of satisfaction. But he had bigger plans in mind. A separate warehouse for specimens, perhaps fronted by a museum where selected ones could be displayed; larger workspaces, equipped with all taxonomic necessities; a gas-lit office; a lecture-hall; perhaps he would even have his own printshop and bindery, as he had had in Neufchâtel, to handle the steady flow of books from his industrious pen....

Agassiz put a brake on his fantasies. All this could only be accomplished from a position of power and prestige. The amount of money he could personally invest was insignificant compared to his dreams. True, his lectures had earned him more than he had ever dreamed possible—in the last four months, over six thousand dollars!—but it was all spent as fast as it came in. Salaries alone for his trained team consumed a large fraction of his income. Add in his purchases from the local fishermen, the normal costs of maintaining a household, the expenses of field surveys, entertaining, and so forth, and you were soon running in the red.

No, only the resources of an institution such as Harvard would be sufficient to propel him to the heights of which he dreamed. He must have the professorship in the new School of Geology soon to be endowed by Abbott Lawrence at the university! His competitors for the seat, Rogers and Hall, were mediocre talents who did not deserve such a prestigious post. He alone, Louis Agassiz,

First Naturalist of his times, was entitled to the professorship!

Approaching the door to the workrooms, Agassiz made a mental note to cajole Lowell into hosting another dinner at which he could subtly lobby Lawrence for the job....

The workroom was humming like a top with activity. As he entered, all his loyal assistants who had accompanied him from Europe looked up from their benches with dedication and admiration in their eyes. There was Count François Pourtales, who had tramped all over the Alps with Agassiz, busy examining a large coprolite with a magnifying lens. Charles Girard, trained zoologist, was gutting a perch while wearing a gutta-percha apron. Artist Jacques Burckhardt was attempting to sketch a live lobster (*Homarus americanus*), which unfortunately was bent on scuttling to freedom across the tabletop. Auguste Sonrel, expert lithographer, was busy with his flat stones. (In an attempt to raise additional funds for science, Agassiz had authorized Sonrel to provide a set of illustrations for a private edition of Mister John Cleland's book under subscription by a group of Boston businessmen.) The only ones missing were Charles "Papa" Christinat, Arnold Guyot, Leo Lesquereux, and Jules Marcou, who all awaited his summons across the Atlantic, which he would issue once he had obtained the Harvard position.

The scene thrilled Agassiz. This was modern science: teamwork and delegation of responsibilities, a tight unit functioning with a single goal—the further illumination of the name of Agassiz!

Responding to the jovial salutations employing his nickname—"*Bonjour*, Agass!" "Agass, come look!" "Agass, zee *homard,* catch heem!"—the head of this scientific factory made the rounds among his workers.

As he was inspecting Pourtales's coprolite in an attempt to discern botanical remnants, Edward Desor emerged from an inner room.

Desor was Agassiz's second-in-command. He had been employed by the naturalist for ten years, since 1837. Of German extraction, originally a law student with facility in languages, he had been tutored in the rudiments of science by Agassiz, although his knowledge never passed that of a half-hearted amateur. His main utility lay in his ability to get things done. He had overseen the day-to-day operations at Neufchâtel, and could bring off the most complicated expedition without a hitch.

Thin and dapper, still under thirty, Desor was inordinately proud of a straggling mustache to which not one hair had been added, as far as Agassiz could determine, since he had come to work for the Swiss. His eyes continually shone with a light that reminded Agassiz of the gaze of a stoat (*Mustela erminea*). After a decade of constant association, Agassiz still felt uncertain at times of the inner mental workings of his assistant.

Agassiz was generally ambivalent about Desor. On the one hand, he was efficient and industrious. He did not need to be continually supervised. On the other hand, he was somewhat reckless and imprudent. For instance, there was that lecture Desor had arranged in England, just before they sailed for America. "Bedlam College," Desor had named the venue, and it had turned out to be an insane asylum, where Agassiz was forced to deliver a talk to the staff amidst the cacophony of caged lunatics....

Still, Agassiz felt that Desor's virtues, on the whole, out-weighed his defects, and, averse to tampering with a fruitful relationship, defended him against all detractors, chief of whom had been Agassiz's wife, Cecile.

Cecile. It had been mainly thoughts of his wife that had plunged him into depression earlier today. Agassiz still felt guilty at having left her and their three children back in Switzerland. But what could he do? He had progressed as far as he could go in his native land, and the Prussian grant—secured by his mentor, Alexander von Humboldt—to travel to America had come at just the right time in his career. He had had no alternative but to take it. Surely Cecile could see the logic in that. Agassiz consoled himself with the observation that she had not cried overmuch....

How devoted to him she had been when they first met! He had accompanied his school-chum, Alexander Braun, to the latter's German home for holidays, and met his sister, Cecile, a perfect specimen of Aryan femininity. Infatuated, she had sketched a portrait of him then which he still pos-sessed. (Had he ever looked that young...?) Years later, they had married and gone on to live happily.

But when Desor came to reside with them, things had begun to fall apart. Cecile had found the ex-law-student vain, crude and irresponsible. He had made off-color jokes which embarrassed her. Agassiz had continued to stick up for Desor, almost irrationally (did the man have some sort of spell on him? he sometimes wondered), and the distance between the naturalist and his wife had thereafter grown wider and wider.

Irritably, Agassiz now put all domestic reverie aside and turned to confront Desor.

"Yes, Edward, what is it?"

Desor preened his incipient mustache. "I just want to remind you, Louis, that my cousin, Maurice, will soon arrive. You recall that we discussed hiring him."

Agassiz exploded. "How could you think of authorizing your cousin's passage when we still have other, more competent people yet to bring over? As far as I remember, we had left his hiring unsettled. What prompted you to take such a step?"

Desor failed to exhibit a suitable chagrin at his employer's ire. "I knew he would be of supreme use to the establishment, and took the liberty of securing his services before someone else did so."

"Refresh my memory as to his qualifications, if you please."

Desor now managed to appear a trifle apprehensive. "He is young, energetic, and eager to serve—"

"But what of his scientific experience?"

"He is an expert in bovine anatomy."

"Meaning?"

Desor visibly squirmed. "He once worked in an abattoir for a week."

Agassiz threw up his hands. "Impossible! But I suppose we cannot turn the ship around, now that it's sailed. Still, if I receive reports of Maurice's disappearance at sea, I shall not languish overlong. Well, we shall deal with Maurice when he arrives. Is there anything else, Edward?"

"No," sullenly replied the assistant.

"Very well, then, you are dismissed."

Desor left in a sulk.

After some further consultations with his staff, Agassiz ventured into the house's kitchen. There, he found Jane.

Jane Pryke was the household's cook and maid, a buxom English lass of eighteen, with a charmingly freckled complexion. Her flaxen hair she conventionally wore in a long braid. In her initial interview for the job she had replied to Agassiz's query about the correct pronunciation of her surname with the verse, "Rhyme it with 'shrike' if you like, but not with 'trick,' 'less you want a kick.'" Agassiz had laughed and immediately hired her.

Now he approached the nubile factotum quietly from behind, as she stood at the woodstove stirring a pot of fish chowder compiled from specimens found unfit for mounting. Grabbing her around the waist beneath her apron and causing her to emit a shriek, Agassiz began to nuzzle her neck.

"In my chambers, after supper," he whispered.

Jane giggled, and lost her spoon in the soup.

For the rest of the afternoon, Agassiz found himself mentally reciting a kind of contrition: Cecile, please forgive me.

But the guilt did not suffice to spoil completely that evening's intercourse.

After the physical interlude, Agassiz fell asleep.

He awoke in darkness to the sensation of someone stroking his face.

"Jane...." he murmured, then stopped.

Jane's hands were somewhat work-roughened, but they certainly did not feel like this—

Agassiz rolled away from the stroking and fumbled for

an Allin-patented phosphorous match on his bedstand. He
struck it, then looked to his bedside.

The hideous face of an ape glowered back at him.

Then the ape smiled, and said, *"Bonjour, Monsieur
Agassiz."*

2

SINUS PUDORIS

Once Agassiz had had a nightmare. In the nightmare,
he was an animal, a deer of some sort. Though
whether *Cervinæ* or *Rangiferinæ* was unclear. (Imagine, the
great Agassiz, splendid representative of *Homo sapiens*, an
animal...!) In that dream he had been trapped, one hoof
pinned in a crevasse. And bearing down on him was a glac-
ier, one of the great ice sheets that had scoured the Northern
hemisphere, whose geological traces he, Agassiz, had bril-
liantly construed, thereby earning himself the title
"Discoverer of the Ice Age." (And damn Charpentier,
Schimper and Forbes as egregious liars, for all their claims
to a share in the discovery!) As he struggled to extricate his
hoof, the speed of the ice began to increase. Soon it was
moving fast as a steam locomotive, tons and tons of blue-
white, air-bubbled ice descending on him, eager to grind
him to a red smear on the gravel, take up his bones and
deposit them in some future moraine....

He had awoken in a cold sweat, found Cecile sleeping
peacefully beside him, and gratefully hugged her to him.

The sensation Agassiz now experienced, as he confronted the repulsive visage of the grimacing French-speaking
ape, was in all respects identical to what he had experienced
as a trapped animal about to be crushed. He was immobi-
lized by fear; beads of perspiration burst through his pores
like the foul exudation of some toad (*Bufo marinus*, say), on
his brow and across his bare hairy chest. All he could conceive was that he was about to be torn to shreds.

The match, burning down, reached Agassiz's fingertips.
The pain jerked him out of his immobility. As the room was
plunged once more into darkness, he rolled out of bed and
began to crawl on hands and knees across the floor, heading
toward the door.

Suddenly, the room was illumined again, this time by an
Argand oil lamp thrust through the open window that gave
onto the seaward side of the house.

"Hallo!" called the bearer of the lamp. "Ist dis not der
house of Doctor Agassiz?"

In the fuller light of the lamp, Agassiz laid his eyes once
more on the ape who, after stroking his cheek, had so shock-
ingly addressed him. After a moment of redoubled amazement, he realized the true nature of the visitor.

Not an ape, but a Negro!

And not a Westernized slave, but a wild African!

The Negro, slight of stature, was attired thusly: a mantle
of sheepskin over its shoulders—fastened in front with bone
buttons through leather loops—and a multilayered raffia skirt
threaded with colorful glass beads. Its arms and legs were fes-
tooned with rings of iron and copper, as well as shell-strung
leather thongs. The flesh left bare was covered with what
appeared to be an admixture of rancid animal fat and soot.

As Agassiz, frozen on all fours, stared in horror at the leering monkey-face of the African intruder, a bulky, pantaloon-clad, booted leg thrust itself through the window after the lamp-bearing arm. A second hand clamped itself onto the window-frame. Then there ensued a period of intense grunting, followed by an exclamation:

"Gott be damned, mine fat zelf ist ztuck! Dottie, come und help!"

The wild blackamoor turned then and moved toward the window. Agassiz was astounded to see that the creature's skirt in back was rucked up over enormous fatty buttocks so huge and disproportionate as to render the very term "obscene" an instance of litotes.

"One moment, Jacob," said the Negro, and the timbre of its speech, in conjunction with the name by which it had been addressed, roused in Agassiz the realization that the savage Ethiop was female!

At the window, the Negro grabbed the wrists of her companion and tugged. The booted foot already inside found purchase on the floorboards, and soon the rest of the man followed.

Big as some bear (perhaps *Ursus horribilis*) from the notebooks of Lewis and Clark, plainly of European extraction, the man wore a dirty white blousy shirt and a conical cap made out of what Agassiz recognized as an animal's stomach. His jocund, sun-cured face was decorated with mustache and chin-whiskers rather in the manner of the British story-teller, Dickens.

Setting down his lamp, the man hastened over to Agassiz and, gripping him under the armpits, hoisted him weightlessly to his feet, all the while issuing a stream of atrociously fractured English.

"Doctor Agassiz, mine greatest apologies for making der disturbance of your dreams in zuch a vild fashion, like rascals in der night, ja, to be zhure, but vee have only chust arrived—mine boat, der *Zie Koe*, she is anchored right outside your vindow—und dere ist not a moment's time to vaste if vee are to find der ztolen fetiche!"

Agassiz stared at the madman in stupefaction. He swivelled his gaze briefly, just long enough to ascertain that the Negro woman—that abominable anthropological specimen whose touch had profaned his face—was hanging back near the window at a suitable, if not entirely comfortable distance. Then, finding his tongue, he spoke.

"Who—who are you? And what do you want?"

The uninvited visitor slapped his forehead and exclaimed, "Vot a dumb zhit! Mine apologies, in zpades! To be zhure, I forget minezelf totally. Your name ist zo famous, und I know of your zircumstances so vell, dot I imagine you zhould know me alzo. Vell, permit me. Mine name ist Jacob Cezar. And dis vun vit me ist Dottie Baartman."

The man leaned confidently toward Agassiz and said, "Of course, her real name ist Ng!datu, but I get to call her Dottie."

The Negro, responding to her click-punctuated name, smiled once more toward Agassiz, her gruesome flat nose wrinkling horribly.

Agassiz shivered uncontrollably, and not from any effects of the warm June air. He snatched some bedclothes up and wrapped them around his waist. Then he faced Jacob Cezar once more.

He was feeling somewhat more charitable toward the intruder, who had exhibited at least enough breeding both to apologize and to praise Agassiz's fame. "Your name, sir, fails to prompt my recognition. And I am still in the dark as to how I may help you...."

"Let us zit down, und I vill explain all. Perhaps dot decanter of zherry I zee dere vould help lubricate mine zpeech—"

Obliging his guest's request, all the while keeping one eye on Dottie Baartman where she squatted on her haunches by the wall, her raffia skirt falling between her legs and revealing more of her hideous black haunches, Agassiz tried to compose himself to listen to the man's tale.

He was not prepared, however, for his reaction to Cezar's opening words.

"I am der zun of Hendrik Cezar, und Dottie ist der daughter of—"

Suddenly, recognition dawned. "The Hottentot Venus!" exclaimed Agassiz.

Jacob Cezar smiled. "Ach, I zee Europe ztill remembers her."

And to be sure, Europe, in the person of Louis Agassiz, still did, though the woman in question had died when Agassiz was only eight years old, in 1815.

In the year 1810, a man named Hendrick Cezar arrived in London and set up a sideshow in Piccadilly. His exhibit consisted simply of a large cage on a platform elevated a few feet above the eager spectators.

Inside was a black woman.

Billed as the "Hottentot Venus," she had been, before her stage career, simply the South African servant girl Saartjie Baartman.

Representing like all her fellow Bushmen a curious hybrid of bestial and human qualities, she was soon drawing spectators by the hundreds, all eager to witness this degraded representative from the lower rungs of humanity.

The guffawing men and tittering women in the audience were particularly struck by her steatopygous traits, those immense gluteal lipoid deposits which Agassiz had noticed in her daughter. This feature was exhibited sans clothing to the audience, who were free to poke and prod it, though, in a gesture of modesty, Saartjie kept her pudendum covered with a loincloth.

(But there were a few members of the audience who claimed in vague terms that the real shock of the attraction lay beneath that ventral covering...)

After a highly successful tour of the British provinces, Cezar and his charge departed for France, where they met with similar acclaim from layman and scientist alike.

But Cezar's captive—who, interrogated once by representatives of a Benevolent Society, affirmed in fine Dutch that she was cooperating willingly for a share of half the profits—contracted an inflammatory ailment and died in Paris on December 28, 1815.

Setting down his glass of sherry, Jacob Cezar proceeded to divulge to Agassiz that portion of the Hottentot Venus's fate that was generally unknown to the public.

"Upon der death of Zaartjie, mine fodder, zaddened und intent only on returning to Capetown, handed over der body of his countryvoman to der French zientific establishment at dere request, in order to zettle a long-time question of natural history. Namely, der existence of der *feminæ zinus pudoris*, or curtain of zhame."

Agassiz blanched. The very notion of the curtain of shame—for decades, he had assumed, merely a racy bit of

naturalistic folklore bandied about when scientists foregath-
ered—was absolutely disgusting to him. Yet, he counseled
himself, as a man of reason he should face with equanimity
all such quirks of the Creator.

It had long been rumored by explorers and other unsa-
vory types that females of the Khoi-san peoples of South
Africa possessed a genital appendage not shared by their
more highly developed female cousins in the civilized portions of the globe. Called the "curtain of shame," it was said
to be a flap of skin attached either to the upper genitals or
the lower abdomen, which hung down like a fleshy apron to
hide the sexual organ.

Steeling himself for Cezar's discussion of this physiological aberration, Agassiz was however once more shocked
by the twist the man's story took.

"Der man who performed der dissection of Dottie's
mudder vas Baron Cuvier."

Georges. God, how he still missed that influential man!
Dead for fifteen years, Baron Cuvier still occupied a hal-
lowed niche in Agassiz's affections.

With tremendous nostalgia, Agassiz recalled how, as an
ambitious twenty-two-year-old, he had dedicated his first
book, *Brazilian Fishes*, to the eminent Cuvier, whom he had
never till then met. This inspired gambit had led to close
contact between the two, and eventual apprenticeship and
collaboration with the elder naturalist, firmly establishing
Agassiz on the road to fame and fortune. Upon Cuvier's
untimely death from cholera, Agassiz had been fortunate
enough to find in the Prussian genius Alexander von
Humboldt a substitute mentor whose patronage continued
to the present.

"I never knew," said Agassiz, "that Georges had anything to do with the Venus of the Hottentots, much less that he dissected her corpse. Why did he never mention it to me?"

"Ach, dere's good reason vie he never zpoke to you about it. First of all, it vas old news, had happened almost fifteen years ago by der time you met. Und zecond, it represented a great disappointment to him. But let me continue vit der story as a few udder people know it, before revealing its zecret zide.

"Your Baron vent like a bloodhound ztraight for Zaartjie's private parts. Dere, he found dot der *dablier*, as der French called der curtain, vas nothing more nor less den der familiar *labia minora* extended by an extra dree or four inches beyond der European norm."

A grunt of disgust escaped involuntarily from Agassiz's lips as he contemplated a whole race whose women were marked by such a disgusting deformity. He flicked his eyes to the Hottentot female not ten feet away from him, and found himself swept by an almost unmasterable compulsion to flee. Only by a superhuman effort of will did he force himself to remain seated.

"Der Baron next pickled Zaartjie's organ, wrote a paper on it, und continued vit udder researches."

Agassiz was aghast. "You maintain that he preserved her *tablier* in formaldehyde?"

Cezar nodded. "Ja. Und he did more den dot. He made a fetiche out of it."

"What!?"

"You heard vot I said. Your hero, Baron Georges Cuvier, vas a black magician."

"This is preposterous—"

"No, it's der plain facts. I have proof dot Cuvier vas a Martinist! Correspondence in his own hand!"

Agassiz had heard rumors of the Martinists during his time in Paris. During the late eighteenth-century, one Martines de Pasqually, resident of Bordeaux, had established a Masonic offshoot organization called The Order of the Elect Cohens. Their rituals and goals, while never precisely revealed, were said to be a cross between those of Rosicrucianism and those of the infamous Abbé Guibourg, Satanist in the court of Louis XIV.

"Cuvier," continued Cezar, "vanted to convert Zaartjie's *dablier* into a dalisman of immense power, much like a Hand of Glory. But he vas unzuccessful. Or zo he thought. He placed der zpecimen in der *Musée de l'Homme* und forgot about it.

"Vot Cuvier did not realize vas dot he vas only vun ztep zhort of achieving his goal. He lacked only vun vital ingredient, a hermetic herb found in mine country.

"Ven mine fodder returned to Capetown, he zpoke to no vun about vot had happened to Zaartjie's remains. Und dot included me, his zun, und Zaartjie's daughter, Dottie, who remained connected to our family.

"Chust zix months ago, mine fodder vas on his deathbed. Den, after all dis dime, he decides to ease his conscience und zpill der beans. I immediately passed dis news on to Dottie. Unfortunately, anudder person alzo got hold of it.

"Dat vun is D'guzeri, zorceror of Dottie's dribe.

"D'guzeri instantly decided dot he vould recover Zaartjie's *dablier*, complete der activation of it, and use it for his own purposes.

"I vas not vorried at der dime. How ist a Bushman going to get to Paris und zteal zomething from a museum? But den, a month ago, I hear from a friend, a Dutch merchant named Nicholas van Rijn, who dravels all around der globe, dot Zaartjic's remains have been ztolen. His zources alzo tell him dot der culprit has fled to America. I realized den dot dis D'guzeri must be ztopped. Zo I get in mine boat, der *Zie Koe*, und zail quick as I can for your zhores."

Agassiz was slack-jawed. He had never heard such a far-fetched load of occult claptrap before. Realizing that such an unstable character could be quite dangerous if provoked, he resolved to humor him while praying that one of his comrades would soon come to his rescue.

"Why," said Agassiz loudly, hoping to wake someone, "should this T'guzeri come to America?"

"Ach, good question. Dottie informs me dot dere are zertain places of zpecial power in dis vorld, und only here can certain rituals be consumated. Dot vas anudder reason vie your Cuvier failed. Und vun of dese places ist here, in dis very state."

Agassiz eyed the door. Where was Desor when one needed him? He was supposed to be continually attentive—"Granted all this, why do you come to me?"

"You are Cuvier's zientific heir, und bear der responsibility for his deeds. It ist your moral obligation to help zet right vot he ztarted. Und you are a man of zome influence here, und can zpeed up der zearch."

Still desperately playing for time, Agassiz said, "I assume you brought along that creature with you for some good reason. Perhaps her animal skills will assist you in tracking down her fellow savage? Can they smell one another at a distance?"

Cezar turned toward the Hottentot and smiled deeply at her. She returned his affectionate expression.

"Oh, zhure, dere's a little of dot. But I chust couldn't ztand to leave her for zo long.

"You zee, Dottie ist mine *frau*."

3

WHALE BONES

When a puffer fish—*Canthigaster valentini*, say—is pulled from the water, its immediate and instinctive reaction is to swallow enough air to turn itself into a startling balloon shape meant to deter a potential predator. Should this boast prove unconvincing and the predator essay a taste of its prey, the puffer will die—if not happily, then at least content—knowing full well that the deadly tetrodotoxin in its cells will exact a full measure of revenge.

Doctor Louis Agassiz, pulled from the calm waters of his assumptions about the master-slave relationship between the South African and the Hottentot, now swelled up and began to spew his triumphant poison at the heinous pair.

Shooting to his feet, unconsciously dropping the bed-clothes that had shielded his nudity—the better to gesticulate wildly—his normally florid complexion reddening to a positively psittacine shade, the veins in his forehead beating like tribal drums, Agassiz thundered out his righteous condemnation.

"By God and all that's holy, sir, as I am a Christian born

and bred, raised in a household of virtue, I brand you as a despicable traitor to your race! How could you! How could you pollute yourself so, and lower the stature of the white race in the eyes of this creature and her no doubt insolent and insurrectionary fellows! By such brutish miscegenation, by catering to your basest lusts this way, you have placed in jeopardy not only your own country, but also four thousand years of civilization, of mankind's struggle upward from the slime! Go! Leave this house as you came, with darkness covering your foul and iniquitous shame!"

As Agassiz finished his fervent peroration a sound of hurrying footsteps manifested itself outside his bedroom. At last, rescue! *Citoyens, aux armes!*

The door burst open, revealing the other members of the scientific establishment, all be-weaponed and ready to defend their leader. Pourtales brandished his trusty alpenstock, while Girard wielded a fearsome microtome. Burckhardt flourished an agressive palette knife, and Sonrel waved a formidable engraving tool. Barely visible behind the foursome crouched Desor, peeping under the uplifted arms of the front ranks.

Cezar seemed undaunted by the reinforcements, as did the Hottentot Dottie, who remained squatting by the window. The hefty Capetowner regarded the poised rescuers calmly, then returned his gaze to Agassiz.

"Vot a bunch of narrow-minded barbarians...."

Agassiz swallowed more air. "Knave! Will you depart on your own, or shall I have my men forcibly eject you!"

"Professor Agassiz, I do not like you now, dough I vas not prechudiced against you before. Yet I need your help to recover mine mudder-in-law's remains, before dey are used

to make a wrongness. If you vill not give me your help vol-
untarily, den I must coerce it. I know you have ingratiated
yourzelf vit the American zientists and public, who all imagine you are zo perfect. Vell, vot vould dey zay if dey knew dot
der man who taught you everything you know und who first
zponsored you vas an occultist? I imagine der penny-papers
vould have a field-day vit the news. Perhaps der *Cambridge
Chronicle* or der *Christian Examiner*, zay? Und der academic
community...."

Generally speaking, the puffer fish may take as many as
five minutes to deflate once the attack has ceased.

Agassiz collapsed in thirty seconds.

Sinking back down into his chair, the naked naturalist
feebly signaled his comrades to drop their aggressive pos-
tures. They complied, casting speculative looks over the
improbable scene.

Upon hearing Cezar's threat, Agassiz had been swept by
a vision of all his careful plans, his dreams of glory and
advancement in the New World, coming to naught, under-
mined by the insane yet lethal charges which the man
seemed prepared to press. Public opinion, that tyrant, could
not be trifled with. Agassiz realized in a flash that he had no
option but to collaborate with the Capetowner—however
repugnant and treasonous to the white race his mating
habits might be—and hope that he would soon remove himself from Agassiz's life.

"Very well," said Agassiz weakly. "You have impressed
me with the justice of your cause, and I will do what I can
to help. But for God's sake, let us save further discussion till
the morning. Edward—"

Danger obviously past, Desor scuttled to the forefront of the watchers.

"Please put up Mister Cezar and his—aboriginal companion—in the spare room."

"Very good, Professor."

Agassiz was soon left alone. He managed to summon up a shadow of his traditional decisiveness.

One way or another, he would end this whole affair as soon as possible. And when the foreigner and his ape-bride were gone, he would burn all the linens, towels and carpets they had touched, and possibly several pieces of furniture as well, depending on what kind of scent-marking habits the Negro revealed.

In the morning, after a restless period of semi-unconsciousness plagued by unrecallable but decidedly unpleasant phantasms, Agassiz joined his team at the communal breakfast table. Jane's peasant disposition had enabled her to sleep soundly through the entire contretemps after she had retired, post-fornication, to her own room, and she now moved swift as a sparrow (*Spizella pusilla*) about the kitchen, serving platters of johnny-cakes, scrambled eggs and crayfish (*Orconectes limosus*) to the appreciative scientists. Somewhat disconcerted at first by the uncouth appearance of the Hottentot, Jane had quickly adapted to her presence, remarking that "she's got better table manners than that heathen Mister Alcott."

Agassiz said little during the breakfast, all the while sorting through his limited options regarding the South African. Cezar, meanwhile, regaled the others with the rousing tale of his storm-tossed voyage in the *Sie Koe* from the

Cape of Good Hope to Boston, his only crew the tireless Hottentot. By meal's end, he had charmed them all.

When his subordinates had left to begin the day's work, Agassiz found himself confronting the Capetowner and his subhuman mate. The Negro smiled at Agassiz and said, "Good meal." She then produced from somewhere beneath her skirt a small bone-handled knife and began to pick her teeth.

Agassiz nearly gagged. He hastily rose and moved to a chair by the hearth, gesturing for Cezar to follow him.

"We must discuss our plans," began Agassiz.

"Ja, to be zhure. But first I must dell you about due men who alzo figure in dis affair. I did not get der chance last night, because of your intemperate outburst."

Agassiz made a dismissive gesture. "Go on then."

"You have heard perhaps of Thaddeus Kosciusko?"

"Of course. The Polish patriot who fought on the Americans' side during their Revolution. What of him?"

"Vere you avare dot he had a zun?"

"No."

"Vell, it's zo. During his vanderings after he vas exiled from Poland, ven der uprising of 1794 failed, Thaddeus stayed vit many nationalist und revolutionary groups around der vorld. He visited der Owenites in Zcotland und America, der Carbonari in Italy, der Fourierists in France und der Philike Hetairia in Greece. But he felt most at home vit der Irish patriots in Dublin. It vas among dese latter dot he fathered a child, a boy named Feargus."

"Feargus Kosciusko?"

"Ja. You are zhure you never heard of him? No? Vell, in any case, der zun is now dhirty years old, und active in both

Ireland und Poland. He fought in der Polish uprisings of both 1830 und last year, und lately he has been trying to zuccor der ztarving Irishmen zuffering from der potato blight. But dis is all incidental. Vot is really important is dot der young Kosciusko is a believer in Polish Messianism."

Agassiz reluctantly admitted his ignorance of this movement.

"Vell, der Polish Messianism vas propagated mainly by Andrei Towianski, who lived in exile in Paris until 1842, ven der French Archbishop expelled him as a drubblemaker, and der poet Adam Mickiewicz. Dey formed an organization called Der Vork of God, vhich maintained dot Poland vas 'der Christ of nations,' whose zufferings vere meant to redeem all mankind. Dey elaborated dis belief vit many zupernatural trappings. In fact, Towianski studied vit vun of der Martinists, der painter Joseph Olesciewicz."

"I fail to see what all this Polish hocus-pocus has to do with your stolen fetiche."

"Ach, it's zimple. Kosciusko has heard of der fetiche und, realizing its potential power, has decided to dry to obtain it in der hopes of using it to liberate his people. My zources tell me he is now in Massachusetts."

"All right. It seems implausible, but I'll assume you know the players in this affair. Who is the other person?"

"Ach, dot one ist Hans Bopp!"

"The German philologist from the University of Berlin who collaborates with the Grimm Brothers? That's ridiculous. I've met the man, and he's a mild-mannered scholar—"

"No, dot's Franz Bopp. Hans ist his brudder, und a chiraffe of a different color! Hans ist der ruthless head of your Prussian patron Frederick's zecret police, murderer of more innocents den dyphoid und yellow fever put together! Und vot's more, he's der last surviving Deutonic Knight!"

"Come now! Them I've heard of. And I know for a fact that the Teutonic Knights are no more. For all practical purposes they died out in 1525, when Albert of Brandenburg accepted the Reformation. Although I believe something called the Teutonic Order existed until just a few decades ago—"

"Ach, dot's vot everyone believes! But der druth is dot not all der Knights accepted Albert's decision. Branding him a draitor, zum kept der old vows made first during der Crusades, und dey formed a hidden core in der organization. Dey never gave up der notion of reconquering Prussia, vhich had vunce been deres. Death and disaffection have vittled avay all but one, Hans Bopp. Und now he dinks he zees the key to making der age-old dream come drue, in der form of Saartjie's pickled quim."

Agassiz looked nervously around, but Jane was not present. "Please, sir, watch your language! I realize that your own 'wife' is a savage, but there is another woman in the house, even if she is a servant."

Cezar winked. "Vimmen are vorse den men in zuch matters, if druth be dold. But vee are getting avay from der topic. Bopp ist now in America also. He has convinced his king dot he ist on der drail of Kosciusko—und in druth, he does hate all Poles, for der defeat dey handed der Knights at Dannenberg in 1410—but in reality, he ist intent on capturing der dalisman for himzelf!"

Agassiz's head was spinning. "Let me restate what you have told me. A Hottentot sorcerer, possessed of a magical relic which must be activated somewhere in my adopted state, is being pursued by a Polish-Irish halfbreed and a medieval Crusader, all of whom we must circumvent in order to recover the relic first."

"Pree-ziscly!"

Agassiz narrowed his eyes on the burly man. "How do you come to know all this, living at the ends of the earth as you do?"

"Ach, Professor Agassiz, I am not a ztupid man, und ven events impinge on me und mine country, I attempt to learn all I can. Chust because I live on der edge of Kaffraria, do not imagine dot I am cut off from information. Dis vorld is not as large a place as it vunce vas. Ven a steamship can bridge der Atlantic in nineteen days, ven dousands of miles of drain-dracks crisscross der globe, ven der darkest corners of der vorld are beginning to be lit by der arc lamps of science, as zpearheaded by zuch brilliant men as yourzelf—vell, den even a zimple farmer like old Jacob Cezar can learn vot he has to."

Agassiz swelled up like a pigeon (*Columba fasciata*). "It's true, people like myself are invaluable in lifting the world out of its ignorance—You know, you seem like a reasonable man, Jacob. Could we not discuss the ethics of racial purity—? I see not. Well, perhaps you'll relent some day. Meanwhile, I suppose we should get busy."

Agassiz summoned Jane back to the kitchen with an imperious shout, his usual mode of command. She returned with a flushed face.

"Lor', sir, I wish you'd speak to Mister Desor about that wicked tongue of his! The tales he's been telling me—I know they're all factual, but it don't hardly seem decent for a lady to hear them. For instance, did you know that your average whale has a male member ten feet long?"

Cezar winked at Agassiz, as if to say, *Zee, I told you zo.* Agassiz grew annoyed.

"Please, enough of such trivial chatter! Jane, you must put aside your normal chores this morning, since we have a tremendous task for you. Observe this—this tribal creature. I need you to bathe it and clothe it so that it is fit to be seen on the streets of Boston."

"Very good, sir. Does she have a proper name?"

Agassiz brushed off the question. "Bah! That's of no matter."

Cezar spoke up. "Of course der lady does. Dottie ist her name."

"Oh, how sweet. I've a cousin named Dottie, back in Letchworth. Well, help me get some water boiling, Dottie, and we'll drag out the old tin tub."

"Let us retire to my study, Jacob, and leave Jane to her formidable task. We must discuss our plans and methods."

In the atelier, Agassiz was about to outline the limits of his cooperation, when he was preempted by Cezar.

"Vie must you be zo cruel to mine vife, Louis? Don't you zee dot Dottie ist chust as perceptive und zensitive as you or I? Zhe understands quite a bit of English, you know, und even if zhe can't follow you vord for vord, zhe can ztill zense your emotions und be hurt. Perhaps if you knew her whole ztory—

"Dottie vas born der year before her mudder left for Europe und given under der care of an aunt. Dot voman had been mine own vet-nurse."

Agassiz repressed a shudder. He must exert every ounce of the self-control that had enabled him to study all night while his peers ranged through the beer-halls of Munich....

"I vas five years old at der dime, und, vit mine fodder gone und mine mudder dead fiom der bite of a horned snake, vas vunce more in der care of mine old nurse. Dot meant dot Dottie und I vere raised together like ziblings.

"Vun day, ven I vas ten und Dottie vas five, vee vere playing dogether down by der Breede River ven I zlipped down a zteep clay bank und into der river, zmack dab into a herd of *zie koes*, der vuns you call hippos. Der mudders, dinking I vas attacking dere young, began to zvarm over me, pushing me under der vater.

"Chust as I vas going under for der dhird dime, zomeding poked me in der head. I instinctively grabbed onto it.

"It vas a branch vhich Dottie had lowered to me. I vas able to use it to climb out of der river.

"From dot moment vhen zhe zaved mine life, I knew I vould marry her zomeday. Und zo I did.

"I have given her der best education possible. Zhe zpeaks, reads und writes Dutch, French und her native tongue. Zhe has been vorking on her English during der drip over here, und has gotten to der point vhere zhe ist ready for der McGuffey's First Eclectic Reader. In zhort, despite dose outvard features of hers vhich you might find offensive, zhe ist an intelligent, quick-vitted voman chust as vorthy of your respect as your own vife."

The allusion to Cecile—like jabbing a bruise—was the final straw. Through clenched teeth, Agassiz made rejoinder.

"*Herr* Cezar, you would be well advised never to make free with the name of my helpmeet again, especially when employed as one of the terms in such an invidious equation. It is enough that I tolerate the presence of your barbaric consort in my home. You must not demand that I accord her equal status with those whom the Creator has fashioned in His true likeness."

Cezar flungs his arms up and apart. "Ach! Your head ist dhicker den dot of an elephant, und your heart ist harder den vun of mine country's diamonds! I von't argue any more, Professor Agassiz. But you mark mine vords: vun day you vill have cause to regret your prechudice."

Agassiz tugged his vest down, as if smoothing his feathers. "Be that as it may, we will operate on my terms or not at all."

"As you vill."

"Very good. Now, you must realize that I have a full schedule of scientific researches which I cannot just abandon for this improbable quest of yours. I will make discreet inquiries among my acquaintances and business contacts as to the whereabouts of this rascal, T'guzeri, and perhaps I will even venture abroad to track down any leads, should it coincide with any of my various specimen-collecting forays. However, you will mostly be operating on your own, though I will allow you to utilize my not inconsiderable name as a reference."

"Oh, Professor, vot a privilege."

"It's nothing. Now, you spoke of a location in this region which possesses certain unique qualities your sorcerer believes will facilitate his rituals. Where is this place? It's plain that by staking it out, we will soon have the thief in our hands."

"Vell, I don't exactly know. Dot's vun ding I vas hoping

you could help me vit. Perhaps if I described it to you. It's vun of der zpots vhere life ist zpontaneously created—"

Agassiz shot to his feet. "What are you saying, man! Are you sure of this?"

"Ja, as zhure as I am of anyding."

Agassiz's compatriots were divided into two camps on the origin of life on earth. One group believed that life had originated in some mysterious fashion one single time, in some unknown cradle, and diffused outward to cover the globe. These credulous people, among whose numbers were Asa Gray, Joseph Hooker and Charles Lyell, also believed in some vague theory called "evolution" (best explained in the epic works *Zoonomia* by Erasmus Darwin and *Système des animaux sans vertèbres* by Jean Lamarck), which held that one kind of creature could somehow over the course of time actually become another!

Agassiz, however, belonged to those sensible types who maintained that the Creator had brought into being all the different species and races separately and fully formed, each in their own country. And as for "evolution"—Well, the fossil record plainly revealed that one kind of creature did not flow into another, but that all the vanished species had died in different catastrophes, whereupon new ones had arisen from the same wells of creation.

And now it seemed that Cezar was affirming that one of these sacred primordial wellsprings—perhaps the very one from which the Red Man, the opossum (*Didelphys virginiana*) and maize (*Zea mays*) had sprung—existed in Massachusetts!

Pacing back and forth excitedly, Agassiz said, "Your search becomes more imperative than ever to me, now that I realize its full magnitude. Why, if I could positively identify this American Omphalos, my name would echo down through the ages!" Cezar looked disgusted, and Agassiz hastened to add, "Oh, and of course, the return of the fetiche to the *Musée de l'Homme* would make me very happy too. Perhaps I was too hasty in limiting my involvement with your quest, Jacob. In fact, I'm sure of it. You may count on my complete cooperation and assistance. Why, together we'll nab this witch-doctor in a trice."

"It von't pay to get overconfident, Professor. Don't forget dot vee've got zome competition in der chase."

"A wild-eyed *sansculotte* and a myth-besotted *martinet*? Don't make me laugh! What chance have they against a scientific Swiss genius?"

"Ja, dot's vot Napoleon zaid before Vaterloo...."

"Come, let's see how Jane is progressing in making your Hottentot fit for civilized eyes. I suggest that we keep your true nationality a secret, so as not to alert T'guzeri that one of his countrymen is on his tail. We'll tell people that you're a latifundian from Dutch Guiana, and that Dottie is a manumitted slave. This town is a hotbed of Abolitionist sentiment, and such a tale is bound to encourage sympathy."

Entering the kitchen, Agassiz and Cezar were greeted by an astounding sight.

Dottie's native costume had been exchanged for the latest mode of American dress. On her head was a bonnet which, appropriately enough, outlined her coal-colored face in a coal-scuttle-shaped frame. She wore a brown glazed taffeta skirt with a fichu of embroidered tulle over a wide crinoline underskirt whose extravagant dimensions completely concealed her natural posterior endowments. High-laced leather boots completed her ensemble.

Fussing with the final details, Jane and Dottie were whispering and giggling together. Upon spying the men, they both broke out in gales of laughter, Dottie's punctuated by queer clicks.

"Come now, Jane," said Agassiz sternly. "What's so humorous?"

This rebuke served only to provoke further hilarity. At last, however, the women calmed down enough for Jane to say, "Oh, Professor, it's just that this crinoline's stiffened with whale bones!"

"And what, pray tell, makes whale bones so jocose? And mind you now, none of your usual lip!"

But this unfortunate turn of phrase sent the women into such tearful hilarity that an answer never was forthcoming.

4

WHAT THE POSTMAN BROUGHT

Ever since, at the age of fifteen, he had outlined in his journal his entire future career, Agassiz had never known failure—or never admitted such. True, some events had transpired in a manner less than absolutely satisfying. His marriage, for one. But there had always been an angle from which to view such partial successes, a perspective which would allow him to salvage radiant victory from black defeat. Never had he been forced to admit incompetence, actually to utter the words, "I've failed."

Yet now, perhaps, that miserable occasion was here.

Much as he hated to confess it, he had found an area of endeavor in which he seemed to possess no skills at all.

That field was detecting.

He had been completely convinced that once he applied his intense intelligence to the problem of the missing fetiche, he would be able to lead Cezar straight to the fiendish Hottentot sorcerer, T'guzeri. After all, what was detecting but a pale cousin of science? In both, one was presented with a motley collection of seemingly unrelated facts from which an overarching explanation had to be cobbled, leading to the ability to predict or extrapolate the actions of one's quarry, whether man or atom. Surely the savant who had read in the grooved rocks of the Rhone Valley the ancient presence of glaciers would be able to follow the clumsy tracks of a primitive blackamoor.

And yet, such had not been the case.

Before casting their net far afield, Agassiz had argued that they should positively eliminate the city as T'guzeri's refuge. As the Hub of the Commonwealth, Agassiz argued, the city should attract the sorcerer, even if it were not the actual Cosmogonic Locus where he would ultimately perform his necromantic rituals.

And so for two days the naturalist and Cezar had combed the cowpath-twisty streets of Boston. In their search they were accompanied by the silent yet alert and inquisitive Dottie, her inky simian features, startlingly incongruous when framed in Western accouterments, attracting stares and catcalls from the lower-class pedestrians.

The trio had made inquiry among various strata of society, searching for any information regarding a half-nude Bushman carrying a pickled portion of feminine anatomy.

First they had tried Agassiz's contacts at the local wharves, reasoning that T'guzeri must have arrived from Paris by boat, commercial or otherwise. On an off-chance, they even visited the McKay shipyards not far from the Agassiz establishment in East Boston, where Donald McKay built his magnificent clipper ships such as the *Flying Cloud* and the *Sovereign of the Seas*, which dominated the China-California trade. But no one they spoke to had seen the Bushman.

Crossing over from East Boston to the Shawmut mainland by ferry, they arrived at Long Wharf, with its marvelous 2000-foot-long, four-story-tall brick warehouse. But there, amid the drying nets of the fishermen and the tethered schooners, barques and sloops, as well as the rare yacht from Newport, bobbing proudly like a peacock (*Pavo cristatus*) among chickens (*Gallus gallus*), they drew a complete blank.

Forced to assume that the wily magician had landed elsewhere on the East Coast, they checked all train and coach stations, questioning porters and ticket-sellers, vendors, pickaroons and mudlarks. From the Fitchburg Depot on Causeway Street to the Providence and Worcester Terminus at South Cove they roamed. No luck.

"Zuppose D'guzeri dravelled overland by vun of dose horse-drawn boats?"

"A canal barge? Let us investigate."

But none of the sweaty roughnecks who guided the horses that pulled the seventy-five-foot flat-bottomed barges along the Middlesex Canal from the Merrimack River to Boston Harbor could supply information about the sorcerer.

The trio of sleuths made a survey of wooden South End row-houses packed with immigrants, to no avail. Hypothesizing that perhaps T'guzeri was using his small stature to impersonate a child, they visited the Home for Vagrant Boys and the many Free Schools. All wards and students were non-Hottentot.

They inquired at all thirty of the city's "benevolent, useful and charitable societies," but enjoyed no success.

Despairing, they journeyed to the Boston Lunatic Hospital at City Point, thinking that perhaps T'guzeri had been captured and consigned there. In the midst of the inmates' cachinnations, Agassiz was painfully reminded of the fiasco Desor had brought about at "Bedlam College." Unfortunately, none of the mooncalves was a Bushman.

At this point, they were at an impasse.

"My reasoning was impeccable. I was positive the rogue would hole up in the city, where his presence was most likely to pass unremarked...."

"Ach, I zhould have gone to zumvun who had experience in dese matters. Like maybe dot writer Edgar Poe. Anyvun who could create a character like dot Auguste Dupin vould be able to solve dis zimple mystery."

"Don't make me laugh! That journalist is nothing but a drunken dreamer, with his talk of a hollow earth and such. And his morals are filthy. Why, he was practically ridden on a rail out of this city."

"Never der less...."

Thus frustrated, Agassiz turned to his network of field correspondents, men and women, amateurs and professionals alike, who had heard him lecture and been motivated to enlist in the great and glorious Army of Science. From them, he daily received packages of interesting natural oddities, which packages, sometimes slimy and reeking, occasionally still buzzing, croaking or rattling, were a source of much anxiety to Jane, who had the task of accepting the post.

Late in the afternoon of the second fruitless day, Agassiz had written the same letter to each of his representatives:

Esteemed Friend of Natural Philosophy,

Your humble Professor now asks you to keep your senses alert for a rara avis *indeed! I have had reports of live African natives of the Hottentot species sighted in these parts, perhaps blown off course during some natural oceanic migration and wafted to these northern shores. I will pay double the usual bounty if you would be so kind as to forward reliable notice of such specimens. Of course, should you be able to trap them, so much the better, and you may count on my paying all freight charges for their speedy delivery, as well as recompensing you for any forage they might consume.*

Yours in taxonomical solidarity,
Louis Agassiz

Now there came a clumsy knock at the door to Agassiz's study. Ah, that would be Jane with the afternoon post. Perhaps there would already be a reply or two from the nearer correspondents....

"Enter."

The doorknob was fumbled, then the door shot open, impelled by a kick, slamming loudly into the wall.

Jane staggered in, her outstretched arms so full of packages as to obscure her face. She tottered toward a sideboard, but, midway there, let loose a high-pitched shriek and dropped all her burdens.

"Something bit me!"

Swooning onto the couch, Jane began to weep.

Agassiz hastened to shut the door, then went to sit beside Jane.

"There, there, my dear, where does it hurt? Show Papa Agass."

Jane unbuttoned the high collar of her redingote down to well below her clavicle. "Here. Look, it's all red!"

"The skin remains unbroken, Jane. It was probably nothing more than the sharp corner of a box. You're altogether too impressionable, my dear. Let me kiss it better—"

As Agassiz lowered his head toward the upper reaches of Jane's bosom, the door opened without warning. Agassiz jumped to his feet and Jane hurriedly began fastening her garments.

It was Desor. The oily German leered knowingly at his employer and attempted to twirl one end of his insignificant mustache. Instead, he succeeded only in plucking out several loosely-rooted hairs he could ill afford to do without.

Agassiz forced himself to repress his rage. It would not appear seemly to inflate this interruption out of proportion.

"Edward, I would prefer that you announce yourself in the future. What if I had been engaged in private matters?"

"I thought you were."

"Nothing of the sort! Jane was only delivering the mail, and chose to rest her feet. Now, what, if anything, is on your mind?"

"My cousin Maurice has arrived, and wishes to meet you."

"Arrived? It was only three days ago that you told me he

had set sail. Has there been a nautical advance I am improbably unaware of?"

"I did not wish you to brood overmuch on his safety, and so delayed mentioning his journey till he was almost due."

"Harumph! I believe you wanted to present me with as much of a *fait accompli* as possible. Well, tell Maurice that his personal interview will have to wait until I have more time. Meanwhile, you can put him to work earning his keep. Considering his skills, perhaps cleaning the stables would be the most suitable chore."

"Nonsense. Maurice is a gentleman. I will have him mount some butterflies."

Before he could be countermanded, Desor left.

Agassiz sidled up to Jane, now standing and ready to depart. He nuzzled her hair.

"All this talk of mounting reminds me of something—"

Jane giggled. "Gracious! Don't make me blush, sir! At least not till tonight...."

After Jane had gone, Agassiz recovered his mail from the floor and began opening it. A missive from his most faithful English correspondent, one C. Cowperthwait, which would normally have received priority, was hastily put to one side.

Only one package pertained to his search. Agassiz did not recognize the sender's name, as it did not belong to one of his regular affiliates.

Sirs:

I heerd as how you was lookin for a runaway nigger of yourn. I got me one here that I come on while it was fleein to Canada. Mebbe its yourn. I am sendin you a token by what

*mebbe you can tell. If so, you will be obliged to come and get it, as
its in no shape to travel. Gold only, no banknotes.*

  Yourn,
  Hosea Clay

Agassiz opened the small parcel that went with the illiterate letter.

Inside was a severed black man's ear, blood dried to a crust on it, a curly hair or two adhering.

Agassiz dropped the box in shock; the ear tumbled out to lie accusingly on the carpet.

My God! Such was the contagious brutality that white men who were forced to dwell side by side with blacks eventually sunk to! What an epic tragedy this mixing of the races was! The whole country was tainted by it, and would be for its entire span of existence. Thank the Lord that he, Agassiz, remained innocent of all culpability in the whole sorry affair, by virtue of his Swiss birth and scientific outlook....

Using a pair of large tweezers, Agassiz retrieved the ear and consigned it, along with the letter and box, to the belly of the room's Franklin stove. Even at this time of the year nights could grow chilly, and a little fire would go unremarked.

The last letter was from Agassiz's mother.

Dearest Son,
  *You know that Cecile has been laboring under many stresses
of late, not the least of which is your unavoidable absence. When
she began to lie abed for most of the day, we expected the worst.
Doctor Leuckhardt has now delivered his diagnosis, and it pains
me to inform you that it is tuberculosis.*

Cecile and the children are relocating to Fribourg, as Doctor Leuckhardt believes the change in atmosphere will benefit her, and as she is very homesick.

Cecile and the children send their love. Your wife says not to worry, as it can do her no good, and will only hinder your work.

With deepest affection,

Mama

The letter slipped from Agassiz's lax hand to the rug. Thoughts and memories, half-formed recriminations and justifications swarmed in his agonized brain like *Apis mellifera* in a field of clover.

After a seeming eternity of confused reverie, the study door opened once more.

Like a nor'easter, the redoubtable Captain Dan'l Stormfield blew in, bringing his maritime perfume.

At first, Agassiz could barely focus on the man's words. But eventually he found himself captivated once more by the fisherman's lively speech, and drawn out of his funk.

"Howdy, Perfesser! Well, ye can damn me for a spineless jellyfish, but I ain't brung ye that miraculous swordfish like I promised. It's like this. My wife found out about the critter, and sorta took him over. Ye see, she's been a-houndin' me for a year to get her one o' them newfangled Howe sewin' machines, and I been resistin', cuz of the cost. So when she learned what that swordfish could do, she just took him over, and what could I say? Now she's got him in a tank in the front parlor, and she's a-workin' him day and night to make herself and all her friends the latest Gay Par-ee fashions. The poor fish is hard put to keep up with the demand, and I daresay it will expire soon. I'll try to get it for ye then,

as a dead fish is better than none, I figger. Meanwhile,
though, I brung you something new."

Stormfield reached under his greasy sweater and pulled
out the corpse of a bird.

"That's a common robin, *Turdus migratorius*. What
would I want with that?"

Chewing the stem of his pipe with satisfaction,
Stormfield advised, "Look a little closer, old hoss."

Agassiz took the bird. Its feathers felt peculiar, raspy and
scaly. There was webbing between its toes, and what
appeared to be gills behind its ears.

"Ayup, it's a sea-robin all right! I netted it smack dab in
Marblehead Harbor itself. Can't say why such queer things
always appear in them waters. It's just like they pop outta
nowhere—"

Agassiz found some ready coins. "Very well, I will buy
this 'sea-robin' of yours for dissection. But if I find it to be
another artifact, you will be in for a severe reprimand."

"Sure as Santa Anna's got a wooden leg, that there bird
is a gen-yew-wine fish. Or is the other way round?"

After biting his coins, Stormfield, on the point of leaving, stopped, plainly alarmed by something outside, seen
through the study window.

"Perfesser, that foreign scow ye got moored at yer dock
'pears to be on fire."

"What?!"

Agassiz went to look. True enough, clouds of bluish smoke
poured from the cabin of the *Sie Koe*, whence Cezar and
Dottie had retreated for a brief rest "und a zpell of dinking."

Running from his study, followed by Stormfield,
Agassiz had the presence of mind to snatch a canvas fire-

bucket from its hook by the back door.

Once on the small dock, he scooped the bucket full of seawater and ran up the boarding plank of the South African ship.

"Hold tight, brave sailors, help's a-comin'!" shouted Stormfield. The fisherman barreled past Agassiz, smashing open the cabin door with his shoulder.

Agassiz tossed the bucket of seawater indiscriminately into the smoke-filled cabin.

A yowl erupted from the cabin. "Mine Gott, vot ist dis inzult?!"

With the source of the pungent smoke apparently quenched and the door open, the cabin began to clear. After a moment or two, Agassiz could see a simple scene.

Jacob Cezar sat in a rocking chair, the loyal Dottie curled animal-like at his feet. Both held long-stemmed pipes, now extinguished.

"Can't a man und his vife have a zimple zmoke vitout bringing down der zecond Flood on demzelves?"

"We thought there was a fire...," faltered Agassiz.

"Don't be ridiculous. Vee vas chust enjoying a pipe or two of *dacka*, to zoothe der nerves und ztimulate der brain."

"*Tacka?*"

"No, *dacka*! You remember me zaying dot first night dot D'guzeri vas going to apply a herb to der fetiche to activate it? Vell, dot herb ist *dacka*, vot grows in mine country. D'guzeri has to zteep der fetiche in a *dacka* tea for two months before he can zay his zpclls over it. Dot's how I know he hasn't used it yet. But der dime is fast running out on us. I estimate a veek or zo left."

"Exactly what is this *dacka*? Do you have a sample?"

"Zhure, I got plenty left. Here."

Agassiz examined the proffered herb and soon recognized it. "Why, this is simply Deccan hemp, *cannibis sativa*. What's so special about it?"

"Ach, *dacka* ist different in every land, depending on der zoil, rain, zun und zo forth. For instance, on der vay here, I ztopped off in Jamaica, und found vot dey call *ganja* to be quite unique. However, only Zouth African *dacka* vill zerve to activate der fetiche."

Captain Stormfield spoke up. "Ye claim this here herb is some kind of snake-oil, good for what ails you?"

"You bet! Vant to dry zome?"

"Don't mind iffen I do." Stormfield began to stuff his pipe full.

"How about you, Louis? I got an extra pipe around here zomeplace."

Agassiz impatiently waved away the offer. "I have more important things to do this afternoon than sit around like a Red Indian passing the peace pipe. I have to visit my patron, Lowell, on a personal matter. I shall expect to see you at supper, where we will discuss what to do next."

"Jah, zomeding vas chust about to dawn on me in connection vit D'guzeri's vereabouts ven you doused me. I'll try to reconstruct it now."

Captain Stormfield, having inhaled several huge puffs, appeared even more animated and loquacious than his wont. "So, old hoss, where do ye and your black crow of a lady hail from?"

"Der Cape of Good Hope."

"And ye sailed this brig all the way up yourself?"

"You bet."

"Well now, that's uncommon fine sailing. Tell me, what kind of sextant do you favor?"

"Ach, I use an old British Hadley vot mine fodder left me—"

Agassiz left the two mariners deep in discussion. After changing into his best surtout and a splendid beaver hat, he set out for the house of John Amory Lowell, his wealthy benefactor.

John Amory Lowell was a member of the American aristocracy, and, while this set was not exactly on a par with the Rothschilds, its members were quite well off: Lowell had a whole milltown named after his family. Along with fourteen other clans, his family formed "the Associates," the secret rulers of Boston, the dwellers in the fashionable Tontine Crescent. The Associates controlled twenty percent of the cotton spindelage in America, thirty-nine percent of the insurance capital in Massachusetts and forty percent of the state's banking resources.

Like all parvenus, however, they were eager to flaunt their intellectual distinction and "taste." It was this lust for cultural currency that Agassiz had been able to so adroitly exploit.

Lowell lived on Beacon Hill, within sight of the State House: specifically in an elegant Park Street townhouse designed by the famed architect Charles Bullfinch.

Toward this luxurious domicile Agassiz now bent his footsteps.

Past the varied architecture of the city he strolled, past the newer buildings on Tremont Street with their trend-setting bowfronts, past the older brick structures, hued in a spectrum of reds and oranges, pale salmon, even black-purple, and past many structures done in rough "Boston granite style." He passed the wooden Gothic structure that housed the clothing store of Oak Hall, the grocery emporium of Batchelder and Snyder, and the Boylston Market.

Several obvious cattlemen, attracted by the Fair at Brighton Market, sat outside the Exchange Coffeehouse, discussing the finer points of steers. Carriages clattered by on all sides, and the general commerce of the flourishing city— nexus of half a dozen railways and as many tollpikes—transacted itself feverishly, as if the whole world depended on it.

Posters soliciting volunteer soldiers to fight in the Mexican War, now in its second year, were everywhere. (Desertions, it was reported in the *Evening Traveler*, were rife, some of the soldiers, recent immigrants, actually going over to the Mexican side!)

Men of Boston!!!
President Polk sounds the call to arms!
Rally round the bold, gallant and lion-hearted
General Taylor!
He will lead you to victory and glory against the vile Hispanic!
Help secure Texas for the Union!
Pay of $7 a month!
Upon discharge, a bonus!
$24 and 160 acres of frontier land!
(Possession of all limbs and a sound constitution
a bonus prerequisite.)
(Land might contain Indians.)

Agassiz arrived at the Park Street residence and was admitted by a servant. Waiting in the ornate parlor, he barely had time to admire the bibelots arranged on the Italianate mahogany sideboard, to flip through a page or two of the latest issue of *Gleason's Pictorial*, before Lowell, a compact and self-confident figure of middle years, plainly attired, stepped in.

"Professor Agassiz, what a goddamn pleasant surprise! You'll have to excuse my tardiness, but I was talking business with Mayor Quincy. Quince and I agreed—the goddamn city needs more land! Too much acreage is wasted in marsh and mudflats. Nothing but goddamn birds and fishes and plants there! Can't have it. Once the waterworks from Lake Cochituate are finished, we intend to double the city's population! Even the fill we took from Beacon Hill and Pemberton Hill didn't create enough land for that! I think we'll dismantle Fort Hill next and fill up the Town Cove. Plenty of Irish donkeys available for that! Can't let the goddamn landsharks get wind of the plan yet, though, or they'll drive up the prices, so keep it under your goddamn hat! Now, what can I do for you?"

Agassiz exaggerated his charming accent. "Mister Lowell, you are aware of the new chair being endowed at Harvard by your compeer, Mister Lawrence?"

"Of course, of course. What of it?"

"Well, I would imagine that you, as my sponsor, would have a vested interest in helping me secure the position. Should it go to one of those rude fellows Rogers or Hall, it would hardly reflect well on your discernment in supporting me, the exemplar of European science. Do you agree?"

"Christ, yes! That job's got to be yours. What the goddamn hell is Lawrence doing, even considering anyone else? I'll twist his goddamn arm—"

"Oh, no, Mister Lowell, nothing so drastic. It would not do to have the slightest tinge of impropriety connected with this appointment. All I ask is that you host a party whereat I may make my case to Mister Lawrence. Rest assured, I will convince him that I am the only man for the job."

"It's done. What do you say to next Friday? I'll have the invitations sent out first thing tomorrow. We'll invite everybody who's anybody in this goddamn town. Maybe you can give a little lecture. Keep it entertaining, though. Work in some of that 'genetic instinct' stuff. Mating habits of the goddamn savages, maybe. Get my drift?"

Agassiz winced. The topic was entirely too close to home. "I will endeavor to entertain as well as educate, sir."

"By jingo, that's my boy! Let's have a goddamn drink to seal the matter!"

Several "goddamn drinks" later, Agassiz made his unsteady way home.

Vomiting over the side of the East Boston ferry did little to increase his appetite for supper.

Nonetheless, he forced himself to sit down at the head of the table. It would not do for the leader of the scientific household to shirk any of his duties. And, he was always a little afraid of mutiny by Desor, should his grip appear to be slackening on the reins of the establishment.

That worthy entered the dining room after the rest of the establishment was already seated, including Cezar. (Agassiz would not suffer Dottie to eat with the others, and had banished her to the kitchen with Jane.) With Desor was his cousin, Maurice.

Maurice Desor turned out to be a plump bantam of a man dressed like a Beau Brummell. His cousin introduced him around. Maurice pulled out a chair, plopped down and lunged for a bowl of boiled potatoes garnished with parsley.

During the course of the meal, the only time Maurice stopped eating was when he was pompously declaiming on the latest intellectual trends of Paris.

"You haven't read Marx, Professor? How can you call yourself educated? The man's a genius, potentially the most explosive intellectual of our time. I have devoured his *Misère de la philosophie*. He's working now on something even more spectacular, with his collaborator, Friederich Engels. I don't suppose you've heard of him either? I thought not. They call it their 'Communist Manifesto.' When it's published, it will spell an end to the reign of wealth and privilege, of all aristocrats, whether endowed or self-made, and their toadies such as yourself."

Agassiz banged his fist down on the table, causing the silverware to perform a tarantella.

"That's quite enough, Mister Desor! I am no sycophant to the rich, I am a man of science, a nobler calling than you can possibly imagine. If you truly object to the way I earn my living, I do not see why you partake so generously of my food and drink."

"Property is theft, so to take from the rich is no crime."

"Bah! You may chop logic like Aquinas, but I warn you—and you too, Edward—that if you want to remain here, you will keep a civil tongue in your head and show some respect toward your employer."

Maurice muttered something that sounded suspiciously like "*Après moi, le déluge*," but Agassiz let it pass. Rising, the Swiss scientist said, "I have had a hard day, with distressing personal news, and you'll excuse me if I retire early."

His four sympathetic assistants wishing him a restful night, Agassiz left the table.

Cezar caught up with him in the hallway.

"Louis, I dink I have a new lead on D'guzeri's whereabouts—"

"Please, Jacob, save it for the morning."

"Very vell. Zleep tight, und don't let der horned znakes bite."

"Thank you."

In the middle of the night, Agassiz was awakened by a strange, albeit pleasant sensation. After a moment's deliberation, he ascertained that it involved the application of someone's oral equipment against his generative member.

Reaching timorously down, he found Jane's familiar braid, and relaxed.

His climax was eminently satisfying, despite an image of Cecile flashing briefly before his eyes.

When Jane was snuggled against him, Agassiz dared ask, "You've never done that before, my girl. Where on earth did you ever learn—"

He stopped.

He suspected the answer.

But he did not want it confirmed.

5

A STICKY SITUATION

The morning post contained only one letter relating to the search for the sorcerer. Unfortunately, it was from Hosea Clay.

Sirs:

I ain't heerd from you in the past twenty-four hours, so I am forced to conclude that you are demandin of more proof that this slave is yourn. Herewith please find enclosed as of this date in response to yourn of the last, which I ain't got yet, etc., etc., another token of its identity. Let this suffice to close our deal, before this creetur is plumb dismantled. Also, you owe for the table scraps with what I been sloppin it.

Yourn,

H.C.

Regarding the unopened package which had accompanied the letter, Agassiz gave a shudder. Letter and package both soon followed the earlier correspondence into the stove. He would issue instructions to Jane to stoke the cast-iron Moloch red-hot tonight.

Still in his robe, sipping coffee from a China cup decorated with celestial carp (*Cyprinus carpio*), Agassiz awaited the arrival of Jacob Cezar. The man and his monkey bride had been still abed when Agassiz arose, and the scientist had experienced distaste at the notion of disturbing them.

The abomination they represented still rankled Agassiz. Every minute he had to remind himself that Cezar was a necessary link to the vast fame that awaited him, Agassiz, as the discoverer of the Cosmogonic Locus, the well of creation. When they captured T'guzeri, Agassiz would need Cezar to interrogate the sorcerer in his native Khoi-San language. But once they had wormed the information from the Bushman, the South African and his bestial mate would be expelled with a few choice vituperations, not to mention some well-deserved corporal chastisement, administered by Pourtales, perhaps, who was a strapping fellow.

Hoping to get a little work done on one of his monographs in progress, Agassiz turned to his sideboard full of
papers.

There, atop one stack, where Jane had doubtlessly put it
while straightening, lay his Mother's letter about Cecile.

What was to be done about his newly invalid wife?
Exactly what did he owe her? Poor fond foolish Cecile....

She had never been the adjunct to his career that he had
envisioned. There was no question, of course, of returning to
Europe to succor her. Europe had plenty of competent doctors. He would send more money. That was it. A bank draft
for a few hundred dollars extra would ease her confinement
and make household life easier. Though it pained him to
divert any money from his scientific enterprises, he would
contact his banker right away.

A knock sounded. "Enter, please."

Jacob Cezar, dressed in a new suit borrowed from
Pourtales (the travel-stained outfit he had worn across the
Atlantic had been deemed distinctly disreputable), advanced
into the study. Agassiz was pleased to see that the Hottentot
did not accompany him. Perhaps the South African was
finally learning some manners....

"Are you ready now to hear mine insight about vhere
Dottie und I dink D'guzeri might be?"

"Yes, my mind is more composed this morning.
Yesterday was an awful day. I can hardly imagine today will
be so bad. Please, what have you deduced?"

Cezar proudly stroked his tuft of chin-whiskers before
announcing, "D'guzeri ist hiding vit der Underground
Railroad!"

Agassiz leapt to his feet. "Of course! What more natural place for a Negro to go to ground? Our prey has no doubt prevailed on the dimwitted Abolitionists to conceal him. It's not hard to pull the wool over eyes full of stars, I always say. Well, well, this is splendid. He's practically in our hands now. All that remains is for us to go to the nearest Underground Railroad Station, expose T'guzeri's imposture and demand that he be handed over to us. It's as simple as that."

Cezar waited for Agassiz to run down to silence. Then he asked, "You know chust vhere der nearest Ztation ist?"

"Well, no, not exactly—"

"I didn't dink zo. Vhere's dot leave us, den?"

"I believe the Quakers are anti-slavery. Perhaps we could seek out a member of that sect and ask him?"

"Dot's like asking a Londoner picked at random to give you an introduction to der Queen Victoria! No, Dottie und I have a fellow in mind."

"And who might that be?"

"Villiam Lloyd Garrison, der publisher of der *Liberator*."

"I've heard of him. A regular rabble-rouser, that one. I understand that some years ago he was actually attacked by a mob here in the city who disagreed with his fiery emancipation rhetoric. I'd prefer to deal with someone more rational, but I suppose that anyone involved with the Underground Railroad is automatically disqualified. Well, shall we seek him out?"

"Ja, chust let me get Dottie."

"Oh, come now, Jacob, is her presence really necessary? The fact that Garrison is an ardent abolitionist does not signify that he has forgotten he's still a white man. I hardly think he cares to meet Negroes socially. A man can keep his private life separate from his politics, you know."

"No, vee need Dottie vit us."

Agassiz threw his hands ceilingward. "I won't argue the point. But if you insist on bringing her along, at least let her wait outside Garrison's office until we gauge his attitude."

"Zhure ding."

Soon, the threesome were making the ferry crossing to the wharves along Broad Street. The harbor, as usual, was exceedingly busy, a moving forest of masts. In mid-passage they were nearly swamped by a steam-powered paddlewheel vessel named the *Jenny Lind*.

"Dottie und I heard der Zvedish Nightingale zing vun night at der Johannesburg opera. Zo beautiful zhe vas!"

"You took that savage to the opera? What a waste! How could she appreciate such a sublime experience?"

"Ach, you underestimate my vife. Besides, ist not music der universal language?"

"Not for beasts."

Cezar was silent for a moment. Then he said with sincere pity. "Zomeday dese views of yours vill give you much pain, Louis. I zee it clearly."

Agassiz said nothing in reply.

From Broad Street, they walked down Congress, took a left on Channing, and soon arrived at Devonshire Street. In the next block they found the building housing the headquarters of that incendiary journal, the *Liberator*.

On the third floor they paused outside the proper door, stencilled with the paper's name.

"Now, remember what I said. Dottie must wait outside, preferably for the entire interview, so that we do not risk offending Garrison."

"All right already, chust go in."

This being the office of a public enterprise, Agassiz forebore from knocking and simply entered.

The entire premises of the *Liberator* was a single cramped room overflowing with books and papers. A desk covered with a mishmash of pamphlets and broadsides occupied one corner. Behind the desk was seated a white man who had to be Garrison. In his lap was seated a black man with his arms around Garrison's neck.

Had the tableau consisted of Medusa and her sister, Agassiz could not have been more effectively petrified. His brain effectively suspended operations, much like the striking mill-girls of the Lowell Female Labor Reform Association.

Garrison and his partner appeared unembarrassed at being caught in such a compromising position. "Welcome to the headquarters of a new world, gentleman," said Garrison. "A brotherhood of all mankind. How may we help you?"

"Mine name ist Jacob Cezar, und dis ist Professor Louis Agassiz."

"Pleased to meet you. Allow me to introduce my best writer and finest friend, Mister Frederick Douglass."

The black man got up off his partner's lap with dignity and came forward with hand outstretched.

Agassiz's immobility shattered. With widened eyes, he began to back up mindlessly, until he hit the wall. His feet kept shuffling uselessly.

Cezar diverted Douglass, clasping his hand. "You must excuse mine friend. He has had many droublesome dings happen to him lately, und ist a liddle on der edge. Allow me to zpeak for both of us. Vee are here zeeking contact vit der Underground Railroad."

Garrison's attitude instantly hardened. "Why?"

Cezar gave an abbreviated explanation of their quest. After Garrison had listened, he swivelled his chair to Douglass and said, "What do you think, Frederick?"

"It sounds most unlikely. I tend to think these two are slavehunters, come to drag our brothers and sisters back down below the Mason-Dixon line."

"And so do I. Gentleman, your transparent subterfuge is an insult to our intelligence. Please go tell your masters, you Judases, that you have failed, and that they will not enjoy their heinous reign of blood, sweat and tears much longer. Soon, for a change, it will be they who will feel the lash!"

"No, really, vee are not—"

"Perhaps I could make an appeal."

Dottie had appeared in the doorway. The addition of this new player appeared to spark Garrison's interest.

"And who might you be, young lady?"

"Ng!datu Baartmann, sir."

Garrison jumped up. "Not Ng!datu Baartmann of Capetown, whose astonishingly perceptive letters I have been printing lo! these many years!"

Dottie looked modestly down at her shoes. "The same."

"Well, this is an honor. Why didn't you two tell me you were connected with Miss Baartmann? This paints the picture in a whole different light. Of course, if Miss Baartmann says you need to contact the Railroad, then I have no compunctions about telling you."

"We do, sir."

"That is all I need to hear. The depot for Boston is run by Josephine Saint Pierre Ruffin, out of her family business, the Ruffin Molasses Works in the North End. Do you know it?"

"Vee can find it."

"Excellent! I wish you good luck locating this nefarious necromancer of yours. Farewell. And Miss Baartmann—keep those letters coming. You're an inspiration to us all."

"A tribute to our race," added Douglass.

"The cause would be nowhere without your efforts, sir."

Gathering the still stunned Agassiz, Cezar escorted him downstairs. The air of the street seemed to partially revive him.

"I told you vee needed Dottie, Louis."

"Never—I never thought I would live to see such a sight! Why, it makes *your* relationship look positively normal."

"Everyding ist relative, Louis. Dot's vun of der lessons life teaches."

"Perhaps. But I am a teacher also, and I never employed the switch so rudely."

"Maybe you never had zuch a dumb ztudent."

"Harumph!"

Journeying crosstown, Agassiz and his companions soon found themselves in the North End: a bewildering congery of crowded streets, formerly fashionable, now filling with Mediterranean, Semitic and Hibernian immigrants.

"It seems a shame," said Agassiz, "that the ancestral lanes of Revere and Franklin should be given over to these lesser breeds."

"Everybody needs a place to live. Und dese are der vuns who are building dis city."

"They could at least show some decency and live like civilized human beings. Look at this tangle of public laundry, for instance. Disgusting."

Agassiz waved one arm to indicate the many lines of drying clothes which were strung across the narrow streets barely above the level of traffic.

"Vun must make do vit vot vun has."

"Following that philosophy, we'd all still be wearing soot and animal fat," said Aggasiz, with a pointed glance at Dottie.

"Your European ztyle of dress, Professor Agassiz, vould not last a day in der bush."

"I have no intention of dwelling in your wasteland. The sooner all such places are subsumed within Western civilization, the better off the world will be."

Ascending dirt-surfaced Salem Street, dominated at its head by the Old North Church, they maintained a prickly silence amongst themselves.

Hull Street doglegged at the top of Salem, a further ascent.

At the crest, they paused for Agassiz to regain his breath, resting at the gates of the Copps Hill Burial Ground. The Swiss mountaineer chided himself. He was getting too stout. Where was the young goat who had leaped across glacial fissures?

They were now at the highest point in the North End. From here they could see Charlestown, connected to the North End by the longest bridge in America. Rearing up in that district was the newly erected Bunker Hill Monument, 6600 tons of stone in the shape of a proudly erect shaft denoting the nation's potency.

Dottie spoke. "I am glad to see this graveyard. Here is buried Prince Hall, a black soldier of the Revolution."

Agassiz harumphed again. "I prefer to note the cenotaph of Cotton Mather, a fine scholar."

"Look," said Cezar, "dere's der Ruffin company."

Across the way stood an impressively wide wooden structure several stories tall, wearing a signboard with molasses-gold lettering that proclaimed RUFFIN MOLASSES WORKS.

"Let us introduce ourselves, using Garrison as our reference, and claim the scoundrel they are mistakenly sheltering. Should they refuse, we will simply threaten to expose their illegal setup to the authorities."

Inset into the large warehouse door was a smaller one. Agassiz tried the latch, but it was locked. He banged on the door.

A narrow sliding panel shot violently back. Outlined by the opening was some fair freckled skin and a pair of fanatical blue eyes.

"Go away! We're closed!"

The panel slammed shut.

Agassiz tugged on a sideburn thoughtfully. "Something seems amiss here. I doubt if that gruff voice belonged to Josephine Ruffin. We must seek an ingress."

"Dottie und I vill go around dis vay, und you go der udder."

Aggasiz found himself venturing down a narrow alley littered with rubbish. In the lurking shadows, he was convinced he saw the glaring red eyes of pestilential rats (*Ratti norvegici*). He wished he had thought to avail himself of Pourtales's alpenstock, with its sharp tip....

Was that a small window above his head? It was. Now, if these discarded crates would serve as a platform....

The window was not secured. Agassiz raised it and cautiously poked his head in. The interior was dark, and he could not see much, but it appeared empty. He levered himself up and hung, half-in and half-out, for a moment. Then with an effort, he boosted himself all the way in, tumbling noisily and unceremoniously to the floor.

Getting to his knees, Agassiz lifted his head.

The barrel of the gun pointed at him approached in diameter the trunk of an Indian elephant (*Elephas maximus*). Or so it seemed.

"Stand up," said the shadowy figure holding the weapon, "and walk ahead."

Agassiz did as he was ordered.

Followed by his captor, Agassiz debouched from the storeroom where he had fallen into a huge space illuminated by upper-story windows and dominated by three or four Brobdignagian wooden vats, their tops accessible by catwalks around them. In one wall was the front door at which he had recently knocked.

Slowly, Agassiz turned.

The man holding the gun on him was clad entirely in black, from his flat, wide-brimmed black hat to his black cape, black trousers and black boots. In sharp contrast stood his pale face framed by longish red hair. Fierce and fiery mustachios half concealed his thin lips.

"Who are you, sir?" asked Agassiz.

The man threw back his head and laughed uproariously and not a little insanely.

"My name is Anarchos! But the world knows me as Feargus Kosziusko."

Agassiz gaped. So, here was the notorious Irish-Polish revolutionary Cezar had warned him of. And he had Agassiz at his mercy. The scientist stiffened his spine. He would show this Byronic Bakuninist that breeding would always have the upper hand over bohemianism.

"What have you done with the owners of this business?"

"Only what should be done to all capitalist swine. I have bound them, trounced them and locked them in their office upstairs. Do you object?"

"Don't be ridiculous. Of course I object to such inhuman treatment, even of abolitionists—"

Kosziusko pounced. "Abolitionists! How do you know they are of that persuasion?"

"Well, I—that is—"

"You are after the fetiche! Admit it!"

Agassiz saw no point in pretending ignorance any longer. "Yes, I am. But for the sake of science, not for personal gain."

" Ah, we are kindred spirits then. You see, I am not interested in personal gain either. I want the fetiche for the cause of chaos!"

" I don't understand—"

"Ah, neither did the Ruffins. I appealed to them first as a comrade in the war against injustice. But their devotion to the movement had been tainted by their stake in society. When I explained what I intended, they refused to tell me where the Hottentot had fled. Yes, don't look so surprised, he's gone. I searched the premises thoroughly, and can assure you of that. But have no fear, it's only a matter of time before I catch up with him and wrest the fetiche away. Then I shall be empowered to do what I have long dreamed of doing— destroying all authority everywhere, and freeing humanity from its chains!"

Aggasiz blurted out, "You—you're mad!"

Kosziusko did not seem offended. "Perhaps. But the purity of my madness gives me my strength. And you too would be mad, if you had seen all I have."

"I think not."

Kosziusko narrowed his eyes. "Do you know how I arrived in this hemisphere, sir? No? Let me tell you, then.

"The 'coffin ship'—for that is what those in the know call such vessels—named *Urania* sailed from Cork in March. It was packed with hundreds of my kinsmen fleeing the Irish Famine. Crammed into the foul holds they were, men, women and children, with no accommodations for common decency. And with them was one additional passenger.

"Typhus!

"It was not a swift trip. Seven weeks it took. And by the time we arrived in Canadian waters, half the passengers were either dead or dying. I shall never forget the things I saw and heard. The gasping of the afflicted, the wails of children, the ravings of the delirious, the cries and groans of those in mortal agony!

"We were sent to Grosse Isle, to be quarantined. Our heartless crew was frantic to be rid of us. They literally dumped us out onto the beaches, leaving many unable to drag themselves from the slime in which they lay, where they finally breathed their last, God have mercy on their souls!

"There were only unheated sheds to hold us, and little food. No doctors, naturally, would visit us. Every day we were told the quarantine would be lifted. Every day we consigned more bodies to the common grave-pits! Every day more ships arrived from Europe, bringing the hopeful to the Land of Opportunity!

"When I finally made my escape, over five hundred had perished.

"This was my introduction to the brave New World!

Like a black slave I arrived, all shreds of innocence burned away, my faith in armed resistance intensified a thousand times!

"But I should have expected as much. Everywhere in my travels I have seen the common man ground down, crushed under the boots of his rulers as if he were no more than an ant! Consider my father's homeland, Poland. Partitioned by the Prussians, Russians and Austrians, its brightest sons and daughters scattered across the globe, its free farmers reduced to serfs! Ah, she has suffered, my country. But her sufferings will redeem the globe!

"Do not think, however, that my heart is concerned only with my maternal and paternal countries. Far from it! I am one with all struggling people everywhere.

"I was there in spirit, cheering, when Louis went to the guillotine, standing beside Marat and Robespierre! I fought next to Touissaint L'Ouverture when he liberated Haiti! I was with the Cato Street Conspirators when the London police broke in and slaughtered them! I battled side by side with Simón Bolivar and Bernardo O'Higgins in South America!

"And even though I have never stood in body on these American shores before, my ardent soul was here!

"I encouraged the slaves Denmark Vesey and Nat Turner to revolt! I died with the Redsticks at Horseshoe Bend! I rode with the Anti-Renters in the Hudson Valley, hanging landlords! I raised my rifle with Thomas Dorr in Rhode Island against the militia come to strip us of the franchise! I manned the barricades during the general strike in Philadelphia and the bank riots in Baltimore! I roused the Journeymen Tailors of New York with my handbills. Listen to what I wrote: 'The rich against the poor! Mechanics and working men! Why do you let the rich decree that they are the only judges of your wants?'

"And not just political rebellion did I support, but also individual crimes, for where the law is on the side of the rich, crime is the only resort of the poor. Highwaymen and murderers are my brothers, the whore and the cutpurse my cousins. I sang along with the desperadoes in California. 'What was your name in the States?/Was it Taylor or Johnson or Bates?/Did you murder your wife/And flee for your life?/Oh, what was your name in the states?'"

Kosziusko accompanied this song with a little polka-jig.

"All this and more I cheered on. And now that I am here in the flesh, I shall do even more! A man named John Brown has plans—But I will not spoil the surprises in store for you. Soon the whole world will recognize my handiwork. Once I have the fetiche, the tyrants will fall by the scores! But for the nonce, I must content myself with smaller acts of rebellion."

Removing some rope from beneath his cape, Kosziusko approached Agassiz and expertly bound his wrists and ankles and forced him to sit in the middle of the floor. The mad agitator pocketed his gun and moved to the base of the vats. There he picked up a long-handled ax.

Agassiz watched in astonishment. "Surely you don't intend—"

"Ah, but I do. Let us say it is an illustration of how the whole system will soon be clogged with the blood of dictators...."

Kosziusko climbed onto the catwalks and began swinging his ax against the metal hoops that bound the staves of a vat. He worked like a fiend. As Agassiz watched, horrified, a hoop snapped and the staves of the vat began to bow outward, a trickle of brown fluid slowly oozing out from between. Kosziusko quickly moved to the next vessel.

Soon, all the vats were bulging outward.

From above, Kosziusko paused to survey his work. Then he addressed Agassiz.

"A million gallons of molasses, sir. Now do you regret the Triangle Trade?"

"I had nothing to do with that!" wailed Agassiz. But it was too late, for, with a swirl of his cape, Kosziusko had fled by an upper door.

Under the irresistible pressure of the treacle, the staves bent, bent, bent—

Then gave way!

The flood of molasses washed over Agassiz like a tidal wave. He felt himself lifted up and carried away. Struggling with bound limbs to keep his head above the surface, he tumbled and spun. Molasses filled his eyes and nostrils, ears and mouth.

He surfaced briefly. Without witnessing it, he had passed outside. The molasses had swept through the warehouse doors as if they didn't exist, and now filled the narrow channel of Hull street, a glistening brown flood deep as the lintels of the second-floor windows, racing downhill as fast as—well, molasses.

Tumbled over and over, Agassiz fought vainly to free his arms. His sticky head broke the surface once, twice—He gasped for air, tried to kick his legs—

Just as he was going under for the third time, he felt his shirt snatched by strong hands. He was lifted partway out of the flood, which still tugged at his lower limbs with grasping viscous claws.

He had no idea who had snatched him. His eyes were gummed shut. He tried to utter his thanks, but couldn't.

Agassiz hung suspended for he knew not how long. He sensed the level of the molasses flood gradually descending. Finally, he was released, to drop a few feet to the ground.

Someone was coming toward him, heralded by the sucking noises of footsteps. Soon, Agassiz felt his bonds being undone.

When his hands were free, his rescuer began to clean his eyes with a cloth. Agassiz found he could open them once more.

Such a scene of devastation he had never before imagined.

Carts and wagons were crushed against buildings slathered with treacle. Dead horses lay everywhere, and also not a few human corpses, of which he should by all rights have been one. People looked incredulously out of their second-floor windows at the wreckage interspersed with brown puddles.

Cezar stood beside him, a sticky handkerchief in hand. Agassiz burst out into fervent thanks.

"I owe you my life, Jacob—"

"Not me. It vas Dottie who saved you. Look!"

Cezar pointed upward. Agassiz looked.

Hanging by her knees from a clothesline, her petticoats immodestly showing as her skirt fell downward, was the Hottentot. It was her strong grip that had lifted him from the molasses stream, as attested to by her wet hands.

Agassiz opened his mouth, but could not repeat the words he had freely given to Cezar.

Cezar did not seem inclined to chastise him after what he had undergone. The big South African only said, "I'm delling you, if vee only had zome flapjacks now, vee'd be all zet!"

6

ONE OR ONE HUNDRED?

Scrub as he would, it took three days for the smell of molasses emanating from Agassiz's person to partially abate. The sweetly cloying aroma took away all his appetites, both gustatory and sexual, and he spent the majority of those hours alone in his study, attempting to divert himself from his problems by idly outlining some embryonic ideas. One of the most promising, he decided, was the notion of creating an organization to be called the American Association for the Advancement of Science. A guild for scientists was an idea whose time was long overdue. Not only would the massed influence of many learned men serve to entrench science more firmly at the trough of public and private endowment, elbowing aside such useless feeders as poets and painters, but such a group would also provide many valuable contacts who would help advance Agassiz's own career....

During his seclusion, Agassiz let his household run itself. He suspected that he would ultimately regret indulging Desor's natural inclination to take charge, but did not have the energy or interest to do otherwise.

Neither did he concern himself during this period with the South African, his Hottentot mate, nor their quarry. He was thoroughly fed up with the whole affair and the burdens it had thrust upon him. Why, he had almost lost his life due to the insane quest! And how it rankled to think that he owed his continued earthly existence to the monkey-like agility of the Aboriginal.... What mordant irony! He still shuddered at the memory of her unclean hands upon his clothing.

As if sensing his attitude, Cezar and Dottie did not disturb the cloistered Swiss savant. How they were occupying their time did not concern him, and he strove to pretend that they had never intruded on his practical and well-regulated life.

But try as he might, Agassiz was unable to entirely dismiss the affair from his mind. There was one facet that still lured him on: the Cosmogonic Locus.

To be able to prove—perhaps even be a direct witness to the fact—that all species were created fully formed, bearing their ultimate shapes; to soundly refute the spinelessly anonymous author of *Vestiges of the Natural History of Creation* and his followers, with their heretical theory that higher forms "descended" from lower ones—Such an accomplishment would be the crowning victory of Natural Theology, and would insure that the name of Louis Agassiz would live as long as men venerated their immortal souls.

By the morning of the fourth day, when the treacly nimbus of fragrance surrounding Agassiz was little stronger than what one might experience had one dropped a bottle of sugarcane-extract in an adjacent room, Agassiz was feeling somewhat more mellow toward humanity in general and toward his personal retinue in particular. He was just on the point of venturing out of his sanctum sanctorum for the first time in days when there came a timorous knock on the door.

Jane stuck her head meekly in. "Sir, you have visitors. Two Frenchmen—"

"By all means send them in. And Jane—"

"Yes, sir?"

"You look exceedingly charming today. Has anyone ever commented on your resemblance to a Constable milkmaid before? No? Ah, what a coquettish laugh you have! Perhaps a little later—?"

"Oh, Lor', sir, you'll turn a girl's head! We'll just have to see, won't we?"

Jane departed in a swirl of flounces, and the visitors entered.

One man was a foppish pot-bellied and spindle-shanked fellow in his mid-sixties, lace at his sleeves and neck, a gold-headed walking stick in his hand. His companion was a younger man in plainer vestments with a hayrick of hair. It was apparent from their relative stances and demeanors that they stood to each other as teacher and pupil, or mentor and apprentice. Both radiated a rather disconcerting aura of otherworldly fanaticism which was perhaps more intense—or simply less well-concealed—in the younger.

The elder of the pair now spoke. "*M'sieu* Agassiz, permit me. I am Josef Maria Hoene-Wronski, and this is Alphonse Louis Constant."

"Levi," interrupted the younger man in a sepulchral tone. "My name is Eliphas Levi, mage of Samath, seer of Unknown Kadath."

Hoene-Wronski appeared somewhat embarrassed. "Ha, ha, yes, very good, many-titled Levi you shall be. Pardon my forgetfulness, your exaltedness. Ahem. In any case, we are here, *M'sieu* Agassiz, as a delegation from an order you have perhaps heard of. Is the name Martines de Pasqually familiar to you?"

Agassiz recalled the accusation made by Cezar on the night of his arrival, that Baron Georges Cuvier, Agassiz's first patron, had been connected with a secret society known as the Martinists. Was Hoene-Wronski alluding to them?

Agassiz pretended ignorance. "No, I think not. Wait— wasn't he the imaginary scholar in Voltaire?"

Hoene-Wronski exhumed a chilling laugh. "Ha, ha, very witty, you make a play on Doctor Pangloss. I appreciate a sense of humor in an opponent. But one must know where to draw the line between what is ha-ha-funny and what is deadly serious. And the matter of the Venus Hottentot's fetiche is most definitely in the latter camp."

Opening his mouth to deny all involvement, Agassiz was forestalled by Hoene-Wronski.

"Please do not insult my intelligence by protesting your innocence. I know that you have already met with my countryman, Kosziusko. That one is an unreliable rogue, I tell you. Even though I share to some extent his beliefs in the inevitable glorious destiny of Poland, I cannot endorse his anarchism. The man is the black night of chaos personified, a walking Armageddon, and I advise you to seriously reconsider any deals you have cut with him."

"Deals? I made no deals. Why, he tried to murder me...."

Hoene-Wronski spread his hands. "There, you see? Trying to murder his partner. Completely untrustworthy, as I avouched."

"Wait a minute, we were never partners!"

"Pah, old relationships are so much water over the bridge and under the dam, not worth the blood they were written in. I take it for granted then that I can count on your cooperation in relinquishing the fetiche to us, should you find it before we do? After all, we represent your Baron Cuvier's old associates."

"I still cannot reconcile to myself the Baron's involvement with your sect. Surely it was but a momentary dalliance..... No, your hopes are futile. I would never surrender the fetich the occultists such as yourself. If I find it, I intend to use it purely for scientific purposes, for the betterment of all mankind."

"Do not try to sell me the same line of shoddy goods you peddle to your audiences of mechanics and clerks, *M'sieu*! I know you seek raw power alone, as do we all. But I warn you, the power contained in the fetiche is more potent than you know, and you will surely be consumed by it."

Constant—or Levi—had been glaring at Agassiz in a decidedly disconcerting manner all this while. Now, of a sudden, his eyes rolled back into his head and he croaked out a string of guttural nonsense syllables. To Agassiz, they sounded like: "Yi-yi, shoob nigger wrath!"

Alarmed, Hoene-Wronski slapped the young man several times across the face. "Alfie, Alfie, come back! Reel your soul in, for Hermes's sake! Do not pass the Seventh Gate!"

After a second or two, Constant returned to reality, trembling and seemingly exhausted.

Agassiz was not impressed. "A splendid show, gentleman. May I join in? 'Yippie-ki-yi-yo, the revenge of Sambo!' Well, this has been great fun. If I am ever in need of entertainment for a child's birthday party, I will call on you.

Meanwhile, I believe our business is concluded."

"You were warned," Hoene-Wronski said as he exited, supporting Constant. "If you come to your senses, you can reach us at the Tremont Hotel."

Once Agassiz had assured himself that the eccentric duo had left the grounds, he headed toward the workroom, eager to see what progress had been made on the various projects underway.

Opening the door to the laboratory, he was greeted with a scene he at first could not credit.

Maurice Desor stood atop a packing crate which held a shipment of fossils from Gideon Algernon Mantell, the respected author of *Fossils of the South Downs*. Seated raptly around him were Agassiz's four assistants. Edward Desor was standing proudly by, as if Maurice were Junius Brutus Booth declaiming Shakespeare, and Edward were his manager.

Maurice was reaching the climax of his speech. "From each according to his abilities, to each according to his needs! Workers of the world, unite! You have nothing—"

"What is going on here?!" bellowed Agassiz.

Maurice paused. "I was merely trying to engage your wage slaves in a dialectic."

"Wage slaves! By God, who paid your passage over here, you insolent ingrate?! I've a mind to thrash it out of your hide! Get down off that box!"

"The First Amendment—"

Agassiz roared, and launched himself at Maurice.

The chubby Marxist belied his girth by dashing swiftly for the door. Agassiz gave up the chase and turned on the audience.

"Well, what are you all gawping at? Are you a school of mouth-breeders? Smartly now, back to work!"

Pourtales, Girard, Burckhardt and Sonrel sheepishly returned to their labors. Agassiz rounded on Desor.

"And as for you—"

"Please, I am not at fault. Maurice promised me he wanted only to inspire the team to greater efforts."

"Inspire them? Any more such inspiration, and I would have been lynched like a disobedient slave! No, we'll have no more of this Blanquist rhetoric in my house. Am I understood?"

"As you wish," said Desor blandly.

Agassiz chose not to press for a firmer promise. "Now, where is Cezar?"

"I hardly know. On his boat, I suppose. Must I manage everything around here, down to the itinerary of visiting savages?"

"That is indeed your job."

Desor made a dismissive gesture, as if his job were a housefly (*Musca domestica*) to be shooed away, and left.

Agassiz ventured out onto the back lawn that sloped away down to his private dock. Above the *Sie Koe* hung a bluish cloud of smoke. Agassiz noted that any mosquitoes (probably *Anophelini maculipennis*) that chanced to pass through the haze fell dead immediately to the deck. Next to the South African ship was anchored another, bearing the name *Dolly Peach*. Although he had never noticed Captain Stormfield's vessel before, he was convinced that the *Dolly Peach* was it. Perhaps the telltale sign was the skeleton of a sea-snake (an anonymous *Hydrophiidæ*) mounted on the binnacle: the vertebrae split and terminated in two skulls.

Once aboard the *Sie Koe*, Agassiz cautiously poked his head into the cabin.

Cezar and Stormfield sat on opposite sides of a low table, both puffing contentedly. On the table a game of checkers was in progress. Each player fielded half a dozen "kingers," some of them triples. As Agassiz watched, Stormfield executed a move resembling the path of a drunken frog (*Rana esculenta*), only to capture a single piece and end up where he started.

Agassiz's eyes roved the cabin for the loathsome Hottentot. Much to his relief, her primitive form was absent.

Cezar spotted the visitor. "Ah, Louis, velcome! Vould you care to choin us in a game of draughts? Dere's always room for a dhird."

"No, I have no time for games. Have you forgotten the quarry we seek?"

"Ach, of course not. But until vee get anudder clue, I'm frankly ztumped! Dere's no use running around chust for der zake of running."

"There's been no further developments in the past few days then, I take it."

"None."

Despairing at this news, Agassiz forced out an allusion to the third member of the search party. "Perhaps your missing wife has her nose to the ground even now—?"

"Unfortunately, Dottie ist chust as dumbfounded as I am. No, zhe's gone to a lecture. Dot former zlave who preaches der vomen's emancipation—vot's her name?—ah, Sojourner Druth—ist zpeaking at der Howard Athenaeum."

"You let your wife attend a lecture by that unnatural and

most unfeminine of creatures? Are you mad, man? Have you read the proceedings of that Women's Convention they held in Seneca Falls a few years ago? Stanton, Mott, Truth—they're all cold-blooded witches! Do you know what they're advocating? They want women to be able to vote, to hold property—even to attend college! How can you let your wife hear such ideas? Why, you'll be lucky if she does not murder you one night in your bed."

Cezar smiled reminiscently. "Vhen vee go to bed, dot's not vot's on our minds."

Agassiz was disgusted, and turned away. "Be it on your own head, then!"

Captain Stormfield sought diplomatically to intervene. "Don't be a stubborn old cuss, Perfesser. If Jake wants to let his hen help rule the roost, then who's to say him no? The times, they are a-changin', and we got to change with them. Why, look at me. I ain't hardly no pantywaist—I licked my share o' hurricanes, human and otherwise—but my gal Dolly pretty much does as she pleases. Consider how she took that there swordfish away from me for her own purposes. Oh, by the way, as I pree-dicted, the poor finny creature expired from overwork. Dolly pushed it harder than a Lynn shoe-factory girl. But before I could rescue the remains, she had consigned 'em to the local taxidermist, outta some kinda sentimental impulse. The results are a-hangin' in my cabin. Would ye care to see the deceased anyhow?"

Agassiz spoke in a perturbed tone. "Captain Stormfield—"

"Please, Louie, we done been friends for a significant stretch of time now. Call me Dan'l."

"Very well. Daniel—"

"Not 'Daniel.' 'Dan'l.' Ye see, my folks was so poor, they couldn't afford the extra vowels when it came time to christen me."

Agassiz was extremely exasperated. "Your foolish personal history is of no interest to me! Please try not divert me again. I simply wish to say that I have no more desire to purchase any of your marine samples, bogus or otherwise. Why, when I went to examine that sea-robin the day after you sold it to me, I found only a pool of wretched slime, even though I had placed it on ice."

"Ah, that's the problem with a lot o' them Marblehead critters. They ain't stable outside o' the region for more'n a few hours. Queer, ain't it?"

"It's more than queer, it's totally unscientific."

"So is life, Louie. F'rinstance, consider this jugged twat you and Jake are a-huntin' for—"

Agassiz clapped both hands to his forehead. "My God, Cezar! You told him about the fetiche? What of our ruse? You were supposed to be a Guianese planter, if you recall."

"Ach, I plumb forgot minezelf, vot vit der camaraderie of der happy-veed und all. Bezides, I figured maybe Danny might be able to help us."

Captain Stormfield squinched one nearly closed eye completely shut in a wink betokening secrecy. "Aye, your faith's not misplaced, Jake. I'll take this secret down to Davey Jones's Locker before I let that dirty Hun or Polack get their hands on your mother-in-law's pisser. And, as it so happens, I got myself a hunch as to where T'guzeri might be a-headin'."

Agassiz was beside himself. "Just keep your blasted

hunches to yourself, Captain. We don't need your lame Yankee intuition. Jacob and I will solve this matter using our superior European wits."

Affronted, Captain Stormfield stood. "Them's almost fightin' words, Louie. It didn't take much more'n that to make us redblooded Yankees kick out old King George. I fought against that swellhead, I'll have ye know, and I don't cotton to tyrants any more nowadays than I did then. Until I gets a suitably humble apology from ye, I'll be a-witholdin' of my valley-bill information."

"It makes no difference to me."

"We'll just see about that. Come on, old Puss, let's be a-goin'. Never let it be said we couldn't reckon when we wasn't wanted."

Reaching down to the floor, Captain Stormfield picked up a leash which led away into a shadowy corner. He tugged on it.

From the corner emerged a huge fish wearing a collar and walking on its stiff fins. By its distinctive barbels, Agassiz recognized it as *Ictalurus nebulosus*, the bullhead catfish.

As the catfish passed Agassiz's ankles, it plainly hissed at him.

Agassiz felt weak. The smoke, the arguments, the futility of their quest—It was all too much. He experienced the need to relax in some convivial setting, preferably with a drink....

"Jacob, if anyone comes looking for me, I'll be at the Culling House Oyster Bar. But please don't send them unless it's of major importance."

"Ja, for zhure. Kick back und let your hair down."

The Culling House stood not a quarter mile from Agassiz's quarters. Outside the sprawling weatherbeaten structure towered a pile of bivalve shells as tall as the masts of a clipper ship, the accumulation of decades.

Inside the rude interior, so unlike the elegant hostelries of Neufchâtel, Agassiz sat himself down amid the boisterous lunchtime crowd of quahoggers and clammers and lobstermen and ordered several dozen oysters and a pint of porter.

After an encore of his order, he began to feel a little better.

It was then that Edward Desor intruded.

"Excuse my impertinence, Agass, but you've just received a letter from your high-hat friend, Lowell. I took the liberty of opening it, since it was marked 'urgent.' He needs to know what kind of arrangements to make for your talk at the dinner-party Friday. It had best be nothing too elaborate, as it's only two days away."

"Hmmm, I haven't even chosen my topic yet.... The salacious moneygrubber ordered something on savage mating habits, as if I were a hack for hire. Well, he'll not get it! I'll stick to natural philosophy. Let's see, what organism haven't I touched on yet in my lectures...?"

Agassiz's eye was caught by a shell hanging above the bar. "Of course, the noble horseshoe crab! I'll make splendid capital of the fact that *Xiphosura* is native to America. Surely that will ingratiate me to Lawrence. Very good. I'll need an easel for my diagrams, and a lectern of course. And why not bring a live specimen? The ladies will squeal prettily, as if a hundred mice were loose! That should do it. Desor! Are you listening to me?"

Desor's attention was riveted on a red-headed barmaid in a lowcut muslin dress who, bending over to wipe a spill, appeared in imminent danger of spilling out her own freckled breasts.

Recovering his wits, the assistant said, "Yes, of course. One hundred. Am I right?"

Listening none too closely himself, Agassiz said, "Yes, correct. See tit—I mean, see to it then."

For the next brace of days, Agassiz worked on his lecture. It had to be perfect. This party was supremely important for his future. Nothing must be left to chance. In spare moments, he added a line or two to the textbook he was working on with Augustus A. Gould, *Principles of Zoology*. It was to be his first American publication, and must be suitably impressive.

By Friday's dawn, no new information on the possible whereabouts of the Hottentot sorcerer had been forthcoming, and Agassiz resolved that, come the morrow, he would apply all his intellect to quickly wrapping up this tedious affair.

When the afternoon post arrived, it brought a letter from Agassiz's Mama.

Dearest Son,

This missive will convey no good news, I fear. Cecile's condition is, at best, stable. She spends most of her day sketching, which pursuit, as you well know, always amused and relaxed her. You will find enclosed a family portrait she recently completed.

The children are well. Alex is rapidly becoming the very paragon of young manhood, and frequently speaks, so I am told,

*of the father he has not seen for so long. Do you think it possible
that some day he, being the eldest, might be permitted to join you
in America?*

My fondest thoughts,
Mama

His son. Agassiz had almost forgotten he had off-
spring.... What would it mean to have Alex with him? Was
the East Boston establishment a fit place to raise a child?
Certainly not under the current manic circumstances. But if,
as he surely would, he moved to Cambridge in connection
with his new position, then a more genteel atmosphere
would prevail.

But a child could not be properly raised in a household
lacking in feminine influence. As Cecile was unfit for travel, he would have to find a suitable substitute. A nurse, a
governess—

A wife.

Agassiz instantly berated himself. What was he thinking? His wife not even dead yet, and his mind speculating on
her replacement...? Was he an unfeeling monster?

Still, it did not pay to be unprepared for any likely even-
tuality.

In his bedroom, Agassiz began to lay out his evening
clothes. He was intent on brushing the lint from his frock-
coat when he was startled by the appearance of Cezar at the
infamous window where he had first materialized, on that
night which seemed geological ages ago.

"Must you make a habit of such unconventional
entrances?"

"Ach, pardon mine rough manners, but vee colonial

dypes live differently from you civilized gentry. Vhy, on der estates outside Capetown it's considered overnice if you pause at der door to kick der chiraffe zhit from your boots."

"I'm sure it's quite pleasant to emulate the savages you so unconcernedly dwell among, if you haven't any higher aspirations. Now, how may I help you?"

"I chust heard you're going to zome kind of ving-ding tonight. Vot's der chances of me coming vit you?"

"Why?"

"Vell, first, I might chance to overhear zomeding dot's relevant to our zearch. Und zecond, I'm a visitor here to dis country, und zo far I haven't gotten to zee anyding. I thought it might be fun to mingle vit der American upper-crust."

"Hmmm.... I suppose you could be of interest to some of the more jaded grande dames, much as a new breed of lapdog might be. And the rest of the staff is coming, so it's only fair. I do have some responsibility as your host—"

A sudden thought occured to Agassiz. "You have no intention of bringing your inky mate, do you?"

"Ach, no. Dottie's not big on dese formal affairs."

"All right then. But you must be on your best behavior. Nothing can go wrong. And please try to remember our agreed-upon ruse."

"Ja, I grow der capybaras on der banks of der Orinoco."

Agassiz snorted. "The people you will soon be meeting are not known for their appreciation of irony. And may I also suggest that you don appropriate dress? See Pourtales."

"Zhure."

After Cezar's departure there came a polite tapping on the door. Agassiz called out permission to enter.

The door swung open upon a startling sight.

Standing in the doorway was a Red Indian clad in full native costume, down to a hatchet held beneath his shell-belt. His imperturbable face with its aquiline nose seemed carved from red marble.

Agassiz's hands went instinctively to his hair. He knew with absolute certainty that he was about to be scalped. Three hundred years of frustrated revenge gleamed in the eyes of the Rousseau-ian Noble Savage. He had known all along that America was unsafe. To think that his personal pelt would soon be hanging as a trophy in some smoky lodge—

The Indian advanced on moccasined feet. Agassiz sought to retreat, but was hindered by the bed.

Edward Desor emerged from behind the buckskinned brave. Beneath his minuscule mustache, he wore a cruel and vindictive smile.

"Agass, what troubles you? Surely you were not frightened...?"

Seeking to recover his composure and the upper hand, Agassiz demanded, "What is the meaning of this intrusion, Edward?"

"I was merely following your behest, Agass. You recall that you ordered me to secure a native guide for our expedition to Lake Superior...? Well, allow me to introduce Chief Snapping Turtle of the Ojibway tribe. He arrived today, forwarded by a Hudson Bay Company agent in Michigan."

Chief Snapping Turtle silently raised a hand, palm outward. Agassiz tentatively did likewise.

"Does he speak any civilized tongue?"

"Not that I have been able to determine. I am trying to secure an interpreter...."

"Well, very commendable, Edward. Now that you have introduced us, you may take your leave."

"There is one small problem. The Chief has no place to stay."

"He can stay here, of course. Inform Jane to set an extra place at breakfast."

"And what's to be done with him while we all attend the party tonight?"

"My God, that's right. We can't leave him alone with Jane. You know the Indian's propensity for raping white women—I suppose we'll just have to bring him along."

And so it was that a most unusual party of nine boarded the seven o'clock ferry departing the East Boston shore. Agassiz and Cezar led the entourage, followed by the whispering pair of cousins, Maurice and Edward Desor. Pourtales, Girard, Burkhardt and Sorel, having adopted Chief Snapping Turtle as one of their number, brought up the rear.

Once on the mainland, they sought conveyance to Lowell's home. Unfortunately, all that was available for hire was an open buckboard.

Seated next to the driver, with the others crouched or standing in the back, Agassiz was forced to stoically endure the shouts and catcalls of all the urchins—and quite a few adults—along the way.

"It's the circus!" "Hey, Mister Barnum!" "Where's the bearded lady?!" "Daddy, I don't see no clowns!"

By the time they reached the Beacon Hill residence of his patron, Agassiz was utterly mortified. He hastened inside to escape the jeering crowd that had trailed them, and announced himself and the others to the butler. Shortly, the nine found themselves being led through the mansion until they arrived at the wide double doors—now retracted into their wall-niches—which opened onto a splendid ballroom.

The enormous high-ceilinged room was lit by chandeliers bearing live tapers, and ultra-modern gas fixtures. Along one wall ran linen-covered tables burdened with dishes of every description: whole pigs, steamship rounds, squabs, buffalo steaks. Silver ladles projected from crystal bowls of champagne punch. At the far end of the room was a temporary stage raised a half-foot or so above the gleaming parquet floor. Close to a hundred people, not counting servants, filled the room, gaily laughing and chatting, drinking and eating. All the men were powerful and stalwart-looking in their suits; the women in their gowns, representing every shade of the rainbow, were sylphlike and delicate.

Agassiz turned to Cezar. "So, my friend, you see how we do things here in my adopted country. Why, this residence even boasts indoor water closets! Not bad, hey?"

Cezar did not seem impressed. "I'm zhure dey vere alzo very zatisified vit demzelves at Nero's court, or Louis der Fourteenth's. But vot do I know, I'm chust a country boy from a *dorpie* in Kaffraria."

"Well, try to show some breeding tonight. Ah, here's our host—"

John Amory Lowell strode decisively across the room. His starched collar stood up almost to his ears, the knot of his black tie was as big as a grapefruit, and a gold chain thick as a string of sausages made a catenary across his vest.

"It's about goddamn time you got here, Professor. Thought you got waylaid by a gang of Irish hooligans or some goddamn thing. Who're all these roughnecks? Never mind, I don't need to know. And an Indian? That's what I like about you, Agassiz, you've always got a surprise up your goddamn sleeve. Well, let them mingle and enjoy themselves. Go ahead, fellows, spread out and sample the grub. You come with me, Louie. There's some people you have to meet."

Lowell grabbed Agassiz's elbow and steered him off. They made a beeline for a knot of people clustered around what appeared to be a midget.

Upon closer inspection, the midget proved to be an exceedingly elderly man who seemed to have shrank with age. Across his bald pate ran a few strands of wispy white hair. He resembled a bundle of sticks wrapped in too much black cloth, like an Indian's teepee packed for travel.

"Abbot," called out Lowell, "here's Agassiz. The goddamn smartest fellow you ever met, and the man you're going to give that Harvard job to. Louie, this is Abbot Lawrence."

Agassiz extended his hand. "I am honored to meet you, Mister Lawrence. May I just say that I think that you and Mister Lowell have done more with your mills to advance civilization than any other non-scientist...."

Lawrence's voice was reedy. "Thank'ee, sir. Don't spare the whip, that's my motto. Hee-hee-hee...."

Lawrence seemed to lose both the thread of his thoughts and all interest in Agassiz. He turned to a glamorous woman beside him and began petting the ermine trim on her cuffs.

"Okay, Abbot, enjoy your goddamn self. Let's go, Louie."

Agassiz was confused. "Do you think I impressed him sufficiently?"

"Hard to tell with old Abbot. We'll hope for the best. Maybe your lecture will bag him. Better make it a corker."

Lowell conducted him on a whirlwind round of introductions.

"Here's a couple of transcendental thinkers for you, Louie. I'd like you to meet Ralph Emerson."

"I've enjoyed your lectures, Mister Agassiz. May I ask what price you've been quoting? We shouldn't undercut each other...."

"And this is his friend, Hank Thoreau."

"Do you endorse the poll tax, sir?"

"Okay, boys, don't pester Louie. Let him circulate."

In quick succession, Agassiz met, among others, Frederic Tudor, the "Ice King," who wanted to know who currently supplied his household; the publishers, George Ticknor and James Field; and the famous orator and politician, Daniel Webster.

"What do you think of the siege of Vera Cruz?" demanded Webster. "Thirteen hundred shells lobbed into the town over two days. That's modern warfare for you, sir. Bomb the rascals back to the antediluvian! It's our manifest destiny to own this hemisphere!"

His head spinning, Agassiz was finally deposited by his host among a group of Harvard professors.

"I'll leave you to jaw with your future co-workers, Louie. I've got to get the goddamn entertainment going. Remind me to tell you later about the new system of bells I've worked out for my factories. I've got them ringing every fifteen goddamn minutes."

Agassiz had already met most of the Harvard men and

their wives before. From his own field, he saw Humphreys Storer, Amos Binney and Augustus Gould.

After making his hellos, Agassiz was commandeered by one man, Cornelius Conway Felton, the classicist.

Felton was a big suety man, jovial and loud, with unruly hair and small spectacles. He was given to wearing checkered vests, bow ties and velvet-trimmed jackets.

"Agass! Come with me. There's someone I want you to meet."

Dreading the very sight of another new face, Agassiz reluctantly complied.

Seated on a chair in one corner was the loveliest young woman Agassiz had seen since coming to America. Her brown hair fell in ringlets around her heart-shaped face. Her eyes were like sparkling brooks.

"Agass, this is my wife's sister, Miss Lizzie Cary. Lizzie, Professor Louis Agassiz."

"I would recognize the esteemed Agassiz anywhere, for I've had the immense pleasure of sitting through every one of his Boston lectures."

Agassiz's accent was suddenly thick. "Ah, if I had known such a gorgeous example of God's handiwork as yourself was in my audience, I would have been unable to speak a word."

Lizzie tittered. "Oh, Mister Agassiz, I hope I won't have that effect on you tonight."

"Well, perhaps if I were fortified with some punch, I could stammer a sentence or two.... You, sir! Two glasses of punch, *vite!*"

Felton spoke. "I'll leave you two alone now. I have to continue my discussion with Jack Whittier about Catullus."

The next two hours passed like as many minutes for Agassiz. He found himself hanging on every word that fell like dew from Lizzie Cary's ripe lips. What a smart, witty, endearing girl she was! She obviously admired him so....

Agassiz paid scant attention to the entertainment, which consisted of a troupe of actors performing a play entitled, "The Miner's Camp, or, What A Girl Did For Gold," followed by a series of amateur tableaux vivants enacted by the guests: *The Lovers Surprised*, *The Mortgage In Arrears*, etc.

"So, my dear," Agassiz was saying, "does a lass of your tender years really find an old fellow like myself attractive?" when he was brought up short by Lowell's hand on his shoulder.

"Time to earn your goddamn keep, Louie. The stage is all set up for you. Though why you needed so many goddamn crabs, I can't say."

Agassiz paid little attention to Lowell's words. "Farewell for the nonce, Miss Cary. I will see you later, I hope."

"Rest assured, I will be eagerly waiting."

Lowell ushered Agassiz toward the stage. Somewhat fuzzy-minded from several glasses of punch, Agassiz suddenly noticed the by-now-familiar sweetish smell of *dacka* floating through the room. What was Cezar up to?

Stepping onstage alone, Agassiz was greeted by a rapidly swelling wave of applause. He bowed gallantly to the crowd, then turned toward his lectern.

Agassiz was struck motionless by what he saw.

A rickety enclosure of chicken-wire had been erected. Inside, like a scene from Dante's *Inferno*, milled a hundred horseshoe crabs (*Limulus polyphemus*) climbing over each other with slow movements, the whole mass churning like a single pullulating organism. The sight was so unsettling as to nearly cause Agassiz to gag.

Damn that Desor! Had he arranged this deliberately, to sabotage the lecture, or was it the result of simple incompetence? Whichever, he would pay for this with his skin!

There was no turning back now, of course. Best to pretend all was going as planned....

Taking up position behind the lectern, Agassiz shuffled through his notes and began to speak. First, however, he made an impromptu addition to his text.

"I would like to dedicate this lecture to the lovely Miss Elizabeth Cary. Now, on to the topic at hand!

"Consider the curious creature known commonly as the horseshoe crab, one of God's little jokes. Unchanged for uncounted millennia, the jolly arthropod bumbles happily along on our North American shores, wagging its humorous spiky tail."

Agassiz gestured broadly toward the pen of crabs. With alarm, he noticed that the hastily formed cage was splitting its seams. It looked like the gates of Hell about to spew forth all its demons.

Continuing boldly, albeit somewhat quaveringly along with his speech, Agassiz noticed a curious change overtaking his audience. More and more of them were turning toward the back of the room, as if attracted by some spectacle there. The scent of burning hemp increased.

Persevering, Agassiz sought to ignore the defections. "—Now used mostly as fertilizer, *Xiphosura* once ruled—"

The air was suddenly split by a chilling war-whoop. Agassiz could maintain his pretence no longer.

"I must now pause, while we ascertain what is causing

this disturbance."

No one paid Agassiz any attention. Everyone was rushing toward the rear of the hall. Descending the stage, Agassiz pushed toward the front of the crowd.

Chief Snapping Turtle was performing a spirited dance, accompanied by Cezar's drumming on a borrowed kettle. Pipes of *dacka* passed everywhere among the audience.

As Agassiz looked on in horror, members of the Boston *bon-ton*, their inhibitions loosed by the potent *dacka*, spilled into the circle, joining the whooping and dancing.

Agassiz vainly sought to restore order. "People, please, we are all civilized ladies and gentlemen—"

Elsewhere, a shouting match had broken out. Agassiz turned to look.

"You claim I sponge off of you all the time?" yelled Thoreau.

"I do!" replied Emerson.

"By God, let's settle this as the ancient Greeks would!"

"Agreed!"

Soon Emerson and Thoreau had stripped down to their drawers and were locked in the intricate embrace of wrestlers. Choosing sides, people began to cheer. "Go it, Ralph!" "Nice move, Hank!"

Something grazed Agassiz's foot. He looked down.

It was a crab. He saw them now, scattered throughout the room, as if on the floor of the ocean. Suddenly, he was convinced he was underwater. He couldn't breathe—

The next half hour seemed an eternity. Agassiz would never forget for the rest of his days the uncanny sights he was forced to witness. Just the picture of Abbot Lawrence riding his female companion like a horse would have been enough to haunt his nights. But there was more. Much more.

He searched in vain for Lizzie Cary, hoping she would serve as a bulwark of sanity. But she had disappeared, and Agassiz could not say he blamed her.

At last, the prospect of order arrived in the form of a squadron of Boston police.

Agassiz rushed up to the lead officer.

"Thank God you've arrived—"

"And who might you be?" asked the man.

"Why, Professor Agassiz."

Agassiz was suddenly grabbed by a number of steely hands.

"I'll have to thank you for saving me some time, Professor. You see, I've got an order for your arrest."

7

SEWING ON A BUTTON

Josiah Dogberry snored. Like a Maine sawmill, like an asthmatic platypus (*Ornithorhynchus anatinus*), like a Michigan beaver (*Castor fiber michiganensis*) uneasily winter-dreaming of Ojibway hunters led by a wild Chief Snapping Turtle, Mister Dogberry roughly rasped and snorted throughout the night, making it nigh impossible for Agassiz to get any rest.

Not that either his mental condition or his physical surroundings were conducive toward sleep anyway.

Agassiz sat on a rude cot cushioned by a cornshuck mattress covered with a scratchy striped material. A pungent blanket—whose aroma was matched only by that of the open chamberpot in a corner—was rucked up at the end of the bed. The cot and mattress occupied one half of a gloomy windowless cell. The cell lay deep in the bowels of the Charlestown State Prison.

He had been brought to the jail in an enclosed police wagon. While being hustled into the back with no apparent consideration of his status, Agassiz had struggled and uttered vain protests against his arrest.

"My good man, there must be some mistake! I am Louis Agassiz, scientist and Swiss citizen—"

The officer who had made the pinch, whom Agassiz had heard addressed as Sergeant Rufus, said, "I already thanked you oncet for not hiding who you was and surrendering so pleasantly. What more do want? A dadblamed certificate?"

"But you obviously don't comprehend—"

"Hold on one minute, old trump. You're the one who don't compree-hend the facts. I am carrying a writ signed by the Governor hisself for your arrest, and his word is law in this state. You ain't in your precious Willy Tell land now, so get your tail in that there Black Maria."

"But diplomatic immunity—"

Sergeant Rufus held a hand palm up toward one of his assistants. "Griswold, pass me the leg irons...."

Seeking to spare himself further indignities, Agassiz clambered into the wagon, followed by Sergeant Rufus, who bore a small lantern. Then the doors were slammed shut on them and barred from the outside.

As they pulled away from the Lowell mansion, Agassiz could faintly hear the raucous sounds of the mad party, which seemed to be approaching some kind of crescendo that could be only guessed at. He grew angry that none of his compatriots had come to his aid. True, his arrest had occurred on the fringes of the fracas, and it was possible that no one had noticed, what with the other spectacles commanding more attention. Still, their disloyalty rankled.

As the wagon rolled on, Agassiz demanded of Sergeant Rufus, "Why did you not fulfill your duty as upholder of the public morals by arresting everyone at that debauched soiree? Surely they were guilty of disturbing the peace, not to mention several kinds of exceedingly vulgar turpitude."

Sergeant Rufus scratched his head. "I got to confess, I ain't never seen the likes of that bash, and I been called to lend a hand at quite a few wild affairs along the Tontine Crescent. What were them crabs doing crawling all over, anyway? Was you staging a race?"

"Those crabs were part of my lecture."

Sergeant Rufus appeared not to hear, so bemused was he by memories of the rampant *Xiphosura*. "Not that I ain't seen animals at parties before. There was that jackass and the actress—But that's neither here nor there. Yet crabs just don't seem to present as much opportunity for fun—"

"Forget the crabs! Why didn't you arrest Lowell and Lawrence?"

Sergeant Rufus looked at Agassiz as if he were mad. "Arrest two of the richest men in the state, just for blowing off a little steam in private? Do you take me for some kind of bloody loon? I might as well just lay my head down on the tracks in front of the New York express! No, I don't mess with the Associates, and I'd advise you not to either."

And with that bit of sage advice, Sergeant Rufus settled back in silence for the rest of the trip.

When they eventually stopped and Agassiz emerged from the wagon, he was struck with the enormity of his plight.

Ahead of him in the night bulked the granite sinews of the Charlestown State Prison.

Its octagonal central portion was flanked by several rectangular wings, their barred windows resembling the vacant eyes of the giant floating casque in Walpole's *The Castle of Otranto*. A six-foot-high wrought-iron fence surrounded the Bullfinch-designed complex. (How ironic, to pass so precipitously from Lowell's Bullfinch townhouse to this creation at the other extreme of the architect's palette.) Fields of prisoner-tended crops stretched away on three sides.

Shivering in the mild June air, Agassiz knew that if he were to enter the prison he would never emerge. He couldn't be sure anyone even knew he was here. And whatever insane bureaucratic mixup had led to his arrest would remain in effect for decades while he withered up into a prematurely aged wretch. He was only forty years old, for God's sake! He was too young to be immured like this, he had so much yet to do, so many honors yet to reap—

Agassiz made a dash for freedom. He was brought low by Sergeant Rufus's flying tackle, ending up with a mouthful of dirt.

"Come on now, Professor, it ain't no use—"

Inside, Agassiz was remanded to the custody of a turnkey who bore a striking similarity to one of the larger species of anthropoids, perhaps *Gorilla gorilla*. This truncheon-wielding Jack Ketch shepherded Agassiz through a labyrinth of cresset-lit corridors until they finally reached a Stygian cell. The guard opened the door, shoved Agassiz in, then banged it shut.

The light filtering in through the Judas-window showed Agassiz a recumbent form. The body stirred, and introduced itself.

"Josiah Dogberry, sir. And you?"

When Agassiz in his stupefaction made no reply, Dogberry said, "Takes a mite of getting used to, doesn't it? Well, see you in the morning." Whereupon he went straight back to sleep, with the aforementioned nasopharyngeal accompaniment.

Now, untold hours later, Agassiz remained in shock. The dank and slimy stone walls of his cell seemed to be closing in on him. He tried to rouse himself to action. What was that cheap novel he had read on the boat to America? Ah, yes, *The Count of Monte Cristo....* How had the protagonist of that romance escaped? Dug his way out with a spoon, hadn't he? Agassiz made an inventory of his personal effects: a pencil (from the Thoreau family factory), his hastily snatched lecture notes, some coins, a pocket watch, and a molasses-scented handkerchief.

His scheme was clear: he would scribble a farewell note, bribe the jailer to deliver it, wait till the stroke of midnight, and then garotte himself with his hanky.

The cell was suddenly silent. Dogberry had stopped snoring. Agassiz braced himself to meet and deal with the hardened felon who shared his incarceration.

Dogberry stretched and yawned. Sitting up, he raised his face into the light. It was a distinctly mild and youthful face, not at all what Agassiz had been prepared for.

"Ah, that was a fine night's rest. Nothing like a good sleep to put you right with the world! How did you snooze, old chap?"

Somewhat reassured by Dogberry's civilized demeanor, Agassiz replied, "Not too well, I fear. My name, by the way, is Agassiz. Louis."

"Well, Lou, they should be by with the morning porridge soon. And with any luck, it won't have too many weevils in it."

Although he feared it was a breach of penal propriety, Agassiz could not refrain from asking, "So—what was your crime, Mister Dogberry?"

"Basically, I'm in the hoosegow for offending an art critic."

"I had not realized that was a punishable offense."

"Me neither. But when money comes in the door, art goes out the window."

"I'm afraid I still don't quite see—"

"Please—read my card."

Dogberry handed Agassiz a printed pasteboard.

JOSIAH DOGBERRY, ESQ.
ITINERANT ARTISTE
PORTRAITS RENDERED
WITH ELEGANCE AND DISPATCH
PROFILES.................10 ¢
FULL-FACE.................25 ¢
TORSO TO WAIST...........75 ¢
DOWN TO THE FEET........ 1 DOLLAR
(HANDS EXTRA)

Above the text was a sample of Dogberry's portraiture. The crude lines of the rendering seemed to limn a hydrocephalic hunchbacked dwarf.

"I see," replied Agassiz, handing the card back. "There was some dispute about your fees...?"

Dogberry sighed. "I'll say there was. I sweated blood to sketch the whole Pickens family, and they weren't hardly satisfied. The father claimed I made his youngest look like a pig. Demanded his money back, he did. Unfortunately, I had spent it all on the vile necessities of life, to wit, kidney pie, a game of skittles and a night's lodging. So, here I am."

"Where did you get your training, may I ask?"

"Entirely self-taught, sir, and proud of it. I started life as a humble barefoot farmboy. In my spare moments, I would sketch the livestock with charcoal on a handy plank. When it came time for me to make my way in the world, I just naturally turned to the pictorial arena."

"Perhaps it would have been better for you to have remained on the farm...."

"Couldn't be done, Lou. I was the youngest of sixteen boys, and by the time I grew up, the land had already been divided amongst my brothers. And it was only two acres to begin with! Not that they had such an easy time of it either. I remember one day when Joshua—he's the oldest—turned to Jeremiah—that's the one with the limp—and said, 'Go fetch Jeb, Jason, Jethro, Jim, John, Jan, Jurgen, Jed, Jabez, Jahath, Job, Joel and Julius—we've got to talk about putting the patrimony back together.' Well, sir, by the time Jeremiah had rounded everyone up—what with his limp and all—the price of corn had dropped another penny a bushel! Sure as taxes, the New England farmer is taking a beating these days. It's all that cheap produce from the west, coming in by the canals and railroads, that's driving us under. I curse the day the Erie Canal was ever dreamed up!"

"But progress—"

"Progress for some is always regress for others, Lou. Take my word for it."

Pondering this new sentiment, Agassiz was startled by the sound of a key in the cell door.

The door opened to reveal the jailer who had conducted Agassiz last night. But instead of bringing breakfast, he delivered these chilling words: "You, the new one—come with me."

"Give 'em hell for all us little folks, Lou."

On watery knees, Agassiz preceded the cudgel-equipped guard. They traversed a maze of corridors, from behind the cell doors of which issued various groans and lamentations, before descending a level. This sub-basement appeared little used: cobwebs graced the nitred walls; rats scuttled with curiously intelligent movements across their path; a stack of crates was stencilled with the legend RELICKS OF YE SALEM TRIALS....

They came to a door from under whose bottom leaked light.

"In you go," growled the guard.

Agassiz laid a hand on the door latch. He was shaking so violently that he actually transmitted his vibrations to the loosely hung door in its frame, powdering his shoes with dust. But at last he managed to pull open the Portal of Doom, whereupon an unfathomable scene met his eyes.

A barely perceptible rumbling, easy to ignore, could be sensed emanating from somewhere. On the floor of the big room was a luxuriant Oriental carpet. Tapestries hid the walls. Centered in the middle of the rug was a long oaken table covered with a damask cloth. In the middle of the table stood a six-branched candlestick of ancient design casting its lambent glow. Two settings of plates and cutlery were arranged at either end of the table, in front of high-backed chairs. The smells of eggs, ham, toast and coffee emanated from various serving vessels.

Seated at one end of the table was a man. He wore high polished boots and the uniform of a Prussian officer, all gold buttons, braids and epaulets. From his belt was suspended an unsheathed rapier. The man's face was as hard and sharp as the stones of the Cuckfield Quarry from which Mantell had gouged his fossils. One eye was concealed by a black patch decorated with the broken-armed cross of the ancient Aryans, primal sun symbol stitched in white.

"*Herr* Professor," said the man in a voice somehow reminiscent of the motions of a King Cobra (*Ophiophagus hanna*), "won't you join me for breakfast?"

Mesmerized, Agassiz took the offered seat.

"Please, help yourself."

Scooping unseen food into his plate, gulping down a huge lump in his throat, Agassiz found his voice. "A-and your name, sir?"

"You enjoy the modest privilege, *Herr* Professor, of addressing a humble representative of the King of Prussia. I am His Majesty Frederick William the Fourth's loyal servant, Hans Bopp."

Agassiz felt a wave of fear wash over him. Here, then, was the second man Cezar had warned him of, the infamous head of the Prussian secret police.

"We have some business to discuss," said Bopp. "But let us wait until we have sampled this novel American cuisine. It is my first visit to the New World, and I fully intend to enjoy it. Come, eat."

Bopp's words and tone brooked no disagreement. Agassiz manfully chewed and swallowed, though he tasted not a morsel. Bopp spoke brightly all the while on inconsequential topics: the poetry of Eichendorff, the music of Mozart (particularly the hidden Masonic symbolism in *The Magic Flute*), and the landscapes of Caspar David Friedrich.... Not surprisingly relaxing a bit under the civilized conversation, Agassiz was actually beginning to enjoy his coffee when Bopp said without preamble, "You are aware, are you not, that you are still in the service of King Frederick, *Herr* Professor?"

Agassiz choked on his coffee. Recovering, he said, "But how can that be? The grant was to last only two years, and that time was up in March. I've spent all the money, but I can give a strict accounting—"

Bopp reached inside his coat and removed some papers. Agassiz recognized with a sinking feeling the agreement Humboldt had mailed him for his signature. Damn his own avarice! But he had needed that three thousand dollars to get to America....

"May I read to you from section four, paragraph sixteen, clause nine? 'The undersigned agrees to offer the Crown first option on his services for a period of time not to exceed two decades after the expiration of this contract. Should the reigning monarch perish (God save him), the option shall pass to his successor.'"

Agassiz attempted a feeble laugh. "Surely such a clause is merely one of those ancient manifestations of *droit de seigneur*, not meant to be actually invoked...?"

Folding up the papers and returning them to his coat, Bopp said, "I'm afraid not, *Herr* Professor. It's actually a modern notion, and quite legal. In fact, it was this very clause which I was able to use—along with my status as ambassador—to convince the Governor to order your arrest. But I don't wish to invoke courts of law quite yet in our discussion, nor the displeasure of the King, which I, as his duly appointed agent, would be duty-bound to express. No, I intend to appeal to your sense of honor and to our common heritage."

The sole surviving Teutonic Knight stood up, his sword clattering on his chair, and proceeded to stride martially up and down the room as he spoke.

"You see, *Herr* Professor, I am going to speak to you as a fellow member of the Aryan race. It's true, you're not technically a member of the Germanic tribes, but as a pure-blooded Swiss, you represent the next closest branch of our noble family. Perhaps you're familiar with Comte de Gobineau, the Frenchman? No? Ah, a pity. He is in the midst of composing a monumental work he intends to call *The Inequality of the Human Races*. I believe you'd find it fascinating. It details the genesis of the Aryans on the Indo-European plateau, their migrations and their proper place as lords and rulers over all other degenerate branches of humanity.

"But this destiny, while ultimately inevitable, is subject, as are all temporal schemes, to setbacks and hindrances.

While the glorious rule of the sons of Ahura Mazda will come to pass sooner or later, it can be delayed. The lesser races, you see, are cunning in a primitive way. They can interpose barriers to our success. If nothing else, they outnumber us drastically.

"By Wotan, they are incredibly fecund! We Northerners, with our concentration on matters of the intellect and the spirit, can hardly match the tropical scum in matters of procreation. It's disgusting how they breed, like maggots in filth! And just as you would crush without compunction a stinging insect that annoyed you, so must the inferior races of the world be brought under the fatherly and wise rule of Germanic efficiency and swiftly exterminated!"

Bopp paused, and Agassiz tried to muster a politic reply. Slowly, he began.

"While I basically agree with you as regards the innate superiority of our white race, I must beg to differ slightly with your aggressive plans for world domination. Surely the wisest and least energetic course is simply to maintain a policy of strict segregation. Let the dark-skinned races be penned up in their portion of the globe, while we keep to ours. For instance, we might begin by shipping all the North American blacks back to Africa—"

Bopp exploded. "And let them squat on the untold undeveloped wealth of that continent!? And what of the possibility of their stealing sufficient arms from us to represent a military threat? No, that will hardly do, *Herr* Professor. It's a fight to the death, believe me. And although it's guaranteed that Aryan forces will ultimately triumph, inaugurating a thousand-year rule, the price of the victory can be high or low, depending on what we do today.

"You see, while German scientific and military prowess lead the world, are at an all-time pinnacle and still ascending—consider, if you will, the miracles of the Krupp munitions factories, the useful accomplishments of scientists such as Baron Liebig, and even the somewhat more esoteric findings of men such as yourself—there is another aspect to our culture that has been much neglected of late.

"I speak now of the religious side, the occult sphere.

"Ever since the Enlightenment, Aryan man has tended to disparage that which could not be weighed or measured. By failing to keep in touch with the spiritual elements in his nature, the inner light of Valhalla which alone gives direction to all his drives, he has cut down the tree of Yggdrasil. Look at the sad state of my own order, reduced first to land-grubbing politicians, then to mere retainers, turning our backs on all the secret knowledge we brought out of Jerusalem.

"I will grant the savages this much: whatever trappings of civilization they mimic, they wisely hold on to their religions. Their ancient gods and rituals still fuel their daily activities and their will to survive.

"It is this pagan spiritual vigor which I intend to restore to the Germanic peoples. And I shall begin by employing the fetiche of the Hottentot Venus!"

Agassiz suppressed a curse. That damnable pudendum! Why had Cuvier ever preserved it? Would it haunt him for the rest of his life...?

Agassiz sought to dissuade this Prussian Paracelsus from his plans. "But surely, *Herr* Bopp, you cannot seriously intend to contaminate yourself with Negro magicks?"

"Why not? What could be more ironically fitting than

to turn the savage's own weapons against himself? Magic, my dear Professor, knows no ethnic taint. I am perfectly at ease with anything that will achieve my ends, whether it be the shamanism of the Red Man or the taoism of the Yellow."

Bopp's lone eye began to gleam. He drew close to Agassiz.

"I have a vision of the German people reinspired with a thousand sects and cults. No more shall the Order of the Rosy Cross offer the sole alternative for seekers after cosmic truth. No, there shall be a hundred orders. The Mystic Aeterna, the Stella Matutina, the Ordo Templi Orientis, the Hammer League, the Thule Society, the Fraternitas Saturni Lodge—The Old Ones shall return! That is not dead which eternal lies! He does not sleep, he only dreams!"

Bopp's mantic trance fled as quickly as it had come, leaving the Teutonic Knight plainly enervated. He rested a hand on the back of Agassiz's chair and slumped. With an effort, he straightened.

"It is your duty, *Herr* Professor, both contractually and as a representative of the Aryan race, to assist me in obtaining the fetiche. I take it for granted that you will contact me at the first definite sighting of the sorcerer."

"And if I should chose not to comply?"

Bopp smiled evilly. "Allow me to show you something."

Moving to one of the tapestries, Bopp lifted it to reveal a door. He motioned Agassiz to open it and enter.

The moisture-scented room was filled with a rumbling that issued from a large water-wheel whose axle protruded from one wall. An underground stream entered from one side of the room through a stone channel, exiting on the far side.

Strapped to the rim of the water-wheel were two figures. With a shock, Agassiz recognized them as his two visitors of a day or so ago: Hoene-Wronski and Levi. With each revolution of the wheel, they alternately plunged into the water and emerged coughing and sputtering, with barely enough time to gather their breath for the next dip.

"Two pitiful would-be players in this great game," said Bopp sarcastically. "I caught them inquiring about the fetiche. Oh, don't be alarmed. I don't intend to kill them, just teach them a little lesson before sending them packing back to Paris. If I were ever to lay my hands on that damn Kosziusko, however, the story would have a different ending! But enough fun—let us go."

Outside the torture-room, Bopp said, "I trust I do not have to spell out the application of what you have seen to your own case, *Herr* Professor? I thought not. Very well, then, you are free to leave. Your guard waits outside to conduct you to the prison gates."

With a hand on the door latch, Agassiz was brought up short by one last comment from Bopp.

"If you still waver, Professor, allow me to assure you that the future of the sub-humans and all their allies can best be depicted by a boot stomping on a face—forever!"

Agassiz found himself on the ground floor of the prison without having consciously made the ascent. The events of the past twenty-fours hours had overtaxed his brain.

Sunlight pouring in through the unbarred windows of an anteroom began to restore him a little to himself. As clerks fussed over the paperwork connected with releasing him, Agassiz sought to reassure himself that the whole interval had been only a horrible nightmare. Surely the affairs of the world were not managed by such madmen....

Another prisoner was brought into the room. It was Dogberry.

"Glad to see you made it through whatever you made it through, Lou, though your face does look like the leeks we used to blanch on the farm. Anyhow, you didn't miss much of a breakfast. I counted fifteen weevil carcasses in the gruel, not reckoning a few wings and feelers."

Grateful for a familiar and friendly face, even of a night's acquaintance, Agassiz said, "I take it you're to be released today also, Josiah?"

"'Pears so, Lou. Though what I'll do when I'm out of here, I can't rightly say. Guess I'll be moving on to ply my trade in a less cosmopolitan town, one where folks ain't followers of this newfangled daguerreotype realism—"

Something about the hapless artist—surely not his minuscule talent—reminded Agassiz of Dinkel, his trusted sketcher of twenty years who had chosen to remain in Europe. Almost without intending to, Agassiz found himself saying, "Josiah, would you like a job drawing for me? The subjects would be animal in nature, which might be more in your line."

Dogberry slapped his trousers, sending up a plume of dust. "Would I! Why, Lou, you're the kind of patron that Rembrandt had with the Medicis!"

"I believe you have Michelangelo in mind, Josiah."

"One Spaniard's the same as another to me, I'm afeared."

Soon, two free men stepped out into the open air of Charlestown. The simple act of breathing had never filled

Agassiz with as much joy as it did right now. He vowed never to forget the feelings of this moment....

Despite the sleepless night and the unsettling interview, Agassiz found himself enjoying the walk through early morning Charlestown. Onboard a ferry heading toward East Boston, he found himself frequently breaking into a foolish grin.

Objectively considered, he knew, his life was a mess. On the one hand, he was forced to play host to a miscegenating colonial and his Bushwoman bride, not to mention a Terpischorean Ojibway sachem. He was simultaneously under surveillance by an autocrat and an anarchist. His wife was at death's door, and last night's fiasco had surely erased all chances for him to secure the Harvard professorship.

On the other hand, he was not strapped to the motive apparatus of a gristmill.

Opening the unlocked door of his house, Agassiz called out, "Pourtales, Burckhardt, Desor, hello! Your leader has returned unscathed!"

Jane poked her head out of the pantry. "Shush, Professor! Everyone's sleeping. They only just got home an hour or two ago...."

"The lazy wretches! And I suppose no one expressed any concern for me...?"

Jane looked hurt. "Master Desor claimed he saw you climbing into a carriage filled with trulls and tosspots. He said you had a slattern in each arm and one on your lap."

Agassiz felt a vein in his temple throbbing. He tried to repress his anger. "I did no such ungallant thing. I spent the night in prison, and this morning nearly escaped a hideous session on the rack!"

Jane gasped, and threw herself into Agassiz's arms.

"Oh, Louis, to think of it nearly makes me swoon! You poor, poor thing!"

Agassiz caught Dogberry watching with rather too much interest. "Ahem, thank you for your concern, Miss Pryke. Ah, allow me to introduce Mister Josiah Dogberry, a new member of the team. I believe Mister Dogberry could use some breakfast."

"I should say! A dozen flapjacks and a rasher or two would sit nicely. But light on the insect parts."

Leaving his servant to attend to Dogberry's needs, Agassiz retreated to his study. He freshened himself by means of a ewer and basin, then had a short nap on the leather couch.

The arrival of the morning post served as cause for Jane to awaken him. Having informed him archly that the rest of the household was still abed—including Mister Dogberry— she waited patiently for Agassiz to read his mail.

Agassiz singled out three letters for immediate perusal. The first bore the return address of the dwarfish yet powerful Abbot Lawrence.

Striving to maintain the devil-may-care demeanor he had felt earlier—there were plenty of other schools that would have him, Yale for instance—Agassiz slit the envelope.

Dear Professor Agassiz:

I can't say when I've had a more delightful time than I had last night. Probably not since Ben Franklin and I painted Philadelphia red back in '88. I consider the success of the whole affair to be attributable to you and your charming staff. Damn

*that fly! Martha! Where was I? Oh, yes. You may count on my
whole-hearted support for your candidacy for the new chair I am
about to endow. Marvelous, isn't it, the divergence of feminine
anatomy...?*

Sincerely yours,

A. L.

Agassiz realized he had been hunched forward tensely
while reading. He now flopped back gratefully in the chair.
Life was good. He was meant to succeed. All his problems
would soon disappear. (But what had Cezar told—or
showed—the millionaire about his African mate?)

The second letter was from Hosea Clay.

You dastardly rapscallion:

*As you well know by now, sir, I was afixin to sever yet
another token from your unclaimed slave when the brute availed
hisself of a poker, whanged me upside the haid and made his
escape. I have been convalesson these past few days, or you woul-
da received my alfred david about this shameful affair even
sooner. Rest assured that my lawyer will be in contack with
yourn, as soon as I employ one. The damages will be treemenjous.*

Hurtfully yourn,

Hosea Clay

Another burden off his mind. Dare he try for three out
of three...?

Dear Louis,

*Please excuse the familiar salutation. I hope you do not con-
sider me unladylike because of it. But I feel I know you so well*

after our heartfelt tete-a-tete *of last night. Your philosophical insights stirred me to the depths of my womanly soul. I look forward to sharing many more such intimate confidences with you.*

With deep affection I remain your good friend,
Lizzie Cary

Agassiz felt a warm glow pervading his nether regions. Thoughts of the lissome Lizzie stirred his genetic instincts.

"Jane, would you mind? I've had such a hard day...."

"Oh, no, sir! I can practice that new trick I tried the other night."

Kneeling before him, Jane began to unbutton his trousers.

At that moment the study door burst open.

Framed in the door was Jacob Cezar.

"Mine Gott, Louie, dank goodness you're zafe! Vee didn't know vot had hap—"

It dawned on Cezar what he was interrupting. "Oh, excuse me, I didn't realize—"

It was too late for the intruder to back out, however. The noise had attracted the rest of the household. Prominent in the front ranks were Edward Desor and Dottie.

Desor said smugly, "So, this is the example you set for your staff, Agass?"

Jane sought an alibi. "No, sir, you don't understand. It's only—that is—I was only sewing a button onto the Master's trousers!"

"A button? Where is it then? And what were you using for needle and thread? Perhaps you swallowed them? And it must have been an extra button, for I see none missing."

"Oh, I—" Jane hid her face and burst into tears.

Dottie hastened to the side of the girl and lifted her to

her feet. With an arm around her, she walked her through the embarrassed crowd.

Agassiz made to rise, realized that he dare not move with his unfastened placket, and settled for folding his hands primly over the offending spot while saying, "Edward, you don't know the real meaning of this innocent tableau."

"Please do not insult my intelligence, Agass. Were matters any more obvious, it could have been one of Sonrel's lithographs for *Fanny Hill*. You may, however, rely on my loyalty and discretion—or as long as you merit them. I will leave you to reassemble yourself now."

Soon, Cezar alone remained with Agassiz.

"Vell," said the South African, "in mine country—"

"Oh, damn you and your bloody country to hell!"

"Dot's not nice to zay to der vun who landed you your new chob at Harvard."

"And exactly how did you do that?" asked Agassiz.

Cezar opened his mouth to speak, but Agassiz raised a hand to cut him short.

"On second thought, keep it to yourself."

Cezar smiled. "Und Dottie."

8

A FISH'S STORY

The delicate calipers looked like toothpicks in the ursine paws of Jacob Cezar. The tips of the measuring instrument disappeared into the woolly curls atop Dottie

Cezar's pate. Chewing on a willow stick to clean her teeth, swigging some native drink from a hollowed-out ostrich egg carried from home, the Hottentot sat patiently submitting to the examination. To pass the time she perused Balzac's *Nana* in the original French, occasionally giggling.

Cezar called out the readings, just like a Mississippi riverboat sailor sounding the depths and yelling out, "Mark twain!"

"Dhree point zix, five point nine, den point dwelve...."

Agassiz, seated at his work table, plotted the figures on an intricate graph, whilst simultaneously recording them in several rows and columns. At last, he held up his hand to signal that he had enough data.

"There," said the scientist, "it's just as I suspected. Craniometrically and phrenologically speaking, your Hottentot mate does not possess sufficient cerebral development to be classified as fully sentient. Like the rest of her race, she falls closer to a chimp in her mental development."

"Vot der hell are you jabbering about?"

Agassiz grew irritated. "Look, man, it's all right here in black and white, mathematically incontrovertible. Why, her Bump of Sagacity is practically concave! Not to mention the distortion along her Node of Intellection, and her hypertrophied Curve of Amativeness. And the overall volume of her brainpan is clearly deficient. If Sam Morton were to get hold of her prepared skull, I wager he'd be able to fill it with only a few ounces of buckshot."

Cezar threw the calipers across the room in disgust. One pointy leg embedded itself in the painting of Agassiz's birthplace. "You're der vun vit der head full of buckshot, Louie! Not zentient.... How can you zay zuch a ding, after practically living in Dottie's lap for a month?"

Agassiz shuddered at the metaphor. "There's no personal animosity involved, Jacob. It's strictly a scientific finding. And you can't argue with science! To be sure, your mate does exhibit certain instinctive qualities which might fool the layman into thinking she can reason like a human. But a closer analysis will reveal that she comes no closer to true ratiocination than, than"—Agassiz struggled to find a suitably unlikely point of comparison—"than *Tursiops truncatus*, the bottle-nosed dolphin!"

Putting down her book, Dottie now spoke up. Agassiz was forced to admit that her English, though still rudimentary, had improved considerably since her arrival.

"Professor Agassiz, suppose I agree with you that I am inferior to the representatives of your white race? Suppose I call myself an animal? Do you not think that even animals deserve moral treatment?"

"Well, yes, within bounds.... Unless some benefit to humanity is at stake, that is."

"Then how do you justify the vile abuse which is visited on the black slaves of your adopted land? The whippings, the separation of family members, the back-breaking labor from dawn to dusk...."

Agassiz coughed and cleared his throat. He took out a handkerchief and blew his nose. He found he could not meet the Bushwoman's gaze. "This is ridiculous. I lower myself to the level of someone arguing metaphysics with a dog! Still, never let it be said that Agassiz ever failed to meet a challenge, however absurd! First off, you impudent thing, the American system is a pre-existing condition, one that I personally had no hand in establishing. I remain morally aloof from the whole question. Still, if one wished to defend the system, one could find many good points to it. First, it has succeeded in bringing Christianity to many souls who would otherwise have languished in spiritual ignorance. Second the material living conditions of American darkies are infinitely superior to their old standards. Wood and brick have replaced thorn and mud. Hearty bread and fresh milk more than substitute for grubs and roots."

"Dere's noding wrong vit a grub if you cook it right," interjected Cezar.

Agassiz ignored the interruption. "And third, their brainless labor, which is basically good for their constitutions, has enabled the country as a whole to enjoy a higher standard of living. If it has to be procured at the cost of a few lashes—never meted out except when truly merited, as I understand it—then their servitude is quite justifiable. How would they live differently if they were free, anyway?"

Straightfaced, Dottie said, "You make it sound so appealing, Professor Agassiz. Perhaps you would care to trade places with a slave, if only for a day or so?"

Agassiz stood up, infuriated. "What a ludicrous suggestion! Imagine me, Louis Agassiz, out amid the cotton plants, wailing some Negro spiritual! You see, Jacob, how little this creature's thought processes resemble those of a true human being? Even you must admit it now."

"All I haff to admit is dot der image of you vit a zack of cotton on your back und zinging der Dahomey hoeing chants is vun I vould pay at least a dollar to zee."

"Bah! This crazy talk is getting us nowhere."

Cezar assumed a gloomy look. "Dot's for zhure, Louis. Vee have no more idea today vhere D'guzeri is den vee did two veeks ago, after you got out of der prison. Und you know vot today marks, don't you? Der end of der period during vhich Zaartjie's quim vas zoaking up der virtues of der *dacka* brew. At any dime now, D'guzeri can go to der Cosmogonic Zpot und put der fetiche to use."

"You needn't remind me of all that. Don't you think I'm worried about it too? But what can we do? I've exhausted my intellect, and still have no idea where to lay our hands on the scalawag. I thought for certain that we would find him in the last place we investigated."

"Tvisting hawsers at der Ropewalk?"

"Well, they do use hemp there.... No, I admit we're totally at sea. All we can hope now is that Kosziusko or Bopp can lay their hands on him before he does anything awful. Although I do not exactly relish the thought of either of those maniacs gaining the fetiche for their own purposes. But perhaps they will tear themselves to pieces, like the Kilkenny cats."

"Dose vuns are both bad news, I'd prefer not to dangle vit dem. Vell, before I get to feeling any lower, I'm going to mine boat for a pipe. Maybe Dottie und I vill dink of zomeding yet. Care to choin us?"

"No. I have some personal affairs to attend to."

After Cezar and Dottie left, Agassiz summoned Jane.

"Can you spare a moment from your household chores, dear Jane? I'm in something of an unsettled mood. By the by, have I ever mentioned before that the blush in your cheeks reminds me of the delicate shade of apple blossoms?"

Jane stared at the floor, grinding with one delicate boot-tip some invisible bug on the carpet. "Lor', Professor, I don't know anymore how to take these compliments of yours. You see, there's been something troubling my thoughts lately."

Agassiz evinced impatience. "Well, out with it then, girl!'

"All right. But you've got to not mind me if I ramble a bit. This is hard for me to say. I don't rightly know my own feelings yet, what with all the new books I've been reading."

"Books? What books?"

"Just some lit'rature that Miss Dottie lent me. Some broadsides by Sojourner Truth and her friends. Pamphlets that talk about how women have always been put down and stepped on, used and abused by menfolk, who seduce 'em and cast 'em aside. How we generate more than half of the world's wealth, but get less than our fair share of it. How we birth and raise all the children, clean all the houses, cook all the meals, then get beaten up for our troubles, laying our bruised bodies down in tears at night! How we must send off all our sons and husbands—worthless as they are!—to damn fool wars in furrin lands, war which we women had no say in startin'! How women are kin to the niggers of the world!"

Jane's voice had been growing steadily louder and louder, until she uttered the last startling sentiment in what amounted to a shout.

Agassiz was dumbstruck. He suddenly realized that his jaw was on its way to becoming unhinged, rather like that of a boa constrictor (*Boa constrictor*), and snapped his mouth shut.

Quivering, Jane said defiantly, "There, I've said it! Now, will there be anything else, sir?"

"Nuh-nuh-no. Uh, thank you for sharing these novel sentiments with me, Jane. Perhaps we could discuss them at greater length later tonight—? No, I thought not. Well, be sure to indulge yourself with a longish teatime this afternoon, Jane."

"I fully intend to!"

When his rebellious housemaid had departed with a slam of the door, Agassiz began softly to swear. Damn that Hottentot to the hottest circles of hell!

To soothe his temper and console his frustrated genetic instincts, Agassiz removed a much-creased note from his pocket and re-read it once more.

Dearest, sweetest Louis,

It seems incredible to me that you are truly mine; that you have chosen me to someday be your wife. You say you long for me to be by your side continually, to grace your home with "my smiling eyes." How I dream of it! No place is home for me on earth but where you are.

I pray each night that the day may dawn soon!
Adoringly yours,
Lizzie

What did he need with the caresses of a scullion when he had the unconditional love of a beautiful, gracious and well-connected young lady of fine breeding, whose cousins included the wealthy and influential Perkinses, Gardiners and Cabots?

Consulting his appointment book and the fine Swiss watch the teary-eyed citizens of Neufchâtel had given him upon his departure, Agassiz saw that it was the hour scheduled for his meeting with the rice planter from South Carolina, Rory Cohoon. The man had obtained an introduction through Lowell—Cohoon was friends with many of the plantation owners who provided the textile magnate with his raw materials—and although Agassiz had no interest in meeting the Southerner, he thought it best to oblige his patron.

Agassiz had time only to add a few lines to his sketch for the grand Museum of Natural History that he intended to build in Cambridge, before Cohoon was announced.

"Howdy, I say, howdy, Professor Ah-gass-ease! Allow me to shake your learned hand, son!"

Cohoon was dressed all in white, including a broad-brimmed hat. A large cigar protruded from one corner of his mouth. His fingers were circled with half a dozen rings. The pearl in his tiepin was as large as the egg of a quail (*Colinus virginianus*).

"I am pleased to meet you, sir. I have not previously had the privilege of greeting one of the South's landed gentry. May I get you something to drink?"

"Do you make a Silver, I say, Silver Horseshoe up in these Yankee parts? If you do so, then bring them on, son. Bring them on, I say!"

Somewhat baffled, Agassiz temporized. "One moment, Mister Cohoon, and I'll inquire."

Summoning Jane—whose red-rimmed eyes and sour expression he could only hope Cohoon did not notice— Agassiz repeated the request.

Jane sniffled. "Do you mean three parts whiskey, two parts bourbon, one part vermouth, a dash of bitters, a splash of branch water, and a twist of lime?"

"Splendid! That's it exactly! What an intelligent, I say, what an intelligent girl!"

"Uh, yes, I agree...."

Jane soon fetched the drinks. After noisily quaffing a huge draught and pronouncing it "mighty splendid," Cohoon broached the topic of his visit.

"I'm a rice planter, son. Fifty slaves and a hundred acres under water. You may not know it, but rice planting requires more intelligence than your cotton. You can't broadcast, I say, you can't just broadcast seed, you have to set out each plant individually. You have to know when to flood and when to drain them. Harvesting is mighty chancey. And then there's maintenance on the dikes and gates and sluices. Taken all in all, it's a devilishly tricky business."

The Silver Horseshoe was beginning to raise Agassiz's thinking to new levels of profundity. "I can well imagine."

"Now, my problem is that your average nigger is hardly smart enough to lace his own shoes, never mind master the art of rice cultivation. I or my overseers have to watch them every minute. They seem to botch things as soon as you turn your back! What I was hoping to learn, I say, learn from you was some way of breeding a smarter nigger. Could you draw me up some scheme to increase their intelligence generation by generation? I know we're talking long-range here, but it would be of immense benefit to the South. And maybe, I say, maybe we could toss in a few other factors while we're at it? Could we get longer arms on them, and maybe a reduction, a reduction, I say, in the amount of sustenance they require? Their damned oats cost a fortune!"

Agassiz gave serious consideration to the interesting request. "Well, we have to consider the inherent limitations of the Negro germ plasm, Mister Cohoon. There's only a limited capacity for mentation in the smartest African, and trying to get more out of them by crosses is like trying to squeeze water from a stone. Now, I take it you're not con-templating adding white blood of the lesser races to the line—"

Cohoon shot to his feet, his face livid. "Sir, what do imply?! Are you repeating, I say, repeating those scurrilous rumors about my darling Lily Belle? If so, then it means der-ringers under the Spanish moss by the river at dawn!"

"Please, sir, be seated! I intended no offense. I was speaking strictly from a theoretical standpoint. I abhor mis-cegenation as much as you evidently do."

Cohoon relaxed and resumed his chair. "Very, I say, very well then. No offense taken. A man's honor, you know—"

Templing his fingers, Agassiz said, "Your idea has many implications. If we could indeed create a new breed of Negroes, both more sensible and docile, it would have vast implications for the nation as a whole. You must let me pon-der this project for some time, and write you with the results."

"Splen—, I say, splendid! Let's drink to it!"

After sealing their agreement, Agassiz and Cohoon passed an additional time in pleasant conversation.

"The family and I are heading north to Saratoga Springs for the summer. It gets so damn hot in the Carolinas that it makes your blood boil. Weather's not fit for man nor beast. I even bring my hounds with me. They're with Lily Belle at the hotel now. Rented the dogs their own room, I did! Of course, life at the plantation goes on. The niggers are out in the fields, I say, fifteen hours a day. Of course, the sun, I say, the sun doesn't bother them. They can't get any black-er, haw haw!"

Agassiz laughed too. More drinks were poured.

"That story, son, reminds me of this one slave of mine. Used to be an infamous free black in Philadelphia until I had him kidnapped. Pretended he was a lawyer, or some other such fool job. Riled me, I say, riled me no end. Well, once I had him in chains, I told him he could buy his freedom back. Took him three years of working overtime, three years, I say! No sooner was he back in the city than I had him waylaid again. Another three years, and I set him free—for a price. Just before I left, the slavers dumped him on my doorstep for the third time. All entirely legal in my state, of course. You should have seen the woolly-headed bastard cry!"

By the time Agassiz could get the jovial planter to leave, it was late afternoon and his head was swimming. Realizing that he had not checked today on his staff, he ventured shakily to his laboratory.

Maurice sat outside the workroom door at a small desk. "Do you have your papers in order?"

Agassiz's head hurt. "Papers? What papers?"

"Your security clearance, your permits and your sponsorships. In triplicate."

"Of course I don't have any such foolish things. What is this? What's going on?"

"We've implemented a new system, an apparatus to administer the resources of the proletariat. In short, the laboratory has undergone collectivization. We have modified Fourier's notion of the phlanstery—"

"Collectivization be damned! This is my laboratory!" Agassiz began to hammer on the door. "Open up in there! Cease this nonsense immediately!"

"It won't do any good to yell. They're on strike."

"Strike?!"

At this juncture the door opened and Edward Desor peered out. "Oh, it's you, Agass. Please go away now, we're busy. And I would suggest not throwing your weight around any more in the future. With what I've seen of your ribald behavior, you are in no position to demand anything."

The door closed in Agassiz's face before he could reply.

"I told you they wouldn't take kindly to being disturbed...."

Agassiz held his head. He was too jingled now to deal with this revolt. Air—he needed some fresh air. When he was his own master again, he would thrash them all—

Out on the back lawn, Agassiz looked toward Cezar's ship. For a moment he thought he was seeing double. Then he realized that the *Dolly Peach*, absent since his insulting of its skipper, was moored alongside the *Sie Koe*.

Agassiz stumbled up the boarding plank of the latter vessel and into the cabin. There sat Cezar, Stormfield and the Hottentot, heads bent in earnest confabulation.

Upon Agassiz's entrance, Stormfield came aggressively to his feet.

"Perfesser, I'm here for that suitably humble apology ye owes me!"

"I just—"

Stormfield interrupted. "Good enough! Never let it be said that old Dan'l didn't know when to bury the hatchet. Now, get your carcass over here. We're havin' a council o' war. Ye see, we knows now where your Well of Creation is, and when that sorcerer plans to be there!"

The fumes in Agassiz's brain cleared immediately. "Where is it? Tell me!"

"Why, where else but goldanged Marblehead?!"

"Your home port?"

"Kee-rect! But I knows ye won't credit it without some explanation, so jest set yerself down and lissen.

"Before the White Man came to this country, there was an Injun settlement where Marblehead stands today. It was shunned by all the neighboring Red Men, the Narragansett and the Pequots, since the tribe in question—the Miskatonicks—had a reputation as bein' unclean and unwholesome. Ye ken, the waters off Marblehead shore were just a-swarmin' with strange creatures—in fact, new ones seemed to be born daily—and the local Injuns were tainted through intimate contact with the queer beasts."

"You mean," said Agassiz hopefully, "that they fed upon the strange flesh, violating certain dietary taboos?"

"No sir—I means what I said! They had carnal relations with the creatures. At least them as was fitted for it."

Agassiz gagged, and had to be refreshed with a sip from one of Dottie's ostrich eggs.

"I knows, it strikes one kind o' hard, unless ye've grown up with the notion as I have. But it's true. The Miskatonicks rogered and was rogered by certain of them fishes, giving birth to various halfbreeds, some o' which lived on land, some in the sea.

"Now, one day in 1629, Clem Doliber was kicked out o' Salem, just down the road from the Miskatonicks. Clem was a mean cuss, bound by neither conventions nor fear. He was booted out, in fact, for havin' congress with a neighbor's prize sow, then shootin' the owner when the affronted fella politely asked Clem to disengage, lest he make the taste o' the bacon go off. Well, with no place else to go, Clem sets out for the Miskatonick village.

"When he gets there, he finds it empty of all humans or

animals or halfbreeds, with kettles still on the boil and blankets warm to the touch. There was no sign of a ruckus or massacree. Alls he could find was a wide trail of slime leadin' into—or outta—the sea. So Clem settles into an empty teepee, and that was the beginnin' of the white man's occupation of Marblehead.

"The followin' years seen an influx of refugees and desperadoes of every stripe. Marblehead became the dumpin' grounds for the whole Thirteen Colonies. Why, it was worse than Rhode Island, and that's sayin' a lot! We had outcasts of any kind you could name, from all over the globe. My own ancestors, for instance, were Manxmen who worshipped Manannan mac Lir, God o' the Sea. Persecuted by the Archbishop of Canterbury hisself, they lit out for the haven of the New World.

"And I'm plumb ashamed to admit it, but these bad white folks had morals as lax as those of the Injuns. They was not immune to the fishy charms of the merfolk, and continued to intermingle their vital essences with them."

Agassiz lifted a hand wearily. "Stop right there, Captain Stormfield. Do you seriously expect me to believe this tall tale? It's absolutely, scientifically impossible for men and fish to interbreed."

"Impossible, is it? Then what do ye make o' this?"

Captain Stormfield pushed back one sleeve of his greasy sweater and showed the underside of his muscled arm.

It was patterned with coarse green scales from the wrist on up. As he twisted it for Agassiz's inspection, the scales sparkled in the candlelight.

"It ain't no razzle-dazzle, Louie. I'm at least one-eighth fish myself, jest like everybody else in Marblehead. If ye be a 'header, ye can't avoid callin' some tuna 'Uncle.'"

Cezar spoke up. "I believe him, Louie. Dey didn't name der Marblehead boys during der Revolution der 'Amphibious Regiment' for noding! How do you dink dey vere able to get Vashington across der Delaware zo easily? Vhy, Danny dells me dot dey chust jumped in der vater und pulled der boats like der drained porpoises!"

Agassiz finally found his voice, although it was but a shade of its normal booming imperiousness. "Please roll down your sleeve.... Thank you. That is a sight no man of science should be exposed to. All right now. Suppose I grant you this incredible tale as prolegomenon. How can you be sure that T'guzeri is planning to carry out his scheme in your absurd town?"

"Why, I was told directly so by them as should know. Ye see, there's always been two factions in Marblehead. There's them mostly human men and women who live side by side with the fishfolk without thinking twice one way or the other about them. They gen'rally give them wide birth, 'cept when a seaweed-draped cousin comes callin', friendly-like. They knows enough to steer clear of certain reefs and shoals, makin' the proper salutes and obeisances when passin' certain bays and suchlike.

"But then there's the other ones, the bent and twisted humans, those with thinner, colder blood than most. They associate with the worst of the fishfolk as often as they can. These are the ones who actually worship the same gods the fishfolk do, gods like Dagon and Pahuanuiapitaaiterai. These rogues collaborate with the mermen in their obscure and diabolical schemes.

"One of these types—not the worst, I'm happy to say— is my cousin, Howard Phillips. He told me jest this mornin'—in general terms, ye understand—about what

T'guzeri and his fellow conspirators have got planned for tomorrow night. Needless to say, I wasted no time in gettin' over here with the news."

Captain Stormfield now folded his (scaly) arms across his chest and waited proudly for Agassiz's reaction.

Agassiz surveyed the expectant trio before him. Did they really expect him to give credence to this cockamamie tale? Baron Munchausen himself had never concocted anything half so wild. Were they playing him a for a fool, only to leave him caught with his pants down, so to speak, at the last moment?

Captain Stormfield said, "Excuse me a moment." He picked up a ladle and scooped water from a bucket near the porthole. Pulling back the high neck of his sweater, he then anointed his highly visible gills.

Agassiz's eyes assumed the proportions of those of a slow loris (*Nycticebus tardigradus*). When he was partially recovered, he said, "The Coast Guard has put a large armed cruiser at my disposal. I shall requisition it for tomorrow night."

9

MOBY DAGON

Agassiz stood resplendently outside the door to Temple Place No. 10, the luxurious residence known as "the Court," home to the chaste and lovely Lizzie Cary. He was dressed in the closest thing to a uniform that he possessed: the red coat and trousers of the *Burschenschaft*, the student club he had belonged to twenty years ago at Heidelberg. A trifle snug, he had thought, gazing at himself in the cheval-glass at home. But he still cut an imposing figure in his old school colors, and he needed all the confidence he could summon up today.

It was noon of the day he was to confront the Hottentot sorcerer in the fishing village of Marblehead, and Agassiz had come to make his goodbyes to the woman he loved and coveted. Although he fully expected to return unharmed to her—after all, what chance did primitive superstition stand, once the blazing light of science was turned upon it?—he could not resist the chance to make a florid declamation of his impending sacrifice.

Within minutes, Agassiz was kneeling beside his beloved, holding both her small hands as she sat on the chaise-longue in the Cary parlor. The long dark curls framing her face trembled with the emotions besetting her, as Agassiz explained—in a carefully edited version, of course—what he had learned and what he was about to undertake.

"Oh, Louis, I'm so frightened!"

"Don't be, my dear. I am brave enough for both of us."

"I can't let you go alone, Louis. If anything were to happen to you, I would surely die of shock. Better for us to perish together in the jaws of some piscine horror than for me to live a moment without your presence!"

"Do you really mean that, my dear?"

"Yes, Louis, I do—with all my heart."

Agassiz came to a quick decision. "Then you shall come with me, darling Lizzie. You shall stand by my side, like a true mate, under the strong shelter of my loving protection. Can you don some suitable rough clothing quickly?"

"I'll wear the outfit I wore when we went butterfly hunting, and tell Daddy that we're going on another such expedition. I'll only be an hour or two."

Good as her word, Lizzie was ready within the stipulated time. Before long, they were descending from a carriage outside East Boston headquarters.

"Our transportation should be arriving momentarily, dear. Let us wait inside."

In the house, Agassiz found a party underway.

Dogberry, Pourtales, Girard, Burckhardt, Sonrel, Maurice, and Edward Desor were uniting their voices in a chorus of "Black Lulu," glasses full of champagne hoisted high. Chief Snapping Turtle shuffled around them, uttering wordless war whoops.

"What's the meaning of this?" thundered Agassiz.

"Our latest monograph has been delivered from the printers," explained Desor.

Agassiz snatched up a copy of the publication. The title page read:

AN INQUIRY INTO THE DIET OF THE
BATHYPTEROIDAE
BY
EDWARD DESOR
AND
HIS ASSISTANT,
LOUIS AGASSIZ

A veil of rage hung before Agassiz's vision like the Aurora Borealis. He prepared to loose the full might of his fury upon the impudent Desor.

Totally unconcerned, Desor merely glance significantly at Lizzie and said, "Had any buttons sewn on lately, Agass?"

Agassiz collapsed like a pricked balloon. "*Touché*, Edward. We shall discuss this later. Right now, I must be going."

"Oh, have no fear, we're all coming with you. Did you seriously think I'd let you hog all the glory? No, your loyal co-workers fully deserve to be with you at this historic moment, so that our names shall redound with yours throughout the history of natural philosophy."

Chief Snapping Turtle, evidencing a new talent for civilized speech, now flourished his bow and arrows and declared, "Chief Snapping Turtle wantum fight Wishpoosh with Great White Father Louis. Giant Beaver God needum good licking."

Realizing the futility of argument, Agassiz merely said, "Very well, then. Let us see if our ship has arrived."

The party paraded out onto the greensward with a view of the busy bay.

Drawing nigh like one of the indomitable Viking ships that had visited Newport long before Columbus sailed was the Coast Guard Survey ship the *U.S.S. Bibb*.

The *Bibb* was actually a small clipper ship, built by the firm of Kennard and Williamson in Baltimore. One hundred and forty-three feet long, four hundred and ninety-four tons, triple-masted, drawing eleven feet forward but seventeen feet aft, she was small compared to the 2500-ton behemoths McKay was currently building. Still, she was an awesome sight. Surely she would strike dread into the hearts of T'guzeri and his Marblehead confederates.

One aspect of her even now struck fear—or at least distaste—into Agassiz: the figurehead, which was cast in the shape of a buxom, gaily painted mermaid.

Anchoring some distance offshore, the *Bibb* lowered a small boat from its davits. Soon it grounded, and the *Bibb's* captain stepped ashore.

A young man of stalwart bearing, the captain strode decisively toward the waiting crowd. Agassiz was immediately impressed with his quiet competence.

"Lieutenant Charles Henry Davis, sir, at your command. May I just mention that I've read all your works, Professor Agassiz, and consider it the highest honor of my short career to accompany you on this mission."

The words of praise slightly recompensed Agassiz for the vile treatment he had been forced to swallow from his assistant. He puffed up visibly. "Rest assured, Lieutenant, that your services will earn you immense credit in the annals of your nation and your race. We sail today for the greater glory of white American science and culture."

At that moment, the disreputable figures of Jacob Cezar and his Hottentot paramour made their appearance on the deck of the *Sie Koe*. Both were only partially dressed.

"Ahoy, der *Bibb*! Vee are almost ready! Vun minute!"

Lieutenant Davis looked quite puzzled. Agassiz sought to explain. "They're, um, experts on the enemy we are about to face. I thought they should accompany us...."

Now Captain Stormfield poked his head out of the cabin of the *Dolly Peach*, which had remained berthed overnight. The Marbleheader was combing his hair with what appeared to be a fresh specimen of the three-spine stickleback (*Gasterosteus aculeatus*).

"I'm a-gonna follow ye in my craft, Captain. Seems to

me we could use a backup ship, just in case. I'll try not to outrace ye!"

"He knows the local waters...," faltered Agassiz.

It took two trips to ferry the twelve members of the motley expedition out to the *Bibb*. But at last they were all aboard. The Bibb lifted anchor, luffed its sails, and they were underway, entering the diamond-scattered waters of Boston Bay, the *Dolly Peach* following.

Lieutenant Davis conducted Agassiz on a tour of the ship, not neglecting to mention their armament.

"We ship several cannon of moderate firepower. But considering the nature of our quarry as you outlined it, I also took the liberty of signing on a skilled harpooner for this trip. Allow me to introduce you."

Lieutenant Davis brought Agassiz up to a somber bearded chap who was neatly coiling the rope attached to the heavy and wicked-looking instrument of his trade.

"Professor Agassiz, this is Mister Melville, a personal friend. I managed to convince him to leave his farm in Pittsfield for a day or two, though he has much plowing to do. Mister Melville has sailed the seven seas—on the fabled *Acushnet*, among other whalers—and possesses a steady eye and hand that will no doubt serve us well. In addition, Mister Melville shares your own literary bent. Perhaps you've read one of his memoirs? *Typee*? *Omoo*?"

"I fear not. But I haven't much time for pleasure reading of any sort. Your hand, Mister Melville—?"

Melville extended a calloused paw. "Call me Herman."

After exchanging a few words concerning the habits of various cetaceans, Agassiz left the sailor-cum-author so that he might rejoin his own party.

His comrades from Europe he found engaged in a game of dice with several Jack Tars. Chubby Maurice was about to roll. "From each according to his means, to each according to his needs! Come on seven!" The noon ration of grog had been disbursed, and much conviviality was in evidence. Agassiz passed them by, with only a baleful glance directed toward Desor.

Chief Snapping Turtle, much to Agassiz's astonishment, had found another member of his race with whom to converse, a tattooed red giant with a topknot.

"—then Queequeg say, "What you mean 'we,' white man?"

"Ho, ho, ho! Kici Manitu himself not say it better!"

By the starboard rail stood Josiah Dogberry, sketchbook and pencil in hand. Agassiz looked over the shoulder of the itinerant artiste: a few scalloped lines stood in for the multi-textured sea; the iron lighthouse on Minot's Ledge was indicated by some verticals supporting a box; gulls were shallow V's; clouds were squiggly circles.

Dogberry turned to face his employer. "I figured a record of our historic journey would be of inestimable value to future generations. What do you think, Lou?"

"The level of detail leaves much to the viewer's imagination...."

"Such is always the case with the best art, Lou."

It was easy to track down Jacob Cezar: the smell of burning *dacka* provided a scent-trail for which no bloodhound was necessary.

The South African was seated on a coil of hemp rope, from which he had cut a length for his own use.

"Vee rushed off zo fast, I plumb forgot mine own ztash.

Dis zstuff ist plenty rough, but as dey zay, any port in a ztorm."

Agassiz paused beside the colonial. Now that the end of their enforced companionship was in sight, Agassiz tried to look back with nostalgia on their adventures. The past month had been a welcome and stimulating change from his accustomed scholarly routine, hadn't it? True, the presence of Cezar's black-skinned mate had been nearly insupportable at times. True, he had nearly been ignominiously drowned in molasses due to the man. True, he had been thrown into a torture pit amidst Iron Maidens and Procrustean Beds for his connection with him. And also true—

Agassiz gave up the attempt to regard the last four weeks with retrospective fondness. It had been an unmitigated nightmare, for deliverance from which he would drop to his knees and praise his Creator.

Still, he could afford at this point to be magnanimous.

"Well, Jacob, your quest is nearly over now, thanks to my help. It seems quite probable that you will be sailing off tomorrow evening at the latest."

Cezar appeared reflective. "Ja, I'll be glad to get back to mine liddle farm. Dis hurly-burly city life ist not for old Jake. Give me der savannah und der vildebeest over der artificial ztone und der policeman any dime." Cezar sighed. "Ztill, it vill be a vhile before I see Kaffraria again. Dere'll be a ztop in Paris to return Saartjie's qvim to der Museum, und who knows vhere else Dottie vill vant to visit..."

"Speaking of the Hottentot, where is she?"

"Oh, zhe's gone forvard to vit your Lizzie to make vit der girl-dalk."

Agassiz took off like a cheetah (*Acinonyx jubatus*).

Dottie and Lizzie stood by the prow, spray sprinkling their faces. Lizzie looked particularly pale, and the Hottentot was half-supporting her.

"Remove your evil hands from my fiancee!"

Dottie replied calmly, "She is simply a little sea-sick, Professor Agassiz. And I thought you were still married...."

"My marital status is none of your affair, you—you heathen pickaninny!" Agassiz wrested the white woman away from the black one. "Are you all right, my dear?"

"Yes, Louis—I'm fine. I—I just need to lie down for a while."

"Let's see Captain Davis about a bunk." Agassiz regarded the Hottentot grimly. "And as for you—"

Dottie smiled, revealing her primitive and hideous dentition. "Oh, there's no need to worry about me, Professor. I feel great."

"Humph!"

The *U.S.S. Bibb* sailed blithely north, beneath the gladsome July sun, its crew and passengers intent on their respective enterprises. The salty air, crisp as lettuce hearts, invigorated all souls. With each passing league, Agassiz felt more and more confident of imminent victory. Past Deer Island they sailed, past Winthrop, Nahant, Lynn and Swampscott. A meal was served. Agassiz unbent enough even to sample a puff off Cezar's pipe—after carefully wiping the stem on his sleeve—but pronounced it unpalatable.

By late afternoon they were anchored off Cat Island, within sight of Peach's Point. Marblehead Harbor, a northward-facing U-shaped bay, was actually to the south of them now. The low and shaggy buildings of the two-hundred-year-old town looked like lichened ruins straddling a buried giant.

Captain Davis regarded the evil village with a cold and calculating gaze, before pronouncing judgement on it. "One of these days they'll go too far, these witches, and the folks in Washington will have to take notice. Why, I wouldn't be surprised if they brought an offshore bombardment down on their own heads one day...."

Captain Stormfield, meanwhile, had anchored alongside and boarded the *Bibb*.

"My cousin Howie is supposed to row out at dusk to meet us and fill us in on the plans of the Deep Ones, as they call themselves on account of they fancy themselves so deep. We'll just have to sit tight till then."

Now the crew and passengers hunkered down to wait. A small knot of old salts congregated around Captain Stormfield to swap yarns. Before long, practically the whole complement of the *Bibb* sat at his feet, mesmerized by his tales, with the falling twilight settling on them like a warlock's black mantle.

"Aye, many's the night I've sat inside my bolted, shuttered house with my dear old Dolly, like all the other good folks o' Marblehead, knowin' that the Deep Ones was a-fixin' to celebrate their unholy allegiance with the sea-critters. They would gather first in Washington Square beneath them contorted and twisty ancient trees with the branches that dangle like nooses. From there, they'd march up to the Old Burial Hill overlookin' the town. There they'd raise up a few choice spirits, such as the souls o' Margaret Scot and Wilmett Redd, who was both hanged as Satan's apprentices. Then back down again, through the twisty, non-Euclidean streets they'd crawl, a-yelpin' and a-howlin' fit to beat the band, some o' the legless citizens a-floppin' their reekin' squamous bodies through the dust! Down to the waterfront they'd hie themselves, there to be greeted by their infamous cohorts from the stinkin' sea-floor. And then—well, ye don't want to know what happened then. Suffice it to say that it'd require a heap o' italics to convey."

Captain Stormfield leaned back where he sat, and poked his unlit pipe into his mouth with dire meaning. There was a stunned silence for a moment. Then one of the sailors spoke.

"What's that there word 'nun-yew-clit-ian' mean?"

Another sailor piped up. "And what about 'squamous'? It got anything to do with Indian squaws?"

But before Captain Stormfield could enlighten his listeners, the lookout in the crows-nest let out a call.

"Rowboat approaching!"

Captain Stormfield rose. "Well, I'd best be gettin' back to my ship. Howie's a mite suspicious of strangers, and there's no way he will tie up to this here clipper."

Agassiz spoke up. "Wait one moment, Captain. Surely you do not intend to meet with this conspirator alone. What if he intends some kind of double-cross?"

"I guess I could take one other brave soul with me."

All eyes—including Lizzie's—now turned to Agassiz. He felt himself irrevocably nominated. With no small amount of trepidation, he said, "Very well, let us be off."

In the darkling air, Agassiz found it clumsy work to transfer himself to the *Dolly Peach*. He managed to clamber aboard after nearly taking an unplanned dip when he set his foot down on the stickleback which Captain Stormfield had been using as a comb that morning. Captain Stormfield hoisted anchor and they sailed off to meet the emissary from Marblehead.

As the crafts converged, Agassiz could discern a pair of shadowy figures in the rowboat. One, sitting, propelled the boat, while the other stiffly stood.

"That's Howie a-standin'," said Stormfield. "I guess his arthritis was actin' up, and he dragooned a young un' to row him."

The creaking of the oarlocks grew louder and louder. Soon the rowboat pulled alongside the *Dolly Peach*. Agassiz hastened to the side to help the men aboard.

As he bent forward, he instantly noticed two important details previously hidden in the darkness.

Stormfield's cousin, the erstwhile Howard Phillips, was dead as the proverbial doornail, and propped up on a tripod of marlinspikes.

Ant the man rowing was Hans Bopp.

Agassiz staggered back. In the next second, Bopp swarmed aboard.

The Prussian spymaster wore a raptor's grin. His hellish single eye seemed to focus and reflect the light from the emerging stars like a lens.

"So, *Herr* Professor, you thought to renege on our gentlemen's agreement? I fear now that you must meet the same fate as the turncoat on the spikes, from whom I extracted all I needed to know. Rest assured, however, that your death will mark a terminus to the contract you signed. We will not be calling on your progeny to fulfill it."

Bopp's hand suddenly held his gleaming rapier. Agassiz watched helplessly as the tip of the sword sketched a pattern of death before his face.

"Louie, catch!"

Something came hurtling through the night air at Agassiz. Instinctively, he snatched it.

He held by its narrow tail the legendary seamstress swordfish, stuffed and rigid, which had previously hung on Stormfield's cabin wall.

The feel of the old garments he wore, along with the heft of the swordfish, plunged Agassiz back twenty years, to when he had been a champion fencer at Heidelberg. Had he not beaten four German students in the space of an hour once? Surely he had lost none of that skill—

"*En garde!*" yelled Agassiz, and lunged.

Bopp parried expertly and effortlessly. "Very good," he said. "This gives me my exercise for the day. And you will die as befits a renegade member of the Master Race, rather than like a mongrel dog."

Now the duel became intense. It took all of Agassiz's concentration to maintain a barely viable defense, never mind press an attack. After a few minutes, he was huffing and puffing, while Bopp was breathing easily. The Hun even began to whistle. Damn that Jane and her rich cooking!

At last Agassiz knew Bopp was merely toying with him. He tried to prepare himself mentally for death. Yet even now he could not quite bring himself to believe that the world would soon be deprived of the genius of Agassiz—

Panting, Agassiz dropped his leaden arm. As he saw Bopp prepare to lunge, he took an involuntary step backwards.

His foot came down on the stickleback and he began to topple. He threw his arms up in a vain attempt to stabilize himself.

Taken offguard, Bopp awkwardly altered the direction of his thrust.

By a fluke—so to speak—the Prussian impaled himself on the waving swordfish. Together, he and Agassiz fell to the deck.

For a moment they lay entwined in a grim embrace. Then Agassiz wormed out from under the dead Prussian.

The bloody tip of the swordfish protruded from Bopp's back. Incredulously, Agassiz noted that it featured an eye, just as Stormfield had promised.

Done to death by a fishy sewing machine—It served the arrogant bastard right.

"Well fought, Louie! I takes pleasure in you avengin' my cousin's murder. As we can't learn nothin' more here, I suspect we'd best be gettin' back to the *Bibb*, for whatever shall eventuate."

Stormfield turned their nose toward the clipper ship. Soon, they had rejoined the others on the deck of the *Bibb*.

Agassiz began to recount his thrilling duel, but was cut short by Captain Davis.

"Another ship has put out from the harbor. We suspect that it's the Deep Ones."

"Shall we intercept them?"

Captain Davis started to reply, but in his turn was cut off by a shout from Dottie, who had been scanning the waters on the portside.

"Something's surfacing!"

"Mister Melville, to your weapon! Gunners, take aim!"

All hands rushed to the portside, causing a slight list in the *Bibb*. Agassiz was carried with them.

The water a few feet away from the *Bibb* bubbled and churned. Something tall and slender poked out of the roiling water. The neck-like appendage revealed itself to be attached to a rising body of some sort. More and more of the creature surfaced, illuminated by torches held by the crew.

Agassiz was the first to recognize it. "Why, it's a submersible vessel, like Robert Fulton's *Nautilus*! "

And so it was. Soon the submarine, at equilibrium, floated peacefully.

A hatch was violently pushed open. A man thrust himself out. He began to gasp deep lungfuls of air.

Agassiz was astounded. "Why, it's that radical, Kosziusko!"

A rope was lowered to the pitiful submariner, who gratefully grasped it and climbed aboard the *Bibb*.

Once on deck, Kosziusko proved hardy enough to exhibit some of his insane *sang-froid*.

"Never trust these international arms-merchants, my friends. They promised me six hours of air, but it turned out to be only five and three-quarters."

Agassiz confronted the anarchist. "Sir, we are embroiled in the midst of a life or death situation. Can we count on you to maintain civilized behavior, or must we clap you in irons?"

"Oh, no, I'll abide by your bourgeois laws as long as I'm aboard your vessel. You have my word as a Polish-Hibernian."

"And I'll hold you to it. Very well. Captain, I recommend that we move to capture this new ship before they accomplish their nefarious goals."

"As you wish, sir. First Mate, prepare to sail!"

Within seconds the highly trained crew of the *Bibb* had her in motion toward the Marblehead craft of the Deep Ones. (The *Dolly Peach*, unskippered and unmanned, save for the unmourned corpse of Hans Bopp, remained near Cat Island.)

The *Bibb* drew nearer and nearer to the Marblehead ship, which sailed on undaunted, as if confident of its superiority against the much larger vessel.

When they were still some hundred yards apart, a new noise rent the ocean stillness: the ominous beat of a tribal drum.

"It's dot D'guzeri! He's zummoning up der voodoo forces!"

"Woo-too?" asked Agassiz.

"No, der voodoo!"

The drum fell silent. Less than a few dozen feet separated the two ships. Shambling figures could be seen crawling among the shrouds and creeping across the deck of the Marblehead craft. At the rail suddenly appeared the Hottentot sorcerer, flanked by squat figures carrying flaring torches.

T'guzeri was approximately three feet tall. He wore nothing but a jackal-skin genital pouch and the hide of a lion with attached skull: the lion's jawless head rested atop his own, its front paws were tied around his neck, and the rest trailed a goodly distance along the deck.

He held aloft in his two hands a glass bottle.

With the fetiche finally in sight, Agassiz grew impatient. Didn't this savage have the good grace to admit when he was beaten?

"Set that relic down and surrender!" yelled Agassiz.

T'guzeri seemed about to comply. He did indeed set the bottle down. When he straightened, he held a long stick in his hands.

"Oh mine Gott!" yelled Cezar. "Everyvun, duck!"

Agassiz turned completely around. "Duck? Why should

we be frightened of a stick—?"

At that instant, Agassiz felt a sting in his arse.

He looked over his shoulder.

A plumed dart was embedded in one buttock.

Before he knew what had happened, he was thrown to the deck on his stomach. His pants were summarily and without invitation pulled down around his ankles, as were his drawers. Someone was sitting on his legs. A knife bit twice into his arse cheek. The whole process took only a second.

"Ow!"

"Don't ztruggle! It's der only vay!"

To his utmost horror, Agassiz felt a warm mouth pressed to his buttock. There was much sucking, interspersed with spitting. At last, he was allowed to stand.

Dottie was rinsing her mouth with water. Her small blade, bearing Agassiz's blood, lay on the deck.

Agassiz nearly swooned. When he saw Lizzie looking on wide-eyed, his humiliation was complete.

"Dot dart vas full of der venom of der horned snake, Louie. If Dottie hadn't moved zo qvick, you'd be dead now!"

Endeavoring to retain the smallest semblance of dignity, Agassiz stooped to pull his pants up. Striving to fasten them, he found all the buttons popped. Plenty of sewing for Jane.... Someone handed him a length of rope, which he clumsily employed. To Cezar, he said, "I almost wish I were."

During this incident, the *Bibb* had continued to advance on the sorcerer's ship. Evidently realizing that he could not halt the *Bibb* single-handedly, T'guzeri had abandoned his blowpipe and picked up the fetiche. He began now to chant harsh syllables of mystic import, an invocation to unseen deities.

"Vee must ztop him before he can finish!"

Captain Davis addressed his crew. "Prepare the grapples and cock your pistols, men. We're going to board!"

Within seconds, the clipper was warped to the other ship. The attackers hurled themselves over.

The Marbleheaders had grouped themselves around the sorcerer, offering their bodies as a sacrifice to permit him to complete his spell. Although more heavily armed, the men of the *Bibb* found the Marbleheaders no mean opponents. The fighting was fierce and bloody.

At last, though, the Deep Ones were all dispatched, and the invaders advanced on the sorcerer.

With a shout, T'guzeri uttered a final throat-twisting vocable and managed to toss the fetiche overboard, before being collared by the sailors.

The small splash was followed by another, larger sound. From the *Bibb*, Agassiz watched as Dottie surfaced with the fetiche under one arm. She swam to the Marblehead vessel and was helped aboard.

Eager to contemplate the fetiche, Agassiz clambered over, followed by Cezar, Stormfield, and others.

A drenched and dripping Dottie proudly held up her mother's relic.

There is a family of marine creatures known as the sea slugs: order, *Nudibranchia*; class, *Gastropoda*; subclass, *Opisthobranchia*. These fringed and limbless, horned and squishy creatures are studded with many curious excrescences called *cerata*. Variously colored, with intricate fringes, folds and convolutions, they prowl through waters warm and cold, twisting their boneless bodies with alien agility.

Saartjie Baartmann's quim with its curtain of shame and attached portions, swimming in its *dacka* tea, resembled nothing so much as one of these sea slugs: specifically, the Maned Nudibranch, *Aeolidia papillosa*.

Agassiz moved to examine the relic that had cost him so much effort.

"Stop right there!"

All eyes swivelled to Kosziusko. The anarchist held a round bomb with a long dangling sizzling fuse.

"I'll take the fetiche, if you please."

Furious, Agassiz accused, "But you promised—"

"Only as long as I was on your vessel. And now I'm on another, which I hereby commandeer in the name of liberation movements everywhere. Back on board your own ship. And don't attempt to follow me, or I'll destroy the fetiche! I go now to ignite a conflagration in a Europe ripe for revolution, the likes of which the world has never seen!"

Now Captain Stormfield spoke up over the anarchist's fanfaronade. "Ye danged lying scalliwag! You're not half the man your pappy was!"

Kosziusko looked astounded. "You knew my father?"

"Aye, didn't he and I fight side by side at Saratoga?"

"How old are you?"

"One hundred and twenty-eight, and I can still lick a tad like ye!"

Kosziusko lowered the sputtering bomb, tears in his eyes. "I never even saw Dad more than twice. He was always off fighting someplace. Mom and I really missed him. To meet someone who actually knew him—"

Stormfield sidled up to the weeping anarchist and put an arm around his shoulder. "There, there, lad—"

"For God's sake," shouted Agassiz, "someone put that bomb out!"

Before anyone could act, there came another interruption.

The sea began to boil and heave off the stern of the Marblehead vessel.

"Not another submersible," groaned Agassiz.

Whatever deity T'guzeri had sought to invoke saw fit now to grant Agassiz's desires. The cause of the disturbance was not another submersible. At least not one of human design.

A head big as a locomotive emerged from the water. It was slope-browed and covered with sleek mottled skin. Its eyes were big as cartwheels. Weeds hung from its open jaws.

The head was supported by a neck thick as one of the Corinthian columns of the Central Congregational Church on Winter Street. The neck pushed the head up, up, up, into the night sky, till it towered steeple-high.

Following the neck was a barnacle-covered body twice as long as the *U.S.S. Bibb*.

The surviving wounded Deep Ones—including T'guzeri, who squirmed in the grip of a beefy sailor—began to sing out the creature's name.

"Dagon! Dagon! Dagon!"

In 1796, long before Agassiz had been born, his mentor, Georges Cuvier, had been summoned to the gypsum quarries of Montmartre. The workers there had unearthed bones of such a size that they could only belong to a species of elephant larger than any extant. After examining the find, Cuvier announced the bones to be those of an antediluvian animal which had been destroyed in some kind of catastrophe. Over the next five years, he had been called upon to examine many other fossils, including the giant Maestricht

jaws brought back from Germany by the army of revolutionary France.

Agassiz himself had seen many of these dusty bones
during his apprenticeship to Cuvier.

Thus the cool-headed Swiss naturalist was the first to
recognize the creature looming before him, though its bones
were clothed in substantial flesh.

"This is no supernatural monster, men! It's only an
extinct fish-lizard, an Icthyosaurus!"

"It doesn't look very extinct to me," muttered Cezar
weakly.

Captain Davis added his voice to Agassiz's. "Give it all
you've got, boys!"

Cannons boomed from the *Bibb*. Melville's harpoon
flew unerringly through the air. A volley of arrows took wing
from Chief Snapping Turtle's bow. Small-arms fire resounded. Finally, Kosziusko's bomb arced through the air, to burst
impotently against the monster's neck.

The Icthyosaurus was as little affected as if the assault
had consisted of so many peas. It swung its huge head back
and forth searchingly.

Now Maurice stepped forward, out of the crowd.

"All you imperialists know is force. Let me attempt tp
reason with the creature. Ahoy, creature! I represent the proletariat—"

Seemingly attracted by the whiney voice of the socialist,
the Icthyosaurus dropped its head down to peer at him.

"You see—"

In the blink of an eye, the horrid beast swallowed
Maurice Desor.

The rest of the humans were frozen. They waited in

stunned silence for the Icthyosaurus to consume them all, smash their ship, or both.

Dottie moved toward the fish-lizard. She bore the fetiche high.

"Down, down, Dagon! Chthulu commands it! Back to your vasty deeps! Sleep for eons yet to come!"

The monster reared back like a frightened puppy. Then it dove, sending up a wave that rocked the two ships almost to the point of swamping them. Men tumbled about like skittles.

Slowly they picked themselves up as the ships stopped rocking. It took a moment for the fact that they had been spared to dawn on everyone. But when it did, they let out a vibrant cheer.

"Hip, hip, hurray for the Hottentot! Three cheers for Dottie! Huzzah, huzzah, huzzah!"

Hardened sailors were crying. Dogberry was hugging Chief Snapping Turtle. Pourtales, Burckhardt, Girard and Sonrel had formed a chorus line and were kicking their legs like music-hall queens. Kosziusko and Stormfield were dancing a jig. Cezar had his arms around the humbly smiling Dottie, who miraculously clutched the unbroken fetiche between them.

Now Lizzie appeared, and threw herself into Agassiz's arms.

"Oh, Louis, you were magnificent!"

She began to kiss him over and over again.

Edward Desor approached. He alone remained aloof from the celebrations. He spoke numbly to Agassiz.

"You and you alone were responsible for my cousin's death. You will pay for this, Agass. Yes, you will pay."

Agassiz tugged at his falling pants and started to reply curtly. He stopped. He could not find it in himself to worry about Desor's threat. Of course the man could make trouble for him. But what could compare to the ordeal he had undergone? With his future wife in his arms, and knowlege of the Cosmogonic Locus secure, his future—and the future of creationism—looked bright.

But Agassiz could not forsee that even now a man named Charles Darwin was at work on a book called *The Origin of Species*, a book which would forever link man and animal, yoke white to black, through Civil War and beyond, and replace Agassiz's beloved creationism with a disgusting notion called "evolution," rendering Agassiz in his old age a cranky, outmoded, derided fossil himself.

In fact, Agassiz's oracular ability did not even extend as far as his wedding night, April 25, 1850, a night when his timid second wife would turn to him and say:

"Louis, I—I have a small feminine abnormality you should know about."

"Nonsense, Lizzie dear. You are the perfect woman."

"No, dear, I'm a little different from most women. I have a kind of birth defect. I never knew the name for it until a few years ago. I'm still rather ashamed to use the common term. Perhaps if I whispered the Latin—"

"Go ahead, dear. And then we'll get to bed."

"It's—it's called *sinus pudoris*."

And they never did have any children.

WALT AND EMILY

1

"MORNING MEANS JUST RISK
—TO THE LOVER"

On the morning of May 1, 1860, Miss Emily Dickinson, the self-styled "Belle of Amherst," awoke feeling uncannily perturbed; so disconcerted by nocturnal phantoms and their ineffable residue of bewildered prescience, in fact, that, sliding quietly out of bed so as not to awaken Carlo, who yet snored canine-wise at the foot of the four-poster, she padded barefoot in her white gown across the rush matting of her flower-papered bedroom to her small cherry-wood table (its surface a mere eighteen inches square, yet easily encompassing the Universe Entire) whereon she daily wrestled with her painful and ecstatic poems, and, pausing not even to sit, dashed off these lines:

Dying! Dying in the night!
Won't somebody bring the light
So I can see which way to go
Into the everlasting snow?;

upon the completion of which, feeling somewhat relieved yet still faintly palsied of soul, Emily crossed to the single window set in the western wall of her corner bedroom in the upper floor of The Homestead (two southern windows looked out across Main Street), and, flinging back the shutters of the open window for a revivifying glimpse of her bee-ornamented garden and the next-door household known as The Evergreens, where dwelled her beloved brother Austin and his wife Sue, she was treated instead to the barely credible sight—which imprinted itself now and forever on her retinas like the last earthly patterns seen by a dying man—of a huge hairy bearded barbarian, utterly and shamelessly naked save for a black floppy wide-brimmed hat, giving himself a bath on her gem-bright grassy lawn.

Emily's heart filled with a mob of feelings no Inner Police could suppress.

The intruder had apparently taken no notice of the movement at the upper story of The Homestead he was so brashly profaning. He seemed utterly intent—in an almost devotional way—on laving his muscled and bulky form, using a cake of soap, a rag and the contents of the rain-barrel set immediately below Emily's window. His simple clothing piled beside him, his voyager's hat perched ludicrously atop his flowing gray-streaked locks, the stranger proceeded unconcernedly with his ablutions, as if he were alone in the midst of some Kansas prairie.

With his manly toes digging into the soil, he soaped his calves, he soaped his thighs—he soaped his reproductive organs! Emily blanched at the heretofore unrevealed sight of that manly portion, queer feelings thrilling every nerve. Reminding herself of her White Election, she raised her eyes with no little effort from that nether generative region.

The giant had moved on to scrub his masculine chest and arms, these latter plainly the well-formed thews of a laborer. Emily wondered if this could be some ignorant new hired man, employed by Father before his departure, who, having wandered from his quarters in their barn, now washed himself yokel-style in public....

All be-lathered, the giant paused now. He lifted his frothed arms up toward the new sun, as if in welcome to a brother. Then, shattering the matitutinal stillness (and whatever remained of Emily's composure!), he loudly declaimed, "Welcome is every organ and attribute of me, and of every man hearty and clean! Not an inch nor a particle of an inch is vile, and none shall be less familiar than the rest!"

This wild unexpected outburst was too much for Emily. She sank to the windowsill in a half-swoon, the sudden fragrance of a few premature lilacs wafting to her and filling her nostrils with sweetness.

In so doing, she knocked over a basket perched on the ledge. Secured by a long string, it was the vehicle by which she dropped sweetmeats to the neighborhood children on those days she felt incapable of leaving her room.

Emily watched the basket fall. It seemed to tumble down with unnatural slowness, taking an Awful Hushed Eternity to drop through the lambent spring atmosphere.

At last, however, it reached the end of its tether, bouncing several times with diminishing vigor, and Time resumed its wonted flow.

The madman's attention was at last caught. He turned and gazed upward, fixing Emily with his deep gray eyes, set beneath craggy brows. Doffing his hat and bowing, he launched into a strangely metered utterance.

"Twenty-eight young men bathe by the shore, twenty-eight young men and all so friendly; twenty-eight years of womanly life and all so lonesome. She owns the fine house by the rise of the bank, she hides handsome and richly drest at the blinds of the window. Which of the young men does she like the best? Ah, the homeliest of them is beautiful to her!"

Indignation replaced embarrassment in Emily. She straightened her back and summoned up her voice.

"If you attempt some peculiar kind of poesy, sir, be advised that it is more effective when delivered by a clothed bard! And I'll have you know that my age is nigh unto thirty, not twenty-eight!"

And with that Emily slammed the shutters on the naked man.

Trembling with rage and frustration, Emily rushed downstairs, her long auburn hair still sleep-dissolute.

In the kitchen, she found her younger sister Lavinia peeping through the dimity curtains at the bather, who was now rinsing himself heartily with buckets of water from the rain-barrel.

"Vinnie!"

Emily's sister jumped. "Emily! Have you seen him too?"

"Of course I have. How could I possibly have missed such a spectacle? My eyesight is bad, I confess, but not that poor. I only pray that Mother hasn't witnessed this horrid invasion. You know her health isn't up to snuff, and I can hardly imagine how she'd react. Vinnie, what are we to do? If only Father were here! One of us must run and fetch the sheriff, Vinnie, and I fear it must be you."

Lavinia regarded her sister with a look of disbelief. "Fetch the sheriff? Why, whatever for?"

Emily returned an equal measure of incredulity. "Is it not as plain as the spots on a tiger-lily? To arrest this jay bird-naked trespasser, of course!"

"Oh, I see. You're not aware then."

"Aware of what?"

"This gentleman and his party are guests of our brother. I assume that our Hercules has wandered over from The Evergreens, although why he should feel the need for such an exhibition, I cannot say."

From outside came the lusty chanting of the bather, along with the plashing of water. "I celebrate myself, and sing myself! And what I assume you shall assume. For every atom belonging to me as good as belongs to you!"

Emily shook her head. "Tish, what doggerel!" Returning her attention to her sister, she counterposed a question.

"Even granted his status as Austin's guest, why should we exempt him from the most basic laws of civility?"

Lavinia's eyes grew wide. "You really do not recognize who he is?"

"Should I have? He was hardly wearing any badges, nor could I see a *carte de visite* on his person."

"Oh, Emily, can't you ever be serious? Even a little housebound dormouse like you must have heard of the scandalous Walt Whitman and his *Leaves of Grass*. Why, the first edition was so shocking, Mister Whittier felt compelled to burn it! And rumor has it that the Boston firm of Thayer and Eldridge are to publish a new edition this very year! That's one reason, I understand, why this 'son of Mannahatta,' as he styles himself, is visiting our New England. But there is another, more secret reason—or so Austin hints."

Emily fell weak-kneed into a ladderback chair. She hardly heard Vinnie's peroration. All she could think was:

At last, He has come.

"DEATH IS THE SUPPLE SUITOR"

Into the trundle-basket Emily lay the sweet dead children, row by row.

Foxgloves, turks-head lilies, pansies, columbines, the early rose. All her darlings fell to her merciless shears, weeping their glaucous tears.

I could not behead you, dears, if I doubted your assured Resurrection. But as children caper when they wake, merry that it is Morn, my flowers from a hundred cribs will peep, and prance again.

When her basket contained a sufficiency to hide what was at the bottom, Emily turned nervously to face her brother's house.

The Evergreens had been erected four years ago, a lavish wedding present from Emily's father to his only son (calculated, Emily frequently thought, to impress the town of Amherst with Edward Dickinson's stature as much as to house the newlyweds). The impressive white Italianate house with its boxy corner turret stood a mere hundred yards away, separated from the ancestral Dickinson Homestead by a small copse of birches, oaks and pines, linked by a narrow well-trodden path "just wide enough for two lovers abreast," as Emily had described it to her good friend Sue Gilbert, upon that selfsame friend's attainment of the sacred status of Mrs. Austin Dickinson.

But at this moment—as at so many, many others—in

terms of Emily's ability to reach it the house might have been situated halfway across the globe, midst the wastes depicted in the engraving "Arctic Night" hanging in The Homestead's parlor.

She did not know what flaw or affliction bound her so strongly to the confines of The Homestead, sometimes indeed forbidding her even to leave the cloister of her bedroom. The face of that cruel Master was always in impenetrable Shadow, strain as she might to glimpse it; though His Hand was always more than real, squeezing her heart with fear and self-loathing, should she try to run counter to its fluctuating dictates.

It had not always been so with her. Why, even as recently as five years ago, she had journeyed to Washington and Philadelphia, exulting in the freedom of travel. (Particularly stimulating had been her first encounter with an old family friend, the Reverend Charles Wadsworth, and the many talks they had had on literature and art, continued now by correspondence.)

But as Emily had grown older, her Father—the dominant presence in the household—had grown less flexible, more demanding, harsher. (His religious spasm of a decade ago, during which he had bullied everyone except Emily into joining the First Church of Christ, had accentuated a certain Calvinism in him.) The Squire's iron rule of his quiet, insignificant invalid wife and his two daughters was positively Draconian, circumscribing all Emily's actions.

Still, Emily knew she could not place the blame for her reclusiveness totally on her Father. After all, Vinnie exhibited no such fear of society, and she too chafed under the Squire's reins. No, there was some congenital defect in Emily's own personality that made the prospect of venturing out among other people, dealing with their naked faces and needs, inherently impossible most of the time, however desperately and paradoxically she might feel the need for companionship....

Yet now here she was, out in the open, late in the afternoon of the day that had begun so oddly. (The egregiously hirsute Mister Whitman had dressed and departed somewhither before Emily could con how to address him after her pert dismissal of his oratory. She prayed now that her hasty impudence would not foreclose further communication between them....)

Steeling herself to walk across those paltry twenty rods and into a house full of strangers, with bold plans to accost one in particular with the secret that resided beneath her flowers, Emily reminded herself: *If your Nerve deny you, go above your Nerve.*

Straining forward, willing confidence to arise, she teetered on her tiptoes, yearning toward The Evergreens. A sensation as of a hot bath tingled along her limbs. Her innards were molten. This was exactly how it had been three years ago, that December when the Sage of Concord, Mister Emerson, had visited The Evergreens, and she had longed to go to him, that noble personage out of a dream, but instead, oppressed by a certain slant of winter light, she had faltered and hung back.

Emily felt poised on the verge of a high precipice, volitionless to fall either backwards into safety, or forward into danger, without some kind of Motive Push.

And then it came.

From out of the primal greenery bordering the connecting path poked the enormous naked head of a strange bird.

Carried a full six feet above the ground, at the end of a

long pliable neck, the sapient avian head examined Emily with quaint goggle-eyed curiosity for a timeless period. Then, giving a soft mooting call, the bird pulled its head back into the shrubs, followed by the sound of its retreat in the direction of The Evergreens.

The most triumphant Bird I ever knew or met embarked upon a twig today....

Emily set out after the apparition.

Halfway down the path, with yet no renewed sight of the fast-moving mysterious bird, Emily felt a sense of unreality sweep over her. Was it really possible that she was doing this? If Father had not been in Boston, speaking with the politicos of the Constitutional Union Party, who wanted him to run for Lieutenant Governor, she doubted that she could ever have braced herself for such a wild flight.

At last Emily emerged from the boskage and onto her brother's lawn.

And there was the glorious bird!

In the open, Emily could recognize the creature for what it was: an ostrich—from fabled Ophir, perhaps, yet still comically resembling a stilted feather-duster. No supernatural messenger, to be sure, but a strange sight nonetheless to encounter in placid, pedestrian Amherst.

At that moment a prepossessing young man, casually attired and roughly Emily's age, appeared from behind the house. Spotting the bird, he hailed it thusly: "Norma, you rascal, git back a-here, or tain't gonna be no supper for you!"

With unnatural alacrity, the big-footed bird hastened to obey the youth, trotting toward him with the zig-zag locomotion peculiar to its species. Soon, bird and man disappeared back around the house.

Simultaneously, the door of The Evergreens opened,

framing Emily's brother within. His thatch of hair the same red as Emily's and his extravagant sidewhiskers had never looked more familiarly reassuring, though the unwonted expression of troubled distraction which he wore was less so.

Searching for the source of the ruckus, Austin's gaze fell on his sister. He molded his features into a forced semblance of hospitality.

"Why, Emily, what a pleasant surprise! Please, come in."

Now that she was fully committed to making her visit, however unwelcome it seemed to be, Emily found within herself the capacity to put some adamant in her limbs. She advanced with unfaltering steps across the lawn and into her brother's house.

Once inside, her brother tried to relieve her of her basket.

"Sue will appreciate these blooms, sister. She's been feeling rather low since her return from Boston." A look of woeful gravity crossed Austin's countenance. "As have I, to tell truth."

Emily resisted Austin's gentle tug. "No, please, let me hold them a while longer. They comfort me." She was not prepared to show what lay beneath the blossoms yet, nor to just anyone. "But what is it that grieves you so? Does it have any connection with the guests Vinnie has told me you're entertaining?"

Austin closed his eyes and massaged his brow wearily. "Yes, in a roundabout way. Although I only fell in with these people accidentally, through my connection with the College. But they and their mission answer a need of mine, a need which has been growing apace this past year."

"Your words confuse me, Austin. What need do you speak of, that I know not? Since when have we kept secrets from one another, dear brother? Come, tell me what troubles you."

Austin opened his eyes and fixed his sister with an agonized gaze. "You would hear all, then? Very well, so be it. I
have tried to spare you prior to this, but shall not refuse your
direct offer of a sympathetic ear. But my story needs some
privacy. Let us step into the study."

Somewhat daunted, Emily nevertheless followed Austin
into the room whose shelves were lined with the lawbooks
of his profession. Once they were seated, Austin pulled his
chair close to Emily's, reached forward to clasp both her
hands (*the sweaty palms of a fevered man*, she thought), and
began his recitative.

"My problems, sister, concern relations between Sue and
myself. No, please, let me speak plainly, before you interject
a word on Sue's behalf. I know that you've ever been her par-
tisan, Emily. Sometimes, in fact, I think we never would
have married, were it not for your urgings. But that's of no
consequence now. Married we are, and married we must
stay. But you must know what connubial life has revealed to
me of certain traits that were perhaps not fully developed in
Sue when you and she were girlish chums.

"Sue is a very ambitious woman these days. She desires
to become the paramount hostess in all of Amherst. Not a
very wide sphere, you might say, and you'd be right. Sue's
ambitions do not stop there, I fear. She has grander dreams,
to be enacted upon a larger stage—a stage which I am to
provide somehow or another.

"Now, you know me, Emily, at least as well as I know
myself. I'm not as driven as Father. I have no desire to venture beyond the pleasant ambit of Amherst as he has, representing the Commonwealth in Washington or parts more
exotic. I'm basically a dreamy fellow, with a nature fully as
poetic as yours. The fabled rushing blood of Grandfather

Samuel has dwindled to a proportional trickle in my veins. Nothing would suit me better than a simple family existence conducted right here for the rest of my mortal days.

"But family life, you see, is just what Sue is dead-set against. She feels that children would be a drag on her social climbing."

Emily considered long and hard before venturing a comment. "I had wondered why the past four years had brought me no little niece or nephew. Father, too, speculates aloud why no heir has yet appeared. But I never expected that it was Sue's reluctance to consummate your union."

Austin laughed mirthlessly. "'Reluctance to consummate!' 'Tis far worse than that, dear sister! The union has been consummated more than once, as a result of certain ungovernable impulses upwelling from both our baser natures. And a year and a half ago, the natural result obtained. Sue became with child."

Emily faltered. "But, I never—Did she miscarry?"

"Far, far worse! She killed it!"

It was as if all the Heavens were a Bell, and Emily just an Ear. When she returned to herself, she struggled to utter the fatal word, but Austin mercifully preempted her.

"Yes, she journeyed to Boston in 'Fifty-nine for a—an abortion!

"And this latest trip was for another!"

With this revelation, Austin burst into deep wracking sobs.

Emily cradled her brother in her arms, his violent sorrow washing away her lesser pangs, until he had cried himself dry. When he raised his face, it was stamped with inexpressible grief.

"The thought of that first death grew and grew in me,

Emily, like a worm. When I learned of the second—although Sue begged to accompany me to the city on my latest trip, I never guessed her intention to repeat the evil deed, and she only divulged it upon our recent return—it nearly did me in. I cannot find it in me to put all the blame on Sue. Not only does she suffer terrible pangs from what she's done, but she's also only acting in accord with her own ideas of what's best for our life, horrible though her crimes may be. No, I account myself equally guilty with her, as much as if my hand had held the bloody instruments of infanticide! That is why, you see, I have taken up with these strangers. There is a Spiritualist among them—"

As if a Cloud that instant slit, and let the Fire through, it flashed like summer lightning upon Emily what her brother intended. Somewhat disdainfully, she said, "You wish to speak to the souls of your unborn children, then, and seek some token of absolution, through the medium of this mystic personage...."

Austin fixed Emily with a wild, dire gaze.

"Speak to them! If only it were that simple!

"No, dear sister, we're going to visit them!"

3

"THE SOUL SELECTS HER OWN SOCIETY"

The difference between Despair and Fear, thought Emily, *is like the One between the instant of a Wreck and when the Wreck has been.*

Her brother's uncanny words had indeed pushed her across the line separating those twinned emotions.

All her life, Death had loomed large in Emily's mind, an insurmountable wall she could only hurl herself against, falling back time and again with bruised mind and spirit.

Hers was not entirely a doctrinal Christian concept of Death; just as she could not bring herself ostentatiously to pronounce her faith aloud as the rest of her family had done, neither could she wholeheartedly subscribe to any church's tenets concerning the Great Clock-Stopper, although her philosophy partook of many schools.

Easer of cares, reward for a lifetime of pain and humili-ation, cruel reiver of friends, coachman to Paradise, cheerful swain, whimsical thief—all these roles and more had that Inescapable Presence assumed in her fancies. Yet none, she knew, fully captured Death's real import. She had become ruefully reconciled to the fact that, try as she might to snare Death in her webs of words, its ultimate nature must forev-er remain a mystery.

And now here was her own brother telling her that he was embarked on a project to fathom that very mystery, to penetrate somehow into Death's Cold Kingdom—but in an insulting, materialistic fashion.

It was almost more than she could comprehend.

Sensing her bafflement, Austin spoke.

"What do you know of the Spiritualist Movement, Emily?"

Proud contempt swelling in her bosom, Emily replied, "I know only this, having read plainly what was often writ between the lines in the penny press: that some twelve years ago, two young flibbertigibbet sisters—by name of Fox and dwelling then in Rochester, New York—decided to pull a prank on their parents—a prank which quickly escalated into a farce beyond their wildest imaginings. By concealed rappings and other sleights, they insinuated that they were in contact with the so-called 'spirit world,' easily tricking their gullible mother and elder sibling, who quickly promoted herself to their manageress. From such an humble beginning, they've gone on to make their fortune by becoming regular stage charlatans, duping thousands of poor bereaved souls with simple tricks that were old when Cagliostro was born, and sparking the like ridiculous behavior in millions across the globe."

Austin's red-eyed face showed a somber mien. "You seem awfully sure of the Fox sisters' falsity and avarice, Emily, and by implication, that of all other mediums. I had thought that you of all people would be sympathetic to the opening of such a dialogue between this world and the next. How can you be so certain there's nothing to their claims?"

"How could I feel otherwise, based on the puerile and ultramundane messages such 'mediums' transmit? Their source is obviously the hoaxer's own insipid imagination. Why, if I were to believe for one minute that the indescribable glory of the next world were to be found in such utterances as 'Mother, do not weep for your little boy, 'tis all peppermint sticks and licorice whips here on t'other side,' then I would have to—well, I do not know what I would have to do. Surely not kill myself, lest I wind up any sooner than necessary among these milk and water spirits!"

"I grant you, sister, that some of the, shall we say, less-inspired revelations of certain untalented individuals plainly betray a modicum of, ah, fabrication. But among the true mediums, invention is only employed when actual contact fades, mainly out of an honest desire not to disappoint the assembled seance-goers. In fact, the medium might not even be aware of the transition from genuine inspiration to unconscious generation of babble. But let us not quibble over the debatable duplicity of some hypothetical Chicago mountebank. Not only is the medium with whom I am involved authentic beyond reproach, but we also have the generous—nay, essential!—offices of a certain eminent scientist to put our whole expedition on an absolutely rigorous footing."

Emily stood up, knowing full well that she was allowing a look of disgust to disfigure those plain features of hers that could ill stand such an additional burden. But so angered with her brother was she, that she didn't care.

"It wouldn't impress me if you and your mysterious friends had a whole academy of bearded and begowned savants behind whatever bizarre scheme you're hatching! And you can chop whatever kind of specious logic you wish—I still maintain that any sort of Spiritualism is a load of bunkum!"

Austin permitted himself a small smile as he played his trump card.

"And what if I told you that your beloved poetess, Mrs. Elizabeth Barrett Browning, was a firm believer in the spirits and in their earthly partners?"

Emily sank back into her seat, shocked. *Her* dear Elizabeth—that noble Foreign Lady who had captivated Emily's soul in youth, whose poems had made the Dark feel beautiful and bred in her a Divine Insanity—the genius behind *Aurora Leigh*—the heroic Female Poet whose given name Emily proudly bore as her own middle appellation—Could it indeed be true that such a superb mind could give any credence to this simplistic new faith sweeping the world?

Seeing Emily's doubt, Austin pressed forward with his

case. "It's quite true. Mrs. Browning's involvement with the spirit world began some five years ago, when she met the famous Daniel Dunglas Home. When she felt the phantom hands he caused to materialize, when the ghostly concertina played, when the spirits placed a laurel wreath upon her brow—then she knew the truth of the matter! Just as all doubters shall be convinced when I and the others journey to Summerland and back!"

Emily knew not what to think. First she had been over-whelmed with the hidden familial discord between her brother and Sue. Then her dogmatic anti-Spiritualist stance had suffered a severe blow with the news that One so admired had been willingly ensnared in what Emily had heretofore taken to be the clearest kind of popular madness. Yet, she reminded herself, much Madness is divinest Sense to a discerning Eye, and much Sense the starkest Madness—'tis the Majority in this, as All, prevail.

Her gaze falling on her basket of wilting flowers at her feet, Emily reminded herself of her real reason for visiting her brother's house. She was surely not advancing her hidden pur-poses by arguing with him, especially from a Foundation sud-denly weakened. And as she did not intend to get involved with his grief-sired insanity, she could afford to let it slide.

"I'm sorry I made light of your new faith, Austin dear-est. I realize now what drives you to embrace such a quest. Though I cannot bring myself to fully endorse such beliefs, I will reserve judgement on them, pending whatever new evidence you have for me."

Austin grabbed his sister's hands. "What a capital girl you are! I knew nothing could ever come between us!"

Picking up her basket, Emily said, "Perhaps you'd care to introduce me to these new friends of yours—?"

"Of course! We're using the back parlor as a kind of headquarters to plan our assault on the hereafter. We should find most of the party there. Come!"

As they walked through the big house, Austin explained how he had chanced to meet his houseguests.

"When Sue and I were in Boston, I saw a poster advertising a Spiritualist lecture and demonstration to be given at Mechanics' Hall. I attended, and the speech and exhibition so impressed me that I introduced myself afterwards to the lecturer and the medium who accompanied him. Learning of their audacious plans, and the imminent arrival of the scientist who was to assist them, I immediately enlisted as one of the party, offering all the help I could give."

"Does Sue have any interest in all this?"

"Not at all. In fact, she tends to avoid our guests, and rather resents their presence."

"I'm just as glad, for I do not know if I could bear to see her right now, so soon after learning of her sins."

"No need to fear that. She's been keeping mostly to her room."

They stood now in front of the closed parlor door. Murmurs penetrated, two male voices and a female. Emily thought that neither of the masculine ones sounded like Whitman's distinctive boom, and sought to learn more of him.

"You haven't yet told me what brings a famous—even infamous—poet into your home."

Austin smiled. "Ah, that was a curious accident. You see, Sue insisted that we pay a visit to Emerson, who was also in the city. I think she had some idea of getting him back to Amherst as her pet performing author again. When we were received by the old Sage at his hotel, we found Whitman with him. It turned out that Emerson was in something of a fix. He had volunteered to put Whitman up on his visit to Boston without first consulting his own wife, who, once she learned of it, absolutely refused to have such an 'immoral beast' in her home! Taking us aside, Emerson begged us to accommodate his friend at The Evergreens, and Sue readily consented, envisioning a social coup. Imagine her disgust, however, when the poet, learning of our Spiritual ambitions, cast his lot with us wholeheartedly!"

This last tidbit disturbed Emily, throwing doubt as it did on the poet's faculties, but she withheld her censure.

"I understand," continued Austin gleefully, "that you and Vinnie had a rather startling introduction to our unconventional Homer."

Emily felt herself blush. "You understand aright."

"With so many guests, there was a line for the bath this morning, and Whitman grew impatient. I told him he might avail himself of the facilities at The Homestead, but had no idea he would—"

At that moment the parlor door swung open.

A large buxom woman filled the doorframe. Draped with colorful shawls, a flowing gypsy kerchief tied around her head, gaudy earrings and bracelets aglitter at lobe and wrist, she struck a dramatic pose, one arm thrust forward, the other pressed against her brow. Although well into middle age and not conventionally beautiful (a distinct mustache graced her upper lip), she exuded the same kind of animal magnetism Emily had frequently sensed emanating from the most sought-after ballroom belles.

"Madame felt the radiance of souls beyond the barrier," declaimed the medium, casting herself in the third person.

"Considering that we were speaking in normal conversational tones," said Emily, "to drag our souls in were rather superfluous."

The medium threw her arms down peevishly. "Faugh! Why do you bring such an unbeliever among us, *cher* Austin?"

"This is my sister, Emily. I wanted her to meet you. Emily, allow me to introduce Madame Hrose Selavy, Paris's most distinguished Spiritualist."

Madame Selavy's attitude immediately grew effusive, though Emily thought to detect a steely glint of remnant hostility in her eyes. "Such an adorable little creature, possessed of a wit fully equal to her esteemed brother's. Let me embrace you!"

Before Emily could protest, Madame Selavy clutched her in a smothering grip. She smelled of perspiration, wool and carnal musk.

Released, Emily reeled back. Before she could fully recover, Madame Selavy clutched her hand and dragged her into the parlor.

"Andrew! William! The much-spoken-of sister has arrived!"

Two men in their late youth—neither of whom was the ostrich herder Emily had seen—were seated at a table on which was spread an enormous chart, its upcurling corners weighted down with strange glass and metal contrivances looking like pronged vials sealed at both ends. A whale-oil lamp had been lit against the declining sun.

Jerking her hand out of the medium's grip, Emily sought to regain her composure. Austin allowed her some time by performing introductions.

"Emily, this gentleman is the author of *The Principles of Nature, Her Divine Revelations*, and *A Voice to Mankind*, and the noted editor of a well-respected Spiritualist journal, *The*

Univercoelum. In addition, he is a clairvoyant in his own right. It was he who predicted the appearance of the Fox Sisters years before their debut. May I present Mister Andrew Jackson Davis."

Davis wore a barbered beard and tiny wire-rimmed spectacles, behind which dwelt disconcertingly unfocused blue eyes. He seemed unused to or removed from common social habits, and merely made a nod in Emily's direction.

"And this other open-minded gentleman, Emily, represents the scientific half of our balance. It's he who shall give our enterprise the intellectual solidity lacking in so many other ill-conceived ventures. I'm honored to present not only the discoverer of thallium, but also a follower and friend of D. D. Home himself. Emily, meet one of England's finest intellects, William Crookes!"

The opposite of Davis, Crookes stepped forward with panache, took Emily's hand, bowed and kissed it. His long narrow face and high brow were not unhandsome. Speaking with a charming British accent, he said, "Your brother has slighted you, Miss Dickinson, for he failed to mention that your eyes were the color of the finest sherry."

Emily was completely flustered, and found herself, for once, at a loss for words.

Luckily, Davis broke the awkward moment. "I don't mean to cut such a delightful interlude short, but may I remind everyone that we have much work ahead of us yet to do, before we're even out of the planning stages?"

Crookes relinquished Emily's hand with a wry smile. "Ah, yes. The spirit world, which has existed for countless centuries, cannot wait a single minute for us. Well, back to the grindstone, I fear. I look forward to seeing you again, Miss Dickinson."

Emily allowed Austin to escort her out of the parlor. As she brushed past Madame Selavy, she plainly heard the words "Little snip!" hissed in her ear, although Madame's lips appeared to remain fixed.

Out in the hall, Austin said, "It only remains for you to meet queer old Walt. He probably out with Henry and the birds."

Gathering her wits, Emily said, "Yes, I'd like that, if you please."

As they headed toward the rear door of The Evergreens, Austin said, "I don't think I mentioned Henry. He's Walt's traveling companion. Sutton, I believe. They used to work together on the *Brooklyn Eagle*. Young Sutton was a printer's devil while Walt was editor. Henry has been invaluable with the ostriches. He seems to have a knack for getting them to behave. Did I tell you about Andy's plans for the ostriches? No matter, you'll learn soon enough. Well, here we are!"

They had stepped outside. A newly erected pen dominated the backyard of The Evergreens. In this makeshift corral, six or more ostriches sat. Watching over them with soft clucking tones was the personable young man she had first seen.

"Hen!" called Austin. "Where's Walt?"

Before Henry could answer, a resonant voice came from behind them.

"The green globe's favorite loafer stands firm right here."

Emily spun around with pounding heart.

Ever since Father had terminated her schooling at Mount Holyoke Female Seminary on the grounds of "constitutional weakness" (in that same year the Fox Sisters were first emitting their rappings), Emily had longed for a renewal of the intellectual companionship and stimulation so fleetingly tasted. When, not long ago, she had begun seriously writing poetry, the need had grown even deeper, an ache that the dull and fusty correspondence with the Reverend Wadsworth could not appease.

And now, standing before her (clothed, thank God!) in full corporeal splendor, was perhaps her first, last, only and best chance for such communion: a living, published poet.

Trembling, Emily thrust forward her basket of flowers.

"My introduction, sir!"

Walt accepted the offering gently. She saw his keen eyes alight on the neatly stitched and ribbon-trussed leaflet of her poetry half-hidden at the bottom.

"Something more than it first appears, I think," said Walt, and winked.

Emboldened, Emily said, "My Basket contains Firmaments, sir!"

"But is it big enough, *ma femme*, to contain me?"

4

"INEBRIATE OF AIR—AM I—"

 On the wall above the piano that stood on the flower-decorated Brussels carpet in The Homestead's front parlor hung an engraving called "The Stag at Bay." The noble venison—caught out in the open and surrounded by silently yapping dogs, the mounted hunter aiming his perpetually poised spear at its chest—was plainly ready to expire from sheer terror.

Precisely so had Emily felt, as soon as Whitman had uttered his veiled challenge regarding the capacity of her trundle.

A sweat had sprung out upon her forehead and her limbs had seemed not her own. The sky—the sky seemed to weigh so much, she was suddenly convinced that Heaven would break away and tumble Blue on her—

So she had fled.

Like a child affrighted by shadows, she had run from the backyard of The Evergreens, through the intervening copse, and into the shelter of her bedroom in The Homestead.

There she had stayed for the next two days, huddling beneath her quilts. Even Carlo had been excluded.

(And what of all further possible embarrassments should come upon her at the same time but her dreaded menses! That Doctor Duponco's French Golden Periodical Pills had somewhat alleviated the curse was small comfort. Where was the Pill she could take for her Nerves?)

Between bouts of self-chastisement and tears, Emily in her head had molded a poem, that the period of pain be not entirely a loss.

A Wounded *Deer—leaps highest—*
I've heard the Hunter tell—
'Tis but the Ecstasy of death—
And then the Brake is still!

The Smitten *Rock that gushes!*
The trampled *Steel that springs!*
A Cheek is always redder
Just where the Hectic stings!

Mirth is the Mail of Anguish—
In which it Cautious Arm,
Lest anybody spy the blood
And "you're hurt" exclaim!

She had intuited Whitman's allegory as soon as he had spoken. The double meanings which tripped so easily off her own tongue and pen still had the capacity to startle her when issuing unexpectedly from another.

Whitman had been proposing—nay, commanding!—a full and open relationship with her. It is not enough, he might as well have plainly said, that you give me these scribbled-over scraps of paper, expecting my opinion in return (valuing what you earlier slighted, in the light of my newly discovered fame). No, if you approach me, you must do so nakedly. You must deal with me as woman to man, as soul to soul, holding back nothing, if you would have the real juice of my fruits, the true meat of my tongue.

And this was just what Emily doubted she could do.

Although she longed to.

Only once had she opened herself up wholly to another.

And look how that had turned out.

Not that dear George had been at fault. There were few men who could stand up to Edward Dickinson's displeasure, and dreamy, intellectual George Gould—Emily's senior, Austin's friend and a crack student at Amherst—had not been one of them. When the Squire had discovered their innocent yet fervid affair and banished George, neither he nor Emily had found it in their power to protest, though both their futures were at stake.

And then had come Emily's self-imposed White Election: her Celestial Wedding, symbolized by her unchanging snowy attire, in place of the earthly one she swore she would never now know.

How, with such a trial behind her, could she find the strength to give to Whitman was he was obviously demanding?

No, it was impossible....

A peremptory knock sounded at Emily's door. Before she could reply, the door swung open.

In stomped Lavinia, bearing a supper tray.

"I swear, Emily—you and Mother will be the death of me! Two bigger babies I've never seen! I've a good mind to marry and be shed of you both! Then we'd see how long this household would stay afloat!"

Emily sat up straight in bed, intrigued by her sister's indignation. "And who would you marry, Vinnie? Is there a potential suitor I should know about?"

"Humph! Don't you worry, I could scare up a husband if I put my mind to it. And I might just yet. Well, here's your supper. And mind you—no complaints that my Indian bread's not as fine as yours!"

Vinnie deposited the tray and turned to leave. At the door, she paused.

"I don't suppose you're interested in news of Father?"

"Is he still in Boston?"

"Further away than that. Although the Party could not convince him to run this year, they prevailed upon him to help their Presidential candidate, John Bell. The Squire's on his way to Washington, and points south and west. There's no telling how long he'll be gone. And we should all be thankful for his absence. If he were here, and forced to witness what Austin and those loco cronies of his are up to, he'd be positively apoplectic! Why, the whole town's in an uproar as it is."

Emily's pain had almost driven from her mind Austin and his wild plans for a journey to the beyond. Now all the strange atmosphere at The Evergreens enveloped her again.

"What's Austin doing?"

Vinnie tilted her nose up and sniffed. "If you want to find out you'll have to get up. I'm not *Harper's Weekly*."

And with that, Emily's sister slammed the door.

Five minutes later, her supper uneaten, Emily was dressed and on the staircase.

At the rear entry, she hesitated. Could she really nerve herself up for another expedition to the mad menagerie her brother's home had become? What if that bestial Madame Selavy grabbed her again? What if the dapper Mister Crookes essayed another buss upon her hand? What if the fanatical eyes of Mister Davis transfixed her once more like a Butterfly upon a Card? What if she met Sue, her Lady Macbeth sister-in-law? What if she met Whitman!? How she regretted now giving him her poems, those Keys to the Inner Chambers of her Heart....

Forcing herself to subdue all these jeering mental demons, Emily threw open the back door.

Heavy-blossomed clumps of lilac, white and purple both, flanked the portal, their sweet scent diffusing like a cloud around the stoop.

With his shaggy bare head buried deep within the drooping clusters, inhaling great ursine snuffling draughts of their inebriating fragrance, stood Whitman.

Motionless, Emily froze and burned simultaneously. It was not Frost alone, for she felt Siroccos crawl upon her Flesh. But neither was it solely Fire, for her Marble feet could keep a Chancel cool.

Whitman withdrew his head from the flowers. Tiny

perfect florets clung to his hair and beard, rendering him a veritable Pan. His open-necked workman's shirt revealed a pelt of chest hair—last noticed by Emily in a soapy state—similarly bedizened.

"When lilacs in the dooryard bloom," declaimed Whitman, "I exult with the ever-returning spring!"

Then, replacing atop his crown the floppy hat he had been holding, and gently taking Emily's hand, he said, "Come, *ma femme*, let us stroll a bit."

Helpless, Emily followed.

They meandered for a short time among the flower beds—the children so lovingly pampered by their mistress—without saying anything. Then Whitman spoke.

"Those were not merely poems you gave me. Not a book alone. Whoso touches them, touches a *woman*."

These words were more than Emily had ever hoped to hear in her lifetime. Willing herself not to faint, she conjured up an ingenuous question in reply.

"You would say, then, that my poems are—alive?"

Whitman gestured widely, to take in the whole green scene through which they promenaded with hands so implausibly conjoined. Would any townsfolk, seeing her now, not think her the Belle of Amherst indeed?

"Is what you see before your eyes this minute not indisputably alive? Are you yourself not alive, the blood pulsing in you and the smoke of your own breath steaming forth? How could anything that issues truly from one alive not itself be alive? Have no doubt! They live indeed! The divine afflatus surges through them as surely as it does through the song of a lonely thrush."

Emily felt her whole being filling with confidence and vitality. The constant anxiety that dwelt behind her breastbone began to diminish. But Whitman's next words brought her up short, deflating her new elation.

"And yet, like the sad piping of that lonely mateless bird, your poems exhibit a grave deficiency, a morbid strain that threatens to wrap itself around the living trunk of your songs like a clinging vine, until it brings the whole tree down."

Emily stiffened and tried to withdraw her hand, but Whitman would not permit it. She was forced to speak roughly while still in intimate contact with him.

"I am not aware of any such grievous flaw as you adduce, sir. But of course, I await the instruction of one so *learned*."

Whitman took no offense at her cold tones, but smiled instead. "I am far from 'learned,' Miss Dickinson, save in what I have gleaned from the streets of Brooklyn and the shores and paths of my native Paumanok. And as my purse and my reviews both well attest, I am no favorite of the academies! Yet my eyes are keen enough to find letters from God dropped everywhere. And what these old eyes—and my heart—tell me about your poetry is this: it is too cloistered, too rarefied, too much a product of the head and the hearth, as if you had no body, nor a world to walk in. You have that fine facility for 'seeing the world in a grain of sand,' as Mister Blake would have it. But you seem unable to see the world as the self-sufficient miracle of *itself*! Everything must represent something ethereal to you. Sunsets, bees and rainbows—self-existent perfections which you insist on cloaking in your own fancies! Nothing can stand for itself alone, but you must bend it to represent a 'Truth.' If you should continue on in this vein, you will, I predict, gradually refine yourself and your poetry entirely out of existence!"

Emily made no immediate reply. So sincere and vibrant had Whitman's voice been, that she was forced to consider the validity of his remarks.

Could it be possible that her constricted life—half chosen, half imposed—was really threatening her poetry with its limited scope? She had been so convinced till this moment that she had a clear vision of what was ultimately important. Were there marvels and wonders beyond her ken? Was she like a color-blind person who thought she knew what color was, but knew not...?

Haltingly, Emily tried to voice her apprehensions.

"What you so glibly condemn, Mister Whitman, might indeed be so. Yet, what if my faults be as you itemize? They are part and parcel of my very nature, a crack that runs through me like the Liberty Bell's. And perhaps that very crack gives me my distinctive timbre. In any case, it is too late for me to change."

Whitman halted and turned to gaze deeply and sincerely into Emily's eyes. "You are absolutely wrong on that score, Miss Dickinson. I know whereof I speak. For all my early manhood, I moved in a fog of false feelings and shoddy dreams, only dimly sensing that I was missing my mark. It was only in my thirty-seventh year that I awoke to my own true nature, and began to shape my songs. It is never too late to change and grow."

"For a man, perhaps, that may be true. Your sex is permitted to test yourself, to hurl yourself into clarifying situations that enlarge your spirit. But we women are not allowed such liberties. Bride, mother or sterile crone these are the limited roles society grants us."

"There is an iota of generally accepted truth to what you say—as much as there is in the assertion that a common prostitute is not a queen!"

Emily gasped at the foul language! But Whitman continued unabashed.

"But I say that a common trull *is* a queen! And I say that a woman is not less than a man, and may do whatever she pleases! Listen to me, Emily!"

The sound of her own given name practically unhinged her. The smell of lilacs was in her blood like wine.

"I—I don't know what to say. How can I venture out into the world? I've been hurt—"

"Do you think the dark patches have fallen on you alone? There have been times when the best I have done has seemed to me blank and suspicious. My great thoughts—as I supposed them—were they not in reality meager? Nor is it you alone who knows what it is to be evil—if that is what troubles you. I am he who knows what it is to be evil! I've blabbed, blushed, resented, lied, stolen, grudged! I had guile, anger, lust, hot wishes I dared not speak. I was wayward, vain, greedy, shallow, sly, cowardly, malignant! The wolf, the snake, the hog were not wanting in me! But I contain them all! I do not repudiate the evil, I affirm it! My poems will produce just as much evil as they do good. But there was never any such thing as evil in this world!"

"Your words, Mister Whitman, contradict themselves—"

Whitman's face was scarlet. "Contradict myself! Very well, I contradict myself! I am large, I contain multitudes!"

Seeking to calm him, Emily said, "But you have not hit on my Deepest Wound, sir. It was—an affair of the Heart—"

Her words seemed to have the desired effect. Whitman grew calm and pensive. "There too I have sad experience. Miss Dickinson—Emily—if I share something private with you, may I ask a favor in return?"

"What?"

"Would you leave off this undesirable formality between us, and call me 'Walt?' I know the difference in our ages traditionally demands such modes of address, but I abide by no such conventions."

Feeling the warmth stealing into her cheeks, Emily hung her head. "It seems a small enough thing—"

"Very well, then. Please, look—"

Emily lifted her eyes. She saw Whitman taking a small loosely bound homemade notebook (much like one of her own chapbooks) out of his pocket. He opened it to a center page, then turned it toward her.

From the notebook stared a tintyped face, that of a handsome woman with dark ringlets, her hands clasped over the back of the chair in which she sidewise sat.

Whitman turned the book back toward himself. He kissed the picture, closed the leaves, then repocketed the precious keepsake.

Emily's heart was nigh to bursting. "Oh, Walt! Is she—is she dead?"

"Far worse! Married!"

Emily was scandalized, yet thrilled.

"We met when I was editor of the *New Orleans Crescent*. I espied her first at the Théâtre d'Orléans, during a performance of Mozart's *Don Giovanni*. Succumbing to the loose tropic influence of that southern port, we fell madly in love. Her electric body exhaled a divine nimbus that wrought a fierce attraction in me, and mine likewise to her. Many were our hours of joy.

"But she was a woman of high society, who could not afford the taint of scandal or divorce. It was the supreme wrenching for us when we realized that our love was doomed, and that we must part. She is the only woman I have ever cherished so grandly, or ever shall."

For some inexplicable reason, Emily grew slightly crest-fallen at Whitman's closing sentence. But not enough to obscure the larger emotions in her bosom. The similarity of Walt's misfortune to Emily's own doomed affair placed a final seal on the affection that had been growing half-cloaked in her heart for the sturdy, grizzled poet.

Clutching Walt's big hand firmly with both of her small ones, Emily said, "You truly know my soul, then, Walt."

"Emily—I have considered you long before you were born."

They found a stone bench and sat for a while, side by side in silence.

But as the minutes passed, a small Fly Buzz irritant grew in Emily's mind, until she finally had to voice it.

"Walt—you used the word 'morbid' earlier in connec-tion with my poems—"

"Yes, Emily, I did. For I fear that you are overly preoc-cupied with death."

Emily opened her mouth to protest, ready with a cata-logue of Death's supreme importance in the scheme of things, but Walt held up a hand to stop her.

"I know all you are going to say, dear Emily. Rest assured that I too have thought long and hard on death. As glorious as it is to be born, I know it is fully as glorious to die. Were it not for death—and it is surely false to even speak of the two as separate—life itself would be meaningless. Yes, I have heard whispers of heavenly death all my life, in the voice of the waves upon the shore and the querulous call of seabirds. But unlike you, I do not long for death, nor give it more than its due. I am too busy living, too busy indulging my holy

senses, to lend death more than a passing nod. While you,
dear Emily, seem more intent on hugging Death to you like
a lover!"

Emily was incensed. "I holding onto death! Who's
involved in this insane scheme of my brother's to penetrate
the shadows of the afterlife? You, not I!"

Walt stood up. "You do not know the full scope of our
expedition to Summerland, Emily. It is not an embrace of
death, but a bold scientific assault on its territory, to wrest
new knowledge that will benefit all the living."

Hoisting Emily bodily up with his bull-like strength,
Walt said, "Come with me, and you shall see!"

5

"MICROSCOPES ARE PRUDENT
IN AN EMERGENCY"

The back parlor of The Evergreens had been converted to an impromptu classroom, or general's briefing
post. A large slateboard rested on an artist's easel, sticks of
chalk on its ledge; a lectern and a single capacious armchair
stood beside it. Tacked to the wall behind the podium was
the large chart Emily had seen flattened out on her earlier
visit; resting prominently atop the lectern was one of the
queer glass and metal devices which had been holding down
the curious map.

Several ladderback chairs had been arrayed before the
lectern. In them now sat five eager listeners, chafing slightly under a ten-minute wait: Emily, Walt and Henry Sutton

three abreast in that order, with Austin Dickinson and the savant William Crookes behind them.

The whole scene forcefully reminded Emily of her brief schooldays. And inevitably with those precious memories surfaced the glorious figure of Leonard Humphrey.

Humphrey had been four years older than George Gould. As a child, Emily, through her Father's close connections with the college, had eagerly followed the news of the broad academic swath the bright personable young man had cut. He had seemed to represent to Emily the proudest hopes of a new generation.

Imagine her delight, then, when, upon his graduation in 1846, Humphrey had been appointed principal of Amherst Academy, the coeducational school which sixteen-year-old Emily and thirteen-year-old Vinnie attended.

Through the Academy's corridors the new principal strode like a veritable combination of Adonis and Socrates, captivating especially all tender feminine sensibilities, Emily's not excluded. (She had gone so far as to memorize Humphrey's valedictory speech, "The Morality of States.") To this day, Emily still regarded Humphrey as her first Tutor, and the memory of those few times when he had stood close beside her still had the power to thrill her.

Humphrey's unexpected and grim death in 1850, when he had appeared yet in the flower of his manhood, had been a Devastation to Emily and the whole town.

She did not know if it was the presence of another masculine Tutor now by her side, or the deathly topic of the scheduled lecture that made the image of Humphrey stand out almost palpably before her, as if straining soundlessly against the thin membrane separating him from the living. But so did he choose to manifest himself in her inner gaze.

I never lost as much but twice—thought Emily, when her musings were interrupted by the voice of the scientist behind her.

"The waste of time is the most damnable thing connected with working with these psychic types," said Crookes. "I had to contend with the same problem with Home. He'd produce the most remarkable effects—levitation, materializations, voices—but only after hours of boredom, the lot of us sitting in the dark with our sweaty hands linked. It's a bloody challenge to someone used to the bright light and clean-cut conditions of the la-boor-ratory, I tell you."

Austin chided his seatmate. "Can't you be a little more circumspect with your language, Bill? We've a lady present—"

Crookes snorted, not so much sneeringly as in admiration. "Me watch my language! Look who your sister's sitting next to, for Harry's sake! If she's read his doggerel, she's already gotten an earful. 'Pent-up aching rivers, man-balls and man-root' indeed! Why, he's got more gall than Rossetti and his whole gang of libertines put together!"

Emily felt herself blushing. She waited for Whitman to bridle at Crookes's speech, knowing how she herself would react to any attack on her verse. But the poet merely bent his sun-browned neck, smiled, and said rather cryptically, "I am surrounded by trippers and askers...."

Seeking to divert the subject, Emily turned boldly to face Crookes. "Why do you continue to pursue your unorthodox investigations under such trying circumstances, Mister Crookes?"

"Only because, Miss Dickinson, Spiritualism is the most exciting, far-reaching subject yet to fall under my attentions. Luckily, thanks to my father's fortune, I am permitted to indulge my curiosity in any fashion I choose, without worrying about earning a living. Otherwise, I'd still be stuck in bloody boring Oxford, as meteorological superintendent of the Radcliffe Observatory. As things stand, however, I'm enabled to travel the globe—and beyond, if we succeed—and to meet such charming young ladies as yourself."

Before Emily could respond, Henry Sutton spoke up.

"Here they are."

From a side entrance emerged the awaited duo.

First to appear was Madame Selavy. Her clothing was somewhat disheveled, one of her voluminous skirts rucked up to reveal an edge of her crinolines. Close behind her came A.J. Davis. The austere author and publicist for the Spiritualist cause appeared rather discombobulated, his vest misbuttoned, his glasses askew and his hair mussed.

Madame Selavy plopped down into the armchair set center stage. She tugged her bodice up more securely beneath her overflowing bosom, then blew out a weary breath which, Emily noticed, distinctly fluttered her mustache.

Davis took up position behind the lectern. Seeming to realize his condition for the first time, he smoothed back his hair and straightened his spectacles before addressing the audience.

"Madame Selavy and I have been speaking to the spirits, in connection with our trip. The audience was an arduous and tumultuous one, as there was much interference along the Celestial Telegraph. Luckily, Madame's spirit guide, the Narragansett Indian Princess, Pink Cloud, was able to ward off all malign influences and deliver assurances of our success."

Madame Selavy interrupted. "*Oui, mon ami*, the auspices from Summerland are good. Soon, we shall be permitted to cross the border into the dominion of *le Moissonneur Hideux*."

For the third time now, Emily had heard mention of this unknown place called "Summerland." The name conjured up for her only one of those perfect July days she lived for, when she could feel a depth, an Azure, a perfume, transcending ecstasy. She resented the appropriation of the term by someone who was in all likelihood a charlatan who had succeeded in hoodwinking her brother, and resolved to speak up.

"Are you preparing to jump us over our beautiful New England spring straight to the dogdays, Mister Davis? Or perhaps you are merely proposing a trip to warmer latitudes of this sphere? Popocatepetl or Tenerife, perhaps?"

Davis stared hard enough at Emily to succeed in disconcerting her before he replied.

"On the contrary, Miss Dickinson. Summerland is a realm more exotic and perilous, yet offering commensurately greater rewards, than any mortal corner of the globe. And we shall reach it by setting sail directly from Amherst—without, in a sense, even leaving your charming little town."

Walt turned to Emily. "Please, Emily, listen to him. This is no simple passage to India we are undertaking."

Davis removed his glasses, polished them, and replaced them. "Allow me, Miss Dickinson, to acquaint you with the history of our mission.

"I am a simple shoemaker's son, born into humble circumstances in Poughkeepsie, New York. In the year 1843, I underwent my first magnetic trance, and began to speak of things I could not possibly have known, due to my meager formal education. Some kind believers saw fit to christen me the 'Seer of Poughkeepsie.' Since then, I have been in nearly constant contact with the spirits of earthly—yea, even unearthly—dead.

"Summerland is what they call their dwelling place.

"Summerland is not paradise, it appears, but rather a temporary stopping place on the way to God's kingdom, where the spirit may rest before making its final ascent. My discovery, as you can plainly see, provides the whole logic and rationale for spirit contact with our world. We are speaking not to perfected angels, but to recently disincarnate entities who have not quite thrown off their human concerns or shapes.

"The geography of Summerland—which I have managed at some pains to map—bears a resemblance to our common landscape." Davis picked up a cane pointer which had been concealed within the lectern and turned toward the map on the wall. Gesturing, he said, "Here, for instance, we see the Chrysoprase Mountains, which run parallel to the Tourmaline Sea. Beyond this range lie such features as the Bog of Effluent Humours, the Crystal Forest, the Beryl Palace and the Ten Silver Gates."

Emily meekly said, "What of the Paris Exposition?"

Her irreverence elicited chuckles from Walt, Sutton and Crookes. Austin, however, was not amused.

"Emily—if you cannot control your tongue, you may leave. I will not have you disparaging my distinguished guests, nor the sacred quest we are about to embark on."

Hearing the hurt in her brother's voice, and feeling a renewed tenderness toward him and his grief, Emily made a motion as of buttoning her lip.

Satisfied with the reprimand, Davis resumed his speech.

"Ever since my discovery of this realm, it has been my one desire to visit it bodily, well before my death. I searched fruitlessly for many years for an entrance to Summerland. Just when I was on the point of abandoning my search, I met the illustrious Madame Selavy."

The medium spoke. "Ah, *mon cher*, it was *I* who met you!"

"As you wish, Madame. In any case, Madame Selavy represented a great advance over all other mediums I had encountered.

"Madame, you see, is able to act as a physical bridge between Summerland and Earth, by means of a curious new material she exudes.

"At this point, I believe I will let Professor Crookes take over. Professor?"

Crookes and Davis exchanged places. With Oxbridge schoolroom crispness, Crookes began to lecture.

"Madame Selavy is a portal between our world and Summerland. Extensive tests and trials have proven that she possesses the unique ability to serve as a channel for the very stuff of which the spirits and their world appears to be made. I have dubbed this new form of matter 'ideoplasm.'

"Ideoplasm seems to be a protean substance—partly organic, partly inorganic—heretofore unknown to science. Issuing from the body of our medium, it is susceptible to her thought commands, taking on whatever shape she wills. A hand, a limb, or an entire spirit can be made manifest. And these ideoplastic creations are quite tangible, as I can personally testify.

"Still, however tantalizing this new phenomenon first appeared to me, I could not see how it might offer us direct entrance into Summerland. The ideoplasm issued forth and returned through the channel of our medium, without permitting any mortal object to accompany it.

"This is where science stepped in."

Crookes now lifted the glassblower's product from the lectern and held it up for inspection.

"This is my latest invention, which I modestly call a 'Crookes tube.' Through its evacuated interior an electric current can be made to flow, from the cathode at one end to the anode at the other.

"When this tube is filled with ideoplasm—captured and detached from Madame Selavy—and activated, a most startling thing happens.

"The tube and its contents, as well as any objects within a certain radius, disappear! It is as if, under the electric shock, the ideoplasm is forcibly ejected from our plane, dragging with it a certain amount of earthly detritus.

"The spirits have told us that they have seen the tubes and their wrack rematerialize in Summerland."

Crookes smiled smugly. "I will now restore the platform to Mister Davis."

When Davis stood again before them, he said, "Our world is in point for point contiguity with Summerland. Here in Amherst, for instance, your familiar grassy Common is, on the other side, coexistent with Summerland's Bay of Seven Souls.

"It is from here that we shall set sail for the afterlife!

"Even as we sit here, a wagon is on its way from the McKay Shipyards in East Boston, bearing a specially designed schooner. After our vessel arrives, we will fit it out with a circuit of ideoplastic Crookes tubes, which we have been filling slowly day by day. Thus outfitted, we will breach the barrier between the worlds, in a voyage more daring than Jason's!"

Out of respect for Austin's dementia, Emily had sat silently throughout this farrago of science and mysticism, despite her rising indignation. Now, however, she could no long restrain herself.

"And how, pray tell, does Madame 'exude' this celestial quince jelly?"

Davis assumed a flustered look and began to polish his lenses once more. Walt gazed toward the ceiling and young Sutton began insouciantly to whistle. Crookes crossed his legs and folded his arms across his chest. For half a minute, the room was as silent as a meeting of the Know-Nothings.

Then the medium herself spoke.

"It is from the *mamelles*, dear sister of Austin. The bounteous tits."

To illustrate, Madame Selavy cupped her large breasts. "It is a kind of spiritual milk, which, with help, I can squeeze out, plip-plop."

Emily was speechless. The most obscene pictures filled her churning mind. *The Brain has Corridors surpassing those of the most haunted Abbey*—

Walt coughed, shattering her inner absorption.

"Mad filaments and ungovernable shoots," said the poet, "play out of the female form, and our response is likewise ungovernable."

"Ungovernable," said Emily, "my foot!"

6

"BY WHAT MYSTIC MOORING SHE IS HELD TODAY"

Lavinia Dickinson tied her bonnet beneath her chin, picked up a large lidded market basket, and, wearing a look of impatience, turned to her dawdling sister.

"Are you coming, or not, Miss White Moth?"

The use of her costume-inspired nickname roused

Emily from her introspection. She had been considering one of the first poems she had ever written, the verse that began: *One Sister have I in our house, and one, a hedge away.*

How treacherous the one linked by marriage had revealed herself to be. A regular Cleopatra! If only Austin could have married sweet Mary Warner, how much better things might have been....

Emily thanked the Lord for the stolid common sense of her blood sister. She could not imagine life without her beloved Vinnie—sour, cynical, acquisitive as she was. How she needed her—especially now, in the light of the unbelievable immorality which seemed to have taken hold at The Evergreens.

Three days had passed since the revelation about Madame Selavy's ideoplastic *poitrines* had caused Emily to beat a righteous retreat to The Homestead. (Curiously, she had not felt compelled to hie herself to the safety of her bed, but had instead frittered the time away in domestic pursuits; enough rye bread had been baked to feed all the gawping spectators at John Brown's hanging! If this represented an increased toughness of heart on her part, she knew not what to attribute it to, nor whether she liked it....)

In that interval, no one from The Evergreens had approached her to apologize or cajole. Save once, when Walt had knocked the very next day at the front door and been received by Vinnie.

"Give him this," had been Emily's response to his arrival, handing her sister a folded poem:

A Burdock—clawed my Gown—
Not Burdock's—blame—
But mine—

Who went too near
The Burdock's Den!

After reading it, Walt had departed wordlessly, and not returned.

Emily had felt a little surprised and saddened that the ocean-deep Bard had not pressed his cause harder. The fires of worship which he had aroused in her—strictly those of one Poet and Free Thinker for another, she reminded herself; had he not admitted that his heart was forever betrothed to that nameless New Orleans hussy whose tintype he carried?—still burned, however banked their coals.

But for whatever reason, Walt had not pled or argued, and Emily had sought to put him and the whole insane menagerie at The Evergreens out of her thoughts.

Yet just this morning had come the incredible news from town which had reawakened all her curiosity about the mad expedition Austin and the others were planning, and which now threatened actually to make her pay a visit to the Amherst she had turned her back on years ago.

"Yes, Vinnie," said Emily, rising from her seat and taking down her Merino Shawl from a peg and donning it. "I shall accompany you to town. That is, I think I can do so, if I may have the comfort of your sturdy arm."

Vinnie seemed touched, and her gruff manner softened. "Why, that's the least you may ask of me, Em. I know this isn't easy for you, but I think it'll do you good."

"You are my Nurse and Confessor, Vinnie, so I shall place my faith in your words."

Arm in arm, the sisters departed by the front door of The Homestead, descended the sloping brick walk, crossed the perimeter of low hedges, through the wooden gate, and turned east, down Main Street's dusty unpaved sidewalk.

For a moment, Emily was reminded of the joyous sugaring expeditions her family and friends had once embarked on, before they had all grown so old and hard. Why couldn't one remain young in spirit forever—?

It was a short stroll into town—Amherst was not a big place—but Emily saw something to amaze her at every step. The simple village life—the children at play, the housewives at their chores, the carriages and horses, dogs and peddlers—It was all as miraculous to her as Heaven Itself.

With a pang, she heard again Walt's admonition that she was refining herself out of existence by cutting the ties that bound her to a common, shared life....

Passing North Pleasant Street, both sisters cast a nostalgic glance at the house where they had spent a portion of their childhood. From its windows, Emily had watched numerous funeral processions wind their way to the nearby cemetery—her first conscious fascination with Death. Out of those sad and mean years when The Squire had been forced temporarily to vacate The Homestead, due to financial setbacks, she yet retained a few happy memories.

Emily wondered how her life might have been different had the family stayed closer to town, been less prosperous, not fortified itself in its castle, The Homestead. Would she have married, even moved away? It seemed so impossible now....

Ahead loomed the Common. Emily noted that most of the foot-traffic abroad this morn was tending toward that open parcel of land, and surmised that the rumors that had drawn her out were indeed true.

As Vinnie had predicted, renewing her acquaintance with the village was indeed proving a tonic. The gentle May breezes were having their old effect. Emily could not meet the Spring unmoved. She felt the old desire, a Hurry with a lingering, mixed—

"Walk faster, Vinnie!"

"Not so speedily, Moth! Ladies do not run in public."

"I'm not a lady, I'm a Queen! And Queens may do as they please!"

Pulling her sister after her, Emily hastened toward the gathering crowd.

The Common was a rectangular expanse two or three acres in extent, fringed and spotted with May-bright trees. Several of Amherst's six churches fronted on the path-laced mall, as did those slightly disreputable yellow-painted structures known as Fraternity Row, among others. The hilly countryside surrounding Amherst held the public seat in its cupped hands, a natural amphitheater, the mountains standing in Haze, the Valleys stopped below.

And now, as Emily could plainly see, the Common sported a new feature.

In the middle of the lawn, secured in its wheeled cradle by thick hawsers, seventy-five miles or more from the nearest harbor, stood a twin-masted schooner, looking as incongruous as trousers on a Sandwich Islander.

Surrounded by noisy spectators, the schooner resembled a misguided barque stranded on a shoal of flesh.

As Emily drew nearer, she espied the trim figure of Professor William Crookes standing on the deck. He was bent over a surveyor's instrument. Following the direction of its barrel, Emily saw Andrew Jackson Davis some yards away, holding a plumb bob.

Eight sweating Percherons in harness—no doubt the team that had transported the craft over the roads from East

Boston—were still attached to the ship's undercarriage. At their head, holding a whip, stood Henry Sutton and his helper, Austin Dickinson.

Neither Walt nor Madame Selavy was anywhere to be seen. Emily suppressed an evil thought.

"We've got to move it fifteen yards further on, Hen!" called out the savant now, above the exclamations and japes of the crowd.

Young Sutton cracked his whip in the air and urged the team on, aided by Austin.

"Hee-yaw! Put yer backs into it, boys!"

Ponderously, the craft began to roll across the turf. At the proper moment, Crookes signaled with a chopping motion to disengage the team, and Sutton did so swiftly by knocking out a wooden pin in the linkage. The ship's inertia carried it on for a short distance before it ground to a halt.

"Perfect!" cried Crookes. "A tribute to Newton's Laws!" Abandoning his instrument, Crookes turned to address the crowd in his regal English manner.

"Ladies and Gentlemen of Amherst, you are privileged to witness today the dawn of a new era, an era in which regular travel between the realm of the living and the realm of the dead shall inaugurate a Golden Age of scientific theology. No longer will life be shadowed by death. Instead, a flourishing commerce between the two kingdoms will permit one and all to live without anxiety or fear, in the knowledge that our souls survive their earthly husks."

From the crowd a rough male voice yelled a flippant rejoinder. "Maybe you and your spooks can solve the Burdell murder!"

The reference to the scandal which had filled the New York papers a couple of years ago set off a gale of laughter.

Crookes weathered it good-naturedly. When it had died out, he simply concluded, "You shall see more, and shortly. This much I promise. Then you may judge for yourselves."

With that, Crookes turned and clambered down a rope ladder, joining his three compatriots, who were planting chocks under the wheels of the schooner. The crowd, seeing that no more immediate entertainment was to be had, began to disperse.

Vinnie turned to Emily. The younger sister's face wore a mottled flush.

"Oh, Emily! I've never been so mortified in my life! Look at Austin, consorting with those mountebanks! How shall I ever attract a husband now!? Not to mention how Father is going to explode when he returns! There'll be hell to pay!"

Emily had never heard her sister swear before. It rather thrilled her. A kind of glorious exaltation had come upon Emily with Crookes's speech. All her life, Emily had secretly considered herself a rebel and even something of a thrill-seeker, though her thrills had been limited to the mental variety. "How I love danger!" she had written in her girlish diary. Now, with this fabulous and improbable ship sitting here like a slap in the face of placid, conservative Amherst, she felt as if her real life were just beginning.

Where was Walt, to share this excitement with her, and urge her on?

Tugging Emily's hand, Vinnie pleaded, "Please, let's go home...."

Emily disengaged from her sister. "You may scurry home if you wish, Vinnie. But I intend to see what else they're up to."

Vinnie appeared shocked. "But Emily—"

At that moment, a familiar resonant tenor thrilled Emily's ears.

"I think that only sailors, far from land, will ever truly appreciate my poems."

7

"HOPE IS THE THING WITH FEATHERS"

 All around Emily, the whispering Leaves like Women interchanged Exclusive Confidences.

And since Emily was a woman too, she could understand what they were saying.

He is true to you. He is here when you want him.

Her heart light as eiderdown, Emily turned about.

Twice as big as life he stood, Walt Whitman, a kosmos, turbulent, fleshy, sensual, singer of himself.

The difference between remembering him and actually seeing him was like the Liquor in the Jug as opposed to the Liquor between the Lips.

Whitman beamed at the women, his bearded cheeks crinkling. "How good to see you abroad, Emily. And you too, Miss Lavinia. The very folds of both your clothes, your style as I watched you pass in the street, and, most especially, the contours of your shapes downwards inspired me deliriously."

Gawking, Vinnie opened her mouth, shut it, then opened it once more.

"Well, I never—! Emily, you can find your way home alone!"

And with that ejaculation, Emily's sister stalked off, swinging her market basket like a truncheon.

Walt was crestfallen. "I fear I have offended your sister. Please forgive me, Emily. It is something that happens all the time. I forget that not everyone is as spontaneous and free as Walt Whitman."

"Oh, don't believe her indignation for a minute, Walt. She was secretly pleased, I'm sure. It's just that she could not show so in public. I myself might have departed just so, a few days ago, in the mock affront demanded by propriety."

Walt laid an assuming hand on Emily's shoulder. "I sensed as soon as I saw you today that a change long under-way in you was well-nigh complete. I am happy to have played a part in it, however small."

For once, Emily chose not to spoil her new confidence by analyzing it to pieces. She shifted closer to Walt so that his whole brawny arm slid naturally around her shoulders. Protected in his embrace, she felt even more assured.

"Let us go see what my brother and his cohorts are up to."

"Exactly where I was tending myself."

Walt and Emily walked up to the wheeled schooner. Under the shade of its elevated bow, Austin, Sutton, Davis and Crookes were prying the lid off a crate that had just been delivered by a local merchant and his wagon. Spotting the duo, the laborers paused. Sutton hailed Walt gleefully, and Austin glared suspiciously at his sister's compromising attitude. Davis and Crookes, after a brief nod, resumed their prying attack on the lid.

"What have we here, Hen?" asked Walt.

Grunting, Crookes answered for him. "It's the ideoplastic tubes. We've got to clamp them to their fixtures on the ship and wire them in circuit. Then we'll be prepared to set out. Perhaps as early as tomorrow."

With a creaking of wood and squealing of nails, the lid of the large box finally gave way. The men lowered it to the ground, and Emily peered curiously inside.

Nestled in straw, layer by layer, were dozens of Crookes tubes, each filled with a misty gray substance that swirled and coiled like a narrow Fellow in the Grass.

Emily's chest pinched with a tighter breathing, and a Zero at the Bone.

"Walt—I don't feel well. Can we go?"

Crookes evinced little sympathy for Emily's distress. "By all means, go. The four of us can manage quite easily to mount these electro-spiritual phials. Why don't you and the lady attend to the ostriches, Wally? That's more in your line, what with all your talk of loving the birds and baboons."

Walt seemingly took no offense at the half-veiled slight. "A splendid suggestion. Come, Emily—let us visit our feathered friends and study their wing'd purposes."

When they reached the edge of the Common, Emily felt better. She sought to explain what had come over her, not wishing Walt to think her a typical faint-hearted spinster.

"The sight of that slimy spiritual stuff affected me queerly, Walt. The notion that it all came out of the gross corporeal form of Madame Selavy—I fear it was too much for me."

"I recall that I too felt somewhat unnerved when I first witnessed a materialization. But such feelings pass, when you realize that nothing that happens on this earth is unnatural. Everything is good in its place, and nothing is out of its place."

Walt's careless admission that he had witnessed an ideoplastic extrusion reawakened in Emily all the repugnance she had experienced upon first learning of Madame Selavy's promiscuous behavior. Stiffening and stopping, she slipped out from Walt's embrace and turned to confront him.

"I suppose you don't think there's anything immoral then in helping to milk that trollop as if she were a prize Holstein! You've doubtlessly enjoyed such scandalous behavior often enough yourself! Why, it's, it's—positively Mormon!"

Walt sighed, and, despite knowing herself in the right, Emily felt saddened to have hurt him. His patient smile that followed somewhat heartened her.

"Morality. I had hoped you were above such small conceptions, Emily. Is the sea moral, or the tree-toad? Is the running blackberry moral? Morality is the bane of small minds, to paraphrase my friend Emerson. I simply eat what is put on my plate, without recourse to praise or blame, thanks or curses. Life is much better lived in such a fashion. And as for our poor, much-hounded friends at Salt Lake—who can say that their way is not as good as—or better than—ours? It's more natural, at least. Does not a single stallion quicken many mares? But if it will put your mind at ease, I am happy to assure you that I myself have never materially participated in assisting Madame Selavy to, ah, form her ejectamenta. That task belongs to Davis and the professor."

Walt's words left Emily feeling both chagrined and relieved, embarrassed and reassured. She was glad that Walt had not participated intimately in the materializations; however, his cavalier attitude toward convention was hard to swallow for one who—however independent—had been reared all her life amongst the contaminating small minds of Amherst.

In the end, Emily let her predisposition toward Whitman have the ascendancy. He was a Poet, and such could not be judged by normal scales.

They resumed their walk, covering the distance back to The Evergreens in silence. Passing through the luxuriant grounds, they reached the ostrich pen. The enormous birds crowded to the fence to greet Whitman, who responded by petting them affectionately.

"I think I could turn and live with the animals," said the man, "they are so placid and self-contain'd. They do not sweat and whine about their condition. They do not lie awake in the dark and weep for their sins. And above all, they do not make me sick discussing their duty to God!"

So neatly did these sentiments tally with Emily's own— she who had oft imagined herself a bee or spider—that she dropped a silent tear or two of joy. When she found her voice, she asked her companion, "I still do not understand what part these glorious fowls play in this expedition, Walt."

"You are aware that our motive power for breaching the dimensions comes from the miracle element, electricity— specifically, a set of Voltaic piles, are you not?"

"I am now."

"Well, the piles hold but a single charge—enough, perhaps, to send us to Summerland, but not to return. They must be continually recharged, by means of a treadmill-powered generator. The ostriches shall serve that purpose."

"But why such exotic draft animals? Surely a horse or two would have done as well...."

"It was instructions from Princess Pink Cloud, Madame's spirit guide. We were informed by the ghost that ostriches were the only animal psychically fitted to make the transition with us to the spirit domain. There is something especially ethereal about them."

"I can believe it," said Emily. "Just look at them!"

"They are beautiful, aren't they? I've named them all after the female cantatrices of my favorite operas, for some quality they possess reminds me of those prima donnas." Walt assumed an air of mock formality. "Miss Dickinson, may I present you to my ladies? Here is Donna Anna and Zerlina, Marguerite and Elsa, Lucia and Alisa, Barbarina, Violetta, Norma, Gilda and Magdalena."

Emily curtsied. "Charmed, I'm certain."

They both began to laugh then, Emily's titters gradually escalating to match Walt's roaring. They were forced to retreat to a seat which circled the bole of a large spreading elm until the shared fit of hilarity had passed.

When Emily could speak again, she said, "Walt, dear, I know why my brother and Davis and Crookes are participating in this expedition. But what are your motives? And what of your young companion, Henry?"

Walt coughed, then said, somewhat disingenuously, thought Emily, "Ah, Hen, he's a splendid lad. He's made much of himself, considering his orphan status and rough upbringing. I've known him since we worked on the *Eagle* together, lo, these ten years and more. Hen was a printer's devil while I was the editor, but we never let that come between us. We were always the best of friends. There is a rare degree of adhesiveness between us, and he is along simply because I value his company."

Emily recognized in Walt's mention of "adhesiveness" the phrenological term for masculine bonding. She could well credit the relationship, having seen the fond glances the two men exchanged. "That explains Henry's presence. But what of yours?"

Walt took Emily's hands, as he had during their first *tête-à-tête*. "Emily, what I am about to confess to you, I have told no others. They think I am along simply to gain general wisdom that will strengthen my poetry. After all, what poet worth his salt would refuse to embark on a voyage to probe the afterlife?"

Emily felt a pang, as if Walt were criticizing her own lack of enthusiasm for the expedition.

Oblivious, Walt continued, "And in a sense, that is not a lie. After all, I have a duty to make my songs as true and brave as I can. Our country, the glorious poem known as America, is entering a perilous period, Emily. I can sniff as much in every Southern breeze, if you take my meaning. And my songs must be strong, to help carry America through her times of trouble.

"But there is another, more personal reason for my wanting to visit Summerland.

"You see, I need to speak to my father."

Walt paused, and took a deep breath before resuming.

"My father died the very week my *Leaves of Grass* was first published. He never got a chance to see it, to see that I was making something of my life. He was a rough-hewn man, who measured success with his carpenter's level, and I was always something of a disappointment to him. Not to my blessed mother—no, she always had faith in her favorite son, and she yet lives and is pleased by my work. But my father—Well, suffice it to say that I feel that there is an unresolved matter between us, and that if only I could speak to him again, I would be able better to live my life and sing my songs. Do you understand, Emily?"

Now Emily was giddy, any slights forgotten. An ecstatic anguish raced through her veins. She should have known that Walt could have no ignoble motive for his involvement with the Poughkeepsie Seer and his entourage, no more than her brother did.

Throwing her arms around his neck, Emily exclaimed, "Oh, Walt! I who have never had a real mother or father I could love or turn to can sympathize with you better than anyone! Please, please, forgive me for ever being so impertinently curious!"

"It is not mine to forgive, nor is it even necessary. But I do."

Thrilled at his words and by his rough-hewn, sweaty, aromatic closeness, Emily shut her eyes and waited expectantly.

At that very moment she heard footsteps approaching.

She and Walt hurriedly disengaged and stood up.

It was only young Sutton.

"The professor says ter kindly wake up the gypsy, Walt. They're a-fixin' to have a say-ants tonight!"

8

"THE SPIRIT LOOKS DOWN

ON THE DUST"

Emily's paralyzing shyness had prevented her from ever attending one of Sue Gilbert Dickinson's "Noctes Ambrosiana," whereat the cream of Amherst and visiting Boston society were wont to gaily disport themselves. Only through articles clipped from the *Boston Transcript* and pasted into her scrapbook—alongside journalistic eulogies, nature essays and comic japeries—did she share the excitement of those *fêtes*.

But she imagined that no matter how thrilling and splendid those parties had been, none could have compared with the tension and excitement generated now by the strange accouterments and atmosphere and expectations in the converted parlor of The Evergreens.

Heavy blood-red draperies had been closed to cut off all traces of moonlight—and much of the natural nocturnal noise. Cabalistic signs cut from paper had been hung with pushpins on the walls. A cone of what Davis had assured them, before leaving the room, was "genuine Hindoo incense" smoldered in a saucer, perfuming the air with pagan mystery. The only illumination came from a pair of thick corpse-pale candles.

Why, it hardly seemed as if they were in New England any more!

A flimsy sidetable had been pressed into service as the main prop. Around it were crammed seven chairs, five of which were occupied: along one side sat Emily and, on her left, Walt; clockwise from the Manahatta singer sat Sutton, Austin and Crookes. The two empty chairs intervened between this latter personage and Emily.

Beneath the table the sitters' knees pressed in an intimacy which, had their purposes not been strictly scientific, would have been most immodest.

Emily could sense a strangeness in the air. It accorded with those rare solitary moments when she had sensed that the veil between the living and the dead was thinner than most people suspected—

Of nearness to her sundered Things
The Soul has special times—

The Shapes we buried, dwell about,
Familiar, in the Rooms—
Untarnished by the Sepulchre,
The Mouldering Playmate comes—
In just the Jacket that he wore—
Long buttoned in the Mold,
Since we—old mornings, Children—played—
Divided—by a world—

Inclined by these premonitions to overcome her natural distaste of Madame Selavy and to give the French mystic all possible benefit of doubt, up till the final test, Emily waited patiently for the medium and her mentor to make their appearance, reminding herself that if her beloved Elizabeth Barrett could endure such foolishness, so could she.

All participants, however, were not so easygoing.

"What a damn fool way to settle a scientific matter!" exploded Professor Crookes, after some moments of painful squirming.

An altercation between Davis and Crookes had arisen, concerning the exact placement of the ideoplastic tubes aboard the ship. Davis had argued for arranging them in a ritualistic pentagram, whereas Crookes had opted for a more Euclidean disposition designed to project their force symmetrically. Finally, both parties had agreed to arbitration by the spirit world—although Crookes appeared now to be regretting his decision.

Before the naturalist could voice further petulance, however, the door opened and in walked the Seer of Poughkeepsie and Madame Selavy.

Davis wore his usual suit and spectacles, but had crowned himself with a purple satin turban, its ends fastened with a large paste brooch. To Emily's eyes, the whole affair suspiciously resembled a lady's sash she had seen in the fashion pages of *All The Year Round*. Barefoot and bare-armed, Madame Selavy wore a flowing, loose-fitting white muslin robe. From the way in which her plentiful flesh jiggled beneath it, she had apparently abandoned all stays and corsets—the better, perhaps, to let the ideoplasm circulate....

Davis raised his hands in a gesture of blessing. "Madame Selavy's meditation has placed her psyche in accord with the higher forces. She is now primed and ready to flow! In the name of Asar-Un-Nefer and Sekhet, of Alampis and Kobah, of Belial and Ishva-devata, let the gates now be thrown open!"

Madame Selavy took her seat at the head of the table, placing her immediately at Emily's right hand. Meanwhile, Davis erected a parchment screen in front of the two candles, plunging the room into further gloom. Then he took the last empty chair, between Crookes and the medium.

"All please join hands, and seek to calm and open your minds. The spirits are extremely sensitive to negativity. And remember—under no conditions must you break the ring until the seance is officially terminated! I cannot be responsible for what might happen should you do so."

Emily thought that Davis had glared at her specifically at the mention of "negativity." But the shadows were too thick to be certain.

In any case, she now did as instructed: with her left hand she gripped Walt's big paw; with her right she submitted to Madame Selavy's plump and clammy grip.

As soon as the circle was complete, a wind seemed to arise from nowhere, causing the candles to shudder. On Madame Selavy's face appeared a look of tortured strain.

Emily saw sweat spring out on her mustached upper lip.

A series of loud raps suddenly sounded from a distant corner of the parlor! At the same time, the table jounced and bucked like a capering colt, through no apparent material intervention.

Davis spoke in hushed tones. "The spirit guide, or epipsychidion, is now entering Madame's very body."

The medium's eyes rolled upwards, showing only white. Then, in a high girlish voice unlike her own deep timbre, she spoke.

"Why Big Chief Davis call-um little Pink Cloud?"

"Princess Pink Cloud! How grateful we are that you could reach us! We realize what an effort it is for you to disengage yourself from the splendors of Summerland to speak with us mere mortals—"

Crookes interrupted. "Enough with the ghostly pleasantries! Ask her about the tubes!"

Davis was imperturbed. "Princess Pink Cloud, my friend, although abrupt, has indeed raised the object of our conference. We need to know the proper disposition of the ideoplastic containers on our vessel. Would you kindly instruct us?"

There was a pause. Then: "Ugh! Is hard to see—Wait! Make-um the sacred seal. But also put-um tubes high and low, to cover-um big canoe like a chief's buffalo hide cover-um floor of teepee."

"Humph!" said Crookes, but appeared mollified at the compromise.

"Thank you, Princess. You may leave now—"

"Wait!"

It was Austin. Emily winced at the contortions of grief evident on her brother's face.

"Please, can you give me a message from my unborn children? Do they know I'm coming to hold them?"

"The little ones which the bad squaw kill-um wait-um for their father in happy hunting ground."

Tears coursed down Austin's face. "Thank you, Princess, thank you—"

Hardening her heart to Austin's grief, Emily now spoke up in accordance with a plan she had secretly devised and kept hidden, even from Walt.

"I too have a question for the spirit, if I may."

Davis hesitated a moment, then said, "Certainly. But I can guarantee nothing."

"I understand. Princess, my question is for Leonard Humphrey, my old teacher. Can you reach him?"

Madame Selavy twisted and writhed before finally replying, "Yes, Leonard be-um with me here."

"Ask him please what he meant when he said to me that my poems were 'dross.'"

"Ugh! Leonard make-um big apology. He say-um that he could not see-um their worth with living eye. But now he see-um they very good chants."

Emily smiled. "Thank you, Princess."

Humphrey had never said any such thing to Emily, had in fact never even seen any of her juvenile outpourings, for she had been too timid to disclose them.

"If no one else has a question—Very well, we shall bring this seance to a close."

Madame Selavy spoke. "Princess Pink Cloud want-um to wave goodbye."

"An ideoplastic manifestation! We are honored, Princess!"

Being closest to the medium, Emily was the first to spot

the manifestation. The shadowy portion of the medium's robe that stretched across her lap billowed and seemed to lift, taking shape as it grew. (Emily hated to think where the "ideoplasm" was supposed to be issuing from this time.) In a few seconds a shiny pale arm and hand wavered above the level of the table.

"Goodbye, goodbye. I see-um you in Summerland—"

Emily leaped to her feet, breaking her contact on both sides, and grabbed the ideoplastic limb.

Madame Selavy screamed! The table was knocked over—by Davis, Emily later assumed, though at the time it seemed to leap of its own will—and general chaos reigned.

By the time Walt had lit the whale-oil sconces on the wall, the tumult had died down.

And there stood Emily, holding triumphantly aloft her prize.

"Look!" she exclaimed. "A light armature on a telescoping rod, draped in wet muslin. I venture you'll find a slit in her robe where it protruded, while she wiggled it with her toes!"

The men had carried the seemingly unconscious Madame Selavy to a couch, where she lay prostrate. From his position of deep concern by her side, Davis now glared at Emily.

"Of course that's what it looks like now! Once you ruptured the link with the medium, without the proper ceremonies the ideoplasm reverted to its nearest earthly semblance! I only hope you haven't killed her, with your sacrilegious disrespect!"

Emily threw down the apparatus. "With such logic, I could make a hummingbird into a dragon! If you believe this faker, you're all loco. I only hope I can keep myself from falling over with laughter when your expedition goes bust!"

Exerting obvious self-control, Austin approached his

sister. "It's a certainty that you won't be there, after this brazen insult."

Emily laughed. "Oh, but you're wrong, Austin. I shall be there, and not just as a spectator, but as one of the crew! It's that, or else I shall wire Father with news of this whole sordid affair! And believe me, a mundane telegraph works just as well as a celestial one!"

Mention of the Squire caused Austin to blanch. The wind had been effectively taken out of his sails.

Now Crookes tried to reason her out of it. "Why are so bent on accompanying us, Miss Dickinson, if you have no faith in our success?"

Emily moved to stand by Walt. "I'm going to protect those I love from being made fools of and hurt!"

Neither affirming nor denying Emily, Walt said, "Are our dreams so shaky, sirs, that we cannot afford a clear-eyed skeptic among us? Her presence will not hinder us, if our theory is sound."

A groan wafted from the couch. Everyone turned to the recumbent medium.

"Let the *petite* unbeliever set sail with us. It matters not. "For she shall never return!"

9

"LAND HO! ETERNITY!"

The parade of ostriches through the streets of Amherst attracted not a little attention, from gentry and mudlark alike.

Led by Henry Sutton, chivvied gently onward from the rear by a switch-wielding Walt—whose informal uniform, for once, fit his role of herder—the big magnificent tropical birds trotted proudly down the dusty thoroughfares, pulling spectators in droves after them.

Emily had to scurry to keep up with the parade of men, women and capering children: not an easy task in her long white dress. Finally, she gathered up her skirts, daringly exposing several inches of ankles and calves, and managed to catch up with Walt.

A little Madness in the Spring is wholesome even for a King, Emily reminded herself. And the Lord knew, this had been the maddest Spring of her life!

It had taken not one but three days to arrange the ideo-plastic propulsion devices to the satisfaction of both Crookes and Davis. So had Emily ascertained, from daily visits to the Common. She had barely suppressed her laughter at the sight of so much useless activity; surely the tubes would prove as much a hoax as Madame Selavy's third arm and hand....

During this time, Austin and Sutton had been kept busy loading various supplies aboard the schooner: tents, bottled water, foodstuffs, ropes, ostrich fodder. Emily was reminded of those Cattle smaller than the Bee, whose tillage is the passing Crumb—

As for Walt, he had simply disappeared after the seance. A brief note had turned up that next morning at Emily's breakfast setting, quoting one of the wanderer's own poems:

> *Afoot and light-hearted, I take to the open road,*
> *Healthy, free, the world before me,*
> *The long brown path before me leading wherever I choose.*

Emily had cracked her soft-boiled egg with no apparent tremor of her hands, while inside she was all awhirl with uncertainty.

She had not meant to state her love for Walt aloud, least of all during such a confused public event as a seance! Yet she had. Under whatever devilish impulse, she had blurted out her true feelings for Walt—feelings she had hardly been willing to admit even to herself.

And now her words, it seemed, had caused the object of her affections to bolt. Was it that he did not reciprocate her deep devotion—or that he felt too strongly toward her to trust himself around her? Probably the former.

My Worthiness is all my Doubt—
His Merit—all my fear—
Contrasting which, my quality
Do lowlier—appear—

Lest I should insufficient prove
For his beloved Need—
The Chiefest Apprehension
Upon my thronging Mind—

Well, there was no way to retract her words, even if she had wanted to, no action she could do take until—if—Walt returned.

So she calmly ate her egg.

But this very morning, drawn to her Main Street bedroom window by the unmistakably unique noise of a passing flock of ostriches, Emily had seen the shaggy figure of her beloved.

Emily made a hasty toilet. Carlo, sensing her excitement

and urgency, barked and bounded. A sudden wave of feeling passed over Emily. She knew with certainty that by plunging after Walt, she was embarking on a grand adventure that might separate her from her pet forever, by elopement or marriage, death or madness.

Emily gave the big dog a hug, then locked it in the bedroom.

By the time she made her way down to the street, the procession was some distance ahead. Hence the need for her indelicate haste.

Now she drew up even with the hirsute shepherd.

"Walt! Wait!"

Obediently, Walt stopped. The flock continued on without him, the crowd encircling them and preventing their escape. Soon, the two poets were alone, the hustle and bustle dying away as the parade disappeared around a bend.

Walt had not moved. Emily came around to look in his face. His placid, manly features, she was relieved to see, revealed no distaste or distress at her appearance, as she had half-feared they would. Quite to the contrary, he smiled gently at her, and doffed his floppy black hat.

"Emily, dearest, I am glad to see you once more before our departure."

"It is today, then! Let's hurry, or they'll leave without us!"

"You do not still propose to endanger yourself on such a chancey expedition, I pray...."

"Of course! I don't foresee any risk—but even if there were, do you think I would let my Master rush into it without me?"

Walt sighed, and replaced his hat. Taking Emily by the elbow, he said, "Let us walk. I can think better then. It is how I have been spending the last several days."

They set out toward the center of town. After a few yards, Walt spoke.

"Emily, I do not think you really know me—"

"Oh, but I do, Walt, I do! Your soul is as clear as ice on a stream to me!"

"I must disagree. We have barely met, and you claim me as your 'Master.' That alone shows how poorly you perceive me. I am no person's master—not even my own, I fear! I am still a mystery to myself, after all these years. How could I be any less a mystery to you?"

"But I love you, Walt! Surely that transcends mere knowing!"

"It does, it does, I agree. But do you and I mean the same thing when we speak of love, Emily? Ever since I left my endlessly rocking cradle, I have been direly perplexed about the nature of love. I have been one that ached continually with amorous love. Does the earth not gravitate? Does not all matter, aching, attract all other matter? So the body of me to all I meet or know! I am not content with a mere majority—I must have the love of all men and all women on this earth!"

"And you have mine, Walt! My whole heart!"

"Emily, listen. Out of the rolling ocean, the crowd, you came to me gently, a drop like myself. You whispered, 'I love you. I have travelled a long way merely to look on you, to touch you.' And this is good. But I respond: 'Now that we have met and looked, we are safe! Return in peace to the ocean, my love. I too am part of that ocean, my love. We are never separated! Behold the great rondure, the cohesion of all, how perfect!'"

All Emily could hear were the words "my love," repeated twice. To travel to Summerland were superfluous: she was in Paradise already.

"Have it as you will, Walt. I am content. Let us join the others now."

"Only if you truly comprehend me, *ma femme....*"

"Yes, be assured. I do."

In silence, they walked the rest of the way to the Common.

The crowd was enormous. Not only did masses of people overspread the lawn, but they hung from the windows of neighboring buildings. The young scholars of Fraternity Row, plainly already in their cups, were singing some raucous ditty about John Brown's body—evidently their idea of the proper sendoff for such a solemn voyage.

Emily was surprised that neither secular nor religious authorities had intervened to stop what was in essence a blasphemous expedition. She could only assume that both money and Dickinson influence had been brought to bear.

The ship itself—sails still unfurled—had been transformed into some kind of bauble-bedecked Tannenbaum. From its rigging and superstructure hung the loaded Crookes tubes, connected by electrical cables. Their suspicious contents seemed to cast a nimbus around each, making the very air waver. It was a spooky effect, and Emily was still unable to conceive through what trickery Madame Selavy achieved it.

The last of the ostriches—Norma, thought Emily—was just being brought aboard, up a long gangplank with a gentle slope. Walt and Emily followed the bird aboard.

The rest of the crew awaited them.

Austin spotted Emily. She mustered her rebuttal to his expected rebuke, but was taken aback by his actual words.

"Although it is too late for you to carry out your threat by telegraphing Father, and so force your passage, you are still welcome to accompany us, sister. Despite your obvious and baseless antipathy toward Madame Selavy, she has graciously interceded on your behalf."

Emily eyed the medium suspiciously, and was returned a mocking curtsy and a smile that resembled the expression one of Vinnie's cats might wear when stalking its feathered prey.

Crookes now spoke. "If all hatchets have been at least temporarily buried, then perhaps we can move to a scientific footing. Our departure time is scheduled for exactly noon, and we still have a few items to attend to. Henry and Austin—please hoist the gangplank. And Mister Whitman—would you do these honors?"

Crookes handed Walt a bottle of champagne. Taking it, Walt replied, "I am privileged, sir," and advanced to the bow.

At the appearance of the poet, the crowd roared, then fell silent. Assuming the dignity that he brought to all his frequent public-speaking engagements, Walt addressed the spectators.

"These are the words of my good, gray friend, William Cullen Bryant, and I deem them meet for today.

"'So live, that when the summons comes to join
"'The innumerable caravan, which moves
"'To that mysterious realm, where each shall take
"'His chamber in the silent halls of death,
"'Thou go not, like the quarry-slave at night,
"'Scourged to his dungeon, but, sustained and soothed
"'By an unfaltering trust, approach thy grave
"'Like one who wraps the drapery of his couch
"'About him, and lies down to pleasant dreams.'"

With his final words, Walt swung the bottle mightily against the hull of the ship, at the same time bellowing.

"I christen thee *Thanatopsis!*"

Champagne and glass sprayed the nearest watchers. A stunned silence reigned. Walt turned to go, then re-faced the crowd.

"The clock indicates the moment—but what does eternity indicate?" he asked them.

No one answered, flippantly or otherwise.

Walt returned to the others. He seemed enlarged somehow in Emily's eyes, as if he were now casting off the restraints of civilization, preparing to match his big soul against death itself, flexing his spiritual muscles in preparation for a celestial wrestling match.

"Well, cameradoes, our ship is nobly christened. It only remains to set sail. O captain, my captain—is it time?"

Crookes consulted a pocket watch. "Nearly. Let us take to our couches."

Davis spoke. "Soon we shall float on the Bay of Seven Souls. Princess Pink Cloud will hail us from atop the Garnet Cliffs, and our fondest dreams will become reality."

Austin said, "Soon I shall hold my babies."

"And *c'est vrai*, no medium shall rival *me* upon my return."

Conducting his crew sternwards, Crookes brought them to a circle of couches incongruously bolted to the deck. Within the circle was the pentagram of ideoplastic containers. Off to one side stood an elaborate arrangement of tightly stoppered metal tanks and a large odd clock. From the tanks ran several rubber hoses, two per couch. Each pair of hoses terminated in a gutta-percha face mask.

"Miss Dickinson, you are the only one unaware of our precautions, so listen closely. We have been warned by Princess Pink Cloud that the transition from earth to

Summerland would drive a conscious human traveler mad. Therefore, we have elected to make the trip asleep, so to speak, as uncognizant of the dangers as one of Professor Agassiz' fossils.

"One of these tanks is filled with ether, a gas possessing the power to incapacitate the brain. Perhaps you have heard of it in connection with some recent childbirth experiments, at Massachusetts General Hospital—? The other contains pure oxygen. The valves of both are controlled by this *multum-in-parvo* clock, a kind of electro-mechanical timing device. Five minutes before noon, the clock will trigger a blast of ether into our masks. At noon, the same device will close the circuit in the propulsion tubes. A mere sixty seconds will suffice to make the transition, at which point we will be awakened by a gale of fresh oxygen. Now, are you willing to entrust your life to such a mechanism?"

The scientist's confident demeanor—similar in kind to Walt's new bravado—inspired Emily. She answered, "If you warrant the contraption, then I place my faith in it—and in you, sir."

Crookes smiled. "Very well, then. The hour approaches! Ladies and gentlemen—couches, please!"

On the horsehair cushions the intrepid cross-dimensional argonauts laid themselves down.

Emily gingerly picked up her face mask and tied it on. Covering her nose and mouth as it did, it imparted a stifling, claustrophobic sensation, as if she were being immured in one of the newest Fisk Metallic Burial Cases.

Truly, she felt already dead, her oldest dreads finally realized.

Walt had taken a couch across the circle from her. Emily caught his eye. He winked, and she felt better.

The sun was directly overhead, and the noise of the crowd came to Emily as a wordless booming surf.

A hiss of escaping gas sounded. Emily held her breath until her lungs nearly burst, but was forced in the end to inhale.

Sleep is the station grand, down which, on either hand, the hosts of Witnesses stand!

As she drained the final dregs of oblivion, she heard a relay click, followed by the very Crack of Doom.

10

"DROPPED INTO THE ETHER ACRE—
WEARING THE SOD GOWN "

Her Dust connected—and lived.

Upon her Atoms were Features placed, august, absorbed and numb.

She was a Creature clad in Miracle.

It was Anguish grander than Delight.

It was—*Resurrection Pain.*

If Death was a Dash, she was most definitely cis-hyphen.

Still recumbent on her couch, noting dazedly that the noon sky above her had changed somehow to sunset hues— a shroud of gold and crimson, tyrian and opal—Emily reached a shaky hand up to her face and struggled to remove her mask.

Above her appeared the figure of Walt, concerned.

"Here, Emily—allow me."

He undid her mask and helped her to sit. Emily forced her eyes to focus on her fellow travelers, who were gradually coming to and rising, weakly doffing their anesthetic gear.

"Are you all right?" Walt asked her.

"I—I believe so. Though I am almost afraid to own this body somehow. What happened? Did we actually pass across death's border?"

"I assume so. But let us help the others, and then we'll see what we can see."

Soon, all seven voyagers were standing, however weakly.

Then, for the first time, they dared to lift their eyes and look outward, beyond the *Thanatopsis*.

What they saw made them move somnambulistically as one to the ship's port rail.

The *Thanatopsis* sat on its wheels in the middle of an apparently infinite, perfectly flat plain, whose circumambient horizon seemed queerly *further off* than its earthly counterpart.

And the plain was covered with emerald-green, almost self-luminous grass, cropped or mown or inherently self-limited somehow as smooth as the lawn of some Vast Estate. Any other feature there was none.

In stunned silence they stood, until from Walt pealed immense gales of laughter, followed by exuberant, near manic speech.

"Oh, my sweet Lord! I was right, right all along! How fine, how just, how perfect! Has any poet ever received surer confirmation of his visions? Please, someone—ask me what this grass is!"

Emily complied. "What—what is this grass, Walt?"

Walt puffed up his chest and declaimed, "A child said, 'What is the grass?' fetching it to me with full hands. How could I answer the child? I do not know what it is any more than he. I guess it must be the flag of my disposition, out of hopeful green stuff woven. Or I guess it is the handkerchief of the Lord, a scented gift and remembrancer designedly dropt, bearing the owner's name someway in the corners, that we may see and remark, and say 'Whose?' Or I guess the grass is itself a child, the produced babe of the vegetation. Or I guess it is a uniform hieroglyphic, the beautiful uncut hair of graves!"

Young Sutton began to clap. "Bravo, Walt! You seen it all before we even got here!"

Now Davis hesitantly spoke. "My calculations must have been off a trifle. This is plainly not the Bay of Seven Souls."

"I should say not," averred Crookes.

"I must consult my maps in the cabin. Certainly such a large geographical feature as this green desert will appear, even if only as a bit of Summerland *incognita*. In any case, there is no need to worry. Once Princess Pink Cloud senses our location telepathically, she will materialize here and conduct us by astral means to the Castle of Cochineal, where we shall sit in colloquy with Aristotle and Socrates, Chaucer and Shakespeare, among innumerable other spiritual luminaries."

Davis turned hopefully to Madame Selavy. "Can you establish contact with the Princess, my dear Hrose?"

Madame Selavy rolled her eyes back in her head and strained her facial ligatures, as if attempting to pass not ideoplasm, but a kidney stone.

"The cosmic telegraph is full of noise. I am overwhelmed by the nearness of so many spirits—"

Emily was about to ask *what spirits?* when her brother spoke.

"Has anyone noticed the sun?"

Everyone gazed now askance at the bloated orange orb, poised a mere degree or two above the horizon. For a full five minutes they regarded it, during which time it moved not a whit.

A tear pricking her cheek, Emily ended the silence. "The Dusk kept dropping—dropping—still. No Dew upon the Grass—but only on my Forehead stopped—and wandered in my Face. I know this Light. 'Tis Dying I am doing—but I am not afraid to know."

"'Tis dying you've done," contradicted Crookes. "This is something quite other."

With that, Crookes, making an obvious effort to shake off his stunned ennui, moved decisively toward the hold where the ostriches could be heard plaintively calling.

"Austin, Henry—come help me manage the birds on their treadmills. We must recharge the Voltaic piles in case a speedy departure becomes necessary. Mister Davis—I suggest you and Madame concentrate on establishing our whereabouts and that of any of Summerland's putative inhabitants. As for our two bards, you may continue to churn out your amusing little lays until further orders."

The party split up into its various factions, leaving Walt and Emily alone at the rail.

Despite their unforeseen and inexplicable circumstances, Emily felt a growing confidence and ease. Whether it was Walt's jubilation, which shone now from every ounce of his brawny frame, or Crookes' captainly aura, or a combination of the two, she could not say. But whatever the source, she found she was not fearful of her fate in this strange place, but rather expectant.

Upon the point of sharing these sentiments with Walt,

Emily espied twin autumn rivulets of tears freshly coursing through his beard.

"Walt, what troubles you?" said Emily, taking one of his hands in hers.

"It's the grass. It speaks to me."

"What is it saying."

"It claims—it claims to be my father."

For a short interval longer, Walt continued to listen to something Emily could not hear. Then, shaking himself, he resumed a less introspective manner.

"Green tide below me! I see you face to face! Clouds of the west! Sun there forever half an hour high! I see you also face to face!" He turned full to Emily. "We have made a crossing greater than any I undertook on Brooklyn Ferry— and I thought those quite supernal! But now we are where time nor place avails not, nor distance either. We are now with the men and women of all generations, past, present and future. This I affirm."

At that moment the three men who had gone belowdecks emerged. All wore various degrees of discomfiture, from Crookes' extreme agitation, to Austin's disconcerted bewilderment, to Henry Sutton's sympathetic incomprehension.

"Captain," called Walt, "what transpires?"

Crookes removed a silk handkerchief from his vest pocket and mopped his brow. His face was white as Emily's favorite wildflower, the Indian Pipe.

"The piles refuse to take a charge. Everything is perfectly in order. We just can't generate a current. It's—it's as if we're operating under a new set of natural laws...."

Emily said, "Does this mean that we're trapped here, Professor?"

"I fear so. At least as far as science can help us. Let us see what the psychic half of our team can contribute...."

Crookes advanced to the bulkhead door that led to the living quarters. There he knocked.

"Mister Davis! Madame Selavy! Please join us. We have something to tell you."

Muffled whispers could be heard from within. The whispers gradually increased in loudness and stridency until they terminated in a plainly voiced "*Bâtard!*" followed by the sound of a palm connecting solidly with flesh.

Shortly thereafter emerged Paris's finest medium and the Seer of Poughkeepsie; the latter bore a florid handprint on his cheek.

Madame Selavy spoke. "I was in contact with Princess Pink Cloud when an evil entity took possession of me. The vile beast materialized an ideoplastic hand and attacked *cher* Davis. It was only by the most magnificent efforts that I was able to cast out the intruder and preserve my sanity."

Despite their troubles, Crookes smiled. "I see. And what was the Princess able to tell you?"

"*Tout le monde* may feel safe. Our appearance here was planned by the spirits. They rerouted our vessel to this green wasteland on purpose. Our earthly souls are not purified enough yet to sustain a *tête-à-tête* with the spirits in their own domain. Princess Pink Cloud is sorry, but there was no alternative. She had no way of knowing this until we actually arrived. After all, our expedition is *un premier*. We are therefore instructed to return immediately to the lower spheres and perfect our souls before essaying another trip."

"I wish I could comply, Madame, as I believe it's our soundest course. But unfortunately, our electrical system is dead."

"What?!" shrieked Madame Selavy, hurling her bulky self upon Crookes and pummeling his chest with blows. The slim savant bore up admirably under the formidable assault. "You lie, you lie, you slimy dogsbody! We can't be trapped in this goddamn place! You got us here, you miserable alchemist! Now you'll damn well get us out!"

The medium's storm of blows dribbled to a halt, and she collapsed to the deck in a faint. Walt and Austin helped lift her to a couch.

"Madame's accent seems to have been our first fatality," drily commented Crookes.

"Plainly another case of possession brought on by the shocking news," faintly defended Davis. "I assume, by the way, that you were not jesting...."

"You assume correctly."

Walt said, "Perhaps we should sit down to a little sustenance, and plan our next move."

"A capital idea."

"I'll set the table," volunteered Emily, happy to have something useful at last to do.

Soon the party of six were sitting down to a simple collation, laid out upon a sideboard she recognized from the Evergreens. They ate in a somber silence. Emily noticed for the first time the lack of insect noises. Apparently, the astral prairie was void of cricket or cicada, beetle or fly.

As they were finishing, Madame Selavy joined them. Making no reference to her outburst, she tucked in heartily to the repast.

When she had finished, Crookes broached their choices.

"As I see it, we can simply sit here on our useless vessel until all our supplies are gone and we die of sheer inanition. Or we can set out across the placid wilderness in hopes of finding something or someone who can help us. Does anyone have any other ideas?"

No one spoke.

"Very well, then. Let us put it to a vote. Mister Whitman?"

"Unscrew the locks from the doors! Unscrew the doors from their jambs! If we be only one hour from madness and joy, then confine me not!"

"I take that as a vote to walk. Miss Dickinson?"

"When Death's carriage stops, one must enter."

"Another yea. Let us cut this short. Does anyone wish to sit tight? No? So be it. Let us make ready."

The decision galvanized all the voyagers, and they sprang into action. The ostriches were lofted from the hold by means of winch and sling. Two of the animals were reserved as mounts for the ladies; the others were quickly burdened with all the supplies. The gangplank was lowered and the haltered birds were driven down it. They were soon joined by the humans, who stepped tentatively onto the alien lawn, but found it to be, as best as they could discern, conventional sod.

"All that remains is to choose a direction," said Crookes, compass in hand.

Walt said, "May I volunteer an encomium from one of my journalistic peers? 'Go west, young man!'"

"Any other suggestions? Very well, west it is."

With Emily and Madame Selavy riding a demure, albeit somewhat slippery sidesaddle—Emily on Norma, Madame on Zerlina—the expedition set out.

Some hundred yards from the ship, they paused and turned to bestow one final nostalgic look on the craft.

"Goodbye, my fancy!" called Walt.

And with his farewell seeming to float in the air, the travelers resumed their journey into the sunset-canopied green unknown.

11

"THE GRASS SO LITTLE HAS TO DO, I WISH I WERE A HAY"

Emily had always loved sunsets. The Housewife sweeping with her many-colored Brooms; golden Leopards in the sky; Ships of purple on Seas of daffodil; a Duchess born of fire; the Footlights of Day's Theatricals— The gaudy aerial punctuation to the day's sentence had always seemed to her like one of God's more inspired authorial decisions.

But now, after eight hours of travel beneath the subtly varying yet essentially repetitive circus of Summerland's riotous skies, Emily was convinced that it would not matter to her if she never saw another colored clown-cloud in her life! The mindless spectacle of the skies now wore on her nerves like the continual moaning of an idiot. Emily could tell that the others were experiencing similar sensations.

Riding beside Emily, Madame Selavy exhibited a downcast apathy relieved only when she chose to cast a malign glare Emily's way. Leading Emily's long-necked and feathered mount, Austin shuffled along with eyes fixed on the unchanging turf, as did the Poughkeepsian Seer, who guided Madame's beast. Crookes and Sutton, each responsible for his own string of pack-ostriches, were plainly preoccupied with their own gloomy thoughts. The only member of the expedition to still exhibit the smallest measure of confidence and vivacity, in fact, was Walt.

The Paumanok Singer had soon assumed the role of pointman for the walkers. Striding out a few yards ahead of the others, he had made the opening hours of their journey pass cheerfully with a recitation of some of his inspirational poems.

"Me imperturbe! Standing at ease in Nature, aplomb in the midst of irrational things, imbued as they are, passive, receptive, silent as they. O to be self-balanced for contingencies, to confront night, storms, hunger, ridicule, accidents, rebuffs, as the trees and animals do!"

Walt would turn and bow comically upon the close of each verse, making a broad sweep with his hat in hand, and the others would stop and clap—urged on loudest by Emily—giving the ostriches a chance to crop at the infinite expanse of fodder, which they appeared to find congenial.

This monotous greensward had quickly become as wearisome as the skies. If only there were just one simple Dandelion amid this infinite Alas, to proclaim that the sepulture was o'er!

But flowers there were none.

When the birds had browsed sufficiently, the humans would resume their walk at a moderate pace, having agreed without speaking that there was no point in hurrying and wearing themselves out.

After the first several hours, they halted for a longer rest. Standing on Walt's shoulders, Henry Sutton was just able to descry the masts of the *Thanotopsis*, apparently unchanged.

Victuals were consumed, as well as refreshing draughts of their bottled water.

"This simple beverage," observed the ever-rational Crookes, "which we never gave a thought to from day to day back in Amherst, now puts an upper limit on our survival. Unless we encounter a new source of water, we shall all expire painfully from thirst long before our food runs out."

"A death almost as cruel as my unborn children suffered," chimed in Austin. "If only we could contact the poor lost babes, I'm sure they would be able to help us. Madame—can't you give it another go?"

The seeress appeared to have regained her Paris tones. "Of course I am willing to try, *cher* Austin. Come, let us form the circle of power."

Seated on the soft living carpet, they all joined hands. Madame Selavy closed her eyes and began her invocation. "Zelator, Sothis, Ullikummi—open the gates! Although we are unworthy, grant us audience!"

The air was heavy with expectation. But despite Madame's energetic grunts—which served to signal her earnest efforts—their hopes remained unfulfilled.

"Well, it didn't hurt to try," said Crookes after the circle had been broken and they were all standing again. "But it's beginning to look as if there are actually no spirits here to respond to our pleas. I'm starting to suspect that this place is merely another mundane world, perhaps orbiting a different star from ours, which we have accidentally reached somehow, and hence no spiritual abode."

Young Sutton now surprised one and all by breaking his usual self-sufficient silence and interjecting a comment. "Nope, I cain't agree with you there, Prof. This place is the afterlife, sure as my Paw wore whiskers. But what I want ter ask you is, how we gonna know when we actually die? If we just go ter sleep extra thirsty and wake up dead, what'ud we notice different about the scenery?"

Crookes laughed heartily and slapped Sutton on the back. "An excellent conundrum, man! Worthy of Thomas Aquinas himself!"

Walt brushed the crumbs of his meal off his trousers. They landed in the grass and lay there looking, thought Emily, unutterably alien, like boulders in the midst of a parlor. Where were the members of the busy minor Nation which on Earth would have carried them away?

The burly poet sought to ameliorate the attitude of defeat that hung palpably over the group.

"Come, my tan-faced children! Follow well in order, for we cannot tarry here! We must march, my darlings! We must bear the brunt of danger, we the youthful sinewy races. All the rest on us depend. We are the pioneers!"

"More like 'prisoners,'" countered Crookes. But he too fell into line with a slight smile.

That brief illusion of hope had not lasted long, however. Footsore slogging soon became the rule of the day. Even Walt had eventually ceased his orations, joining the others in silent dejection.

For Emily, the most brutal physical aspect of the trip so far had manifested itself as an embarrassing soreness in her posterior. The downy cushion of Norma's back had soon become a rock-hard seat of torment. Emily had switched to walking for a while, but found herself becoming too fatigued to keep up with the others. Her daily housebound existence had not fitted her for such a trek, and she was forced despite her aching buttocks to resume her mount.

Now, Crookes raised a hand to call another halt. He took out his pocket-watch and said, "By Amherst time, it is now eight in the evening. I propose we make camp for the, ahem, 'night,' and set out again at 'dawn.' Agreed? Fine. Let's get the tents set up, men."

The ostriches, temporarily freed of their burdens, were hobbled to graze. Three tents were broken out of the rest of the equipment, and unfolded onto the lawn.

"Austin, Davis and myself," said Crookes, "shall share one lodge. Walt and Hen will make a pair. And the ladies will have their own shelter. Now, let's get our encampment in order. Although the sky does not seem to threaten rain, this lawn must be watered somehow, sometime."

Nothing could have been less welcome to Emily than the prospect of spending a night side by side with the disagreeable and, she had realized from prolonged proximity, the noticeably garlicky Madame Selavy. Yet there seemed no alternative, or at least she was too tired to think of one.

Emily watched the men drive stakes into the lawn and rig ropes. After a few minutes, a sudden breeze—the first to make itself felt in Summerland—caused her to turn.

What she saw left her Lungs Stirless, their Cunning Cells incapable of even a Pantomime breath.

Less than a dozen feet away from the encampment, an oval patch of grass had come alive with motion.

It was if the soil were a-boil with the activity of a hundred thousand wriggling earthworms. The earth rippled and churned. And the grass itself was not immune from this bewitchment. Every blade seemed possessed of its own will, dancing and intertwining with its neighbors like the tendrils of a squid.

It seemed forever that Emily watched appalled, though it must have been only seconds. At last, finding her voice, she called out weakly, "Someone—help!"

In a trice the other members of the party had surrounded her. Emily pointed wordlessly, and they gasped as one.

For now the grass was cohering! Acquiring shape and solidity, the individual blades were losing their identities, growing and weaving themselves into a seamless fabric.

And that billiard-table-green fabric, molding itself around an invisible armature or skeleton, soon assumed the luster of green flesh—and the form of a perfect naked male child!

The transformation of the turf over, he lay there on his back, breathing, with eyes yet closed.

The babe of the vegetation.

No one gave utterance to his or her astonishment, till Walt spoke.

"The prairie grass dividing, its special odor breathing, I demand of it the spiritual corresponding. I demand the blades to rise in words, acts, beings, and go with its own gait...."

As Walt trailed off, the green child opened his eyes and gazed upward with mild wonder at the sky.

Walt took a step toward the boy.

Emily grabbed his sleeve. "No, Walt, don't! We don't know what manner of creature he is—"

With a note of gentle reprimand, Walt answered, "If I wish to speak to anyone I see, who shall say me no?"

Emily reluctantly released his sleeve, and Walt closed the distance between himself and the boy in a few decisive steps.

Squatting down beside the child, Walt said, "Son, can you hear and understand me?"

The child's voice was sweet as clover. "Yes."

"Where are you? What has happened to you?"

The child blinked, its green lashes sweeping over green eyes. "I—I was old. Sick. Dying. I—I died."

Emily drew breath sharpened like a stake. So it was true. They were in Summerland, the anteroom to Paradise.... Old religious tremblings overtook her.

"What year did you die?" queried Walt.

"Year? Oh, you speak of time. The year was nineteen—nineteen ninety something—I can't remember."

Now Crookes found his tongue. "This is preposterous! How can we be talking to the spirit of someone who hasn't even lived yet?"

"Time is not a simple matter," Davis warned. "It is quite conceivable that Summerland is coexistent with all ages, past, present and future. Such a theory would explain the precognition exhibited by certain spirits...."

"What was your mortal name?" asked Walt.

"Name?" said the child, as if it were the most foreign of words. "I think I had a name. It's all fading so fast. Allen. Allen Ginsberg. Is that a name?"

Walt laughed at the sound of the mundane syllables amid so much strangeness, and clapped a hand on the boy's shoulder. "Indeed it is, and a fine Hebraic one at that."

At Walt's touch, a look of amazement transfigured the child's features. "You're Walt Whitman!" he said. Then, as if overcome by the knowledge, the boy swooned away.

Alarmed, Walt quickly scooped the child up in his arms and stood.

Where the boy had been born, the prairie was clean of grass in a neat outline of his form, revealing the fecund brown earth below.

But even as they watched, new grass thrust its spears up through the soil, stopping its accelerated growth when it was level with its cousins. Soon, nothing distinguished the spot.

Walt carried the boy into the circle of tents and sat him down with his back against a bundle of equipment. Unstoppering a bottle of water, he sprinkled some into the face of the child.

Allen—for so Emily now found herself thinking of the child—opened his eyes.

"The sea," said the boy. "I must find the sea and join the others in it...."

Allen got to his feet and began to walk toward the setting sun.

"Wait!" exclaimed Davis.

Allen obediently halted, his small unclothed form yet seeming to strain west.

"Is this the Tourmaline Sea you speak of?"

"It has no name. It is simply the sea. And I must go to it."

Austin reached out a hand toward the child, as if he wished to cradle him. "You seem to have gained knowledge of this land somehow, Allen. Can you help us find our loved ones here?"

"If they have reached the sea already, you seek them in vain. And why do you call me 'Allen?'"

"But—you told us that was your name before you arrived here—"

The boy regarded them with utterly ingenuous frankness. "I was never anywhere but here, forever. I know only Summerland."

12

"HOW ODD THE GIRL'S LIFE LOOKS
BEHIND THIS SOFT ECLIPSE"

A fire would have been pleasant. A fire would have kept away the fear. A fire would have dispelled the gloom.

A cheerful blaze it would have been, as on a winter's night in The Homestead, when the entire Dickinson family would gather for a Bible reading, the three children still young, the Squire relaxed, Emily's mother less indisposed than nowadays. Perhaps it would even have been one of those rare occasions when Emily had been invited to climb into her father's lap, where he sat in his massive chair beneath that engraving of "The Forester's Family," a happy brood so unlike her own. And perhaps the Squire would have unbent enough actually to cosset his daughter, pet her hair and tell her she was a good girl, despite her being such a disappointment, too simple at age ten even to read a clock....

But there was nothing to burn here in Summerland, lest it be their own equipage.

And if there had been, would they have dared to start a fire that would inevitably scorch and damage this miraculous grass, an entity apparently capable of giving birth?

And would the grass *have even let them*?

So the disconsolate travelers were forced to sit in a circle around the wan glow of a single whale-oil lamp—much diminished by the glory of the polychrome sky—discussing their next "day's" moves in the light of recent events, prior to turning in.

Outside the range of the light, the huddled ostriches muttered petulantly, as if their dim brains were finally registering the abnormality of their surroundings.

Beyond the birds, Allen stood.

The strange, inscrutable child faced west, his long unchanging shadow reaching almost into the camp. Still as a jade statue, he appeared to be communing with someone or something the humans could not perceive. He had maintained this immobility for an hour, and seemed intent on continuing so for many more.

After confounding them with his response to Austin, the boy had made as if to leave.

"Please," pleaded Crookes at the last minute, "you must stay and help us."

"I will if *he* wants me to," said Allen.

And the green child pointed to Walt.

"It amazes me how he has fixed on you," said Crookes.

"It happened when we touched," said Walt. "There was a flow of intelligence between us. I daresay it would have happened with anyone else as well." Addressing the child solemnly, Walt said, "It would gladden my heart to hear your valved voice a while longer yet, my son."

"Then I will stay," said Allen.

It had seemed a major victory at the time.

But now their talk revealed how far from solving their problems they were.

Nervously twirling a bit of string around a finger, Crookes said, "Assuming Allen can help us reach the shore of this nameless sea, what do we gain? The *Thanatopsis* will be many miles away, so we will not be able to set sail—even if such a course should seem worthwhile. Granted, we might meet these other resurrectees, if Allen is to be believed. But if they are all as naive as he—"

"Maybe," said Austin, "there will be elders among them who will be able to help us...."

"What disappoints me most," said Davis, "is that the dead apparently forget everything about their earthly lives. And I was so looking forward to discoursing with Alexander the Great...."

"And I with my children," Austin echoed.

"Bah!" spat Madame Selavy. "This *enfant vert* is not one of the real spirits! He is some kind of unhuman devil, bent on leading us astray! Why, imagine—he did not even react when I mentioned Princess Pink Cloud! No, you may rest assured that I will know the true ghosts when we meet them. Have I not spoken with them for years?"

Crookes threw down his bit of twine and stood. "Well, this talk is getting us nowhere. Let us retire, and perhaps things will look brighter in the morning."'

They all betook themselves to their assigned tents.

Beneath the lowering canvas assigned to the ladies, Madame Selavy moved quickly to establish her dominance.

"I will not put up with any snortling or fidgeting, *Mam'selle.* Watch your elbows, occupy only your half of the tent, do not snatch the blankets, and we will get along fine."

So saying, Madame Selavy flopped down on their rude pallet, arrayed herself grandly in three-quarters of the coverings, and, shifting onto her side so that her hams overhung Emily's portion of the mattress, began within thirty seconds to manufacture a mustache-fluttering snore.

Squeezing herself into the remaining space and trying to keep as much room between herself and the pungent seeress as possible, Emily lay sleepless on her back.

Neither she nor Walt had had much to say during the discussion just past. The miracle of Allen's birth seemed to preclude ratiocination. Emily knew that the true meaning of the manifestation could only be apprehended poetically, and she longed to hear what glorious thickets of verbiage Walt might have effused from the miracle....

After half an hour of such ruminations, Emily stealthily rose, and left the tent.

No one else stirred within the encampment, where the lamp still burned untended.

Emily approached Walt's tent. Timidly, she lifted a flap.

Young Sutton slept alone, his cherubic face peaceful.

Dropping the flap, Emily moved beyond the bivouac's fitful flame.

She found Walt sitting cross-legged beside Allen. The poet was as mesmerized as he had been aboard the *Thanatopsis,* when he had first heard the grass speak.

Gingerly, Emily touched his shoulder.

Walt started, then turned his face upward.

"Emily," he said, in the tones of one recognizing a childhood friend not seen for decades. "'Tis vigil strange I keep here this night. I am glad for human company. Come—sit here beside me."

Awkwardly, Emily folded her legs beneath her skirts and sank down to the velvety turf.

Allen paid no attention to the actions of the humans, but continued to stare off in the direction of the ever-setting sun.

Walt took one of Emily's hands in his. Her pulse raced like spring torrents.

"I am at peace now with my father," said the man, "even though I have seen not seen his soul clothed in human form, as I foolishly longed to. I have realized what I always knew, but had forgotten. My father is all around me, in the mossy scabs of the worm fences, in the heap'd stones, in the elder, mullein and poke-weed. I need search no further."

Emily felt ecstatic tears scald her cheeks. "Oh, Walt, I'm so happy for you."

Walt transferred his hands to her waist. "Let me share my renewed joy and strength with you, Emily."

And then he kissed her.

George Gould had kissed her once. But that was years ago. And he had been a smooth-faced youth, not a virile bearded *man*!

Walt broke away and whispered, "You villain touch! What are you doing? My breath is tight in its throat! Unclench your floodgates! You are too much for me. My sentries have deserted their posts...."

"Mine also...," said Emily.

And she drew him down with her onto the lawn.

Walt's hands were busy beneath her clothing. "Urge and urge and urge, always the procreant urge of the world. Out of the dimness, opposite equals advance. Always substance and increase, always sex. Always a knit of identity, always a breed of life. Learn'd and unlearn'd feel that it is so. To elaborate is no avail—"

"Don't, then!" hissed Emily.

Walt was atop her now, his face buried in her neck, his weight like a treetrunk splaying her legs. She smelled the scented herbage of his breast.

Emily clutched him tight, her mouth against his ear. "My river runs to thee, blue sea! Wilt welcome me? My river waits reply, oh sea—look graciously. I'll fetch thee brooks from spotted nooks. Say, sea—take *me*!"

Walt said, "*Ma femme*—" then pressed with slow rude muscle against her.

Emily cried, and bit her lip.

In the sky, a cloud bled alizarin.

Walt was moving slowly. "Ebb stung by the flow, and flow stung by the ebb. Love-flesh swelling and deliciously aching. Limitless limpid jets of love, hot and enormous. Quivering jelly of love, white-blow and delirious juice. Bridegroom night of love working surely and softly into the prostrate dawn, undulating into the willing and yielding day. I am lost in the cleave of the clasping and sweet-flesh'd day!"

"Yes, Walt—I am the day, and you are my night!"

"And now comes the dawn!"

Walt howled a barbaric yawp, and sagged onto her, eclipsing the sky.

Emily didn't see how the others could have failed to hear Walt's climax. Surely they would be venturing out to see what the commotion was. But she made no move to escape Walt's embrace. She was not scared of their censure, here on the edge of dying in this strange land. Let everyone see what a royal hoyden she was!

Title divine is mine! The Wife without the sign!

Twisting her head slightly, Emily realized that her limited field of vision included the small feet of the green child. Upon resolving them, she had the strangest feeling that he was the improbable son of their just consummated union.

She waited for the others. But they never came.

Enchanted or exhausted, they had slept through Emily's coronation.

Finally, Walt stirred and removed his bulk from atop her.

"We should return, Emily, before we worry the others."

"Whatever you say, Walt."

As they walked back toward their separate tents, Emily felt a little sad and worried and tired, her exaltation fading.

"Walt?"

"Yes?"

"Did the Harebell loose her girdle to the lover Bee, would the Bee the Harebell *hallow* much as formerly?"

"I am for you, and you are for me, Emily. Not only for our own sake, but for other's sakes. You awoke to no touch but mine."

"Oh, Walt!"

13

"THERE WAS A LITTLE FIGURE PLUMP FOR EVERY LITTLE KNOLL"

 When Emily awoke, this was how she felt.

If all the griefs I am to have
Would only come today,
I am so happy I believe
They'd laugh and run away!

Lost in an eerie borderland between life and death with no prospect of rescue, she should have felt as miserable as her unlucky companions.

But Walt's attentions and embrace had allowed her to transcend her immediate condition.

At last she had captured her soul-mate, forging with

him those immemorial carnal bonds which time could never snap. And what a catch! A tender yet rugged male deep enough to match her female needs, a wild poet with roots in the hidden wisdom of the universe.

Finally, Emily knew how her esteemed Elizabeth Barrett had felt when she had found her Robert. At that moment, Emily realized she had been secretly rather jealous of "the Portuguese" all these years.

Now she could easily let such juvenile emotions go.

As she stretched luxuriously in the otherwise empty tent, her long chestnut tresses undone and in rare disarray, Emily praised Walt for doing so much for her. She swore she would do as much for him. Whatever he wanted or needed, wherever he roamed, whatever he did, she would stand by him, as support and inspiration.

Great I'll be, or Small—or any size at all—as long as *I'm the size that suits Thee!*

Suddenly Emily could wait no longer to see her beloved. Hurriedly, she left the tent.

The others were sitting around the extinguished lamp, partaking of a light breakfast.

Walt loafed on the grass, one arm resting on a bedroll, legs extended. His gaze was fixed on a single plucked blade held between thumb and forefinger.

"Ah, Miss Dickinson," called out Crookes, "we thought you had sneaked into the ether, so soundly did you sleep! But you have awakened just in time, as we're about to break camp. Walt, perhaps you'll tell Miss Dickinson what you've learned."

Now Walt looked up at Emily. His face betrayed none of what had passed between them last night, showing only his general benevolent and sunny impartiality, somewhat tempered by the stresses of their situation.

What a considerate lover, thought Emily. *He seeks to hide our relationship and spare me any possible embarrassment. I will have to tell him in private that there is no such need. I would shout my love from the rooftops of Amherst....*

Walt discarded the grass. "I have been speaking with Allen. During the 'night,' he learned more of what he has to do. He must find six of his peers to accompany him to the sea. Only as a unit will he and the others be able to achieve their destiny, and move on to the next plane of existence."

"It makes excellent sense," said Davis. "Seven is the mystic number supreme. Seven planets, seven days, seven metals and seven colors—As the properties of seven are powerful on earth, so must they be in Summerland."

"In this sense, then," Crookes extrapolated, "our own expeditionary force was incomplete and unbalanced until the late fortuitous addition of Miss Dickinson."

Madame Selavy hurriedly disposed of a pickled egg so that she could declaim, "I myself would have preferred to be *un peu* discomboobled, rather than have along such an unsympathetic intellect."

Even Madame could not fluster Emily this morning. She bestowed a gracious smile on the seeress and directed her words toward Crookes.

"I would not have missed this outing for the world, Professor."

Now Austin spoke up gloomily. "Unless Allen and his compatriots can help us get home, dear sister, that exchange might be precisely what we've bartered."

On this note of urgency, and without further delay, the exiles assembled their gear and were on their way, led today by the preternaturally obsessed and silent Allen, Walt in second place.

Somehow, Crookes had ended up with the reins of Emily's mount, while Austin had taken a string of pack-ostriches. Finding themselves somewhat apart from the others, the Professor now engaged Emily in conversation.

"It seems to me that if we can project our first day's experiences with any justification, then we should witness the rebirth of a new soul out of the grass every twenty-four hours or so. Reckoning thus, it should take approximately a week to assemble the company required by Allen. I believe our supplies will stretch that far, with just a little caution. Though much beyond that point, I cannot hold out hope."

Emily appreciated Crookes talking so frankly and intelligently with her. He was really quite a nice man. Though of course not so splendid as Walt. She tried to reply in similar fashion.

"What astonishes me, Professor, is that we are not literally stumbling over one child-soul or another at every single step."

"Whatever do you mean?"

"Consider. How many millions and millions of dead have there been in the past, and how many millions more in the future? If Summerland is receiving any portion of them on a regular basis—though how the time disjuncture between the worlds figures, I cannot speculate—then the soil should be exploding with revenants every few feet. Ancient Romans and Greeks, Persians and Medes, not to mention future dwellers such as Allen."

Crookes was plainly awestruck by Emily's analysis. After a moment's cogitation, he replied, "I see no flaw in your reasoning, Miss Dickinson, and only two possible answers. Perhaps most of eternity's dead have already made the transition to Summerland. This would mean that we have arrived here at a special time, a unique moment in the history of the afterlife. As a scientist, however, I tend to regard every situation as representative, until proven unique. Therefore, I lean toward the second postulate."

"Which is?"

"That Summerland is practically infinite in extant. The dead are indeed arriving moment by moment in their teeming myriad—but scattered across a billion billion hectares."

"Then our meeting Allen so soon was sheer chance? And our prospects for meeting any of his necessary companions likewise dim?

"It appears so. Unless, of course—"

"What?"

"We are assuming that the dead manifest themselves randomly, much like dandelions popping up in The Squire's front yard. There is another alternative—"

Emily supplied it. "That some Higher Principle ordains where they shall appear. That we were meant to meet Allen. And that our fate is in Unknown Hands."

Crookes looked disgusted. "How I hate to imagine some bearded Jewish elder as big as Mont Blanc continually peering over my shoulder and nudging my elbow! But I suppose anything is possible."

"Only events will prove which hypothesis is correct. After all, a rainbow convinces more than all philosophy."

Crookes laughed. "Miss Dickinson, you're quite a rare woman! Allow me to place my services at your complete disposal, should you ever need them."

"Thank you, Mister Crookes, but I already have a protector."

Crookes smiled slyly. "Ah, so that's how it is. Well, I wish you and your beau the best of luck. You both may need it."

Before Emily could completely decipher what Crookes implied, a shout rang out.

"Rebirth ho!" pealed Walt's clear tones.

Emily glanced significantly at Crookes, who shrugged as if in mock defeat. Together, they hurried with the others to where Walt and Allen stood.

The grass had already finished its transformation when they arrived. Congealed out of the thrashing warp and weft of the chlorophyll, the figure of a girl-child lay. As the spectators watched, she opened her eyes.

"Don't touch her," warned Crookes. "Remember the adverse effect physical contact had on Allen—"

Emily bent over the sweet-faced child. "What was your name, dear?"

"Sill—Sill—Sylvia...."

"Is that all?"

"All I remember."

Emily wanted to hug the little girl, but refrained. "That's fine, darling. Look, here's a friend for you—"

Allen stepped forward and helped Sylvia up.

"The sea," she said as soon as they touched.

Without any reference to the humans, the pair of naked toddlers resumed their determined westward progress.

"Is it possible," asked Crookes, "for something to be both alluring and horrifying?"

"Have you never seen," asked Walt, "a common prostitute in the city of orgies, with her charnel-house body of love?"

Austin blanched and said, "Sir!" Madame Selavy tittered. Davis dealt with a speck on his glasses. Young Sutton chuckled.

Crookes turned to Emily with a lifted eyebrow, as if to say, *Good luck indeed with this mad beau!*

14

"AN EAR CAN BREAK A HUMAN HEART
AS QUICKLY AS A SPEAR"

The slow perpetual Day moved along, but arrived nowhere. Emily heard its Axles go, as if they could not hoist themselves, they hated motion so.

No Seasons were to her, it was not Night or Morn. It was Summer set in Summer, centuries of June.

She was on an infinite trip down Ether Street.

Emily had lived an eternity in Summerland. This was simple fact. There had never been an Amherst. Lavina, Mother, The Squire, Carlo—all were figments of her imagination. All that had ever existed were the unchanging landscape, her human companions, and the gaggle of children.

There were six of them now: Allen, Sylvia, Hart, Delmore, Anne and Adrienne. Planted in the soil of Earth by their ignorant mourning loved ones, they had tunneled like industrious grubs, emerging out of their chrysalis, the mould, in Summerland, wearing the bright forms of youth, with Lethe-smoothed minds.

Never tiring, needing neither to eat nor sleep, the children would plainly have moved on toward their however-distant mystic sea without pause, had they not been constrained by the humans. The bond formed between Allen and Walt, however, still held, and the children would halt when the humans did.

At such times—irregular as they had become, as the travelers grew detached from earthly rhythms—the children would form a silent circle of introspection. Emily remembered the farcical seance conducted at The Evergreens; the children's circle resembled that imbroglio as Parliament resembled a caucus of crows.

What would happen when the seventh child was added, no one could predict. Even Allen claimed not to know....

Emily had no idea what kept the others going on this mad quest for escape from the afterlife. In her case, it was only love for Walt, and a dream of how their life together back on Earth could be.

Emily and her Paumanok Paramour had not enjoyed another tryst since the first. Emily had not gone seeking Walt for another "midnight" assignation, and he had not come for her. This was fine. Even on the far side of death, it was well to observe propriety. Emily was content to know that their imperishable love still burned like a hidden volcano beneath the surface of their cordiality.

How red the Fire rocks below, how insecure the sod. Did I disclose, it would populate with awe my solitude!

She pitied the others their lack of such a bulwark, and tried to share her strength and cheer.

But on this day—perhaps the seventh since their arrival, perhaps the seven-hundredth—there was precious little hope to be found among the weary travelers.

When Walt's familiar shout shook them out of their torpor, they moved only sluggishly toward the reincarnation, despite its climactic significance.

"Our last tiresomely perfect child," drawled Crookes as they surrounded the ultimate babe of the vegetation. "Does anyone hear the Final Trump yet?"

Walt regarded the male child queerly, a look of rare unease on his face.

"Something startles me where I thought I was safest! How can it be that this ground itself does not sicken, so full of dead meat is it? Where are the foul liquids it is stuffed with? If I run a furrow with my plough, I am sure to expose some of the foul meat! Every mite of this compost once formed part of a sick person, generations of drunkards and gluttons!"

Walt fell to his knees and dug his fingers into the soil. "The very wind should be infectious!"

Emily hastened to Walt's side, dropped down and hugged him. "Walt, please! We need you! Do not succumb to delirium—for my sake!"

Gradually, his sobbing abating, Walt recovered. He stood and brushed soil-clotted hands on his pants. "Very well. I am not an earth, nor the adjunct of an earth. I am the mate and companion of people, all just as immortal and fathomless as myself."

"Much better," applauded Emily.

While Walt had been experiencing his moment of the terrible doubt of appearances, Madame Selavy had been circuitously approaching the newest child. Now, kneeling beside him, she spoke with saccharine sweetness.

"Tell us your name, *petit bébé*."

"My name is Ezra—"

Madame Selavy now shrieked, "Listen, Ezra, you devil! You're going to damn well get us out of this hell, or I'll kill you again myself!"

The seeress clamped her hands around the child's throat—

And froze, as if pinned by Galvanic forces.

From Ezra's mouth emerged Madame's voice, clear as a Unitarian church bell.

"My name is Maude Frickett. I was born to an unmarried fishmonger in Fulton Market, New York. At age seven I was orphaned, and forced to live on the streets, taking shelter at night on a barge in the East River. At age ten, I was raped by sailors. At age thirteen, I became a prostitute. By fifteen, I had added picking pockets and serving gin to my skills. I put away money enough to open my own brothel by age twenty. When the police shut me down, I changed careers. I set up in Albany as a medium. That's where Andy found me. He thinks he's using me, but it's the other way 'round. Nobody uses old Maude! Nobody's smart enough. They're all marks, everyone, just fit for plucking—"

With an enormous effort, Madame Selavy yanked her hands away from the child, breaking the flow of secret speech. For a second or two, she remained kneeling. Then her eyes rolled back in their sockets and she collapsed in a swoon.

Davis rushed to aid the stricken seeress, as did the others shortly thereafter. The children, meantime, calmly took charge of Ezra, who had likewise lost consciousness.

After Madame's unmoving form had been laid out comfortably among the tethered ostriches, Crookes voiced their common realization.

"A form of thought transference—"

Walt put it more poetically. "There was a child went forth, and the first object he looked upon, he became...."

Davis objected. "Surely you don't believe that the nonsensical biography the child spouted pertains to Madame Selavy? It was plainly a case of a stray psychic broadcast from an errant soul, registering itself on the conjoined minds of Hrose and Ezra...."

Austin shattered Davis's defense. "Come off it, Davis. Even if you are truly blind to the woman's deceptions, you cannot expect us to continue so. You and Maude—as we should now refer to her—have been wrong about everything connected with this place. And don't forget the time I found you compounding your 'ideoplasm' in my kitchen! God, what a fool I was to accept your jejune excuses! My grief must have made me mad and blind!"

Davis broke down. "It's true! God help me, it's true. The ideoplasm is only raw cotton soaked in various salts and minerals which somehow glow. But there was never any intention of real deceit. Maude has a genuine talent, whatever her origins. We just wanted to help people deal with their sadness. We took only enough money to sustain us in a modicum of comfort—"

Crookes was cupping his chin thoughtfully. "We must attempt to quantify your ideoplastic recipe, Mister Davis. It would put our whole transdimensional expedition on a more scientific footing...."

"Interesting as these confessions are," interjected Walt, "and good as it is to unburden the conscience, they have little relevance to our plight. It appears that there will be no further developments until little Ezra awakes. May I suggest that we use this interval to get some rest? One of us should watch the children—"

"I volunteer," said Davis.

"I will watch with you," said Austin. "I don't care to be deceived or tricked again."

"Mister Dickinson, I assure you—"

"Please, spare me. Let us start our vigil."

The two moved off to within a few yards of the patiently waiting children, who were clustered around their recumbent comrade. Quickly, the remaining humans erected the three tents.

"I shall maintain a close eye on Maude," said Crookes, once the still-unconscious woman had been placed under his direction in his own tent. "I have some small medical knowledge, and should be able to minister to her. I am sure Miss Dickinson would appreciate not having to share her quarters with such a patient."

Under this new arrangement, all retired.

Emily was restless. Try as she would, she could not summon sleep. What would happen when Ezra awoke? How had the charade conducted by Davis and Maude turned into grim reality? Would any of them ever see home again, or would they all die here, trailing off into madness first?

With these thoughts and more bedeviling her, Emily resolved to seek Walt's comfort and guidance.

She arose from her pallet and left her tent.

At the closed entrance to the tent shared by Walt and Sutton, Emily hesitated.

A husky whispered voice filtered out.

"O camerado close! O you and me at last, and us two only. With my arms draped around you, I am satisfied. What? Is this then a touch quivering me to a new identity? Flames and ether make a rush for my veins! The treacherous tip of me reaches out to help them. Unbuttoning my clothes, holding me by the bare waist, behaving licentious toward me, taking no denial, immodestly sliding my senses away! The udder of my heart drips sweet milk! Part the shirt from my bosom-bone! Settle your head athwart my hips, and gently turn over upon me!"

Henry Sutton laughed, and replied, "Ya talk so funny, old man! But I loves yer anyhow."

Then all speech ceased.

Emily stumbled backwards, an arm raised across her face.

No, it could not be—She must be mistaken.

From the tent came the unmistakeable noises of pleasure Emily remembered from the night of her surrender to Walt.

A queerly disturbing image from her schooldays surfaced: an ancient Greek statue of two naked Olympian wrestlers, ecstatic sinewy limbs intertwined—*To learn the Transport by the Pain, as Blind Men learn the sun! This is the Sovereign Anguish! This—the signal woe!*

Tears obscuring her vision, Emily fled to her last refuge.

Throwing back the canvas door of Crookes's tent, she was on the verge of spilling her distress when the disorderly scene within registered on her senses.

The pretend seeress seemed partially conscious, like a lazy sleeper fighting Morpheus, or a languorous debauchee. Her upper garments were pooled about her waist, exposing her generous endowments—quite normal in appearance, no leakage of ideoplasm evident.

These attractions Crookes was slowly caressing, no resistance forthcoming.

"Imagine—a common trull. Yes, you shall not refuse me—"

Emily choked on an ocean of bile. Gagging, she fell back.

She wanted to scream, but it was as if an invisible membrane had been stretched across her face, keeping all the horror inside.

Was it her mind that was coming unhinged, or those of the others?

At that moment, her brother's shout rang out.

"Quickly! The child awakes!"

Emily staggered blindly toward Austin's voice. If there had been so much as a pebble in her path, she would not have made it. But the grass offered no obstacle, and somehow she reached her brother's side, falling into his arms.

"Emily, what's wrong—?"

Love's stricken "Why?" that breaks the hugest hearts was all she could speak.

Before Austin could query further, the trio was joined by the other four.

Crookes was half-supporting a hazy Maude, one of whose breasts was still exposed. Walt and Sutton wore only their long buttoned undershirts, which luckily hung to their thighs.

"Allen," called out Walt. "What is happening?"

The children had formed a circle. Within, the air seemed shimmery, as around the *Thanotopsis's* ideoplastic tubes.

"Now that we are whole, we are going to the sea," replied the child.

"Take us with you!"

There was a moment of silence, as if the children were communicating. Then: "Very well. Enter the circle."

Breaking hands with one partner, Allen made a gap.

Slowly, knowing they had no choice, the humans shuffled within.

Emily thought about hanging back, letting the others go, so she could die alone in her misery. But at the last second, she found her feet moving in synchronization with the others.

The circle was reformed.

The air around the humans seemed to thrill and vibrate. Emily thought, *There is a morn by men unseen, where children upon remoter green, keep their Seraphic May. And all day long, with dance and game, and gambol I may never name, they employ their holiday. Ne'er saw I such a wondrous scene. Ne'er such a ring on such a green—*

There came now a hum felt only in the bones—

Humans and children stood on the seashore.

Yet it was not a shore of sand.

A vast tongue of water lapped a gently sloping bank of grass.

And the water itself was green as a spring apple, and unrippled as a silken shroud upon a corpse.

The instant transition left Emily stupefied, and the others plainly also. Too much had happened too fast. Her limbs went to jelly, and she dropped down on the turf.

The children separated into a line, facing the ocean.

Allen turned to Walt. "Goodbye, father."

The reborn souls began to walk into the sea.

The slope must have been precipitous. Only a yard from the shore, they were submerged up to their chins.

A step more, and the water closed around their heads.

They were gone.

The humans' last hope for escape had disappeared....

Emily felt someone brush past her.

It was Maude.

Like a sleepwalker, drawn perhaps by the remnants of her intense connection with Ezra, or by simple desperation, the seeress was heading for the sea.

Before anyone could stop her, she had entered the water.

Two steps only, and it was up to her waist, lifting her dress around her like a jellyfish's mantle.

Davis began to rush forward to rescue his partner, but was stopped by Crookes' decisive restraint.

"No, don't! Can't you see what's happening, man? She's not sinking—she's dissolving!"

It was true. Standing only where the shorter children had gone under, Maude should not have been so swamped. Indeed, she had stopped moving, yet the water was still crawling up her! Inexorably it swallowed her, as the horrified onlookers watched. Exhibiting no pain, but rather a transcendental bliss, the woman melted into the ocean's embrace, till only her empty clothing was left floating on the placid sea.

Davis wailed, "Maude!" then collapsed.

Emily had passed all bounds of shock. Betrayed, bedazzled, bereft, her mind was now working in some kind of cool and rarefied zone, like a little bird carried by a storm into the highest reaches of the atmosphere finding it could somehow still breathe and fly.

Emily giggled softly to herself, hysteria bubbling under.

I started early—Took my Friends—
And visited the Sea—
The Mermaids in the Basement
Came out to look at me—

But no Man moved Me—till the Tide
Went past my simple Shoe—
And past my Apron—and my Belt
And past my Bodice—too—

And made as He would eat me up—
As wholly as a Dew—

Coincidental with the intrusion of Maude into the greedy sea, there now came a deep rumbling noise from the plain behind them, as if in response.

Austin helped Emily up, and Crookes aided Davis. Together, the six climbed the slope until they had gained the gramininferous flatland.

There was a green Mountain breaking the tableland now in the middle distance. Its magnitude obscured for a moment the fact that it possessed a familiar human profile.

Then the Mountain rose from the waist.

Only Walt dared speak. "We seemed to have awoken someone—"

For a moment, the Mountain sat upon the Plain in its tremendous Chair, its observation omnifold, its inquest everywhere—

At last it saw the humans.

The Mountain got to its feet and began to walk.

In no time it was towering over the expedition, casting a cold shadow across them.

The Mountain, observed Emily, was a hermaphrodite.

Divided down the middle, its left half was naked Emily, its right half naked Walt.

Beard and breast, split genitals—was this then their own magnificent reborn soul, somehow conjoined for eternity? Or was it rather a convenient guise for something beyond their comprehension?

Emily felt a curious wisdom emanate from the gigantic being. It seemed to sense why they were here, seemed to grasp their whole lives from start to unseen finish, much as a person might comprehend the entirety of a mayfly's short existence.

And from the Mountain radiated pity.

Then the giant reached for them, with a hand as huge and green as Amherst's town common—

There was a roaring in Emily's ears, as of the sea. Something was clamped on her face. Where was she? What had happened?

She scrabbled at the impediment to her breathing, succeeded in clawing it off.

It was a gas mask.

Emily got weakly to her feet.

She was aboard the *Thanotopsis*, which vessel still sat on its cradle in the midst of the grassy town lawn, its bow still dripping with champagne. Above stretched the welcome blue sky, and a sun at normal noontime height. The familiar buildings of the town bulked reassuringly around them. From the hold came the muted cries of the ostriches.

The louder noise was that of the crowd who had come to watch them depart. Now their cheers were turning ugly.

"Start the show!" "When's the sailing?" "I seen 'em shiver like, but then they came back!" "Hoist yer sails, lubber!" "Where's the ghostly gale?" "Show us some skeletons!" "Heaven or bust!"

Emily's shipmates were now off their couches. All seemed as dazed and bewildered as she herself felt.

"Of the dead, I dreamed," said Walt. "Passing strange it was—yet even now it fades, fades, fades....."

Crookes said, "I too half-recall an adventure almost beyond words. Was it the ether only, or was it...?"

"Did I get to hold my babes?" asked Austin. "Someone, tell me, please! I don't think I can go back to Sue without knowing—"

"Where is Madame Selavy?" Davis asked with some urgency.

Emily noticed now that the medium was indeed missing.

Davis rushed to the ship's side and addressed the crowd.

"Did anyone see a woman leave the ship? Speak up, for God's sake!"

"Not me." "She musta jumped ship if she ain't there." "I think I seen her go overboard." "Say, now that you mention it—" "Yeah, I seen her hoist her skirts and run off." "She couldn't take the failure—"

Davis returned, massaging his brow wearily. "It does not seem possible that Hrose would have fled. But the alternative—I can't quite envision it, but it's something too horrible to contemplate. Perhaps I will find her back at The Evergreens...."

Austin said stiffly, "I fear you will not be welcome there long, Mister Davis, nor will Madame. This whole affair has proven an expensive and embarrassing fiasco. If you will be so kind as to pack your belongings, I shall be happy to pay for your ticket back to Poughkeepsie."

"And I too shall be leaving," said Crookes. "This fruitless sidetrack off the road of science has lasted too long. My laboratory beckons."

"Henry and I also shall be going," said Walt. "Manahatta's million-footed streets call." The burly poet draped an arm around his young companion, who smiled with animal amiability, as if he had simply been for a walk around the block. Then Walt turned to Emily.

"Would you consider accompanying us to New York, Miss Dickinson? Although I cannot guarantee you an easy *entrée* to literary society, you might find the writerly company at Pfaff's Saloon congenial. And, with a little luck, it might very well lead to the publication of your poetry...."

Here was the invitation she had lived long years for, uttered by the man who had shown her the most respect and admiration.

So why was a wave of repugnance engulfing her?

Something she had learned, something about Walt and young Sutton—

No, it was gone. The cause was invisible, but the sharp-edged feeling of distaste remained.

Emily spoke coldly. "I fear my sensibilities would not permit my easy entrance into the circles you frequent, Mister Whitman."

Walt smiled sadly. "As you wish, *ma femme.*"

She almost relented then. But her rock-ribbed New England soul could not burst its straps of iron.

The men dropped the gangplank, and the travelers descended. Halfway down, Emily spied Vinnie waiting for her, and waved.

As Emily's foot touched the grass, a sudden vision overwhelmed her, full, broad and comprehensive.

She saw her future days in their entirety. Years going by with no male company other than The Squire and Austin. Keeping more and more to her room. Tending her garden, tending her parents as they began to decline in health. Writing letters, writing poems. Vinnie somehow staying with her, growing bitter and convoluted. Her own eventual death, her corpse carried out the back door and across the fields—

And the rebirth she dreamed of?

An image of a green sea rose from somewhere. It was strangely comforting.

Sad and lonely those years would be, stretching long and cold, yet not lacking a certain icy glory....

This trip, however abortive, had been the turning point. Now there was no going back.

What if she had truly spurned Whitman and his

beguilements, when he had first serenaded her below her window? Snubbed him utterly, instead of chasing after him? Would it have made her future easier to bear?

No. She could have done nothing different.

But the cost of the knowledge of who she was seemed rather steep—

> *For each ecstatic instant*
> *We must an anguish pay*
> *In keen and quivering ratio*
> *To the ecstasy.*
>
> *For each beloved hour*
> *Sharp pittances of years—*
> *Bitter contested farthings—*
> *And Coffers heaped with Tears!*